CRIMSON STEEL

CASCADE WOLVE
CRIMSON SERIES

By
M.A. Kastle

Books by M.A. Kastle

Cascade Saga
Bone Chimes
Dark Awakening
Warrior's Crown

Cascade Wolves – Crimson Series
Crimson Moon
Crimson Steel

Moonlight Territory
Wolf Within

Horror
Tales of Woe (Collection)
A Curse Revisited – The Legend of Noah Blyth (Novella)

CHAPTER ONE

Please don't be hurt.

With their pleas ringing in her ears, she raced across the highway, up the embankment— then hit the steep incline and rough terrain. Boulders and ground cover, wet from dew, glittered in the sparse sunlight while tree roots stabbed up from soft soil, doing their best to trip her and slow her run to a crawl. Stopping to catch her breath and shake dirt from her running shoes, she hunted for a path, and frantically searched for evidence someone had gone through the brush. Anything. Broken limbs, smashed grass, trampled flowers, or leaves. With her hands on her hips, Clio inhaled, drawing a breath to catch the missing woman's scent, and hopefully her blood, if she had been hurt.

Each inhale was ladened with various traces of the woods and its inhabitants, causing doubt to rear its ugly head. She consoled herself knowing there was a GPS chip in her identification badge, the electronic device actively sending her location to communications located in the Enforcer's office at Foxwood, Baron Kanin's estate, and to the enforcers' terminals. Cascade's version of law enforcement. Or, as the rest of the territory saw it, the pack's military.

Backup is on its way, she told herself. The deeper she hiked, the thicker the trees became, which left the midmorning sun fighting to penetrate the canopy. The shaded area kept the soil moist, the undergrowth thick, healthy, and blooming, and made singling out one scent impossible. Over the last few months snowstorms, thunderstorms, and heatwaves struck without warning, making the weather unstable and unpredictable. Each storm left a different kind of disaster in its wake. Clio was looking at the woods riddled with fallen trees, broken limbs, and peppered clumps of thick grasses. The vastness of the forest, the wind through the treetops, and the feel of wildlife surrounded her.

She mumbled her frustration as her resentment with her half human and half werewolf weaknesses reminded her she was a Wight—a person of a specified kind and regarded as unfortunate, or a creature. *Work harder.* If she couldn't scent her, then she would have to track the woman. Because three different statements and, *up there*, didn't tell her anything. After scouting ahead, she found several broken branches, smashed undergrowth, and footprints left by boots. Like they had been running. "Found you," she whispered. Adjusting the med bag over her shoulder and heading deeper into the woods, she trudged farther up the mountain.

Minutes earlier, she had been driving to a luncheon when three backpackers, decked out in light jackets, cargo pants, and boots, charged out of the woodline, down the embankment, and nearly tumbled into the road. She skidded to a stop, the tires of her crossover squealing, her heart in her throat, and her stomach somewhere in her seat. She could have killed them. They swarmed the driver's window, and talking over one another, frantically explained their friend had fallen down a ravine. They weren't sure if she was conscious, they couldn't see her, and she wasn't answering their yells. After telling them not to worry, she used her terminal to contact communications, relayed her position, and the mile marker.

Communications immediately reported it to the ranger station, human search and rescue, and medical services. She explained she was an emergency room doctor, then dutifully advised them she was non-human, and waited for their reaction. Human and werewolves, all magic-born, lived together, their relationship affable, but it didn't mean they were going to let one, a stranger, help a wounded friend. Humans feared the lycanthrope and therianthrope viruses, not understanding how it was transmitted. However, the three of them were scared, and with panic, fear, and uncertainty racing in their veins, they didn't seem to care.

That'll change, she figured. *Always does.* She parked her crossover on the shoulder of the road, then from the trunk switched her sandals out for running shoes, grabbed the med bag she always had with her, and ran in the direction the hikers had come from. Clio couldn't stop herself from laughing when she thought about the med bag and why she carried it and enough equipment to supply a small ER. Mistress Jordyn Langston, soothsayer for the pack, had a way of getting into situations, and Clio never knew when, where, or by what means Mistress would get hurt.

She adjusted the med bag, pulled at the hem of her skirt, and kept scaling the mountain side, her smile quickly fading as frustration moved in. Tombstone Mountain sat an hour and a half outside of Trinity, home of the Cascade pack, the city named for the encampments that once imprisoned all magic-born. The remote location along twenty miles of two-lane, rural roadway lined by trees meant cell phones were useless. If they were going to backpack in and camp, they should have checked in with the park station, followed an established trail, and carried a satellite phone for emergencies. As if giving the woods and her search a sense of foreboding, the thick treetops continued blocking the sun from the fern and grass covered ground, and a chill settled on her bare arms. Then the trail ended.

Damn. Lifting her face to the breeze and inhaling, she tried again to catch the woman's scent, if there was blood, and a direction. A faint trace of bitter iron drifted—she was injured—followed by the distinct aroma of human, and Clio sensed fear. Not just fear but terror and panic. "Dusti!" she yelled, her voice getting lost in the immensity before her. She remained still, not wanting to miss hearing the wounded hiker, and waited. One second. Two. Three. Four. Nothing. Out of habit, Clio adjusted the med bag on her shoulder, gripped the scent trying to allude her, and started hiking.

"What the hell is she doing at Tombstone Mountain?" Ansel growled as he drove the narrow stretch crowded by firs, pines, oak trees, and dogwood flowers. When Mandy, Director of Communications, alerted the enforcers of Clio's report, he took charge, put Deimos' team on standby, and left Foxwood.

Ansel pushed his silver 4x4 with Cascade's crests on both sides faster than the posted speed limit. He was confident human law enforcement wouldn't bother stopping him; they didn't want to talk to him. They knew Detective Jordyn Langston, soothsayer for the Cascade pack, worked for the Organized Paranormal Investigations, and her association to law enforcement gave the enforcers and Cascade's patrols a wide berth. Another corner and the screen refreshed and dinged. He checked the terminal for an update and saw there wasn't one. No cell service. No contact with Clio. The chip in her ID card giving her location in sporadic intervals.

How did he survive for over a hundred years without knowing exactly where everyone was? He didn't know. Communications, the terminals, cell phones, and state-of-the-art computers were convenient, there was no doubt, but he felt depending on technology was going to be their end when they finally failed. As if they needed proof, and a warning, winter in Trinity had been harsh, knocking out electricity, forcing them to use generators. Then in April a round of snowstorms left the city a white wonderland ... only to have a thunderstorm blaze through with its rain, thunder, lightning, and warmer temperatures, turning the winter landscape into a mixture of frozen tundra and rainforest. April turned into May, bringing two more thunderstorms, flooding, lightning, a forest fire, and an earthquake. Geologists warned the shift in weather and the earthquake effected the tectonic plates and had the potential of catapulting Mount Shasta, an active volcano, into action.

Just what they needed. A volcanic eruption.

Rutger, Director of Enforcers, and his mate, Jordyn, thought the radical changes in the weather were part of the Emanation, the rise in magic. Armed with a stack of papers containing twenty years of weather statistics, they made their case to Baron Kanin, who didn't waste time putting a plan into action. When the weather cleared, construction started on Cascade's weather station and fire lookout equipped with firefighting equipment, Argentine Rock, at Butte Springs. Despite the tragic history of Butte Springs—they had rescued Jordyn from a coven of murdering witches who were living in the dilapidated cabins left behind by miners—its location served their purpose.

Ansel followed the curve, his truck pushing into the corner. When he spotted the familiar pearl-white crossover on the shoulder, the sunshine making it sparkle, his heart lodged in his throat. With his approach, three backpackers stepped out from the tree line to stand beside her car where they waited for him. Rolling up to the back, he parked a foot from the bumper, marked he was at the location, and a second later Mandy reported search and rescue and medical were fifteen minutes out, and an airship was in the air. It would take minutes for it to reach them.

"I don't have cell service. Communication is by radio," he stated as he activated the handset, clipped the mic to his BDU top, and put the plastic piece in his ear.

"Confirmed," Mandy replied.

He killed the engine, got out, and straightened to his six-four height. His muscled build intimidated some. Then his black BDU top—with his name, rank, and Cascade's crest—jeans, boots, and dropdown holster intimidated the rest. By the looks he was getting when he approached the three, they weren't immune.

"Captain of Enforcers Ansel Wolt, Cascade," he announced with his hand on the butt of his gun.

"She said she was non-human, she didn't say she was from Cascade, or that she was a lycan, and she didn't say anything about enforcers," a man responded. His pale brown eyes narrowed. His sandy blond hair was back in a bun, while strands sat against his tanned neck, the ends on the collar of his jacket.

"Would it have mattered?" Ansel asked but didn't wait for an answer. "Search and rescue are on their way and a medical airship is in the air. Are any of you hurt?"

"No, just Dusti," a girl answered as she sucked in a breath, her eyes spiderwebbed with red. "I hope she's all right."

"Where is Doctor Hyde?" She better be all right, or there was going to be problems.

"She went up the mountain. We weren't on a trail. How is she going to find her?" Man Bun asked.

By the fear your thundering human heartbeats left behind, he wanted to answer. "She'll follow the trail you left."

"We didn't leave one," the girl mumbled.

"If you walked through brush, you left a trail. I'm going to follow her. When search and rescue arrive, they've been advised to contact Cascade. Dr. Hyde is being tracked," Ansel explained.

"How?" Man Bun asked.

"Does it really matter?" a male questioned. "Dusti could be hurt."

"I can't believe you're arguing," the girl accused.

They clearly didn't need his assistance, and he wasn't going to listen to them. Leaving them to themselves and their argument, he crossed the street and ran up the embankment. When it leveled out, he pushed through brush, then trudged into the underbrush and trees. As their voices drifted, he heard their names while they argued—Jason, Trish, and Eric—then they were talking about how he looked normal, not like a lycan, and Clio looked human. Part of her was.

Humans. Shaking his head, he walked a little farther, and when he was confident they couldn't see him, he stopped, brought his wolf forward, his eyes gleaming bronze, and knew he was going to regret what he was about to do.

It had taken months of denying himself, discipline, and ignoring her to build walls around the instinct to possess his mate and train himself and his responses when he saw her. Forced to see her day after day, pretending they weren't fated mates—hadn't kissed, he hadn't held her against him, they hadn't made plans—and not losing his shit every time a male talked to her, pushed him to an edge he might topple over. He kept telling himself it was for her safety. Like when he watched her townhouse at night and kept track of her location during the day. He shadowed her because Bronte, a dhampir, assassin, and ex-lover, tried killing him by setting him on fire, and then drugged Clio. Thankfully her human side, the part she hated, saved her life. The thought sent fear down his spine as he pictured her hiking along only to have Bronte find her. He needed to find her. Protect her.

The cost of exposing himself was going to feel like he was flaying his defenses and it was going to be the end of his sanity. Then feeling her would have his wolf howling for its mate, his body demanding to touch her, the need coiling in him like a starving beast. With his walls lowering it took him a heartbeat to lock on her, his wolf finding its mate, and his head jerked in her direction. As if following an invisible path, he started up the mountain, then he caught Clio's scent— cinnamon and spice with a pinch of sweet. His wolf howled while the emptiness where Clio should be blackened to the point of pain. Shoving the feelings down, because they were going to derail him, he noticed her scent didn't hold the chemicals or the sterile crispness from being at Nearctic, the med room she oversaw at Foxwood. She hadn't been to work.

What was she doing? Why was she there?

Ansel would have to ask her when he found her. Hiking through brush, over fallen limbs, and boulders, his height giving him long strides, combined with his speed, he closed in on her location in seconds.

"Dusti!" Clio yelled. She shook her head in frustration with the hikers' lack of knowledge of the area. It was not a ravine. And how Dusti fell was beyond Clio. With her bare knees on the rock, her hands on its edge, she searched the narrow fissure, saw red fabric clinging to the sharp edges and pro-truding roots, and straight down it opened to the ground. This was the place the girl went over; her scent saturated the air, as did her fear. Clio had no idea how large or small the area was. After changing to a sitting position, she shifted the strap to cross her chest; she didn't want it falling from her shoulder, nor did she want the med bag to cause her to fall. She didn't need to add to the wounded.

As if the weight of a presence drifted over her, a chill feathered her skin, and looking to the right, left, and behind her she didn't see anyone. It was an odd feeling and one she should have been used to. She was convinced there was a phantom following her. First it was in her dreams, the dark figure watching her, then it was in the quiet she used to center herself. Clio refused to tell anyone, especially Dr. Carrion, her therapist. He would tell her it was an emotional reaction to having been drugged and then forced to watch Captain Wolt being set on fire. Like her amnesia. She called BS on that, too. There was something else going on, she could feel it. Shaking the feeling loose to focus her thoughts on the decline, she took a step, then another, her hands on the rocks on either side of her, another step, and she looked down.

Thirty feet, maybe forty. Too damn far to fall. And the girl was human. Clio couldn't hear her heartbeat—not a total surprise, but not good. She hated where her thoughts were going and stopped them. She scooted down the side of a rock, making sure her steps were firm, then her skirt caught and while she worked to pull it free, the med bag hit an out-cropping that shifted her weight and knocked her to the side. Nearly losing her footing, Clio stopped herself from tumbling down, her hair falling in her face, the rocks cutting her skin, leaving a sting, and she steadied herself. Secure on a larger rock, she took a second to examine the abrasions, cuts, and reddened areas that would turn into bruises, and mumbled curses. She couldn't afford to get hurt. As a Wight it would take shifting into her wolf form to heal, or days to heal naturally, her human side slowing the process. Frustrated she had gone back to her default setting, resenting both halves, she tucked her strawberry-blonde hair behind her ears, the mass of curls down her back, yanked her skirt free, heard fabric tear, and continued her descent.

With Clio's yell, he made a right and started running, his dropdown holster hugging his thigh moving against denim, the radio and equipment on his tactical belt jostling. Covering the side of his face in the crook of his elbow, limbs whipped his forearm as he charged through the woods like a bull. He broke branches, upturning dirt and crushing foliage as he went. Then he caught the scent of blood, a sweet iron he knew too well ... human, werewolf, his mate. His wolf howled, and pressing on the thinning barrier between it and the world urged him to run faster while his blood rushed in his veins. He kept to the invisible path, then skidded to a stop when he reached a rock point and cliff. Clio's scent hung in the air, and while he knelt, her spice threaded in his memories. She was in front of him, chained to the ground, her knees in mud, her cries carrying on the air thick with kerosene, smoke, and burned flesh. And Bronte's stench. It was a painful reminder of why he betrayed her the way he did. If anything happened to Clio, his life was over.

The end.

There wouldn't be a second chance. Ordered by the Highguard to standdown, he was forced to give up his hunt for the dhampir, live with his festering revenge, and keep Clio at a distance. He told himself he was content with staying in the shadows to watch her, that it was better than nothing. While his thoughts bombarded him and his selfishness reached new levels, he stared at the crevice, the boulders, rocks, and dead bushes as they turned white and blurred under the sun. Ansel jerked himself from his thoughts with her voice and jumped to the first rock big enough to hold him.

Not wanting to scare her—she didn't know if the woman was conscious or not—Clio softly announced her presence, "Dusti, can you hear me? I'm Doctor Hyde, I'm here to help."

Dusti lay in a crumpled mess of hiking gear while her backpack arched her back off the ground. The woman's eyes were closed, her hair covering one side of her face. Dried crimson stained her cheeks and neck, and the ground glittered behind her. Clio froze when the eerie feel of the phantom's presence crashed into her.

"Sh-Shit," she stammered as she jumped back, not so far as to go near the ledge, which was damn hard. "You just shaved five years off my life."

Softly landing a few feet from her, he straightened to his full height. The area wasn't more than ten by ten, littered with loose gravel, the edge a sheer cliff. The girl was lucky she landed where she had. Between bounding through the woods and jumping down the rock face, he needed to adjust his tactical belt and holster. After doing so, he saw Clio's knees were scratched, her skin red, puffy, and there were cuts and scrapes on her bare legs. The pale blue skirt she wore had been ripped on one side, all the way to her hip, and there were brown smudges on the thin material. So thin he could see her creamy skin and the outline of her toned muscles. His wolf reared, the instinct to touch her, to pull her to his body and hold her, became a physical pressure he battled. Touch would make him feel better, would assure him she was safe, her heartbeat a rhythm for his ears only, but he couldn't. He shut down his walls, trying to close her off from him, and shoved his wolf to his depths.

"Doctor Hyde, it's impossible to shave years off your life. As a werewolf, you're immortal."

Half, she wanted to point out to Captain Good Mood. She didn't when, she had no idea how you could be half immortal. How did he make her feel like an idiot every time he was around? Giving him a hesitant glance, she caught his cinnamon eyes narrowing on her, as bronze shards rose from the deep, like his wolf was searching for her, trying to drill into her. She felt his presence as if it was gale force winds churning in a storm, its rain-heavy clouds building an impenetrable wall between them to block her out. Through the cracks she felt the chill coming from the darkness in its center, the threat he was, and fear slid down her spine. The cold did nothing to erase the phantom's presence she felt moments before. The warning coming from him was the opposite of what he had done. *He tracked me. Not another enforcer, not a patrol, but Captain Wolt,* she thought as she pulled gloves from her bag. And he found her. *Shut up, Clio. He's doing his job. Captain Good Mood has no interest in me, never has, never will.* More than once, Clio had told herself she focused on him because he was unattainable, untouchable, so far out of her reach she would never have to worry about getting close to him. Because she didn't have the time for a relationship.

"Have you examined her?" Ansel asked.

"No. It took me a while to find her."

With Dusti's heartbeat in her ears, she cut her attention from the captain and gently moved the girl's arm. Before she started relaying the injuries, she heard Captain Wolt giving search and rescue her identification information, and they could confirm it through Cascade's communications or with Eachan Grimm, Head of Personnel at Celestial Medical Center.

She waited another second before beginning. "I don't smell disease, cancer, or internal injuries ... she's in good health. The patient's skin is cool, clammy, her heartbeat is racing, she's in shock. There are lacerations and abrasions on her face. Left wrist, deep contusions and swelling around the closed fracture, multiple fractured digits on her right hand—index, middle, pinky fingers—and bleeding under the skin. Right leg, there's an open fracture, tibia, bleeding, extent unknown. Head injury, blood loss." She gently lifted eyelids and checked for damage. "Subconjunctival hemorrhage in both eyes." After taking a penlight out of the bag, she swiped the beam over the left and then the right. "She's unresponsive, has unequal pupils."

Her voice held her confidence, knowledge, and a hint of the warmth that made her a healer.

"The flight nurse has the information, and is ready for her," Ansel reported just as the sound of the airship's blades slicing through air grew closer. Meeting Clio's azure gaze warmed by honey streaks, he continued, "There's no way we can get her out of here from this location. The airship is going to hoover, and they'll lower a basket. You need to stabilize her."

"Copy." Clio started unpacking the med bag, grabbing a cervical collar. She would secure the girl's neck before treating the laceration on her head, the closed fracture, and then the open fracture.

With the medical airship thundering above them, its blades sending gusts of wind through the treetops, the reverberation cascading into the basin below, she lowered her head, and looking up at the dark being, met Captain Wolt's stare. His focused concentration drilled into her, and she felt herself slipping into the quiet, a muted space she used to protect herself from Bronte's voice, the sound of flames sweeping over Captain Wolt's flesh, the ruined hospital of her nightmares, and the invasion of having been taken. It buffered the worst of her fears, the frayed edges of her anxiety, and the phantom's shadow offered protection. The unconscious hiker, the severity of her wounds, and the human airship registered but wasn't the reason she grasped onto the protective silence and the being that couldn't be real. With her next breath, the roaring saturating the air and the thump of reverberation above her began fading, leaving her with her heartbeat, her pulse in her ears, and her focus on the patient. Holding his cinnamon gaze with shards of bronze longer than she should have, she took in his rugged looks, the set of his jaw, and the ends of his auburn hair grazing the collar of his BDU top. She knew the truth and didn't want to admit it, let alone face it and her fear. The cause of her fear. It wasn't Bronte, not totally.

It was him.

It was the cold he embraced.

The strength he possessed.

The control he held onto with a steel grip.

She was protecting herself from Captain Wolt and the storm raging inside of him. It was an instinct she couldn't deny, but at the same time she wanted to leave herself open if he needed her. Inside the quiet she felt safe, the world buffered, as if she pulled herself out from the revolution of life.

Battling the fear he created and herself, she yelled, "Help me with the backpack." Her words shattered the quiet like it was thin glass and flooded her with noise, breaking the moment. The choice had been made.

Ansel watched her, the change, and nodding his response, wanted to ask what she saw when she looked at him with that concentrated glare. A monster? A thief who had stolen her right to choose? A coward? Did she see the reason for her fear? Or was there a chance, slim as it was, that she saw her mate?

With tension in her voice, because she disagreed with him, Jordyn had told him Clio's instinct to recognize him was buried under what he had done to her. What he had done and what put him in debt to the Fellowship of the Stone. *Their dog on a leash.* With the thought, the collar around his neck, the medallion nothing more than a corrupted crest, felt heavy and burned his skin. Jordyn didn't know it had been a spell, its caster Leonidas, demon spawn of Eros, the Greek god of love, devout member of the Fellowship. It took the albino demon with pearl-white eyes seconds to shroud Clio's memories in a shade laced with evil colder than ice, making him a stranger and those memories dangerous. If she touched the venom enshrouding them her instincts forced her to back down.

The conversation with Jordyn, as she faced an interrogation by the Highguard's Justice Talbolt, had been against proper etiquette. Captain of Enforcers didn't rate speaking with Cascade's soothsayer and Prime's scion. It didn't stop Jordyn from telling him to talk to Clio, to open communications, because she would fight back, destroy the vault holding her memories and find out what he had done. That's who she was. She wasn't scared of a challenge or getting hurt. What was going to happen when Clio learned the truth? He didn't know. He relied on his cold control and on his fantasies, her body against the length of his as he slept, to keep him from reaching out to her. Bending down, his arm brushed hers, sending fire into his shoulder. He let the burn scorch his insides as they began removing the backpack from the limp body.

Acute awareness, like a scalpel through her flesh, cut into Clio's senses with Captain Wolt's touch, his closeness, his wolf's strength, his smell of pine, smoke, and the richness of his skin. Wild. Dark. Forbidden. A silent mystery to her. A threat. Save for the bits of his past she learned from Dr. Carrion—Deviant, a human with magic-born traits, and therapist at Celestial. She didn't know anything about Captain of Enforcers. Pureblood. Domineer. Werewolf. Ansel Wolt was a one-hundred-and-forty-one-year-old man with an unknown past. Locked in a self-created cell of isolation. Parts of her battled for their place but it was her wolf's demand that won. Rising, its fur brushing her skin, she felt the need to heal him, to touch him and bring him back, give him a home. Forgiveness for his sins.

Assassin.

Bronte.

Lovers.

The three words were like arctic water over her warmth, and freezing her skin, they seeped into old wounds to create images better left forgotten. Despite her denial, his bronze eyes were holding her, *I won't leave you*, and flames crawled over his body and a knife slashed across her mind. The sting was enough to reinforce her focus, the memory a danger, and the silence she created, where she believed her phantom watched over her, veiled her, canceling the world. With the backpack to the side, she carefully placed the cervical collar around the girl's neck. Moving on, she took a medicated pad, placed it on the seeping wound on the side of the girl's head—she was lucky her neck hadn't been broken—then wrapped it with gauze. With her mind on her tasks, she didn't notice when Captain Wolt stood, leaving her to wrap a binding around the closed fracture, then strapped a brace in place around the wrist. Clio checked the fractured fingers, treated them the best she could without doing further damage, and tapped them together, making them immobile. Lastly was the open facture. It was ugly, the tip of the bone pushing up and against Dusti's cotton pants, wet and stained from blood. She didn't cut the material away to treat the fracture; the nurse on the airship would have the proper equipment to stabilize the injury.

Minutes later, Ansel held the metal edge of the basket stretcher, and doing his best to control it, lowered it until it rested on the ground. He took the spinal board from the basket and set it next to the woman while the blades and roaring engine rose to a crescendo. He met Clio's gaze and saw a rawness that tore at him. There was the thrill of doing what she loved, the moment written on her face, then there was another and it was like she was skinning him alive. It was the innocence in her, a type of naivety. Its appeal drew him in, and despite wanting to protect her, he wanted ... needed to absorb it. Steal a sliver for himself. Unfortunately, there were things he couldn't change. His past. His relationship with Bronte. His betrayal. He couldn't touch her.

"Ready?" he asked.

Rather than yelling at him, Clio nodded her response. They were both kneeling beside the woman, and on the silent count of three, moved her from the ground to the board. Immediately Clio went to work on the straps.

"Is she stable?" he asked without raising his voice.

'Affirmative,' she mouthed. Trying to yell over the air-ship's engine was futile, and Captain Wolt was watching her, his bronze gaze tracking the slightest movement. She buried her feelings, wiped any emotion off her face, and wore a neutral look. At least she hoped. She was a fool, and she didn't need him knowing she was thinking about him more than she was the human waiting to be transported. Clio could fix broken bones, stitch skin, close wounds, cure the sick, but she had no idea how to cut the captain loose. The fear he created with his presence should have been enough, but no, and she couldn't heal her own damn heart, or fix her missing memories.

When Ansel stepped in to help lift the girl, a man wearing a Paradise County Search and Rescue uniform appeared from the rock cleft. Ansel pointed to the board as Clio stood and took her place along the wall of rock. When he under-stood the situation, he dropped his gear, and approached Ansel. Taking his place at the girl's side, and gripping the hand holds in the board, Ansel waited for Search and Rescue to do the same.

"On three," he said loud enough the human nodded. "One. Two. Three."

Together, they lifted her and gently placed her in the bas-ket. Clio was at the girl's side in a second to make sure her bandages remained in place, the brace on her wrist, her hands were secure, then she stuffed material around the open fracture to immobilize it. Satisfied, she backed up and out of the way. Ansel grabbed the first strap, and following his lead, Search and Rescue took the next until Ansel fas-tened the last one over the girl's leg and backed up to stand beside Clio. He grazed her arm with his, he couldn't stop himself, and her skirt brushed his jeans while the human talked into a radio as the basket and girl began to slowly rise.

Seconds turned into minutes as the sun caught the metal sides and sent glittering sparks into the air. The three of them held their breath as it rose, and when it was close enough, they watched half a body, then an arm extend, capturing the basket and girl, and both disappeared into the airship. Ansel released the breath he had been holding and watched it clear the treetops, the blades slicing through air as it departed.

The man turned his hat from facing backward to forward, the bill blocking the sun, then picked up the med bag and slung it over his shoulder. When the airship couldn't be heard, he said, "Captain Jim Barnes, Paradise County Search and Rescue."

"Captain Wolt, Cascade Enforcers," Ansel stated.

"Doctor Hyde, Celestial Medical Center," Clio said as she bent to gather the supplies. While the human's presence disrupted the tension and loosened the threads of her fear where Captain Wolt was concerned, it did nothing to the need to appear human. It nearly overwhelmed her as she shoved everything into the med bag. Her position at Nearctic, personal physician to the Kanin family, wasn't something she advertised, and wasn't something the human needed to know. Personal doctor to Pureblood werewolves wasn't human.

"The girl is lucky you came along," Captain Barnes started. "There's no cell service here, gets a lot of people in trouble. How did you get help?"

"Enforcers have terminals in their vehicles. Connects us to our communication center," Ansel answered, his voice flat.

"And she's an enforcer?" he asked as he eyed Clio.

Clio took her place beside Ansel, making him feel like the man he wanted to be for her, the wolf protecting its own, and answered before she had a chance, "Doctor and en-forcer." She always would be.

Captain Barnes watched them, gauged them, the two ly-cans in front of him. "I see. Impressive gear, Doctor. Do you always travel with that kind of equipment?"

"Affirmative." Clio adjusted the strap across her chest, se-curing it for the climb. Wanting to get out from under the captain's attention, she met his brown stare.

"All right. I guess it's time we get out of here." He gave them another questing look, grabbed the backpack, slung it over his shoulder, and headed to the rock cleft in silence.

When he was out of sight, Ansel met cobalt eyes subdued by honey, and framed by blonde lashes painted in black. "I'll go up, then help you."

"Awe, my knight in shining armor?" Clio teased and felt the silence crowding in and pushed it back. She made it down, she could make it back up. When his lips curved into what might be a smile on his formidable face, and his cinna-mon eyes glittered, her heart hit her sternum. *Stay strong*.

Yes, tesoro. He saw the laughter in her eyes playing with her innocence and didn't answer her. Ansel turned to the rocks, jumped to the first, and facing her lowered his hand. "Trust me?"

Negative. Looking up at him, Clio's fear crushed the ease with which she teased him, the break created by the human's presence, and worked to choke the life out of it while the quiet threatened to mute his presence. No. Her wolf flowed through her, fighting the fear, and she wasn't going to cave in. She wasn't scared of him, and the fear, it felt real, but it couldn't be. It was Bronte. The nightmares. She wasn't scared of Captain Wolt. He was pack and wouldn't hurt her. He served as a reminder of what happened. Nothing more.

"Trust me?" he repeated. Ansel saw the battle raging in her eyes and knew the spell was doing its job. He wouldn't be allowed to get close to her as long as she feared him.

With my life. "Affirmative." She raised her hand to his. His fingers circled her wrist, their warmth soaking into her skin, and she held him with her left, as he pulled her up, her body against his.

They stood together on the rock, the silence between them palpable when he turned and jumped to the next. Their dance, jump, body-to-body tension racing between them continued the entire way up the rock face. Just as she thought she was going to go insane, they reached the top, and backing away from her, he gave her space, and he stood in the shadowed woods. The sun breaking through the canopy cast pale yellow slivers across his stern face, slicing one bronze eye, and across his chest. When he turned and headed down the mountain, she followed, and as if sensing her anxiety, the quiet moved quickly to surround her. With her next breath the wind through the treetops disappeared, the branches breaking with her steps, the feel of soil sinking under her—there was nothing but the quiet.

As they made their way down, she focused on not falling, her footsteps sure, while ahead of her Captain Wolt moved through the woods with grace and a prowess she didn't possess. Wouldn't since she was a Wight. Like jumping the rocks instead of climbing them. He was a dark mystery with a storm circling him, and even as the quiet suffocated her senses and warned her he was dangerous, she wanted in. She yearned to feel the lashing winds, the pelting of rain, hear thunder roar in the sky and see lightning torch the land. She wanted inside the walls of his protection to see the man behind the mask. He was cold, remote, and a phantom. Why did she long to heal him and give him a home and for-giveness? Because she couldn't stand to see the darkness created by the pain in his eyes.

He doesn't acknowledge your existence, she screamed at herself. Yes, she was chasing a phantom.

At the embankment Ansel stopped, faced Clio, and while she was choosing her steps, she was lost in thought. She was clearly trying to bury her emotions, still they rolled from her at the same time her thoughts crossed her face like the webbed sunshine through the trees. She was light to his world of dark, innocence to his guilt. She was too good for him, that he knew. He understood some of his feelings came from adrenaline—its effects simmering, its intensity coursing through him—as the events that brought them together lin-gered in his thoughts. He continued to watch her, the way her hair tumbled over her downcast head, her hands clutch-ing the strap across her chest, and the sway of her torn skirt.

If I had found her hurt or worse ... A growl rumbled in his chest. He would have lost his mind, then himself to blood-lust.

With her approach, she met his gaze, hers darker than usual. "Here," Ansel said as he extended his open hand. *Take my hand, tesoro.*

Without hesitation, Clio placed her hand in his to have him wrap his lean fingers around her, once again, and they descended the embankment to find Captain Barnes and the three hikers waiting. Slipping her hand free from his, his fin-gers grazing the inside of her palm, a tingle skated down her spine.

Ignore it. Ignore it. Ignore it. Ignore him.

They crossed the road.

"Is everyone all right?" she asked.

"Yes, and they have something to say to you," Captain Barnes replied.

The woman took a step forward, her eyes going wide, and sucking in a breath she calmed herself. "We wanted to say thank you, Doctor Hyde. You saved Dusti."

"You're welcome. I'm glad I was here." Clio smiled, trying to make it look real, like she hadn't been put in the spotlight, like it wasn't coming from humans. She hated people telling her thank you; it was her job to heal. She couldn't stop herself if she tried. With nervous jerks she shifted the med bag and gripped the strap.

"Captain Wolt, Doctor Hyde, if you would write up a report, I would appreciate it," Captain Barnes said.

"You'll have them by tomorrow," Ansel replied, his voice even, stern, and carrying his authority. "If you have any questions, this is my email and phone number." He extended his hand, a white card with black print and Cascade's crest held between his soft, brown fingers. His skin color from his ancestry—his father Native American, his mother Italian. The captain reached for it, his eyes on Ansel, then took it. With his hand resting on the butt of his gun, Ansel took an unintentional step closer to Clio.

"Have they given you an update?" Clio asked. She was mentally going over the procedures, and the time it would take to get Dusti to the nearest trauma center while her senses targeted Captain Wolt and his closeness.

"She's conscious and they're treating her. Oak Run Trauma Center is waiting," Captain Barnes answered.

Their location put them between Trinity and Oak Run, making her assume they would have taken her to Edgewood Regional Medical Center, located in Trinity. It was one of the premier trauma centers in the state. It was where she had taken Detective Watt when the witches, the ones holding Mistress Langston prisoner, had shot him. That had been interesting. "Why Oak Run?"

"Her father, Sheriff Samuels, is the Sheriff of Paradise County. He requested she be flown to Oak Run," Captain Barnes explained.

"She's in good hands," Clio replied to say something. Oak Run was the county seat with the county legislature, courthouse, sheriff's department headquarters, hall of records, correctional facilities, and was the hub for state and county highway maintenance. The center for Citizen Base, or CB, a database of all shapeshifters, magic-born, and paranormals throughout the nation, was part of the hall of records.

"Trish, come on, we'll go to the hospital," Eric insisted, as he grabbed her sleeve.

Nodding, she looked at Clio. "Thank you again." Trish gave her a weak smile and turning, walked away.

"I'll be looking for the reports," Captain Barnes began. "This is the first time I've worked with Cascade. Thanks for the assist."

"You're welcome." Ansel's anxiety was about to short circuit his brain if the captain didn't leave. He had an interrogation to get to.

Captain Barnes tapped the card against another finger like he was considering something. "If we needed your assistance again?" he asked.

"All you need to do is call," Ansel responded. "We have people available, twenty-four hours a day." He watched the three hikers climb into the SUV and wanted to order Captain Barnes to follow them.

"Can those people track?"

"Affirmative. They hold state certification in law enforcement and are certified paramedics." Ansel gauged the man and the chance he would actually call Cascade for help.

"Good to know," he replied as he lifted the card as if putting emphasis on having Ansel's information.

Ansel didn't know how the captain felt about the enforcers, or if he took Ansel's position seriously when he lingered for a moment longer, then he also got into the vehicle. When the red and white SUV pulled onto the road and disappeared, Ansel turned to Clio. "Why do I feel like he was staring at me like I'm a hound dog?"

Clio giggled at his words and the natural sound of his husky voice as if his defenses had been lowered. "Don't worry, you're a big, bad wolf." She surprised herself with the ease in which she laughed and teased Captain Good Mood.

Your big, bad wolf.

"What are you doing here?" Clio asked. With the construction on the weather station and the fire lookout progressing, not to mention the new recruits, she figured he would either be at the construction site or supervising the soldiers and enforcers.

He couldn't tell her he had to know what she was doing and to make sure was all right. "You're the Kanins' doctor. You should have the best." Was he teasing her? What was he thinking?

"The best? Wouldn't that be Quinn?" she countered and fought to keep the smile off her face. Actually, it would have been Aydian, who was directly under Captain Wolt. He was the best, but possessed zero tolerance for humans and zero compassion.

Right. Ansel had to swallow the growl when she said another man's name and reminded himself the man was pack.

There was one thing left to do—his interrogation. "What are you doing here?" he demanded, his voice rough, stark, as he ignored her question.

She felt his defenses snap into place as he ignored her. As if he had spoken another language, Clio stared at him, disbelief in his question, which wasn't a simple question. "I was driving," she replied. The moment over, she gave him her back and marched to the back of her crossover, noticed how close he parked to her, and opened the trunk to toss the med bag inside. Her sandals sat side by side, and she debated changing her shoes—she wasn't wearing socks, and could feel dirt around her ankles and blisters—then decided it wasn't necessary since she was going straight home.

"Driving where?" Ansel pushed, and hoped he softened the edge in his voice.

"How is it any of your business, Captain Wolt?" Clio countered, with her hands on her hips, her frustration plain in her stance. He took a step closer, his cinnamon eyes with bronze shards drilled into her while his six-four height felt like it was towering over her.

"You haven't been to Nearctic and you're not working today," he started, his mind searching for a good excuse. "You never take time off." *You're wearing a skirt.*

If there was one trait Captain Wolt shared with Director of Enforcers, Rutger Kanin, it was his need to interrogate everyone. If she refused to answer his questions, he wasn't going to let her leave. She suddenly felt sorry for Mistress Langston having to live with Director Kanin twenty-four-seven. "Pack business. I was headed to Oak Run for a meeting. The Coulter Coalition," Clio answered as she tilted her head to look at him and block the sun from her eyes. "They had to have given up on me by now."

Oak Run was three hours from Trinity. The Coulter Coalition—made up of coyotes, black-tailed deer, gray foxes, and cougars ... they can keep the cats—were under Baron Kanin's authority. They were mostly Wights, with a few Illuminates, the alpha of the coalition being one of them. None of them were Purebloods or Domineers. However, they were building their own faction, the mixture of species like a rag tag group of magic-born were strengthening their foundation in the territory and getting attention. The unconventional coalition was proving you didn't need a pure pack to survive and changing tradition. Why Clio was going to see any one of them he didn't know, unless she was going there because she was a Wight. Maybe she thought she would fit in. While he hated the thought, he considered her as strong as any Pureblood. Hopefully, it wasn't a date with a male he would have to kill.

"Meeting?" he asked a little too harshly. Damn. It wasn't any of his business.

"Affirmative, Alpha Crevan Stone. We were supposed to have lunch."

He was a dead man.

"And the provosts of the sets. They have a functioning clinic but fear as their coalition continues to grow, it could become inadequate. They feel they need to expand, and seeing Celestial as the pinnacle, want a hospital of their own. They wanted to ask me questions. This was not a good way to start."

No, no, he wouldn't have to kill anyone. He was going to do a background investigation on the alpha. "Once you explain, they'll understand," Ansel assured. He was positive no one at the missed meeting would have a reason to be angry, and if they were, he would talk to them, and they would change their minds. Even apologize to her.

"I hope so. This is a great opportunity to connect Oak Run with Trinity on a personal level. I would love to have their medical staff intern at Celestial," Clio explained. With magic changing them and the environment, uniting the factions was in the best interest of Cascade. And medicine healed and was a good way to extend the olive branch. "No one said anything about the Emanation, but it's at the forefront of everyone's mind."

Teacher, helper, healer. Too good for him. A killer. A liar. Nodding his head in acknowledgement, his thoughts crumbling his response, he went to his truck, got in the driver's side, and leaning over, grabbed the flannel he had thrown in a few days before. By the time he walked back, she had closed the trunk and was waiting for him, the sun brightening the strawberry in her hair, the freckles over her nose, and the blue in her eyes. The scarlet was drying to crimson on her shirt and there were dirt smudges. While he sensed her lingering fear, she didn't back down from him, didn't give under the pressure. She stood up to him, and his wolf howled.

"Here. Thought you might want to wear this."

Captain Wolt was handing her a blue and gray flannel shirt. "Why?"

"Your top is stained with blood and is stuck to you. The tear in your skirt goes up to your hip," Ansel replied. Not that he stared at the tear, her pale skin, and the shape of her thigh as she walked.

His voice was uncompromising and hard edged as ever. How the hell did he manage to make her feel unbalanced? With threads of fear Clio twisted at the waist, and fumbling with her skirt saw the pale blue linen material torn and frayed, then her white silk top stained with grime and blood. And that was nothing compared to her running shoes. "Dammit, this fucking sucks! I just bought this," she mumbled. "I wasn't paying attention." Her focus had been on getting to Dusti, like tunnel vision.

Ansel couldn't stop from smiling ... one second a healer and the next her pink lips were curving around her seething curses. A part of him was glad no one had seen her in the skirt and top. Especially Alpha Crevan. She belonged to him. Fitted to her, the top hugged her breasts, flat stomach, and narrow waist while her skirt accentuated the flare of her hips. The body he had held against him. "They are ruined, but you saved a life today."

"We all saved a life today," she said as she looked up. "I'll take the shirt." She wasn't stopping, wasn't planning on seeing anyone, but that didn't mean anything. She hadn't planned on climbing the side of mountain to scale a rock face either. No one needed to see the blood and muck, or her thigh and panties.

Oh my gosh, my panties. Pale blue, to match her skirt, the string bikini panty seemed like a good idea at the time. Heat kept up her neck to stain her cheeks in scarlet. She was standing there talking to Captain Barnes, Trish, Captain Wolt, and the two other men, acting like a doctor confident in her field. That's a signature Clio move. Total disregard for herself. "Thanks. I'll give it back to you in the morning."

"No rush." Ansel held his breath as she took it from him, and drawing the sleeves up, rolled them to fit her better. The hem covered the tear and ended below the curve of her butt. Releasing his breath in a slow exhale, he realized Clio was wearing his shirt, his scent, and when she gave it back to him, he would have her scent. His wolf howled and clawed at his insides while demanding its mate.

This was nothing short of a slow death.

CHAPTER TWO

From the driver's seat of her crossover, Clio watched Captain Wolt turn his truck around, and when the silver 4x4 marked by Cascade's crests was ahead of her, the weight of his presence weakened and the quiet sank back. As she drove, the terminal dinged, and music played in the background while she analyzed his questions. The way he looked at her. Each of his touches. She knew she was reading too much into the attention he had given her.

She needed to stop. He treated everyone with the upmost respect, his kith and kin, and would protect every one of them with his life. She wasn't any different. She wasn't special. Doctor Clio Hyde's purpose was to serve the pack while Captain Wolt's was to make sure she did her job. Forty minutes into the drive her cell finally chimed, alerting her she had service and could make a call. Her nerves were going to eat her alive. Dreading losing the signal, and having to wait longer, Clio entered the number in the terminal and waited. One ring. Two. Three. Four. Five. Voicemail.

"Dammit." A spike of fear grated down her spine as his low voice and somber words told her to leave a message. Just because Crevan Stone, alpha of the Coulter Coalition, didn't answer her call didn't mean he was angry with her, thought she ditched him, or she hated thinking he didn't warrant Cascade's attention. After leaving a detailed message, her deepest apologies, she entered another number.

"Alpha Stone's office, Bess speaking, how may I help you?"

"Bess, this is Doctor Hyde from Celestial. I had a meeting with Alpha Crevan today," Clio started, and explained what happened. As she described search and rescue and the airship, her mind went straight to Captain Wolt, the shirt she was wearing, and how, without doing anything, he made her question her abilities. "*The tear in your skirt goes up to your hip.*" Like she planned that. "Let me know if he would like to reschedule."

"Yes, ma'am. I can assure you, he'll understand, and as soon as he is back in the office, I'll give him the message," Bess replied.

"Thank you." Clio ended the call and felt better. About the meeting, anyway.

The Coulter Coalition carefully holding onto the specification was one of three of its kind existing in the state of California. While the others were smaller and protected by a traditional pack or faction, the coalition had grown and gained respect. Alpha Crevan Stone was one of five Domineers, and each set governed by their own provost. However, Coulter Coalition with its diverse kith and kin wasn't a fundamentally pure pack as defined by the Highguard's criterions. With the coalition's demarcated by the criterions, Alpha Crevan and the provosts were denied the classification of Domineer. Despite the Highguard not giving them the entitlement, Baron Kanin recognized the alpha as well as the provosts as Domineers and responded to them accordingly. It gave Alpha Crevan the authority he fought for, the Coulter Coalition the legitimacy necessary to continue to grow, and because of Cascade's status with the Highguard, it also gave them a higher level of protection.

When a representative from the Coulter Coalition contacted Baron Kanin's office to request a meeting, logistics and security were discussed between Baron Kanin, his staff, and Director Kanin. It had taken three weeks and included the risk involved, where the meeting would be held, who was allowed to attend, and what kind of information would be shared, before she had been told it was approved. The baron's staff—eight people—occupied an office in the Enforcer's building, kept up with his schedule, special requests, meetings, social events, public interest, and the association with human politics. Errando Lynch, Wight, werewolf/human, had been assigned to her case and working with him they compiled a packet containing information she was allowed to share with the coalition. While they deliberated over details, he gave her the report of the background investigation conducted on the alpha, provosts, including the ranking officers in the coalition. Clio hated missing the meeting. She wanted to meet the faction of Wights and Illuminates who united their strengths, and she wanted to get out of Trinity. She hoped the different environment would have settled her nerves, and she needed distance. If only for a little while, from Foxwood and Captain Good Mood.

Did her a lot of good.

Not knowing anything about Alpha Crevan, besides rumors—he was respected, and admired by women—or about the Coulter Coalition, she read the file front to back, and memorized the information. Crevan Stone, a Shasta Indian, single, age forty, six-two, black hair he wore styled, gray eyes, Illuminate, coyote/mage, was the owner/chef at North Mountain Grill. The establishment served as a neutral meeting place for magic-born much like the Timber House in Trinity. Owned and operated by Weston Roth, a Pure-blood werewolf, he made sure everyone got along and followed the rules. Lunch, a cocktail, and relaxed discussion with Alpha Crevan, about her favorite topic, the medical field, would have been outstanding and calming. What she would do to have an easy conversation without worrying about the strict rules Baron Kanin had placed on the pack.

A blinker flickered, brake lights came on, and Captain Wolt's truck slowed to take a right turn as he headed back to Foxwood.

"No doubt going to give his report to his BFF Director Kanin," she groaned. What was he going to say about her? She ripped her skirt. Didn't make the meeting. Low-key went to her default setting and wanted to work with the humans. No, she doubted that. He didn't know she had a default setting. Thank the gods. Knowing Captain Wolt, he would state the facts and only the facts. Nothing personal. She didn't care.

Sure she didn't. Clio's thoughts went back to the alpha where they should be. Alpha, owner, chef, and single. There had to be something wrong with him. Arrogance if the photograph was any indication. Arrogant and determined. At age twenty he created Coulter Coalition, stating those without a faction needed a place to belong, kith and kin. His work and the sacrifices made were recognized when at age twenty-five the Highguard validated the coalition and confirmed Crevan as its alpha.

"Twenty-five," Clio mumbled. The challenges would have been brutal, mentally and physically. A fight to the death, as well as the Highguard's tests, its strongest tearing him apart, ensuring he was resilient enough to hold the coalition. Alpha Crevan was coming up on his twentieth anniversary. It was an achievement. And to further prove his strength and status he was contacting Cascade to secure the wellbeing of his people.

Clio slowed, and stopping, hit the button, and watched the garage door rise, her mind on the day, and not on the landscaping, rose bushes, river rock, and perfectly trimmed grass. When there was enough room, she drove inside, parked, and sat back, the motion releasing a wave of pine, and a heady bite that if she had been standing would have dropped her to her knees. In a futile attempt to forget about Captain Good Mood and his shirt, she focused on her next move, and if he was going to reschedule. Tired, Clio remained in the car. The rescue burned through her adrenaline, then the anxiety from dealing with Captain Barnes, and the unrelenting need to be seen as human, weighed on her. It made the captain's weighty presence in her thoughts impossible to stop. She knew he was trying to be kind, but he had no idea what he was doing when he gave her his shirt, and what it was going to do to her resolve to be covered in his scent. To wear one's scent meant there was a relationship developing. She was sure that was not what he intended. She tugged the collar closer to her nose and inhaled pine, the raw scent of his skin, and a tangle of smells from it sitting in his truck. Her stomach clenched, and her heart ached. He didn't know she was a single female let alone low-key in love with him.

"Should have said no," she mumbled into the soft material, then letting it fall, embarrassment and guilt simmered. She had been too flustered to think that far ahead, and she wanted to cover her rear and the blood staining her top.

It wasn't like nudity bothered her. Clio had seen it all, treated it all, stitched it all up, and was a werewolf who discarded her clothing in order to shift. Had done so in front of her pack when they gathered for the full moon runs. She didn't have anything to hide, but it wasn't about that, and she knew it. It was about appearing human and acting human around the humans. How quickly she slipped into the *accept me as one of you* mode. Not quite as bad as it used to be, but she hadn't kicked it loose, and the state of her clothes added to the feeling of not being good enough. Damn Captain Good Mood. Clio cursed, a string of colorful words, and after getting out, walked to the passenger side door where she retrieved her things, then stomped up the stairs and into her townhouse.

She walked the short entryway, stopping to set her purse on a side table, her keys in a crystal bowl, the clicking echoing in the empty house, then turned to the panel in the wall. Clio entered her code, deactivated the alarm, and when the lights were blinking yellow, she went to the center of the townhouse, the kitchen, where familiar scents greeted her. Cinnamon from her candles, the fading aroma of garlic and chicken from the night before, and spice that was uniquely her. A mix of wolf, human, female, and her body wash scented with vanilla. She wondered if the captain noticed it the way she noticed him and needed to slap herself for letting her mind go there. Soon silence surrounded her, promised peace, and she put her water bottle on the marble counter. Going through the living room, she eyed an over-stuffed chair. The warm afternoon sun turned her graphite couch a softer gray and made the antique cherry wood flooring glitter.

In the hallway, framed photographs—some black and white, some color; landscapes, and faces of her family— hung on cream walls. Farther down one door led to another, and passing the first, she walked to the open door and entered her office. When her position changed from ER doctor at Celestial, to chief physician at Nearctic, her workload tripled and so did the paperwork. She found herself in charge of making sure the enforcers, soldiers, and patrols' paramedic certifications were up to date, and they received the appropriate training. Add the time she worked at the Hollow, a secret hospital and containment building, and her administrative duties to all three, she did nothing but work.

"You never take time off." She guessed she didn't. Even going to Oak Run had been work.

I have no reason to take time off, she thought as she dropped her satchel next to her desk. Without looking at the stacks of papers, binders cluttering its top, and a pile of folders, she turned around to walk out and stopped. Boxes, packed with the furnishings of the room, sat along the wall, the mattress against another with a side table and lamp.

The spare room turned office was sufficient for the time being, but eventually she was going to have to sell her townhouse and buy a house. She wasn't kidding herself. She didn't need the extra room because she had a social life ... no, she didn't have guests, besides her parents, and wasn't going to have a relationship as long as she was contented with pining for Captain Good Mood. She needed a real office. Bookcases. Filing cabinets. A desk large enough to accommodate her computer, and every other electronic device she possessed. Inhaling and exhaling, she shook her head, not knowing when it was going to happen. And it was her decision. She didn't have a reason to take off work and didn't have anyone to talk to about selling her house. Her first home. Happy to leave the mess behind her, she left the room and hall, the antique cherry flooring gleaming, then crossing the vintage, red Aubusson rug went through the living room. The townhouse was updated, immaculate, not hard when she was never home. A friend of hers, a real estate agent, told her it wouldn't take long to sell, had practically begged her to put it on the market. Maybe she would start looking at houses and go from there.

Sure. Because she had the time.

Back in the kitchen she shrugged the flannel from her shoulders, draped it over the back of a bar height chair, stared at it, imagined its owner wearing it, and her heart danced like it was trying to kill her.

Stop thinking about him, she ordered. Stop thinking about the way he tracked you, found you, helped you up the rock face, and then told search and rescue you were an enforcer. *Yeah, stop thinking about him*, she repeated as she took the bottle of tequila from its place, poured, and picking up the glass, sipped to taste citrus tangled in warmth. With the second sip the stress of the day eased, the rough weight eased, and the tension in her shoulders slowly began unraveling. Before she decided to sit in the overstuffed chair and call it quits, she set the glass down. She needed to get out of her clothes and see what the damage was.

In her bedroom, she kicked off her running shoes, causing dark soil to sprinkle the carpet, and continued to the bathroom. Looking in the mirror she saw dirt smudges on her cheeks and forehead, and her hair was tousled on one side; the airship hadn't helped that. Crimson stained the right side of her white silk top while dirt colored the left. She shook her head as she pulled it off, and dropping it on the counter, made sure it hadn't stained her bra. After unbuttoning her skirt, she let what was left of it to drop to the floor. It took another couple of minutes to clean the grime off her face, then grabbing a sanitizer she cleaned the blood from her side and legs. If Dusti had been sick, which she wasn't,

Clio wasn't worried about illnesses being transmittable, she was a werewolf and her body fought diseases. But she had worked at Celestial for years, not all magic-born were capable of fighting viruses, and now working at the Hollow, she treated blood as the carrier it was. Clio ran a comb through her hair, her curls bouncing back, and swept its thickness up in a messy bun. With both her shirt and skirt in hand, she went to the kitchen, regretted the loss, tossed them in the trash, and intending on going back to her room because she needed clothes, she eyed the flannel.

He let her have it.

"No rush." His words.

Slowly walking over to it, she touched it, her fingers feathering the material like it might report back to the captain or bite her. "Screw it," she mumbled. Clio took the flannel from the chair, pulled it on, fastened a couple of buttons to keep the front closed, and smelled him all over again. "Yeah, 'cause that's what I need." Self-torture.

Grabbing her glass, she headed to the couch. She needed a couple of minutes to relax, to filter the day, go over her reactions, the treatment of the patient, and if there was room for improvement. Then there was Captain Good Mood and missing the meeting. After she processed everything, she would take a shower and wash it all away. Clio was staring out the large picture window at the rooftops, the mountain ridges eating the sun, the azure sky broken by thick, white clouds, and heard herself terming the woman's injuries when the muffled ringing of her cell broke the silence.

Where did I leave it? She uncurled from the cushion, padded over to her purse, and retrieved it.

"Doctor Hyde," she answered as she toyed with a button.

"Sorry for disturbing you, it's Captain Wolt," Ansel greeted. His office—a silent cave with white walls, a bookcase, filing cabinet, and two chairs—surrounded him. He hadn't added any personal touches, wasn't the decorating type. The only color was from the varied office supplies, the computer with Cascade's crest sitting before him, but then it blinked black, clicking off the color.

Clio reclaimed her seat, cringing while guilt threaded through her because she was wearing his flannel, a bra, panties, and nothing else. *In my house.* It was his shirt. *"No rush."* "How can I help you?" she finally asked.

"Am I disturbing you?" She sounded distracted. Stressed. "Are you all right?" He knew about her issues with humans; she wanted to work with them, had expressed her desire to work at a human hospital. Maybe today opened an old wound. She hated being a Wight, thought it made her weaker. And it had been a stressful rescue. Or it was him ... she feared him and their past. He was the reason Bronte tried killing her. Since then, he hadn't spent any time with her, and worked to keep his distance. Unless he was watching her townhouse. Selfish bastard. He stayed far enough away she didn't know he was there, because it hurt to be near her.

Just wearing your shirt. "I'm fine, and you're not disturbing me."

Okay. He didn't believe her but wasn't going to push. It was none of his business. And yet it was his business. "I received a form from Captain Barnes. He would like us to fill the report out. I've emailed it to you. When complete, you can either email it back to me, or send it directly to him," Ansel explained.

No casual conversation here. "I can send it to him. I'll work on it tonight." It might take five minutes since there wasn't much to tell. The initial call to communications and the contact with human resources would be handled by Fox-wood's communications. Or Captain Wolt.

"Copy. I'll let him know." Ansel sat back in his chair, making it squeal, and staring at the black computer screen saw his reflection. Bronze eyes glowed and he saw the monster living inside of him. The thing the Fellowship of the Stone was confident their magic would release from his depths. It kept him from saying the dozen things he had on his mind—she did a great job, was the strongest woman he ever met, was the one thing keeping him from drowning in his lies, and he needed her. Like the blood in his veins. Yet the monster staring at him reminded him he was a danger to her, and he wasn't his own man. He was owned like a dog and kept on a short leash. And if Bronte should hurt her ... "Enjoy your evening, Doctor Hyde."

"You too, Captain."

The only response was silence. Clio set her cell on the side table and picked up her glass. "He didn't sound good," she said to the room, then took a sip.

Not my problem. So not my problem. He doesn't know I exist. Let him have his distance. There's no reason to invade his privacy and nothing good is going to come from chasing a phantom. It's eventually going break me. She repeated the words like they were her motto; she was infatuated with an idea of who he was, not the man.

She didn't know him, not really, and struggled with the fear she sensed when he was near her. At a distance, he was safe. He would never approach her, and she would never have to tell him no. She would give her heart to her phantom, have her Pureblood Domineer all to herself, all while protected in her fantasy land.

"Safer that way." Even as her mind screamed it was a bad idea, she was setting herself up for a letdown, she grabbed her cell.

"Captain Wolt," Ansel greeted absently. He clicked the mouse to erase his reflection, to dissolve the monster tempting him, and stared at the crest, his mind lost in his sins. *Clio isn't broken. She isn't one of us.* White eyes with scarlet diamonds stared at him as if in silent protest, then he felt fangs slide into his skin, cool lips moving on his flesh, creating a chill that sank into his bones and turned his stomach with the invasion.

"I wanted to say thanks for the backup and telling Captain Barnes I was an enforcer. Sometimes I miss that." Clio's words rushed from her before she could change her mind. "Thanks for the shirt."

The nightmare lingered as Ansel's heart stopped for what felt like an hour before it pounded in his chest. *I would give you anything.* "You are an enforcer and you're welcome, on both counts." Was she wearing his shirt while she talked to him? The truth didn't matter. He pictured the blue and gray flannel draped over her breasts and resting on her skin, her fingers toying with a button. She wasn't broken. Wasn't scarred. However, she would be if he allowed himself to get close to her.

Now what was she going to say? "Thanks again. Goodnight," Clio blurted out, and ending the call tossed the cell to the couch like the apparatus was haunted and it might call him back.

Sipping the liquor, she watched the sun decline, its absence ushering in a steel blue cloak over the land highlighted by gold. Twilight wasn't day. Wasn't night. As if time, for breathless seconds, teased another world, a precious chasm always out of reach. Then night crept in, its darkness leisurely veiling the landscape, taking the un-known, and giving her the real world. Clio relaxed against the cushion, and holding the glass in both hands, relished the soft cotton sitting against her flesh and the pine and wolf marking her.

Ansel held his cell for several seconds, then gently set it on the desktop, while fighting the urge to throw it across the office. Jordyn had been right. Not that he doubted her, the soothsayer, but he wanted to believe his lies would last for-ever. Clio seemed determined and strong enough to unravel the spell and regain her memories. She would break the vault wide open and rip every single one of them out and understand what he had done. Time was ticking down to an explosion. And when she found out, would she walk away?

He had been living a fantasy, close enough to her to ap-pease his wolf, and with a cold divide between them, they didn't interact. It was bound to fall apart. He would have liked to have Bronte dead and buried ... more like burned at the stake, returning the favor. He would be happy if she was at the Highguard's Crystal Palace, Хрустальный дворец, in the Siberian tundra, preferably frozen like an ice cube. One mile underground and hundreds of acres of square footage, it held every kind of magic-born, creature of myth, and those who had gone insane. Like Bronte. He would take anything to secure Clio's safety. Before it crashed down on him, he had to open communications with her. Maybe he should ask if he could talk to her. The last time he asked her to leave her townhouse in the city, she gracefully declined. That was before ...

"This. Us. Is it real?" she asked, her blue eyes drinking him in while the smears of honey turned to heated shards.

"I hope so, tesoro." Ansel's hands worked up and down her sides, then stopping at her hips he gripped her and pulled her closer to him. "I need to make sure you're really here," he whispered.

"Mmmm, let me help." Clio leaned into him, her hands clutching the cushion behind him. Then, lowering, she held his side, their bodies touching, his muscles tense against her.

He betrayed his pack—Rutger, Jordyn, Baron Kanin—his lies going deeper than anyone suspected, but when Clio found out it was going to destroy the fragile trust she had in him. *Trust me? Affirmative.* She held his gaze as she battled the fear planted there by a spell, then clasped his hand and allowed him to lift her from rock to rock, their bodies touching on each of the narrow ledges. He paused, held her, and looked at her with the mountains behind her, her eyes bright, her hair loose around her shoulders. He didn't deserve her.

Three knocks jerked Ansel from his thoughts, and he looked at the door as if he could see who was there while his senses told him it was Rutger. Pushing his cell to the side—he didn't need a reminder of his lies—he entered the code into the keypad in the desk, the locking mechanism sounded, and Rutger marched in.

It had been nearly two months since the Director of Enforcers had been taken off the street in broad daylight, tortured, infected by an incantation, and brainwashed to believe Jordyn was a doppelganger and a threat he needed to eliminate. The methods Jordyn used to find him were proof of the strength of her magic, and why the powerful were targeting her or wanted her on their side. The means she used, a physical fight, to break the incantation's hold on Rutger proved she would risk her life to save her mate. While he hadn't been allowed to witness what happened—very few had been—Rutger mentioned she tried kicking his ass. He had a hard time picturing Rutger's six-four height and thick build against Jordyn's five-two and petite frame.

Ansel met burnt gold eyes as a shadow passed behind them and his muscled bulk sat down in the chair across from him. He gained the muscle he lost and maybe more, if that was possible, but with Rutger, who had shifted into the forbidden Bestial form—a seven-foot hybrid created from human and wolf to utilize the dangerous traits from both—anything was possible.

"I see you're living the dream," Ansel said, breaking the silence. They were repairing the incisions in their relationship, created by their lies. However, their personal hells created walls no one was allowed to breach.

Rutger grunted, then replied, "What happened today?"

"Doctor Hyde was driving to Oak Run when three humans stopped her along the Tombstone Mountain range and reported a woman, another hiker, had fallen from an outcropping and into a ravine. It wasn't, and she's damn lucky to be alive. Clio alerted communications, and Mandy notified the Ranger Station, requested Paradise County Search and Rescue and medical. While waiting for the airship, Clio treated the woman, we loaded her up, and the airship took her out. Captain Barnes from PCSR drove the others to the trauma center," Ansel explained. He left out the part of running through the woods searching for Clio like she might disappear. Although if anyone understood the drive to protect their mate, it would be Rutger.

"Any trouble with Search and Rescue?" he asked.

"Negative. Captain Barnes thanked us, and I think he liked the idea none of his humans had to scale the rock face."

"We can use that, our relationship with human agencies, as the incident will go public. I noticed you said Clio, how is she?"

"Yeah, can't stop myself. Besides scratches and bruises, tearing her skirt and ruining a silk top that hugged her every curve, she's fine. She's filling out the form the captain emailed us," Ansel explained.

"Her every curve?" Rutger asked with a grin, the darkness fading from his gaze. "You could talk to her."

"Don't start. However, I'll say and do whatever I have to in order to see you smile, brother." Ansel sat forward, glanced at his cell as another message lit up the screen, and he wanted to tell Rutger he had no right to talk to her. Resting his elbows on his desk, he watched Rutger shake his head. "You look like you're healing."

"You sound like Jo. And I am. Doctor Hyde didn't meet with Alpha Crevan?" Rutger asked, getting back to business.

Ansel regretted it but understood.

"Negative. The rescue took a couple of hours, and her clothes were ruined. If he's serious about receiving the requested information, he'll reschedule. Why does the Coulter Coalition want to talk to her?" Ansel asked.

"They're serious. Doctor Clio Hyde is the face of Cascade's healthcare and is the personal physician to the Kanins." Rutger stood, as if unable to sit still. "Errando Lynch has been assigned as the liaison between her and the pack. While precautions have been taken, keep an eye on her."

With his words the darkness came back, wrapping the usual soft tawny with gold flakes in cold bars. "Count on it," he promised. "How's the list for Pyramid Empire coming along?"

Pyramid Empire, a mining region sitting on the border of California and Nevada, drew Baron Kanin's attention when the alpha, Gersh Shaw, a Pureblood Domineer, began losing control over his pack. Of course, the profit the mines were making didn't hurt. Yet it was the search for sunstones—a mineral capable of bringing down the strongest magic-born, which Ansel believed were myth—pushing the baron and making it difficult to create a team.

"One minute it's a takeover, and I can deal with that, the next it's a negotiation and I won't touch it, that's Gavin's area of expertise. I've done what I can by proposing a team and I've given him my reports and my opinion. The baron is hesitant to make a decision since Gavin is in talks with Alpha Storm," Rutger explained, his low rumble giving away his frustration. "If it's a takeover, I'll recruit the Domineers in her pack."

"Alpha Storm. Isn't she a Pureblood?"

"Affirmative. An alpha and Pureblood Domineer of several hundred werewolves and has an interest in Gavin. She's beautiful, dangerous, and I think he's scared of her." Rutger laughed. "My younger brother doesn't think he can compete with an alpha."

Ansel chuckled. He could picture Gavin, his silk suits, button-up shirts, and ties, trying to escape the baron and the alpha. "Speaking of brothers, how's Tanner?" He liked talking to Rutger, hearing him tease his brothers, challenge his father, the alpha, and seeing his eyes light up when he talked about Jordyn. It was a reminder of better times. A sad reminder of what he would never have.

"Doing his job. Having Tanner and Bailey living within the Lassen Range has bridged the gap between factions and nearly erased the border. Alpha Storm is allowed to travel as she pleases. Pretty sure that's the baron's way of getting her to visit Cascade and Gavin." Rutger walked to the window with views of the parking lot and the baron's mansion, the lights doing nothing to inhibit his wolf's eyesight, and after looking out for a second, he faced Ansel, his eyes dark, his face losing any softness from before. "Baron Kanin's ability to hold the territory and authority is unmatched, and with Jo being part of the Highguard, her alliance to Prime and relationship with Shadow Lord, they see Cascade as a zenith. With that kind of power, the territory will continue to expand, and they'll expect our protection. We don't have the manpower."

"You talked to Baron Kanin about this?" Ansel asked, knowing the answer. Rutger was thorough, down to the last detail. If he was worrying about manpower, it was a fact.

"Affirmative. Whether it's a takeover or Alpha Gersh gives his confidence, it's another pack that will increase Cascade by hundreds. Now Coulter Coalition is reaching out, I give them a week, and I'm being generous, before they give their confidence. That will be one alpha of a coyote pack, three provosts, each ruling over their set. With a radical coalition aligning themselves with a traditional pack others will follow. There will be a need for security, a committee, a body to represent the factions, and a spokesperson from each to explain the unique needs of their territory."

"Cascade has incorporated the Unseelie court, Seelie court, the Lapis Lazuli coven, and the Fellowship of the Stone, the biggest factions, and has allowed them to keep their traditions and govern themselves. It will become imperative to band them together with the increasing population," Ansel added.

"There will need to be a person and a team in every major city. Cascade could rule the entire state of California and territories in Nevada." Rutger's shoulders tensed under his black BDU top and he turned his back to the window. "Security will be an issue as long as Krijgers are active. As the territory expands, it won't be beneath them to use anyone from Coulter, Lassen Range, and Pyramid Empire. And we've seen firsthand they'll use magic against us."

Like they used it against Rutger. "What about Allied Territories? Are they going to work with the pack?" Ansel asked. He had been forced to step away from the security company Rutger created to hide the existence of his team of mercenaries, Dark Rouges, made up of magic-born from every sect, when the Highguard investigated him. Allied Territories was currently working independently of Cascade. Much to the dislike of the baron.

"Negative. I'm keeping them impartial for as long as I can. There are humans submitting packages for employment. If they're qualified, I'll hire them. That will add to the legitimacy of the company and eliminate the separation between human and magic-born. And I'll have the loyalty of the humans. It will also detract attention from Dark Rouges. I'm having them monitor the temperament of the territory and watch for outsiders. The Krijgers being priority."

"The non-believers included?" The Emanation was creating a divide within the pack. It hadn't reached extreme levels yet, but it could.

"Affirmative. There are some who are talking more than others. I need to know what they're saying and who they're trying to convince. The baron isn't taking them seriously at this point, but I won't be caught unprepared."

"He can ignore them knowing you're not. It gives him time to work on Pyramid Empire and Lassen Range." If Cascade controlled California, its people might be able to stall the civil war between magic-born and humans while reducing casualties on both sides, if and when magic manifested itself. "Has Jordyn sensed anything?"

"You mean when she isn't chasing down bad guys with Detective Watt?" Rutger countered, his hate for the human ... correction, Latent evident. The detective was a human with magic-born in his lineage, and whose magic had been dormant, but was now manifesting itself. The human wasn't thrilled about it and depended on Jordyn for help. Rutger did not like it. "Affirmative. The weather has its own energy and it's continuing to build as if it's being fueled. She hasn't said this, she won't until she's positive, but I fear magic will use Mother Nature as a conduit."

"Like the earth opening up and letting creatures from hell free to ravage?"

"A little dramatic, but yes," he answered, giving Ansel a sideways glance and a half grin.

"You know me, all drama." They were the least dramatic people on the planet. "What's her timeline? When will she leave the Latent and the OPI and start working for us?" Ansel asked. If Rutger was worried about manpower, they needed Jordyn.

"Not soon enough. She says a month, maybe more. The longer she's there, the more magic-born are trusting the Organized Paranormal Investigations. While I'm not thrilled with the prospect of our own calling the OPI over patrols and soldiers, it'll lessen our load, and gives us time to add to our numbers. And she's watching the detective. Says he a good man, and she wants him on our side. It doesn't change anything. The training schedule has been posted and we'll be in and around Butte Springs. Jo will continue training with the slayers."

"I can't believe the baron authorized that and you're taking her up there. You don't think she'll have a setback?"

Butte Springs had been where a witch, sociopath, Flint Platt, had taken Jordyn and kept her prisoner for days before trying to sacrifice her to his god. Flint failed, fled in the chaos of the rescue, and after another failed murder attempt on Jordyn's life, he committed suicide. Even with his death and those of his followers, it hadn't been easy for Jordyn to get over the trauma.

"Negative. The original buildings are gone, there's nothing left, and with new growth over the years and construction she won't recognize it, and she can handle it. She's been through worse since then." Like finding, then saving him. Rutger stopped, his eyes holding his pain, his face more defined than it had been, and giving Ansel his back, he stared out the window. "She's stronger than anyone believes."

Ansel didn't doubt her strength and knew Jordyn had been handling a lot of things—pack politics, Prime, the leader of all magic-born, and Shadow Lord, an egotistical vampire with his own empire. "Clio sealed Jordyn's medical records and the baron won't give anyone access. Do you know why?" Ansel asked, changing the subject. The more they knew about her and her traits, the better they could protect her.

Meeting Ansel's gaze, he replied, "She hates the freak file. And Jo stated her case with facts knowing Baron Kanin wouldn't listen to an emotional plea for privacy. It's for your protection. If you know what she's capable of, you could become a target. They could use you to get intel about her. It goes for everyone save for Doctor Hyde."

"Who protects Clio?" he asked with an edge to his voice.

"While she has treated Cascade's soothsayer, is seemingly on friendly terms with her, Doctor Hyde isn't part of the inner circle. Jo doesn't associate with anyone outside of the Langston or Kanin family, and wouldn't socialize with a Wight and an employee. Doctor Hyde doesn't have the status and isn't at risk," he stated.

"You're using peoples' prejudices to hide their relationship."

"To protect their relationship. Who knows about the records being sealed?"

Lies in plain sight. "Team leaders. They asked about the information that had been deleted from the reports." Ansel's instincts told him no matter what Rutger said and the guise placed around Jordyn and Clio, she was at risk, and he was going to make sure Clio stayed safe.

"Lieutenant Bouldin?"

"Negative. While he is receiving updated information on Jordyn because he trains with her, sensitive material has been left out," Ansel explained. Jordyn's ability to heal, her connection with the pack, Rutger, her telepathy. Ansel experienced it once, felt the weight of her power, the pain it promised, the darkness roiling inside of her, and fearing for the baron and baroness pulled a gun on her. She could have killed him before he fired.

"Does he know?"

"He hasn't said anything and hasn't questioned anyone, but he must. He'd be an idiot if he didn't. Bouldin is sharp, that's why he's a lieutenant and head of security. He might be waiting to see what happens to Tracy. In the meantime, when Jordyn trains with him the sessions are recorded, and there is someone watching them from the observation room. The recordings are watched for discrepancies, her offense and defense tactics, kept for seventy-two hours, then deleted. There are others in the gym while they're there. Their presence isn't unusual, so it isn't causing a problem," Ansel explained.

Tracy, Lieutenant Torin Bouldin's wife, had been one of Jordyn's sentinels. Her time with Jordyn was riddled with challenges, disagreements, and questioning Jordyn's orders. While at Foxwood training, Tracy and Lieutenant Bouldin got into a verbal argument that escalated into physical violence and threats against Jordyn. Several soldiers, who had been training, stopped the fight from progressing and reported it directly to Baron Kanin. They broke canons when they argued in public, and then fought. Since Tracy incited the fight, insulted her husband, derided the sanctity of their relationship, and disrespected a Domineer with status in the pack, she was taken into custody. While those charges were added to her file, it was the threats against Jordyn, the doubt of her power damaging Tracy's future. The punishment for her crimes; she would never be employed by the pack, was placed on house arrest, and wasn't allowed near Jordyn. After an extensive investigation, Tracy regained her freedom and had been assigned a shadow to watch her movements. The severe punishment was meant to send a message to the pack, klatch, and the Cloaked that no one was untouchable and if you threatened one of your own you were going to be held accountable. Claudia, a shadow, and girlfriend to Jason, Executioner of the Slayers, the pack's assassins, was keeping in contact with the shadow following Tracy and updating Jordyn as necessary.

"If anything changes let me know. When are you heading out?" Rutger asked as he stood by the door, his hand on the butt of his gun, his stance tense.

"A couple of minutes," Ansel replied, holding his gaze, and hoped to hell Rutger didn't see the betrayal in his eyes. The messages lighting up his screen weren't going to be good news.

"Then I'll see you tomorrow. Have a goodnight." Opening the door, he stopped and faced Ansel. "You could talk to her."

"Get out of my office," Ansel ordered with a smile on his face.

Rutger shook his head, walked out the door, and closed it behind him, leaving Ansel by himself. Taking his cell phone, he checked the messages, three more since the last one, and reread the orders. Strong Lord of the Fellowship of the Stone was a mystical shapeshifter whose animal form was the half body of a lion and half of an eagle, and he held Ansel's leash. Ordered to meet with him, the medallion— gold with a wolf's head—felt heavy against his skin. Like background music in his mind the conversation with Rutger played, keywords provoking a response while he reread the order as if it might magically change.

CHAPTER THREE

Pine, oak, and cedar trees blocked the scant light from the winding, two-lane road. They began thinning and finally opened to a valley with tall grasses that swayed in the evening's breeze. The snow-topped mountains glittered under the crescent moon's silver light, its glow turning the snaking black asphalt a dull gray that led Ansel farther away from Cascade.

The first time he met with Strong Lord had been at Ansel's request. *Desperation*, he thought. He stood at the shore of Shasta Lake, the blue water lapping at his boots, the birds chattering as they flew, the Strong Lord's feathered mane bright white while his mocha skin drank in the sunshine as he agreed to Ansel's deal. In one heartbeat he secured their doom and gained a master.

"It's there, Principe," he mused. *"Know this, your legacy is blood, and your crest is stained scarlet."*

Instead of accepting Clio's invitation to go to her swanky townhouse in the city to celebrate the end of her administrative leave, and the fact she passed the damn psychological evaluation, he went home. Like a coward, he couldn't be there and watch while her privacy and safety had been invaded, and her memories buried. He sat on his couch, the front door open, the whispering woods the only noise, and while night's embrace wrapped around him, he drank his fill of bourbon. The end came in form of a message on his cell ... *so says the covenant.* A blood vow had been made, his freedom negated, and his servitude to the Fellowship had begun.

"I took a part of her," he whispered to the inside of his truck. That's why he confirmed she was at home, drove to her townhouse, and parked where she couldn't see him to make sure the area was secure. He sat there for a couple of hours, then headed to his meeting. The terminal dinged and chimed as if reminding him it was there. He wasn't worried anyone was tracking him because he signed off, made himself unavailable, and was on his own time. He laughed, the rough sound resembling insanity crossed with sorrow. He didn't have his own time.

Taking a left, the tires crunched on dirt and rocks, and continuing for several more miles, he made a right. The road narrowed and the trees shielded him from the moon while dirt drifted behind the truck. When there was a wider area, he pulled over well off the one-lane, dirt road and parked. He could have driven, at least another hundred yards, but he needed the walk. The air on his face, his body in motion, and the wolf in the woods.

His steps were heavy, his anger simmering, and kicking up red dust the cloud drifted over his black boots and clung to the cuffs of his jeans. Before leaving Foxwood, he had discarded his gear, dropdown holster, and black BDU top ... anything identifying him, and wore a plain white T-shirt, its sleeves snug around his arms. He wasn't there as Captain of Enforcers, wasn't there with Cascade's authority, just a dog called to heel. Unconcerned with the noise of his approach, he marched as his anger turned to rage and his wolf clawed at him. The night weighed on him to torment him with his sins, his betrayal, and the fated mate he would never possess. Clio stayed with him day and night, but opening himself to her and feeling her waiting for him, and then tracking her, pushed his control to the breaking point.

When he interrogated her, she hadn't backed down, and her strength hadn't helped his wolf's demands for its mate. The half that would soothe the need for touch while making him stronger. It called a primal part of him while revealing a vulnerability he thought had been buried under the deaths of his parents, the years of serving Bronte, her torture, the blood he spilled, and the lives he had taken over the century of his life. He thought he lost his heart, soul, the parts capable of saving him from himself. As if a door opened, he realized a fated mate wasn't a weakness. It was a strength. Rutger and Jordyn were the perfect example. They strengthened one another when nothing else could.

Ansel stopped and shoved his thoughts down, not wanting his regret, raging fury, or his grief staining his face and giving away his weaknesses. When he trained his face and gathered his control, he jumped to the rock ledge and found he was alone. Standing on the highest part of the ridge, the slice of moon teasing the land with light, he looked at the vastness of the mountains, the sea of trees buffering the contours, making them appear smooth like rolling waves. The location of the meeting, on the border of Cascade, had Ansel's instincts screaming something bad was going to go down. As if Strong Lord wanted to talk to him about his past, his mother, her power, and the monster living inside of him.

The thing responsible for killing his parents.

When the breeze shifted and moved Ansel's hair, the ends grazing his nape, he waited for the seven-foot shifter to lower himself then land in a semi humanoid form.

"Principe," he greeted as he shook his shock of white hair and feathers, the thickness laying down his back.

He hated the term. "Strong Lord." Ansel dipped his head in respect, then met yellow eyes the color of the sun. "What is this about?"

Turning toward the valley, Strong Lord let the silence stretch out between them before answering. "I have something you want."

Ansel was sure no one with the Fellowship possessed something he wanted, except the keys to his collar. "You don't have anything I want."

"I do. Nothing is given freely. You must provide compensation of equal value." His eyes blazed white in the dark. "Do we have a deal?"

"Negative. What kind of fool do you take me for?"

"You are indebted to me."

Ansel's rage hit a new level. "How am I supposed to compensate you when I don't know what *it* is?" Ansel's fury coursed through him, tangling with his doubt and the fear the blind deal would take more than a pound of his flesh. And he hated Strong Lord's games.

"Soothsayer's weaknesses. How she saved the Second."

"I don't know her weaknesses." There was the pack. Rutger. Trying to save them all. Trying to protect them all. Her heart.

"You lie."

"They're werewolves, fated mates. They have a bond, and she found him," Ansel replied. "The connection and the strength of it between mates is no secret among the magic-born."

He scoffed, his features sharpening. "Stop lying to me. There were wards." He nearly screamed the words, his mouth turning to an eagle's beak. Several seconds vanished into the night when he calmed himself, and his human features, what there were of them, returned. "At her ascension, she stated you were her brother, and one she protected when she faced the Highguard's Prosecution Administration. Family. You must know your di famiglia secrets, Principe?"

Ansel ignored the use of his mother's native language and couldn't believe Jordyn told Strong Lord he was her brother. As pride and belonging filled the empty voids inside of him, he became her weakness. He understood the need to restrict who saw her medical records. Who knew the depth of her relationships with her pack. Clio's friendship with Jordyn had to be kept a secret. "Any proof of a strength or a weakness is sealed. No one except Director Kanin and Baron Kanin have access. They guard it with their lives."

"You have your ways. The wards?" he insisted.

"I know nothing of them. I wasn't allowed to be with Mistress Langston. Had no way of seeing her or knowing what she was doing. I was ordered to put my team on standby, then I was given a location, and ordered to go there, by another enforcer," Ansel lied. He may be broken. A murderer. An assassin. And betrayed his fated mate. However, he wouldn't help in bringing the pack to its knees. Using her blood as an offering, Jordyn used the Collective to find Rutger, then twisted the wards until they were her own and saved the man she loved. "How do you know there were wards?"

"Nothing is free. You'll learn her weaknesses."

"Nothing is free. What are we negotiating for?" Ansel held the yellow gaze narrowing on him and felt he was losing the game.

"Milanka Telep."

Fuck me.

His breath stopped, his lungs ceased to operate, and his heart stilled in his chest. He wouldn't recognize her, Milanka Telep, until her blood was draining from her to soak the ground. If he killed Bronte, Clio would be safe, and she would be his.

"You know where she is?" Ansel questioned. He didn't trust Strong Lord and wasn't going to get his hopes up.

"You want her. I know you want to kill her to protect your mate." Looking at the sky, he mused, "Soothsayer's weaknesses are worth it? Are they not?"

Ansel's mind raced with hope and the consequences of his actions. He would sacrifice his life to protect Clio, knowing she might walk away from him. But knowing Strong Lord there was a good chance it was going to be a trap, one that would tighten the collar around his neck. "You've protected her. Hidden her from the pack and the Highguard's canons. You've harbored a fugitive. A murderer. The Highguard isn't going to forgive the offenses. Especially when you're a threat to Mistress. Prime doesn't tolerate those conspiring against his scion," he explained like the enforcer he was, his voice stern, disconnected from the emotion coursing through him.

Strong Lord looked at Ansel, his head cocked to the right, his eyes flashing white then yellow with his emotions. It was the first time Ansel witnessed him losing control of his anger and ... jealousy. He didn't know her importance to Prime.

Pushing further, he warned, "Prime will punish anyone who thinks about harming her." What had Jordyn done to secure the ruler of all magic-borns' protection? No one knew. No. One.

Strong Lord seemed to consider his warning. "Principe, pray I don't order you to the stronghold."

"Why haven't you?" Ansel was living on borrowed time, this he knew. The Fellowship hadn't made any demands of him, except for attending meetings. He hadn't been asked about the pack, the baron, anyone ... until now. And Strong Lord demanded Cascade's prize possession, Jordyn. Did he care if he ever destroyed Bronte and ended her evil? Affirmative. Clio's safety overruled everything, including his life.

"I haven't had need to."

Why? "You want Mistress Langston." It wasn't a question, and his bronze gaze met sunlight white in challenge. "You want her for yourself."

"Baron Kanin has become obstreperous. If they are justly alpha and soothsayer, and their link is unquestionable, all I have to do is bring Soothsayer to her knees. The baron will fear the Fellowship's power once more, and she will be humbled," he replied, his tone like steel. "Once she has been rebuked, and proven unworthy of Prime's attention, she'll understand her station. I'll have no reason to care what she does. I want your magic, and your loyalty to the Fellowship. You'll help us strike the final attack on Cascade."

Negative. There was no fucking way he was going to do anything against Cascade. He was stunned Strong Lord would threaten Jordyn's life. Ansel didn't believe she would be rebuked, humbled ... no, Strong Lord wouldn't allow a threat like Jordyn to remain alive, he would kill her. In doing so he would eliminate the pack's foundation, Rutger, Second to the Alpha, he would cripple Baron Kanin, and infuriate Prime.

"You're risking Prime's wrath," Ansel warned. There was no reason to mention the pack was stronger than it ever had been. He wouldn't believe Ansel anyway.

"You trust the reverence he has given the soothsayer is more than a man with a toy. I am a true power of lore and have eminence in the echelon of the Highguard. Prime will have to get another to entertain him."

Strong Lord was jealous of Jordyn. He wouldn't have believed it if he hadn't witnessed it. "You've threatened my Mistress." Strong Lord believed his status with the Highguard was going to protect him. How wrong he was. Even if Prime and Shadow Lord didn't protect Jordyn from the Fellowship, the pack would protect her with their lives. They would fight back. The same couldn't be said for him. If they found out about his connection to the Fellowship, and why they wanted him, they wouldn't hesitate to kill him. Eliminating the problem.

"You have no mistress, Principe." With a talon, Strong Lord pointed to the medallion resting against Ansel's chest. "I own you."

His past cascaded through him. No one owned him. At least that's what he told himself. With strong casts from the fae, his mother served as a priestess to the pack's lord, took council with him, held status with the upper echelon of the synod, and possessed a title with the Highguard. With the breeze circling him, Ansel heard his mother, her lyrical accent curving the stories she told by candlelight as the centuries separating him from his past drifted on the wind. He and his mom weren't so different. Strong Lord wanted Ansel's magic the way his mother's lord wanted hers.

Despite facing punishment from the synod, the lord's fury, and having her status as priestess taken from her, Priestess Gaia rejected Lord Alessandro's demand for her to mate with him. The rejection was quickly followed by intimidation and threats, but Priestess Gaia, Ansel's mom, didn't back down, she never did. Having embarrassed Lord Alessandro, he withdrew her from the echelon and Gaia was imprisoned for her defiance of authority, refusing her lord, and not adhering to the edicts of the synod. That's when the Highguard handed down their punishment and revoked her title. As a disavowed priestess her worth meant nothing, her magic and traits deemed invalid. She spent two years in the dank stone cell in the belly of Lord Alessandro's castle before convincing a girl, whom she'd become a mother figure to, to help her escape. When she was free, Gaia fled, and boarding a ship, sailed away. She didn't stop until she landed in the US where she met River, Ansel's dad.

Years later, a dozen soldiers dressed in black and wearing masks came in the middle of the night, took his parents from their bed, and home, and dragged them to their yard where others stood with torches. Their scent circled Ansel as one of them shoved him to his knees beside his dad. They watched a man wearing a red cloak rip Gaia's magic from her. What they didn't know, what no one knew, was Gaia had given him her magic years before and buried it so deep within him its feel was mute. Strong Lord believed Ansel inherited his parents' magic when they died, but when he tried to reach inside himself to feel its presence all he felt was cold, a dark, empty void. It was as if his mom had carved a crater inside of him instead of giving him her power. Watching the being that held his leash, his instincts told him Strong Lord wasn't powerful enough to force it from him, but it didn't mean there wasn't another who was. Ansel was going to have to report everything to Rutger. He wasn't going to put Jordyn's life at risk, lie and betray his brother. Not when they were healing their relationship.

"Her weaknesses," he demanded, his voice strained.

The Fellowship of the Stone were the extreme creatures of myth and legend, their features cut from their species, forcing them to live in the shadows as part of the Cloaked, those living in hiding. They were the strongest among their kind, but the Fellowship were outcasts who had broken their factions' canons and had been ostracized from their own. The blatant disregard threatened the safety of the Cloaked and all magic-born. To live under Baron Kanin's authority, each member signed a covenant with Cascade and a pledge with the Highguard vowing to obey the canons and understood the punishment for disobeying was death. Ansel wasn't surprised Bronte ran to them for help. She was an outcast, even among other dhampirs; their society and their cultured ways making her bloodlust and need to kill an atrocity. Bronte was created by her sire—a vampire, her mother a mage—to be the coven's daywalker, guard, assassin ... a weapon to use and to discard. When it came time to eliminate her, she fought back, and both her sire and mother died at her sword. Ansel couldn't stop from feeling remorse and loss decades in the making. There had been similarities between them—their parents were gone, they were alone, and neither of their lives were their own.

"I see you as I see myself," she whispered as she drew him closer, her fingers around his neck, her lips on his skin, a tinge of iron wafting to his nose. *"We live in two worlds and belong to neither."*

"If you're prepared to betray her, Bronte did something to you." Ansel shoved the memory down with the feel of her fangs as she took his throat. Against his will. "Or you're done with her."

"Time is not on your side." With his words, his body glowed in the night, and a second later a half lion and half eagle took to the sky.

If he betrayed Jordyn, he could have Bronte. He could end her once and for all and erase one sin staining his conscience. The temptation was like a flame. Ansel gazed out at the expanse of wilderness and felt it closing in on him. Revenge was in his grasp. Was he going to choose his mate? His loyalty to the pack? Or betray a woman who called him brother and was the symbol of Cascade's hope?

Clio padded barefoot back to her bedroom, set the cup of coffee on the nightstand, and crawled under the thick covers. The dream from the night before wove through her thoughts as she adjusted the pillows, and after pulling the hem of the flannel she wore from underneath her, grabbed the coffee and leaned against the headboard. Captain Wolt's presence tangled with the phantom sitting at the edge of her mind. She assured herself she wasn't dreaming of him, it had been from seeing him and working with him. And his shirt.

Beside her, her cell sat silent on the nightstand, her tablet blinking as it updated her email, messages, and schedule. She ignored it, ignored her dream and its affects, drank her coffee, and mentally planned her day. Despite the list of appointments, the evaluations she needed to write, paperwork needing her signature, then going back over the information she planned on sharing with Alpha Crevan, she couldn't forget to restock her med bag. All of that couldn't compete with Captain Wolt. Her dream. She was a damn hopeless fool.

"You're kidding yourself," she mumbled as she took a sip of the roasted notes, hoping they stopped her mind from continuing.

He didn't care she was alive. Didn't see her as anything besides Dr. Hyde an employee of Cascade who wore scrubs. And he saw her when she was at her worst. Torn skirt. Bloody shirt. Trying to impress humans. The bruise inside of her, the one she pretended hadn't been caused by his absolute denial of her existence grew with her thoughts. Why did she care? Because something told her it shouldn't be that way. It was as if she had left something undone. She forgot something.

Stop! She needed a forehead slap. So why did he interrogate her about why she was there? *Because Bronte is free,* her mind threw at her. Captain Good Mood didn't need any more guilt and something else connecting them. A situation that might break through his barricade of isolation. When the shrill ring of her cell blasted through the silence, it made her jerk, and she spilled her coffee on the comforter.

"Great." If this was the start of her day, she was staying home. After setting her cup on the nightstand, she wiped the majority up with the sleeve of the flannel, then grabbed her cell. "Doctor Hyde."

"Good morning, I hope this isn't too early," the throaty but somber voice greeted.

Sitting straighter, she answered, "Of course not, Alpha Crevan. I would like to apologize for yesterday."

"Please, no apology necessary." A rough chuckle, as if he couldn't believe she apologized. "I heard about the rescue, it's big news here, as you saved Sheriff Samuels' daughter. I understand it was a nasty fall."

She couldn't get over the easy sound of his voice, how freely he spoke to her, and the friendly tone inviting conversation. A distinct difference from Captain Good Mood and the military regime the enforcers and soldiers had become. "Yes. Considering what happened, she's lucky to be alive. It's a good thing the airship's ETA was a matter of minutes." *They should have followed the rules, and checked in with the ranger station,* she wanted to add.

"She's lucky you were there. The reason for my call is I'm wondering, would it be possible for you to visit this afternoon?" he asked. "I understand if it's short notice."

"Not at all. I can rearrange my schedule," she replied. The evaluations could wait, Lieutenant Bouldin wasn't in a hurry, he had his own problems and was busy training with Mistress Langston. The rest of her appointments were standard oral interviews with the doctors working at the Hollow and Nearctic. She had no doubt Baron Kanin would agree to the meeting, the alpha was priority.

"Excellent. North Mountain Grill, I'll have something special prepared, and we'll toast to the successful rescue. How about four?"

Something special prepared and a toast? She swallowed the embarrassment clawing its way up her throat and answered around the lump, "I'll be there."

"Looking forward to it, Doctor Hyde."

The line went silent, and making sure he'd ended the call, she closed her screen and leaned back. "Couldn't be a hiker from out of town or some nobody. No, it's the damn sheriff's kid," she groaned. *The last thing I need is attention*, she thought as she opened the screen and dialed.

"Good morning, Doc, how may I help you?" Mandy asked.

"You're too cheery this morning," Clio responded.

"A pot of coffee gives false joy."

Laughing, she explained, "Advise Baron Kanin I won't be at Nearctic this morning." She didn't want to see Captain Wolt, even in passing, and wasn't prepared to give up the flannel. "If needed, I'll be at Celestial for a couple of hours and then I'm meeting with Alpha Crevan."

"Copy. Everyone has heard the news of you and Captain Wolt rescuing the sheriff's daughter. You're quite the hero. Baron Kanin would like to talk to you."

Clio rolled her eyes. "It's my job. Do I need to see him today?"

"Negative. The meeting with Alpha Crevan is priority. Once I have a day and time, I'll message you."

"Understood. Thanks." Clio ended the call and made another one.

"Good morning," Danette greeted.

An Illuminate, wolf/fairy, she was over seventy, didn't look a day over thirty, and was organized, and sharp as a tack. She had to be when her command center consisted of one monitor displaying the doctors and nurses in Clio's team, specifically chosen to respond if there was an emergency. Another one keeping up with Clio's location, which was necessary like the day before, and Dr. Baines—a witch from the Lapis Lazuli coven, son to the Esme, and her second in command. Clio's secretary worked from home, a security precaution, because she kept up with sensitive data of the inner workings of Celestial, Nearctic, and the Hollow, and the personal information of the staff, including Mistress' records. Baron Kanin, Director Kanin, Mistress Langston, Dr. Baines, and team leaders knew Danette worked for Clio.

"I need you to tell Doctor Baines to handle the oral interviews at Nearctic and the Hollow," Clio explained. "Since they're going into day four, I suggest he takes donuts or cookies to the Hollow. No caffeine."

Thankfully, there were only two employees at Nearctic on Foxwood. Wyatt Gautier, paramedic from Dulac, Louisiana, Pureblood werewolf and Shade. Deviants, humans with magic-born traits, were progenitors, the originators of wraiths who were the originators of shades. When a Deviant experienced true death, their body dying, their soul drifted, and fighting to live once more, they became a wraith to roam in search of a suitable host. Prior to Wyatt's birth, his father had become a host and the wraith's presence made Wyatt part Shade. The doctor on call was Dr. Shahla Ramsey, Pureblood werewolf, whose family was part the upper echelon of the pack. With Nearctic being within the walls of the enforcer's building they weren't alone, having plenty of people to talk to.

Where Nearctic was social, with soldiers and enforcers coming and going, the Hollow—unknown to humans, the pack, klatch, and the Cloaked—was not. The medical staff, five doctors, eight nurses, and ten soldiers, had been hand-picked to work in the underground facility. While they rotated in and out, five soldiers, a doctor, and two nurses, stayed at the underground facility twenty-four hours a day for six days with four days off. The medical staff didn't fraternize with the soldiers and keeping to themselves meant they needed a break from one another. It wasn't ideal for shapeshifters to stay in confined spaces. Arguments between species were common; the elves, fairies, werewolves, therian shifters, and witches lived to antagonize one another. Dr. Baines needed to talk to everyone and make sure they were mentally and physically healthy, and there was no animosity among them.

"Noted." Clio heard keys being tapped then silence. "Confirmation Doctor Baines understands. Anything else?"

"I'm heading to Oak Run later in the day. I'll have my cell, but through Tombstone there's no service." Like zero as she found out the day before. Clio imagined Captain Wolt's 4x4 truck parked directly behind her luxury crossover, the silver and pearl white gleaming in the sunlight. "Beauty and the beast," she mumbled.

"Pardon me, Doctor, did you say something?"

"No," Clio responded quickly, and rolled her eyes.

"Very well. Marked. I'll have notifications sent to your cell and your terminal."

"Thank you. When I'm on my way back, I'll notify you." Clio ended the call, tossed the cell to the bed, and grabbed her coffee. Her heart raced with anticipation. A meeting with Alpha Crevan, a discussion about a future hospital, a relationship with a coalition and its provosts, was going to establish Cascade as a tolerant territory. There would be every kind of magic-born making them stronger while sharing knowledge throughout. Her thoughts stalled when, from its place on the comforter, the cell's shrillness broke the silence. She saw the caller and snatched it up.

"Mistress, is there anything wrong?" she asked, the question rushing from her.

"Stand down. I'm going to have to call you more often to prove I'm not always in trouble," Mistress teased, then grew serious. "Just heard who you rescued. I know how much you love attention and being in the spotlight, so I was making sure you were doing all right."

Closing her eyes, Clio held back tears that suddenly started building up. The day before had been stressful. Taking a deep breath, Mistress Langston, soothsayer, surprised her. She had been kidnapped, poisoned, wounded, had saved her mate, Second to the Alpha, from torture, and was the target of a group who wanted her dead, and she was making sure Clio was all right. Mistress Langston hadn't been exaggerating or lying when she told Clio she would risk her life for her kith and kin.

"I'll survive. Thank you for checking on me."

"You're welcome. Look, I know I should probably be telling you this in person, but I'm not going to pull any punches with you. Enough people do it to me," she mumbled the last part.

Clio couldn't imagine what it was and for a breath let the quiet mute Mistress' voice as she searched for her phantom's presence. "I appreciate the honesty ... I think."

"It's not bad. I hate discussing things of this nature over the phone, but you're going to talk to Alpha Crevan, so I feel it's best. I believe you have empath qualities. Obviously you've followed your intuition by becoming a doctor, but I think it's increasing, you're sensitive and intuitive."

An empath. Sensitive. Intuitive. She doubted it. Doctors were empathic by nature, possessed good listening skills, were observant, and were understanding, had to be if they wanted to help their patients heal. She believed hers were stronger because she was a werewolf with heightened senses, and concentrating on those that would help her strengthened them. Was it possible? Maybe it explained why she felt the need, instinct, to help Captain Wolt when he clearly wasn't interested. And the need overrode the nightmares from their ordeal, and the fear she felt when she was around him.

"Why do you think that?"

"At least this way you can't look at me like I have two heads. I sense it, Doctor Hyde. When I'm near you it reaches out to me," she answered, her voice perfectly cultured, her words clear like the Pureblood she was. "It's like you're reading me."

Clio laughed an uncomfortable sound. "There isn't a magic-born who would tempt your defenses."

"Not if they know what's good for them," Mistress replied.

It had Clio thinking about the times they spent together, and as they played in front of her, she heard Mistress' questions, and her answers, then their overall interaction. "You tested me at your ascension party. You're always testing me."

"Affirmative." Clio heard the smile in the word. "When you talk to Alpha Crevan and the provosts, don't be afraid to use your senses, and let your instincts guide you. While the alpha appears to want to move froward in a relationship with Cascade, if one of the provosts disagrees or hesitates, we cannot have them within our ranks. Their negativity will poison others, and the pack doesn't need any more opposition than it has. Do you understand?"

It was all or nothing. "Yes. I'll do my best." A direct order from Mistress Langston to question Alpha Crevan and the provosts and low-key try to sense their authenticity. No pressure.

"Excellent. Damn, I have to go. Arson investigators think a magic-born is responsible for the last forest fire. If there's a firebug on the loose, I'm going to be pissed." Exaggerated exhale, slow inhale. "You can do this, Doctor Hyde, and if you need anything call me. If you need to get away, I'm available and I always have wine, or as you prefer tequila."

Clio held the cell to her ear seconds after Mistress ended the call, letting silence thicken while she stared at the wall, the pictures, dresser, everything blurring. Yeah, she would have stared at her like she two heads, she did that a lot when she talked to Mistress. After setting the cell on the table, she took her coffee and sipped. It wasn't bad news ... no, she hadn't been diagnosed with something that might end her life. It was news, and Mistress had known for a while, and was being open and honest with her. Empath. *"It reaches out to me."*

"In search of strength."

"It's like you're reading me."

"In search of knowledge." She knew it like she knew her wolf. Mistress embodied strength and knowledge. Sitting for a minute longer while she processed the meeting, her role, and Mistress' diagnosis ... revelation, she sipped her coffee, calmly. Because this was her job. No different than Mistress investigating an arsonist or entertaining the most powerful magic-born in the world.

"Time to go to work." She set her coffee down and climbed out from the warmth, comfort, and security of her bed.

Two hours later she had dressed in gray slacks, a pastel pink, button-up blouse, heels, had done her makeup, hair, was wearing earrings, and looked like the doctor in charge of things. She didn't feel like it. Her travel coffee mug sat beside the screen of the desktop computer, the evaluations staring back at her, a stack of files with notes scrawled on green paper sticking to them. The stack increased from an inch to three, and she was sure if she ignored it for another day or so, it would reach epic proportions and weigh a ton, making it impossible to budge. There was no need for her to drive to Celestial when a carrier would deliver the files to her office at Nearctic. She visited the medical center to check in with staff, the paramedics, and to keep up with friends. Today, though, she was hiding from Captain Wolt.

Her mind wandered to a home office. She could do admin work from there. The thought had her reaching for the phone. Clio dialed a number, drummed the pen on the desktop, her heart doing flips as she listened to the rings and stared at the next name on the list. Chenoa Matten, female, Pureblood werewolf, thirty-three, newly promoted to the enforcers, and assigned to team Ares, under team leader Aydian Collins. Last name updated to Riordan. Promoted and assigned to a team, and to Aydian's, she had to be prior military, and used to strict practices that Aydian enforced at all times. Clio was sure Director Kanin wouldn't assign her to Ares if she wasn't qualified or couldn't handle Aydian's cold detachment. Right?

"Twin Lakes Real Estate, Jess speaking," a voice greeted.

Pulled from her thought, she replied, "Hello, it's Clio Hyde. I was wondering if you had the list of houses ready?" She was mildly surprised by the lightning bolt of excitement that shot through her. It dimmed when she thought she should have talked to someone about it. There was no one. She was single with no prospects, save for pining over a phantom. And if she talked to her parents about it, they would tell her she would make the right decision, she always did.

"Clio, finally. Tell me I can put that gorgeous townhouse on the market and make you some money." As Jess listed the features, as if Clio didn't know, and the possible listing price, she sat back and stared at the screen. "All right, all right, I'll let you answer."

"Yes, I'm ready to put it on the market." Clio wasn't worried about the money. The townhouse was paid off, she made investments, saved where she could, worked twenty-four hours a day, and received a raise when she became the chief physician at Nearctic. Money wasn't a problem. The problem was, she was about to sell the first place she called hers by herself. "*I* need a new home." She needed to walk into it and know it was hers. A safe place.

"That's what you'll get. Now, let's go over what you want. One story or two?" she began.

Clio answered her questions. Two story was all right, office space, spare rooms, large master, laundry, garage. Did she want land? Her townhouse was part of an association—the amenities including a pool, tennis courts, fitness facilities, and landscaping because she was never home. She wanted the option of working from home, which meant time to play in the yard, maybe have people over.

Cool your jets. She was getting ahead of herself.

"Yes, I want land." The screen and list of names were forgotten while she listed her wants, needs, and she lazily drew a doodle in a notebook, as her mind whirled around what she was doing.

"There's a two story on Setzer Road, five acres, wraparound deck, garage, and it has dedicated office space. Do you have time today?" Jess asked.

"No. Is it landscaped?" Clio wrote the name down.

"The front yard is. The back is a blank canvas."

It needs work, she thought, and looked forward to creating her own space. "I have tomorrow after two," Clio replied.

"Three o'clock it is. I've made the appointment. I won't be there, but my partner, Elroy Starks, will meet you at the property," Jess explained and gave Clio the address.

Writing it down, she nodded her head. "Perfect. I'll see him there."

"Let me know when I can send a photographer to your place. Then we'll go over the contract."

"Of course." After Jess said good-bye, Clio placed the handset in the cradle and sat back in the chair with the paper in her hand. She was doing this ... really, truly doing it. Staring at the address, her eyes zeroed in on the street, which could be her street with her home. "Where do you live?" she asked the room. "On Setzer." She saw the road leading from the city to the outskirts of town, the mountains, the open sky, and further she wouldn't hear the familiar noises of people or feel the pulse of the city. Her heart stopped and she felt her lungs releasing air as if there was a slow leak.

She was a flaming idiot.

CHAPTER FOUR

Ansel kicked the dirt with the toe of his dust-covered boot as he stared at the screen of his cell. He needed to make the call, get security to the property, make a report for evidence and human law enforcement, if it came to that, but he stalled. After spending the entire night staring up at his ceiling fan, his mind racing and Strong Lord's voice sitting heavy in his head, repeating Milanka Telep, he decided he was going to tell Rutger the truth.

The truth. It meant exposing why the Fellowship was interested in him and that would lead to his parents. Who and what they were. He couldn't do this by himself, and he wasn't going to lie to Rutger. Not again.

He pushed the thought aside. He would face telling the history of his parents if and when it happened and concentrated on Bronte and revenge. Every time he closed his eyes, he saw her gaze—white with scarlet diamonds—and when sleep took him, he felt her hands on him, her lips on the sensitive skin of his inner thigh, her fangs puncturing him, her nails deep in his flesh to hold him in place as she swallowed his lifeforce. His blood. She stole from him, and he had been helpless to stop her. A sheen of sweat covered his chilled skin as the nightmare dredged up emotions he thought he buried under the years. With the feel of invasion and the loss of control, his wolf prowled his insides, clawing at him with its need to protect, to fight for him. Ansel fought the chaos, grappled for control, and clearing his throat touched the green circle and the cell came alive. He listened to the ringing, each one telling him he had time to end the call, think of another way around the truth he was going to spill.

"Director Kanin," his rough voice greeted.

"We have a problem," Ansel started, keeping it business. "Humans have been at Butte Springs."

"You're sure?"

"The tracks are from a car, not a truck, and their scent is everywhere. The male scent is strongest, the female weaker, meaning there were more males than females, and they snooped around both stations. Nothing is missing. They could have been being nosy, but I doubt it," he explained.

A meteorologist, Douglas Brien, Illuminate, werewolf/fairy, who Baron Kanin hired agreed the storms were another effect of the Emanation and been put in charge of monitoring the weather. Ansel stared at the equipment, the drill rig, and land they cleared for what would become the weather station and the second, a fire station. The forest fires proved they needed to be able to protect their territory and the woods, because human bureaucrats overseeing fire protection agencies were concerned with who was in charge, how they looked in their uniforms, and not into actually fighting fires. And with their mismanagement they would let the mountain burn. When nothing was left but charred stumps and ash choked the land, they would make excuses and walk away, leaving the victims to deal with the aftermath. Cascade would protect their woods and mountains, the essence of the territory giving them energy, the same way they protected their kith and kin. Which reminded him of Strong Lord and his demand.

"At least there's no instruments, it's all construction equipment."

"Affirmative. Make a report, then advise patrol what to look for. And have a dual patrol posted, with vehicles. I want them visible, like blinding lights in the night. I'm going to have a surveillance system installed, should have from the start," Rutger said more to himself.

"I forgot as well." Rutger had been dealing with his recovery, the construction at Butte Springs, and the baron's needs, and it made Ansel reconsider telling him about Strong Lord. But he couldn't, wouldn't lie, not to the man he loved as a brother. "I need to talk to you, in private."

"When you're done there, meet me at the warehouse. I'm leaving Foxwood now," Rutger replied.

"Copy." Ansel heard the rush of wind as Rutger stepped out of the office, and hesitating, closed his eyes and blurted out, "I need Jordyn there."

"Why?" His tone somber while his wolf threaded through the one word, a growl trailing it.

Picturing Rutger standing still as if made from stone, his eyes rolling gold, and his shoulders tense, almost made Ansel change his mind. Since the rescue his rage had been on razor's edge, and needing Jordyn was going to push the alpha werewolf to protect what was his. While he wasn't going to back down from confessing his sins to Rutger and would benefit from the truth, he was tightening the collar around his neck and pulling the leash taut, so much so he was going to hang himself. The threat, one he hadn't thought of with his mind in chaos, the truth may set him free, but it might open old wounds created by lies and hurt and destroy the remains of their relationship. If he was going to destroy what he had sacrificed for with Rutger and Jordyn and lose his place in the pack, then it was going to be as a man. An honest man. Not a coward. Not a dog on a leash.

"This concerns her."

"Done."

Ansel expected him to demand a reason for needing to see Rutger's mate, fated mate. The woman who risked her life to save his. "Thank you."

"Don't thank me, I want answers."

The cell went silent, and shoving it in the breast pocket of his BDU top, he stomped to his truck with Rutger's words in his ears and wondered how far he was willing to go. His contact with the Fellowship was a direct betrayal of his mother's order and last wish. Now to think about telling Rutger and Jordyn about her, a tale he hadn't whispered in a century, made him feel like there was a knife in his heart. And twisting the blade until it flayed him open was Clio, her innocence, her passion. Her safety without question was his first and only concern and he knew whatever Rutger and Jordyn might think of him, they would never allow anything to happen to her. Jordyn especially. Once inside, he started the diesel engine, and when the terminal dinged back into existence, he typed his findings, ordered patrol, and sent them to communications. The reply was quick and short, security was on its way, his report had been given to patrol, they were en route and he was free to leave.

Ansel took one last look at the skeleton structures that would become stations, the equipment, and vehicles with the ridges and azar sky as a backdrop, then put the truck into gear and started down the mountain. The trees slid by as his tires crunched rocks and kicked up dirt, leaving a hazy cloud behind him. The scenery blurred as his thoughts circled the Fellowship, Strong Lord, Rutger and Jordyn, Clio, his lies, and Bronte. He didn't know what he was going to say, or how he was going to explain what he had done to protect the woman chosen to be his mate, while never being his, and what the Fellowship wanted in return. Then there was Strong Lord's demand for Jordyn's weaknesses, and knowledge of Bronte's whereabouts. She was with them, had been with them his instincts told him, and he should have questioned them first. But he hadn't wanted contact. He did, however, want to keep the uneasy distance between them.

It's all I have, he thought as the medallion moved against his skin.

Months ago, the Highguard ordered Cascade to withdraw from the hunt and then ordered him to stand down. He laughed a rough sound, its serrated edges grating his throat, as the realization squeezed his chest, and inhaling, he exhaled, "Fuck me." The Highguard had known she was there the entire time. It explained Strong Lord's confidence, and his brazen threat toward Jordyn. He really thought he was untouchable. It didn't matter, not anymore. Would Strong Lord hand Bronte over? If there was a chance, he needed Jordyn. To have Jordyn he needed to go through Rutger. He had been protective of her before, and now if anyone looked at her wrong his human features turned Bestial.

Through the city limits he drove to the industrial district, his heart pounding in his chest, his confession twisting in his mind, and doubt leaking into his veins. Seconds slipped into the past as they pushed him forward, toward his confession. How was he going to tell Rutger Strong Lord wants to destroy Jordyn because he wants Baron Kanin to fear him? He didn't know. The front of the warehouse came into view, the renovation replacing old metal with new, the company name replaced with the name of the security company, Allied Territories. Per Baron Kanin, Cascade's crest identified it as part of the. pack. The repaved parking lot was a black mat broken by a white lines and light posts. Ansel drove through the empty lot and around the warehouse to the back where a black square took the place of the metal roll up door. There was enough room for four vehicles to park, or two ARVs, Armored Rescue Vehicles. With dual rear wheels, armor plating, bulletproof glass, and capable of defending against small arms fire and explosives they took up the parking area. Offices, holding cells, a communications room, an armory, bunks, a kitchen, everything to make it self-sufficient, took up the square footage of the warehouse. There were final touches needing to be completed, but it was open and operational.

It had him thinking of Jordyn and how she risked her life to save his from the Highguard's prosecution, and now he was about to demand her secrets. Entering the warehouse, he parked beside Rutger's black 4x4 with its grille guard, light bar, and Cascade's crests on its sides. He killed the engine, got out, and took several breaths as he met Rutger's gaze through the ballistic glass of his office. He stood, hands clasped behind his back, his cut jaw, and tense shoulders warning Ansel it wasn't going to take a lot to push the man into the wolf.

Taking a second to gather as much courage as he was able, he walked to the stairs. Before he reached the door, he turned to see a ruby red 4x4 enter the warehouse. In the dim overhead lighting her raven hair gleamed, then her face was in the shadows as she parked on the other side of Rutger's truck. Her presence was either going to calm Rutger or was going to push the human down and release the beast. Ansel did not want to see his Bestial form or feel the sharp edge of his anger. He opened the door, stepped into the office, met a gold glare, then closed the door behind him, knowing Rutger hated open doors. They both sat down, the tension increasing while they waited for Jordyn. Since the last time

Ansel had been at the warehouse, Rutger added a second computer, and recognized it as Cascade's.

"Just heard from security. The humans were searching for evidence of the bear," Rutger commented as his gaze went to the woman walking toward the stairs.

"Bear? Like the ant and bear?" Ansel asked. "That's months old."

"Affirmative. They believe Cascade is responsible for the bear coming out of hibernation, accusing our animals incited the incident. We're polluting the forests with our non-humanness. They searched two other locations, stating they were monitoring the wildlife."

"I take offense to that, the wildlife likes us," Ansel replied. Rutger chuckled, and he wanted to believe they were having a normal conversation, but knew they weren't, and it hurt his heart more than he wanted to admit. The risks were stacking up and time was running out. "They didn't find anything, everything at Butte Springs is basically human. The Forest Service has lookouts. Are they satisfied?"

"Affirmative. They won't be back, there's nothing there, and they met four lycans who weren't in the mood to help them. This is the perfect example of why we need to guard ourselves where humans are concerned. If the truth of the ant ever got out, there would be anti-paranormal groups crawling all over Cascade's properties," Rutger explained. "Once they think they can trespass they'll take it a step farther and target our residences."

"You have your people monitoring them?" Ansel asked. By his people he meant Dark Rogues.

"Affirmative."

"Good. I can't believe Fish and Wildlife buried the case, not to mention the highway patrol, and the Organized Paranormal Investigations."

"Agreed. I don't think they want to be responsible for the consequences of having a magic ant on the loose. The OPI is actively recruiting magic-born, and the state is using them as their paragon. They'll do what they must, to ensure the public sees the agency is working with not against magic-born," Rutger stated with a growl running through his words. "No matter how they try to cripple us."

Ansel was going to reply when Rutger's eyes blazed gold and amber, and fading returned to their natural color, at the same time the door opened and closed.

Jordyn, wearing dark jeans, low heeled boots, a Glock 19, 9mm handgun holstered at her waist, and black, button-up shirt, walked by him and around the desk. Lowering her head, she nudged Rutger's to the side, and when he let her have access, she kissed him behind his ear, and he whispered, "Mea."

Ansel's heart stopped as he thought about what he was asking, what he was wanting.

When she straightened, Rutger's fury ebbed, and she walked to the empty chair.

"Ansel," she greeted as she sat down.

"Jordyn," he replied as he met cocoa brown eyes capable of turning onyx and causing death.

Rutger gave them both a glare. "We have an understanding," Jordyn began explaining. "I need intel, not a title."

"Understood." Rutger focused his attention on Ansel. "Why do you need Jo?"

Where the hell did he start? "Strong Lord has intel on Bronte's location." Good enough.

"He told you this?" Rutger asked.

"Affirmative. Last night." And it began, his confession, his lies brought to light, his betrayal out for them to hear and feel.

"Why did he talk to you?" It was Jordyn who asked, her tone firm, the opposite of the black lined eyes, soft features, and cultured mannerisms.

He couldn't ignore Rutger's sharp gaze on her and the way his wolf sat in its depths.

Without answering, he unbuttoned the top three buttons of his BDU top, and pulling on the chain, the gold medallion escaped his T-shirt. "Because I'm his dog on a leash. And he knows I want her."

Jordyn stood, and taking the gold in her hand, looked at the wolf. "What is this?"

"My legacy is blood. My crest is stained scarlet." He met her gaze, as she dropped the medallion, gold landing on his black T-shirt, and sat down.

"He makes you wear it. Is that the price you paid to have Clio's memories erased? A collar?"

Her words stung, but knowing she was piecing it together sent fear down his spine. He couldn't lie to them any longer. "They aren't erased. They're locked in a spell, and whenever she thinks about me, it creates fear. It forces her to stay away from me." *That she defies time and time again.* He saw her staring up at him, then she gave him her hand, with a trust so pure it burned, while her blue eyes warmed by honey held onto him.

Jordyn openly stared at him like he committed a horren-dous crime, which he had. "What do you have that they want?"

"Enough to risk breaking the canons?" Rutger asked from behind his desk.

"They want two things from me. The first is my parents."

"Your parents?" Rutger asked.

"Your magic," Jordyn whispered, it wasn't a question. "It's old. Something holds it, it's like a magical hand." Her eyes bled onyx, her body tensing. "They won't be able to reach it, the hand is solid, tight. If they try to force it from you, will it kill you?"

"How?" he asked, his lips barely moving around the word, as he stared at her.

"You're mine. And I sense it," she replied. "Will it kill you?"

He didn't know if she was telling the truth. While his senses didn't feel her lie, she was capable of concealing herself. "It's a possibility." This was not how he saw it happening. "It's believed once it's accessed it can be taken from me. My mother, Gaia, was a Pureblood with strong traits, like you, and because of her power she served as a priestess for her lord." Ansel told them about Gaia's refusal to mate with her lord, her imprisonment, her escape, and how she fled to the US. The entire story, his life, kept a secret for a lifetime tore from him in a rush of words, emotions, the past rising up to weave into the present. He didn't stop or try to hide his emotions when his voice broke when he spoke of his father and the magic he held as shaman for his tribe. He told them of the life they had, his parents' love for one another, for him, and when the lord's priestess and guards arrived to drain his mother of her powers. "I've held her magic inside of me for over a century. When the fire destroyed the farm, everyone thought I died with them. River and Gaia were dead along with their son, their legacy nothing but ash."

"How did Strong Lord find you?" Rutger asked.

"I don't know," Ansel answered. And he didn't. He didn't hide his name since no one knew River had taken a last name, and he assumed no one would connect him to Gaia.

He left with Bronte, and after escaping her, moved west where no one knew him.

"You've been on their leash for months. What else have they demanded?" Rutger questioned.

"I go to their meetings."

"What happens at the meetings?" Jordyn asked.

"They discuss the Emanation. They sense the increasing magic and the change in magic-born. They're in contact with other factions and the leaders are welcome to attend meetings. They have a wide range of communication. While I know they're doing surveillance on the pack and factions, they're watching me."

"Are they bargaining your magic for Bronte's location?" Jordyn asked.

"Negative. They've demanded something else."

"Is that the second thing?" Rutger growled as if he knew.

"Affirmative." Ansel inhaled, knowing he couldn't go through with it. Wouldn't put them through any more pain. They suffered enough, and magic, the Emanation that would push humans and magic-born into a civil war hadn't begun. "Jordyn."

"What is it with these people?" Jordyn asked. "Does he want his brain turned to mush, because that's what's going to happen."

"He wants your weaknesses," Ansel answered. Confessed. "He says you need to be humbled."

"Humbled. What does that mean?" Jordyn's eyes darkened while surprise marked her face.

Jordyn's question was overshadowed by Rutger's roar and his fists hitting the desk. "Negative. No."

"Wolf." Jordyn glared at him. "If you give him my weaknesses, he'll give you Bronte's location?"

Jordyn didn't look at him; she kept her eyes on Rutger, leaving Ansel staring at the side of her face. "Affirmative."

"Jo, no. Not going to happen. He threatened you. And I'm not the only one who will be against this. Baron Kanin will agree with me, and you know it," he countered. "Strong Lord is a security risk."

Scooting to the edge of her seat, she placed her hands on the desk's frame. "Don't you want to see Bronte pay for what she did? Tony's death? Lado? Daniel? What she did to Doctor Hyde and Ansel? She invaded our territory and tried to destroy the relationships we have with the factions," Jordyn challenged. With her hand raised to stop Rutger from answering, she continued, "I want the Fellowship to know they can't threaten us. They don't own this land, I do. The pack does. We lie. We'll make up some weaknesses."

"Mea, you know I agree with you. But if they believe the lies, what will stop them from coming after you?" Rutger asked.

"You. And I'm not helpless." Sitting back, she crossed her arms over her chest.

Ansel watched them, saw raw worry in Rutger's eyes, and tension in his shoulders, and then listened to Jordyn state her case for him. She was willing to risk her life for him. He didn't deserve the loyalty they were giving him. "I can't ask that of you," he said to Jordyn, and meant it, then to Rutger, "I wanted you to know what was said. You're aware. Strong Lord is jealous of the attention Prime gives Jordyn and didn't know Prime referred to her as his scion. I warned him, if any harm came to her, Prime would act. They do fear him. Even if they do have the information, they won't go against Prime. This about bringing Cascade to its knees."

Jordyn bowed her head, her raven hair falling forward as she stared downward. Ansel couldn't guess what she was thinking. What did she possess that Prime would take claim of her? As if sensing his question, she looked at him, and then Rutger. "By protecting Bronte, they broke the canons. The pack has every right to—"

"Prime called you his scion?" Rutger interrupted, his voice low.

"Negative. Justice Talbolt referred to me as Prime's scion," Jordyn replied as she shrugged.

"That changes everything," Rutger mocked, his words tight, and sat back. "You're right, though. They have broken the canons, the covenant, and soiled the trust between Cascade and the Fellowship. We have to tell the baron."

"Agreed," Jordyn quickly answered.

"Agreed." Ansel sat back, realized he was a free man, his secrets were out, and his leash was little looser. "I don't know how I can thank you."

"You're a brother," Jordyn replied.

"We protect our own," Rutger added. "And like Jo said, this isn't their territory. They have threatened Jo's life, and Baron Kanin's."

"They need to be taught a lesson. Be humbled," Jordyn seethed.

"Mea."

His heart was going to explode if he stayed there any longer. "I'll head to Foxwood," he started as he placed his hand on Jordyn's shoulder and squeezed.

Lifting her hand, she covered his and looked up at him.

Rutger's cell sounded with a notification, and he ordered, "Wait." He took his eyes off Jordyn, straightened, tapped keys to Cascade's monitor, his eyes roaming the screen, and met Ansel's stare. "The security alarm at Doctor Hyde's place has been activated. Go check it out and advise backup."

"Copy." It took him a second and he was in his truck, his mind racing with the what ifs, Bronte, and if Clio was hurt or worse, and what if she wasn't at her townhouse, because ... Bronte. She hadn't been to Foxwood, he checked, and he checked to see if she was at Celestial, she wasn't. The terminal dinged with updates, and he saw Rutger had put him en route to the call. He hit the number beside her name, listened to her phone ringing, and then her voice, its resonance only he should hear, tell him to leave a message.

"Dammit, Clio." Out on the road, he went as fast as he dared and called her again. Voicemail. He was going to roar.

Clio turned the engine off, stared at the parking lot, inhaled, then grabbed her satchel from the passenger seat. She was going to discuss a future hospital with Alpha Crevan, a possible alliance with Cascade, and following Mistress' order, use her senses to gauge their honesty. "Easy."

Once out of the crossover the warm summer breeze wrapped around her, taking the gentle chill from her skin and brought the tangled scents of flowers and smoked meats. Clio adjusted the satchel's strap over her shoulder, crossed the parking lot, her heels clicking on pavement, and approached the double glass doors. The restaurant all raw edged beams, natural wood, and windows, with river rock skirting sat in the midst of flowers of every color, bushes of emerald green, and trees casting shade along the sidewalk. It looked natural in the urban setting, and at the same time she knew it would look natural tucked away in the woods. Like the Timber House, off the road and hidden among tall pines, oaks, and cedar trees. Opening the right side, she stepped inside, and a wash of cool air infused with the varied scents of coffee, fried foods, and magic-born mixed with humans met her nose. A sense of comfort wrapped around her as she walked up to the hostess station, and waiting behind a couple, magic-born, took in the interior. Half walls painted a soft honey broke up the bar from the formal eating areas, while industrial lighting gave a muted glow, and music and chatter played in the background.

"A table for one?" the hostess asked. Her name, Grace, stitched over the right side of her red, button-up blouse stared at her with green eyes.

"I'm here to meet Crevan Stone," Clio replied, as she adjusted the strap of the satchel, more out of nerves.

Grace gave her a once over, turned, and led Clio through the middle of the restaurant. Several feet from a table of four, a tall man with black hair and gray eyes stood, his chest filling out a silk, black, button-up shirt, the collar open to expose bronze skin, the curve of his neck leading to board shoulders, and the sleeves rolled to his elbows. Tucked into a pair of dark jeans ending in shiny, black boots, he smiled, the curves playing on his lips gave away his confidence and told her he knew his effect on women. Clio absolutely understood why he was admired, when he wore casual style with tailored elegance like a second skin.

Plastering a smile on her face, she forced herself not to stare. She was there as a representative for Baron Kanin, Cascade, and didn't need Alpha Crevan reporting she was unprofessional. She wasn't hunting for a man. Gods knew she didn't have time. Then there was her fascination with Captain Wolt.

"Alpha Crevan," Clio started, her voice strong, confident, nothing giving away her jumpy nerves.

"Please, Doctor Hyde, just Crevan, you're here as a guest." He gave her another dazzling smile, his eyes glittering silver, and sweeping their weight from her turned to the two men and one woman sitting at the table. "This is Sean, provost of the gray foxes. Casey, provost for the cougars. And Allyson, provost for the black-tailed deer."

"It's a pleasure to meet you," Clio said as she met their gazes.

"Please have a seat."

Clio smiled as she placed her satchel on the floor beside her chair and sat down, anxiety skipping along her nerves and under her skin. She didn't know what she was doing there. A representative with Baron Kanin's authority. A spokesperson for Celestial.

"How was the drive?" Sean asked.

She met his narrowed gaze of stony blue and answered, "Uneventful, thankfully."

"Everyone is talking about Doctor Hyde and Captain Wolt from Cascade," Crevan began. "Does the Captain of Enforcers usually respond when there are patrols available?"

Captain Wolt does what he wants, she wanted to answer. However, she had wondered that herself, but not for the same reasons. "Affirmative, so does Director Kanin. It helps them stay connected to the pack and klatch, and they understand the feel of the territory. Do you want to see the reports I brought with me?"

"Eventually. I promised food and drinks." Making eye contact with a waitress, his smile dimmed, giving up to his authority. He was an alpha and owned the restaurant. When the woman, Lily—curly, blonde hair up in a ponytail, her azure eyes on Crevan—stood at the table, he said, "We're ready. Doctor Hyde, what do you like to drink? I have a rosé that will match the ahi tuna perfectly." Another smile curved his lips.

"Chief's choice sounds wonderful," she replied. Wine, ahi, and his smile. She was going to indulge.

After checking with the others, the appetizers had been ordered, and the waitress had taken their drink orders, she left them. Clio watched the waitress move through the tables while several patrons stopped to watch them.

"You have to give my gratitude to Baron Kanin for allowing Cascade's premier doctor out of his territory." Crevan met her gaze, the smile returning as if closing the conversation to only them.

Damn he's good, she thought. Baron Kanin hadn't let her out of his territory without a thorough security check. Clio laughed an easy sound with the compliment. "I will. However, I'm part of an incredible team," she replied. "We rely on one another."

"Now you're being modest. You're the chief physician at Nearctic, an administrator at Celestial, I understand you're on the junior board, and you're the Kanins' physician. You're one of a select few who are allowed near Mistress Langston," Crevan pointed out. "You have incredible status and authority for someone who isn't yet thirty."

She was twenty-nine, she wanted to point out, and stopped when all eyes were on her. "Baron Kanin has given me the opportunity to follow my passion while serving the pack."

"As a doctor, being an empath must benefit you?" Allyson asked, her eyes turning from rust to dark chocolate. "Although it's a natural step."

"Affirmative." Clio lowered her shields, allowing her senses to feel and caught the threads of their emotions. The strongest, like a wall of power and subtle sexual appeal, was coming from Crevan. He wasn't hiding his magic, animal, or his feelings from her.

"I thought I felt it when you walked up. It's like a gentle breeze on my senses. I'm sure people are drawn to you, Clio Hyde, you are pure of heart," Crevan noted.

As surprise crossed her face, Allyson laughed a soft sound. "I'm sorry, that's my fault. It must feel like we're ganging up on you. I'm an empath, I feel your truth, and Crevan is a mage. Like he pointed out, you have status, authority, and the Kanins have chosen you over others. You haven't allowed your importance to corrupt you. When he said you were being modest, and you were, you don't take compliments well. You are humble of heart. It's very telling," she explained. "That's a valuable characteristic."

"That's what we wanted to know. Being sanctioned by the Highguard, Mistress Langston recognized by Prime, and fated mate to Director Kanin, Second to the Alpha, the Kanins' power and authority has increased exponentially. As Cascade maneuvers to attain more territory and its factions, it makes us, the weaker, question where they stand with Cascade. Will we get swallowed up and drown or will we remain independent?" Casey asked.

"Why me?" Clio demanded, feeling like she had been set up. Her heart sank as if they had disrespected her and her status. "You could have had a meeting with anyone from Cascade. Someone from Baron Kanin's staff, a pack representative, Director Kanin. One of the Elders. Even Baron Kanin himself." Clio held their gazes as her authority and anger filled her eyes.

"You heal the wounded and care for the weak," Sean replied as if it explained everything.

"You're a healer," Casey added.

"Forgive me. We are absolutely interested in the information you have brought, and are taking the steps to build our hospital, Promise Medical Center. I am interested in seeing Celestial, if that's possible, as well as understanding how your team works," Crevan explained. "By allowing you to come here, unguarded, Baron Kanin has shown us respect, and has proved he trusts us with someone he cares for. Having said that, he had to assume we would question you."

He did, and had Errando warn her. Although she was sure it was going to be about a hospital. "This was a test?"

"Of sorts," Casey answered. "We are sorry. We did what we thought was best."

"I could leave now and tell Baron Kanin exactly what happened," she threatened. She wasn't the threatening type. Even as it left her mouth, Clio contemplated the name, Promise, and thought it suited them. Like Celestial. She considered the medical center heavenly, and a sanctuary for those in need, where the doctors were guardians, and healers of the weak. While they stated their case, she understood their caution, she was going to wait before telling Crevan that Baron Kanin wrote up an official invitation to Foxwood, and the guarantee he would have safe passage into Cascade. Did she believe Crevan? Yes. Did she believe the others? Yes. Clio felt their truth reaching out to her. It didn't change their deception. As they stood by their alpha and respected their leader, they would be held accountable for their actions.

"Please don't leave. We offer our apologies, as one," Allyson pleaded.

The coalition's strength didn't come from one of them but all of them. Crevan, alpha. Sean, second. Casey, third. Allyson, fourth, while being their conscience. Clio met their gazes and didn't respond.

"Doctor Hyde, as alpha, please offer my apologies to Baron Kanin. As your host, please forgive me," Crevan implored with a slight grin.

Clio wanted to smack the look off his face. "Yes, Crevan, you're forgiven. As are all of you." She gave him a tight smile, a little sweet, a little evil, that she saved for unruly patients. Basically Mistress. "Next time I expect you, all of you, to be upfront. I don't play games," she warned. *I'm not going to pull any punches with you.* And that's how she liked it. "Baron Kanin especially hates games. They waste time."

"You have my word," Crevan replied as he crossed his heart.

"You have our word," Sean promised.

Silence reached out, threading through them as they stared at each other, and she heard her cell vibrating. Not the time to answer the call. After the awkward silence ended, she would check her messages.

"I didn't intend on offending you and ruining this afternoon. Let me make up for it. I believe are our appetizers and drinks are ready. I hope you enjoy the stuffed tiger prawns, I added a pinch of red chili flakes."

She let her anger settle but wasn't going to let her guard down. As the waitstaff approached and the smell of food drifted, Clio found herself thinking maybe she would like the chili flakes, spice went well with her tequila. "I'm sure I will." She was easy. When he smiled in victory, she wondered how was he single?

In minutes, four plates were deposited on the table, all teaming with food, their rich aromas promising decadence. Then her cell vibrated. Again. She internally groaned, and taking it from the satchel's front pocket, saw the image, and groaned again with regret and then fear slipped over her.

"If you'll excuse me," she said to Crevan. "Captain Wolt, how may I help you?"

"Where the hell are you?" Ansel demanded. He raced to her townhouse, found it empty and her crossover gone, and imagined the worst of the worst possibilities. Dead. Kidnapped. Bronte. Standing in her bedroom, he hadn't left to check his terminal, and hadn't bothered to call communications, he wanted, needed to hear her voice. And he wanted to yell at her.

"I need to take this," she mumbled, knowing everyone heard him, including the humans on the other side of the restaurant.

They nodded their response, save for Crevan who was staring at her, like the alpha he was, his gray eyes liquid silver, his magic swirling in them.

Clio speed walked away from the table, and when out of earshot—at least they wouldn't hear Captain Wolt's side of the conversation—replied, "Oak Run. I'm in a meeting with Alpha Crevan and the provosts. Why?"

He didn't know relief could feel so good. He knew the meeting was important but didn't know it had been rescheduled. "I'm sorry for the interruption. Your security system alerted communications there was an intruder," he explained. While his worry was fading, his anger was front and center. He was losing the battle with his wolf and his mind.

"W-Was there? D-Do I n-need to leave?" Clio stammered as she turned back to the table to see Crevan staring at her while the others were eating and talking to one another.

Ansel smiled like the predator he was with her fear. "Negative. I checked the premises, cleared the interior, and there's no sign of a break in. I'm waiting for the tech guy to come and check the system." He picked his flannel up from her perfectly made bed, with its thick, white comforter with splashes of soft pink, and held it to his nose to inhale her scent—spice, cinnamon—then put it back.

Tech guy? He was in her house. Giving the group her back, scarlet crawled up from her chest to her throat and into her cheeks where embarrassment burned. Her house was clean, her dishes washed and put away, everything was in its place, except the office; it looked like an atomic bomb blast had gone off. It was the flannel. His flannel. She left it draped on her bed, because she was going to sleep in it again before washing it and giving it back. If he searched her bedroom, he had to have seen it, couldn't miss the blue and gray on white. She saw her comforter, pillows, and throw blankets, making her a girly girl, all pastels, then the photographs on the walls, and the antique mirror, combs, and jewelry box sitting on the dresser. More images flew through her mind, and shoving them down she felt like an idiot.

"You don't think anyone was there?"

"Negative, I didn't smell anyone. Once tech has a reason for the alert, I'll message you," he stated, keeping the hard edge to his voice. *Wouldn't want to interrupt your meeting,* he wanted to add.

Maybe Captain Good Mood didn't notice it, he certainly sounded like he was at call, nothing more. It wasn't like he was there to judge her place. "Thank you. I don't know how long I'll be."

"Understood." Ansel ended the call and shoved his cell back in his pocket. As he cleared the house, he went from room to room, and found her office. The cluttered desk and boxes had to be driving her nuts. Clio liked everything neat, like the rest of the place, showroom perfect. Then he found the file on Alpha Crevan Stone and his photograph. One word stuck out, single. He heard the rumors of the alpha's conquests, his looks, and how women flocked to him. Clio was there with him. Ansel growled as he stomped to the front door and opened it to let the tech guy inside as if he owned the place.

"Is everything all right?" Crevan asked.

"Yes. My home alarm sent an alert to communications, so they sent someone to investigate. It's nothing, tech is going to check it," she replied as she sat down. Clio eyed the glass of rosé and wanted to chug it.

"Someone like Captain Wolt?" Crevan asked, his eyes darkening. "Called you. He sounded angry."

She wanted to roll her eyes and tell them he always sounded like that. "Yes, he didn't know where I was," she hesitantly answered. Saying it made her feel like he really had called to make sure she was all right. "He confirmed there hadn't been a break-in, then called tech support."

"After what happened to the both of you, I wondered if he would feel protective of you. I guess I have my answer."

Everyone stopped eating and all eyes were on her again. It was a matter time before Bronte came up. But Captain Good Mood protective of her? Nope. Not possible. She wouldn't make matters worse by believing it. "As Captain of Enforcers, he's protective of everyone, as are all of the enforcers."

"That is their reputation," Casey said, to have to others nod their agreement.

"But you're different," Crevan insisted, his silver eyes on her.

Clio wanted to hide. "Thank you, but I'm sure communications alerted him to the situation." Was she even making sense?

Crevan held her gaze for a second and let silence stretch out, then grabbed his glass and held it up. "A toast to Doctor Hyde. Thank you for accepting my invitation and for rescuing Sheriff Samuels' daughter. The act of selflessness extended a friendship between non-humans and humans and strengthens our place here."

Relief swept through her like a strong wind when the subject of Bronte didn't continue, but it didn't change her reaction to the depth of his toast. Friendship between humans and non-humas was tentative at best. It would take one magic-born to commit a crime and the fragile friendship would shatter as if it were made from crystal. As her thoughts plummeted into chaos, Clio raised her glass, clinked the edge to Crevan's, and met his questioning stare. He wasn't done, she could see the questions concerning Bronte and Captain Wolt waiting to be asked. With each of their gazes seeming to look at her as if she was something more than she was, scarlet colored her cheeks, and she worked to put a smile on her face.

"Thank you for the invitation," she replied.

When the tech guy, Paul, completed the system check, he explained it was an alert to notify communications there was a problem. A wire short circuited, and while it sent the alert to communications, it didn't notify Clio, explaining why she didn't know what was going on. Ansel immediately messaged her a short explanation, received a thank you in return, and he headed back to Foxwood, his heart in his throat, and his worry out of control knowing he was going to face Baron Kanin, Rutger, and Jordyn. And a lifetime worth of lies.

"Wolt," Ansel said as he answered the call.

"Is Doctor Hyde's place clear?" Rutger's rough rumble asked.

"Affirmative, tech fixed the problem. I'm heading back to Foxwood now."

"Negative. Baron Kanin rescheduled the meeting for tomorrow morning. Jo is responding to a call, nothing serious, and won't be able to be there," Rutger explained. "You're unavailable."

"Copy. Have a goodnight."

With the reprieve, at least for a night, his nerves became a low roar, taking the edge off his anxiety. Now that his workday was over, Ansel checked on Clio, saw she was moving, and headed to her place where he backed his truck into a dark parking spot across from her townhouse while keeping it in view. His terminal dinged, chimed, and updated the enforcers' status, and he sat back and waited. Soon minutes turned to an hour, then two, and with his patience burning to ash he nearly left his spying spot to search for her. Did he believe the alarm short circuited? Affirmative, Paul said it happens. It didn't mean he wasn't going to make sure Clio was safe. Bronte, even with her association with the Fellowship, and her possible imprisonment, lived for revenge. He survived. Clio survived. In one night, Bronte lost her Covey, her team, and failed to take out her target, twice. She wasn't going to give up, Ansel knew this.

"Where are you, tesoro?" he whispered to the silence. With the windows down, his elbow resting on the edge, the breeze carried various scents from flowers and lawns and then a mixture from the warm evening into the cab. He looked at the passenger seat to his gear, his thoughts drifting, his cell, then back as headlights skated across the expanse hitting vehicles, trees, and flowerbeds, with white light.

For a terrifying heartbeat he feared they would reach him and expose him. Safely out of their grasp the pearl-white crossover turned and stopped as the garage door began rolling back. His pulse slowed to its normal rate, he released the breath he had been holding, and the light gave him the inside of her garage, finished with white walls and storage shelving. It was neat and clean like the interior of her house. Checking the time—it was after three in the morning—he growled as he imagined her with Alpha Crevan, the man making her laugh, making her feel important, valued, and treating her as an expert in her field. Which she was.

"I shouldn't be here," he mumbled into the night. The unfairness of it wasn't enough to make him leave.

Being near her was breaking down the barricade he hid behind, and caused his mind to torture him, while his wolf fought him. It was clawing his insides, demanding its mate and her touch, knowing it was the piece he was missing to fill the void inside of him. Ansel knew he couldn't have it both ways. Clio at a distance while expecting her to be faithful to him. It wasn't fair to her. She deserved a life with a mate who wasn't being hunted, wasn't a broken-down shell of a man, and wasn't a dog on a leash. Like Alpha Crevan. Growling, Ansel hated where his head was, and hated knowing he needed to abandon his dreams where they ended up together. It was the right thing to do. When the crossover parked, the brake lights switched off, and the interior light came on, he held his breath and froze.

Clio left her satchel on the passenger side floorboard, and the containers filled to the rim with food Crevan sent home with her on the seat. She was stuffed, the sumptuousness of the dishes sitting on her lips, and couldn't believe she stayed long enough the provost leaders left them. When they were alone, she barely noticed the busy restaurant, then he ordered coffee, and relaxing with one another, they talked for another hour. She hadn't realized she needed the conversation, to interact with someone, and then be near them. There was no doubt she enjoyed talking to Mistress, everyone at Celestial, the Hollow, and Nearctic, but it could be tense, and was always work related. She told herself she was going to make getting out more a priority, and would visit with her parents more. Walking to the sidewalk, she stood at the curb and looked at the lot, the cars neatly parked, streetlights, and the different townhouses and apartments surrounding her. Silence sat thick as everyone was asleep and allowed her to enjoy the early hour without interruption.

"Not going to miss it," she whispered, her imagination picturing a view free of buildings.

Fascinated, Ansel watched her stand under the halo of the streetlight with her blonde and strawberry hair gleaming, her azure eyes warmed by honey glittering as she stared out at the dark embracing the early morning. He mused over the look of concentration holding her face and wondered what she was thinking, what she was deciding, and if it had any-thing to do with the meeting, the alpha, and the provost leaders. Then scents warmed by summer's night found him, and trying to ignore them all, magic-born and human, rich food and drinks, he was going to roll up the window but hesitated when he couldn't risk her hearing him. He didn't know how he would explain himself if she found him. The breeze stirred the tangle, and in his next breath, his thoughts crashed and burned, his wolf howled its rage the jealousy echoing in his veins. There was one scent clinging to her, and it pushed him over the edge and challenged his wolf. Not just a scent. The mark of an alpha whose animal had been close to the surface as if both man and animal wanted to know Clio. The alpha wanted his animal near her when he had been fucking close enough to touch her. Embraced her. She smelled like him. Wore his scent. Trying to control his reaction to the truth, he gripped the steering wheel, his knuckles turning white while it gave under the pressure, his eyes blazed bronze with his wolf, and he wanted to roar.

On the drive home, she thought about the house versus townhouse and decided she was leaving the city for views of the mountains and a level of freedom. An outside area she didn't have to worry about who saw her, free of parking lots and lights, and space to spread out, home office and a place to entertain. Alpha Crevan was in her thoughts, and she imagined the smile he flashed her, and thought about Setzer Road. Shaking her head, she rubbed her neck.

It doesn't matter, she told herself. She was only looking, and it was one house on a list of many. Clio ran her fingers through her hair, gave the lot her back, went to her car, and made the first trip inside, then went back for the food. Once inside, she put everything away, and going to her room saw the flannel draped on the edge of the bed and picked it up. Clio drew in her phantom's scent, felt his lingering presence in her room, and knew it should have sent heat to her cheeks while it scalded her in shame. It didn't. She didn't know if it was the late hour, the contentment she was feeling, or knowing he made sure her place was secure and the alarm system was working properly. Taking the flannel with her to the bathroom, she ditched her clothes, the smells from the restaurant clinging to them, and there was Crevan.

He hugged her, held her to his body, which in the coalition was normal, but it wasn't to her and caught her off guard. It hadn't been normal for over a year as the pack turned from being touching and friendly to rigid and cold. Maybe it was the touching that calmed her wolf, eased the tension from her, and made her content enough to accept Captain Wolt had been in her house and had to have seen *his* flannel on *her* bed. Maybe. In comfy pants and the flannel, she went to the kitchen, poured a tequila, and going to the couch, curled her legs under her, and sipped. Clio sank into the cushion behind her, the liquor warming her as it eased the edge of the day, the drive, and the time. With sleep creeping up on her, the phantom haunting her dreams waited in the shadows, then through heavy lids she watched headlights cut through the curtain of the early morning, their white beams streaming across the parking lot. When a sense of awareness drifted and the phantom beckoned her, Clio let sleep take her to him.

The alpha reminded Ansel he had no claim, no means to right his wrong. He wasn't an alpha, didn't have a crest, and his life wasn't his own. Alpha Crevan was stable, strong, respected, working to prove the strength of the provosts and sets, and validating the coalition. The time had come.

"I have to let her go," Ansel whispered, and his heart sank, as his wolf's sorrow overwhelmed his senses and turned his insides cold. He never heard of a fated pair denying one another and surviving the emptiness where their wolves should be joined. Lowering his head, he closed his eyes. He was the only one denying anyone anything. He could have Leonidas—not just trap his memoires in a magic net, but erase them all together, so he had no idea who Clio was, could have been, would never be. "Ask for another favor," he mumbled to the cab. The Fellowship and Strong Lord would tighten his collar and shorten his leash.

"No," Ansel growled the word. He needed the pain as a reminder of his sins, what he deserved, and what he didn't deserve. And as a selfish bastard, he wanted to feel her.

Ansel forced his focus from Clio and her time with the alpha, to the meeting with the baron, the lies he was going to have to face, and the possibility he might have Bronte. When Clio's window went dark, he started the truck and hoped like hell she was wearing his flannel. With the teasing thought, Ansel bowed his head from the pain. Like a vice around his chest it crushed bones, and wringing him dry made his eyes water and blurred his vision. He had to get out of there and away from her.

CHAPTER FIVE

First thing in the morning Clio washed Captain Wolt's flannel, folded it, and set it beside her satchel, intending on taking it back. The fantasy was over. She was a representative for Cascade, and hoped to continue to be the liaison between Crevan and Baron Kanin, and didn't need her phantom's clothing in her house. Especially when Jess called to confirm she was going to go to the townhouse to have a photographer take pictures for the listing. It sent uncertainty through her at the same time the excitement was like lightning in her veins. Like the appointment she had with Mr. Starks, Jess' partner at the office, to see the first house on the list.

Setzer Road.

Clio drove through the gates of Foxwood, her report for the baron in her satchel, the flannel beside it, and her thoughts on the success of the meeting. As she parked her crossover in her space, she saw Captain Wolt's silver truck. Her heart fluttered for a second, and she knew she didn't wash and fold his flannel because the fantasy was over but because Jess was going to be in her house. Multiple people were going to be traipsing through her home and judging everything from the bathrooms to the flooring she chose. Clio thought about hanging it in her closet—one more day she told herself—then decided it was sad clinging to the phantom's shirt. She was going to cling, and while she knew it wasn't good for her mental health, sad even, it was a safe habit. She didn't have time to date, let alone invest in a long-term relationship with anything other than a phantom who didn't reciprocate the feeling. Totally safe. However, it didn't mean she needed physical proof to ensure someone found out.

She grabbed her satchel, the shirt, and her travel mug, closed the door, and started toward the enforcer's office when Captain Wolt walked out. His muscled body, from spending time in the gym, combined with his confident gait, carried his authority, his legs taking long strides, while his jeans fit snug around his hips and butt. Clio watched for a second as his shoulder-length auburn hair caught the sunlight, its ends grazing the collar of his BDU top, his hand resting on the butt of his gun holstered at his thigh. Yeah, she was going to cling, and not because he was nice to look at, stare at ... no, she was clinging because she wasn't going to leave him on his own. As he started across the parking lot and toward the baron's mansion, a spike of fear struck her, like a warning not to get close to him, the whisper a soft breeze through her mind that she quickly shoved down.

If she stopped him now, she wouldn't have to go to his office, get tongue tied, and make a fool of herself. As if sensing her—she knew it couldn't be real—Captain Wolt slowed his walk, and turning his head, his cinnamon eyes with bronze shards met hers and she waved at him.

Please stop. Please stop. She didn't want to go to his office. The cinnamon rolled to full bronze for a second, and giving her the side of his face, he hurried his walk to a march, and left her where she stood. Stunned by his dismissal, Clio remained where she was, her thoughts going in a thousand different directions. It would have taken two seconds to give him the shirt. Two seconds. All right, he was meeting with the baron, was obviously in a hurry and didn't want to stop.

Yeah, yeah. Clio was staring at the mansion when a truck pulled up close to her. She turned to see who it was, and Mistress waved at her. Clio waved back, and stepping out of the parking spot, waited for Mistress to park.

"Good morning," Clio greeted with her approach. Mistress wore a white, button-up blouse, jeans that ended in low heeled boots, and there was a handgun holstered at her waist, beside her Organized Paranormal Investigations badge. Her raven hair was loose, its ends in the middle of her back, and her cocoa eyes held an eerie darkness like she knew things no one else did.

"Good morning," Mistress replied, her gaze narrowing on the shirt. "Nice shirt."

Clio's cheeks heated, and Mistress smiled. "It's not what you think." She couldn't believe she said that.

"No?" Mistress questioned with a curve tugging at the corner of her mouth.

Not even a little bit, when he just ignored her. "No. During the rescue, I tore my skirt, and my shirt was stained with blood. Captain Wolt let me borrow it. I'm returning it to him. That is all."

"I didn't say a word," Mistress teased. "How did the meeting with Alpha Crevan go?"

Shaking her head, Clio answered, "Excellent. I'm giving my report to Baron Kanin. Will you be there?"

"Affirmative. I have meeting with him now. Is it true what they say about him?"

"If you mean overly confident, good looking to the point you can't help but stare with a dangerous smile he knows how to use, and makes food that would make you follow him back to his house, then yes, it's true. He sent me home with four containers. I'm going to have to diet," Clio explained as she patted her stomach.

"He gave you food. He's making a move on you, Doc," Mistress teased.

"No, he was showing off. He does it well, I might add." Clio laughed as she thought about the fit of his shirt, as it accentuated his toned upper body. "This is strictly business. I wouldn't do anything to jeopardize the relationship between the coalition and Cascade, and the future hospital."

"Maybe after they give their confidence."

"I don't have time," Clio began, then stopped.

They both turned when a black, lifted 4x4 pulled up, its diesel engine rumbling, Cascade's crest on its sides, grille guard, winch, and light bar, and it parked beside Mistress'. A second later Director Kanin stepped out of the cab, his height and build thick with muscle, the opposite of Captain Wolt's leaner form. His magic filled the atmosphere, and Clio felt the power of an alpha on her skin as he nodded to Mistress, then herself. After acknowledging them, he marched across the lot, the same determined gait as Captain Wolt, and toward the mansion.

"He didn't look happy. How is he doing?" Clio asked. She had been one of four doctors at the Hollow to witness the match between Mistress and the director. It was brutal, but in the end, Mistress took a snake out of his chest and saved his life.

"He's happy and he's doing well," Mistress replied as she stared at him. Standing at the door, which a sentinel held open, Director Kanin faced them, his mahogany gaze burning gold, then he walked into the house and the door closed on him. "He might be a little pissed at me."

"What did you do?" Clio asked as Mistress met her gaze.

"Disagreed with his hard headedness." She inhaled and exhaled. "He hates admitting defeat."

"I can only imagine. It must be a male thing," Clio replied. "Changing the subject, I'm putting my townhouse on the market and going house hunting."

"Congratulations."

"Thank you, it's pretty exciting. I have an appointment to look at a two-story log home on Setzer."

"Setzer?" Mistress asked as she raised her eyebrows.

"It's first on the list. I need to see what the land looks like. I haven't had to worry about landscaping for years," Clio explained as she ignored the part about Setzer. "Someone wants you."

Mistress faced the mansion and groaned. "Duty calls. Keep me updated."

"Will do."

Clio watched Mistress cross the lot, and meeting Director Kanin who was waiting for her, she slid her arm around him as his height towered over her. He shook his head, his tawny hair moving, then he wrapped his arm around her, and they walked inside. Jealousy's green eyes blazed within her as she wondered if she would have what they shared and what it would be like to wake up next to someone who loved her. Have someone to confide in and rely on. Like backup. Did she have to have someone? No. She was doing pretty damn good all on her own. *But to have someone* ...

Could she see Crevan on a personal level once everything was finalized? *I don't know*, she thought as she walked to the Enforcer's office, slid her card, and entered her code. Through the lobby, and at the steel doors, she repeated the process, and entered the heart of the Enforcers. Walking the hall, she noticed Captain Wolt's door, his name and status, saw his bronze eyes, and passing made her way to the stairs and toward Nearctic.

As alpha of the coalition, Crevan emanated dominance, strength, his leadership stern, but not so much he didn't value the opinions of the provost leaders and the needs of each set. When the leaders were getting ready to leave, he had given Allyson a hug and kiss, and then grasped Casey and Sean's forearm, showing them respect. Then he hugged Clio. His confidence was infectious, she felt it, and clearly the coalition trusted him to protect them and to negotiate a covenant with Cascade.

At the double doors of Nearctic, with Cascade's crest on one side and the Rod of Aesculapius, the serpent-entwined rod belonging to the Greek god Asclepius—a deity linked to healing and medicine—on the other, she slid her card and entered her code.

"Doctor Clio Hyde, authority code One Heka."

In an instant, bright LED lights glared down at the same time locks disengaged, and panels that had blended into the wall slid open, revealing touch screens. Clio made a left, and placing her hand on the palm vein scanner, locks sounded, and opening the door she walked into her office and to her desk. She set the satchel on the floor, the travel mug on the desk, and going back to the door, she hung the flannel on the coat rack. Clio didn't bother closing the door as she grabbed her lab coat with her name embroidered on the right side and Cascade's crest on the left and pulled it on. Knowing she was going from work to the appointment with Mr. Starks, she wore makeup, left her curly, blonde hair loose, and dressed in a floral blouse, slacks, and low heels. Not her usual T-shirt, zip-up hoodie—Nearctic tended to be cold—scrub pants, and running shoes.

Crevan's words drifted through her thoughts. He saw her as someone with status with the pack, having the baron's respect, and a high-profile position in Celestial and Nearctic. She never considered herself one of the elites, or better than anyone else—she did her job, worked hard, and challenged herself to be better. Clio served her pack to the best of her abilities and would have done so even if she wasn't a doctor. Then again, it was easy to remain humble when she was around Mistress Langston, who had been given status and prestige by the ruling leader of all magic-born, Prime, was a Lady in Waiting with the Highguard, and she held herself with grace. It wasn't just Mistress, no, it was all of them. The baron and baroness, the ambassadors working with different factions, soldiers, enforcers, staff at Celestial, the Hollow, and their mates, and families. They were a pack. They took care of one another.

As a doctor, Clio couldn't shake the nagging feeling that the military strictness they were adhering to was going to hurt the pack and klatch, emotionally and mentally. Pack animals needed one another. Shapeshifters needed one another. Conversation, touch, a sense of being part of a family and having unity and feeling you were never alone. Lost in thought, she scrolled down the roster on the monitor, her eyes drifting to the flannel.

"Did you ignore me?" she asked the empty room. "No." It was the meeting with the baron, he didn't have time to stop and talk to her. And if Director Kanin and Mistress were involved, it had to be serious. "That's it." Why else would he walk away from her? Because she wasn't anyone important to him. He had a job. Before she left for her appointment, she would check his office. If he wasn't there, she would leave the shirt with Tabby, and the receptionist could give it to him. It was out of her hands.

Clio jumped when her cell blasted through the silence, and grabbing it, answered, "Doctor Hyde."

"Did I catch you at a bad time?" his throaty voice asked.

She could hear the smile he was wearing and wasn't going to fall for it. "Not at all. How can I help you, Alpha Crevan?"

His rough chuckle made her smile, and she trained her face, as if he could see her fighting to remain serious. "It's Crevan. Just Crevan. I don't fish for compliments, ever, so don't tell anyone I called to ask if you liked your food. The chef in me is dying."

Clio laughed then, an easy giggle. She couldn't stop herself, he had to be kidding. "Crevan, the food was incredible, you know that. Keep the stuffed tiger shrimp and lobster raviolis coming and your secret is safe."

"Blackmail, I like it." He laughed, and she sat back. "Have you talked to Baron Kanin?"

"No. I have a meeting with him in an hour," she replied.

"I know there are requirements we are expected to meet. I also know they allowed you to interview us because you're an empath and were told to sense our truth. I hope our honesty and integrity proved we're serious about our intentions."

Bold of him. "Yes, you demonstrated your sincerity," Clio responded. And didn't expect anything less from the alpha. "It's my opinion, it would be in Cascade's best interest to pursue an association with the Coulter Coalition."

"Excellent. If Baron Kanin agrees with you and we're given permission, we're prepared to give him and Cascade our confidence. It would be an honor to sign the covenant. To make this statement I would like to have a conference call."

Clio sat straighter. "Of course. How much time do you need?"

"Fifteen minutes should be fine. I'm going to be at my office or at the restaurant," he replied.

"You'll be messaged fifteen minutes before *if* Baron Kanin agrees," Clio explained, knowing the baron was going to agree. She then gave him the number communications would use to send the message.

"I look forward to hearing from you," he replied. "Enjoy your day, Doctor Hyde."

"You as well, Crevan." Clio set her cell down, and after getting the satchel, took the file and her report from the pocket and set both on the desk. She opened it, looked over her statement, and added to her assessment of Alpha Crevan.

"They're harboring a fugitive. A murderer," Jordyn argued, standing behind Rutger, her hands on his shoulders. "They broke several canons."

"I won't have a frontal attack and accuse the Fellowship of harboring a fugitive," Baron Kanin began.

"Why not?" Rutger questioned. "You accused them of my abduction."

Jordyn squeezed his shoulders, and letting go of him walked to the back of the office, to the window.

"I wanted a reaction from them. Anyway, we all knew they had nothing to do with it, and Prime was entertaining me. We can use this to find out more about them. Strong Lord demanded a list of Jordyn's weaknesses, in order to weaken her and myself?" Baron Kanin asked for the third time, as if needing confirmation. His disbelief the leader of the

Fellowship would dare encroach on Jordyn or Cascade was evident in his voice.

"Affirmative," Ansel replied as guilt and betrayal tangled in his middle, and he shoved his hands over his thighs. "He's jealous of Mistress and Prime, and believes because of the attention the Highguard is giving you, you don't fear them. They aren't the ruling power here."

"Because they aren't," Jordyn said from her place by the window.

Baron Kanin's eyes narrowed on her as if seeing her onyx gaze for the first time, then shifted back to Ansel. "And you're indebted to the Fellowship because one of them put a spell on Doctor Hyde, so she has no memory you're her fated mate?"

"Affirmative." He felt like a coward and knew it sounded weak. He could smell the alpha on her, the scent permanently embedded in his head, the serene expression on her face as she gazed out at the night, and he wanted to growl.

"Who cast the spell?" Baron Kanin asked.

His insides caved. "Leonidas, demon spawn of Eros."

Baron Kanin raised his eyebrows and chuckled. "Of course. I'm going to revise the covenant and demand they keep me informed who and what are residing in my territory."

"After the Prosecution Administration's hearing, I found a photograph of Bronte and I stuck to my table with an ivory-handled knife. She had been at my house. Between the invasion and her boldness, I couldn't risk anything happening to Doctor Hyde, so I called Strong Lord for a favor."

"Why?" Baron Kanin asked, his authority and a shard of betrayal in the one word.

"I didn't want to involve the pack if I didn't have to. I had already caused enough problems and I knew you would never allow me to betray Doctor Hyde the way I had." *She's going to hate me.* "They've been after me for years," Ansel started, and plowing forward explained his mom's magic, how she gave it to him, and his dad's magic as a shaman. "They think they can take it from me."

Grunting, the baron sat back in his chair. "You're right. I never would have given you permission to do what you did to Doctor Hyde. They want to use you and are doing a good job. You've kept your past and the deal you made with them a secret, and have followed their orders thus far, and because they have you on a leash, they're arrogant enough to think you'll continue to do so."

"It could be my imagination, but I believe they used Bronte and our relationship to get to me from the beginning. The property across from Elder Macario is owned by Griffin Enterprises. The Fellowship owns it," Ansel explained and hoped he didn't sound crazy, like a conspirator, or arrogant. Bronte's Covey, her team of assassins now known as Crimson Moon, used the property to stalk the Seelie court's elder, then shot his nephew. The attempted murder was the first part of her plan to take everything Ansel had worked for away from him. His pack. His respect. His honor. His rank as Captain of Enforcers. Clio, his fated mate.

Baron Kanin leaned forward. "Or seized the opportunity when it presented itself and decided they would use her. The only way I'm going to allow this is you're going to spy for us."

"Negative." Rutger's expression was thunderous. "Absolutely not. You cannot send Ansel straight to them, and you can't give them Jo's weaknesses. They want to hurt her to destroy you."

"This is what I think," the baron started. "When Bronte failed, they took her in, protected her, knew you would go to them for help, and thought they could use her against you. Only now, Cascade is stronger, we take care of our own, and are prepared to eliminate problems without worrying about the Highguard intervening. Hence, Strong Lord's jealousy of Jordyn, and his need to weaken the pack. They hadn't expected Bronte to stop being a threat to you, nor did they predict she would become the Fellowship's liability."

That's what he thought, except the part about Bronte being a liability. "They got what they wanted ... I'm on a leash, so there's no reason to keep her," Ansel replied, and hated admitting to betraying the pack and Clio and looking weak in front of the baron who treated him like a son. "She has faced people wanting to get rid of her her entire life." He rejected her. Ansel couldn't stop from feeling he created the monster she became. Then he shook it loose. That was a hundred years of guilt and emotional manipulations talking.

Rutger turned in his chair to look Ansel in the eyes and he felt the weight of the director's resolute stare. "Is that sympathy? Because, brother, she killed, set you on fire, and drugged Doctor Hyde. Yeah, that makes her a pain in the ass no one wants." Sitting straight, Rutger said, "Besides conspiring against us, if that's true, why now? The Fellowship could keep her hidden forever. Or kill her. No one would know."

Ansel looked at the side of Rutger's face and let his use of brother settle in his heart where it helped steady him. "Strong Lord knew about the wards Kerrick used to protect your location. He questioned me about them. He doesn't know how they were broken."

Jordyn laughed from her place beside a bookcase. "Bronte is a liability because Strong Lord is feeling pressure."

"From who?" Rutger and Baron Kanin asked in unison.

"Us. I told him it was better to work with us than against us," she answered. Ansel and Rutger both turned in their seats to see her smiling and her wolf in her copper gaze. "And protecting Bronte is actively working against us."

"When?" Baron Kanin demanded, his voice low.

"At my ascension party. With Shadow Lord making a scene with his overlords and generals and Prime's reverence, verifying we're protected, I reminded him the Fellowship is in our territory and teamwork makes the dream work. Strong Lord did advise me that he's more powerful than I am. But he doesn't know for sure, and this might be a way to test that theory. No one knows what my traits are, let alone my weaknesses, and Rutger's rescue created more questions than answers. It's possible this will do two things ... one, establish our power base, forcing them to recognize us as equals, which means they have to cease their plotting, and two, because Cascade is protected, they have to leave Captain Wolt alone. At this point Strong Lord is a thorn in our side. The immediate problem is Bronte. The only way Captain Wolt and Doctor Hyde are going to be safe is to eliminate her. And knowing she can't be good company, rather than killing her outright, they'll try to use Captain Wolt's need for revenge. They know we all want her for what she did."

Ansel watched Jordyn, then glanced at Rutger to see him staring at her with full blown pride on his face. She needed to quit the OPI and work as an enforcer.

"Prime knows. He let them hide her," Rutger stated as he tore his gaze from Jordyn and faced Baron Kanin. "He was here, the Highguard was here. They lied to us, and that gives Strong Lord confidence."

"It would appear that way," the baron replied with frustration.

"What do we do?" Jordyn asked, her hand on her gun, her badge flashing in the light, as she walked back to stand behind Rutger's chair.

"Ansel, you're going to stall while trying to get Bronte's location. If we can find her, we can eliminate her," Baron Kanin answered, his elbows on the desk. His eye rolled gold. "That's the priority. With her out of the equation, the Fellowship will have nothing. What we need to do is find a way to cut your leash."

"If we have proof they're protecting her—" Rutger started.

"Harboring a fugitive," Jordyn interrupted, her hand at the back of his neck, her fingers in his hair. "And it's goes against the canons. Just reminding you."

"Right, Detective Langston. Harboring a fugitive, and it's against the canons. We could use it to blackmail them. Release Ansel or we tell the Highguard," Rutger finished as he turned his head, a sliver giving Jordyn better access. "As simple as it sounds, they can't dispute evidence, and we'll have to confront Strong Lord."

"That depends on the agreement the Highguard has with the Fellowship. None of that matters if we don't find Bronte." Baron Kanin sat back, his arms crossing his chest to pull his charcoal and white pinstriped button-up shirt tight. "The fact he knew about the wards is distressing. We don't know the full extent of Strong Lord's powers, the others, or what others there are. They could have felt the wards. Or felt them when Jordyn destroyed them."

"I'm betting it was when I destroyed them. I wasn't very careful," Jordyn admitted. Rutger raised his hand and covered hers, then held it.

"I'll set up a meeting with Strong Lord," Ansel said as he stood.

He needed to get away from Rutger and Jordyn, their closeness, and Baron Kanin, the kindness and respect they had for him despite his lies. More than that, his mind was toying with him and giving his fantasies life. Bronte dead, and the freedom to have Clio. His fated mate. He said it again, in his head, as if holding onto it he was holding onto Clio, and his wolf howled. Would their plan be enough? Or was it too little too late and he was going to lose Clio to Alpha Crevan, or another man? The instinct to recognize him as her mate tangled and corrupted by a magic he didn't know how to undo. And if he did, she would find out he lied to her. Betrayed her. She was going to hate him.

"I have the rest of the day off. The storms did a number on my backyard and pond, and the geese aren't having it."

Baron Kanin laughed, a rumble from his chest. "Understood. Let me know what he says."

"Affirmative, sir." Ansel met Rutger's gaze, then Jordyn's, and lastly the baron's. "Thank you."

"You're our clansman, kith and kin," Jordyn said before anyone else.

Her words drove into him, and he knew he made the right decision in telling them the truth. Jordyn needed protecting. Clio needed protecting. But he hadn't divulged everything, and he lied. He hadn't asked the Fellowship for a favor and in return he became their lap dog. He signed a covenant, a blood bond, the Highguard would uphold, and Baron Kanin would be forced to recognize the agreement as binding. What he did and what he was going to do was breaking his vow and was punishable by death. He knew Strong Lord wasn't interested in killing him, the death threat being a minor deterrent to stop him from disobeying. He wanted the magic Ansel possessed, making him worth more alive than dead. So what was going to happen to him when Strong Lord found out he set him up, deceived him, broke the covenant, and challenged his authority in front of witnesses? Strong Lord would prove his power, and flexing his strength, would make an example out of him. Ansel was going to be punished. Tortured. Pain was going to be his companion for an unknown amount of time. At the door, he opened it and escaped into the hallway.

Over his heavy footsteps he heard music drifting from the family room, and Baroness Kanin humming along, while the scent of roasted coffee infused the air. The mansion could have been cold, sterile, to showcase Baron Kanin's power, but it wasn't. It was warm and comfortable and had become like home to him, the baron and baroness his family. At the double doors Troy opened the right side and held it open. "Thank you."

"Have a nice afternoon, Captain Wolt," he replied.

Ansel started across the parking lot, his mind racing with Bronte, Strong Lord, Clio, and the countdown to his demise. Closing the distance to the office, he saw Clio open the door. Stepping out, her hair shone in the sunlight and highlighted the strawberry threading through her curls. Gods, what was he doing? He didn't want to see her. Couldn't with his mind muddled with hope and despair. He used his werewolf speed to race to the back of the building, and after sliding his card, entered the guarded inner access, and then through secondary doors to the Enforcer's office. Farther to the left another set of double doors marked the entrance to the jail—prisoners wouldn't be escorted through the reception area, then into the heart of the Enforcers. On the other side was the receiving room, where they checked in the detainees, took their personal property, and gave them clothing identifying them as inmates of Cascade. Once processed, they were escorted to an elevator and taken one hundred feet below to the one thousand square feet of cells, cages, and interrogation rooms. He stepped inside the office and into a rush of cool air that swiftly washed June's warmth from his skin. Ansel took a right, headed down the hallway toward his office where he would grab his things. Behind him the gym buzzed with people and rock music; however, he preferred the blues. Then there were the stairway and elevators to the dorms and Nearctic, Clio's office.

"Captain Wolt."

Stopping and turning, Ansel rested his hand on his gun, and waited for the enforcer.

"Do you have a minute?" Luke asked as he pushed black hair from his forehead. The team leader of Hades and one of Rutger's Eight was dressed in a gray T-shirt, the front dark from sweat, a pair of shorts, and running shoes.

"What do you need?" Ansel wanted to get his gear and go home. He had a phone call to make that would initiate the countdown to his capture. And the meeting with the baron. What he asked for was selfish and yet they were going to help him hunt Bronte so he could cut his ties with the Fellowship. They were going to help him right his wrongs and asked nothing in return. If he lived to see the plan through, there was a chance he would be free. Freedom meant Clio.

"Do you have time for some sparring?" His molasses eyes glittered with an amber undertone while his shoulders lifted and lowered with his inhales.

Ansel looked into the gym to see Luke's team, some of them using the weight machines and others grappling.

Negative, he didn't have the time; he needed to call Strong Lord. He was going to tell the team leader no, it was a waste of his time. "Give me ten minutes."

"Yes, sir." Luke smiled, turned, and heading back into the gym said, "He's in. Prepare to have your asses handed to you."

Ansel shook his head and started toward his office. He had no idea what he was thinking.

CHAPTER SIX

Clio walked across the parking lot, folders in hand, one with her recommendations, her endorsement of the Coulter Coalition and Alpha Crevan, and upon Baron Kanin's acceptance of their confidence, an outline of training for the medical staff that would work at Promise Medical Center. The request to have the staff do their internship was tucked inside as well. She was suggesting, even advising Baron Kanin to allow outsiders within the walls of Celestial where they cared for their sick, wounded, and the weak, the most vulnerable part of Cascade.

There was a chance Alpha Crevan or one of the others might betray them, and if it happened it would be her fault, blood on her hands. That's why there would be safeguards in place, like added security. Having been an enforcer it was natural to see the possibility of deception and plan for it, but she couldn't think that way. She trusted her instincts; Crevan and the provosts had nothing to hide and weren't deceiving her. The priority was teaching and cultivating a relationship with the coalition. With her racing thoughts her nerves jumped under her skin, firing into the anxiety roiling in her middle.

"I can do this," she mumbled. She heard Crevan's voice as he stated her accomplishments.

Before she reached the double doors, Troy opened the right side and held it open for her. "Good afternoon," he greeted, his smile curving his lips, his sand-colored eyes watching her. He wore the sentinel's uniform of white polo shirt with Cascade's crest and his name, tactical pants, shoulder holster, and boots. With his dark blond hair styled, and his build, he looked like an all-American football player. Under his boyish appearance, easygoing bearing, and charm was a trained sentinel the baron counted on for protection.

"Good afternoon. I'm expected," Clio replied, tightening her grip on the folders.

"They're waiting for you in Baron Kanin's office," he explained.

"Thank you." Clio walked the hall, her heels clicking as if ticking off the seconds, the hem of her slacks swishing around her ankles. It felt like her heart was in her throat, and with her pulse in her ears she barely heard the music playing.

The displayed framed and matted photographs of Cascade, Shasta, and the surrounding area were Mistress' and had Clio wondering how a person with a passion could leave it to do something else. Especially a detective with human law enforcement. Clio was a doctor, and helping people, healing people made her who she was; it completed her and gave her a foundation. Like realizing she was an empath. The pieces slipped into place to create a finely tuned mechanism. Clio softly laughed, as if she didn't want anyone hearing her and she would disturb the atmosphere with her nervous giggle. Finally, she understood she had come to terms with being a Wight.

High five for it not taking my entire life to accept the facts. She shook her head. Her place was at Nearctic, and she belonged with Cascade, her pack; they were her family.

"Doctor Hyde, how are you?" Baroness Kanin asked, her velvet caramel eyes holding a combination of gentleness and wisdom as she stopped in front of her. She was the mother of three men, one of whom would be an alpha one day. She was the mate to the baron of Cascade and alpha of the pack. Nothing about her—her lithe frame, the perceived tenderness, and her quiet demeanor—betrayed her three hundred years and the tragedies she witnessed. Director Kanin's abduction, the attacks on Mistress, and the time the baroness spent in the encampments. The city of Trinity was named after three encampments built as prisons for the magic-born, and their families. They lived behind miles of steel walls and were treated like animals. Both the baron and baroness' families had died inside of the encampments.

"I'm well, thank you," Clio replied as she clutched the folders. She felt like child in front of an adult she idolized.

"Would you like a cup of coffee? I was about to check with the office."

She didn't name anyone, just referred to them as the office. It made Clio smile despite the pterodactyls making rounds in her stomach. "Would love some. Do you need me to help?" Clio asked. She couldn't, didn't want the baroness serving her coffee.

"Not at all. I'll bring it to you," she replied. "Tell the baron I'll be a minute."

"Ma'am."

Baroness Kanin smiled, and turning, her thick, mocha hair moved along her shoulders, and the hem of her loose, white top fluttered around the waist of her light blue, cotton capris. She walked away in silence, her bare feet on the marble flooring. She wasn't much taller than Mistress and was the exact opposite of Baron Kanin, his six-four height, which his sons inherited, and thick build. The Kanin men liked their women petite, elegant, and as powerful as they were beautiful.

Clio watched the baroness disappear and lightly knocked on the dark stained walnut door and waited. A second later, it opened smoothly with a soft swish of air, and Mistress stood on the other side, her level gaze holding Clio's as the scents of vanilla edged with tobacco, the musk of werewolves, drifted around her. There was another she knew intimately, and it wrapped around her, and struggling to ignore it, she failed and pictured his flannel. Clio didn't want to think about his scent, his shirt, and the way he ignored her. Although, if the tension in the office was an indicator, the meeting Captain Wolt had with the baron, the director, and Mistress hadn't been good. It was the proof she needed to convince herself he hadn't ignored her, but was concentrating on the meeting's subject. What it was, Clio had no idea, and wished she could help.

"Come in, Doctor Hyde."

Clio smiled, knew it had to be crooked as her nerves went into overload, and entered the office. "Thank you," she managed.

"Please, have seat." Baron Kanin waved to one of two chairs facing his large, walnut desk. To the left, pens, papers, books, and a journal cluttered the top while a computer dominated the right side.

"Baroness Kanin said she'll be a minute. She's bringing coffee." Clio sat down, crossed her legs, placed the files on her lap, folded her hands, and put them on top.

"Excellent. Jordyn explained she thinks you're an empath," Baron Kanin began, getting straight to business. "Do you feel this is true?"

Clio prepared to answer when Mistress sat beside her, and they were both staring at her. "Yes, I do believe it. The provost of the black-tailed deer, Allyson, is an empath, and she recognized me as one." Said I was honest and true.

"Is this a change? Or do you think you've always had this trait?" he asked with his heavy gaze holding hers, the directness in his eyes targeting her. The feel of his authority circled him, his power a low hum.

She hated talking about herself on a good day, and with his attention on her, she hated it even more. Clio felt her nerves kick up a notch, which should have been impossible. Having to answer, she inhaled and exhaled. "I've always been intuitive. I believe the trait has helped me as a doctor. My senses have never been strong, since I am a Wight, but this ... this is different. My senses were sharper than usual, and rather than feeling a person's injuries or their fear, I felt their truth. As if their intensions were in their words."

"If your traits are strengthening, I would say you're a Potent. Do you agree, Jordyn?" Baron Kanin asked.

Potent. The magic-born whose traits were increasing as the Emanation, the rise in magic, continued. When it was going to stop and what the end result was going to be, no one knew. War between humans and the magic-born. A race of super magic-born. No. One. Knew.

Clio watched Mistress transform, her ability to heal, her strength, telepathy, and was low-key jealous. It stung the wound she carried around with her because she was a Wight. She always wanted to be more. More werewolf. More human. More. Then accepted what she was, her place, and it changed. *Be careful what you wish for.*

"Affirmative. It was the reason I told her. Again, it should have been in person, and I could have explained what was going on," Mistress replied to the baron, then shifted in her seat to meet Clio's wide eyes. "Don't be scared. You're going to experience changes. Since your traits are centered on healing, I suspect your senses, instincts, and intuitiveness will increase in that area."

"Any other changes I should know about?" Clio asked hesitantly. She was going to make an appointment with Dr. Barsacq, Pureblood elf, and a High Privilege empath with the Seelie court. If Baron Kanin trusted him to work at the Hollow, a state-of-the-art underground medical facility hidden from the pack, klatch, the Cloaked as well as the Highguard, she could trust him. She needed to talk to someone who understood her from a doctor's point of view, and as an empath. With her decision to contact Dr. Barsacq, her fear eased. She would get the help she needed. Her heart raced with the implications—stronger senses, instincts, she would be able to help more people.

"Not at this time. Just stay aware," Mistress replied.

"Now to the business of Coulter Coalition," the baron started. "How was the meeting?"

"They consider Celestial the apex and are interested in building a hospital, Promise Medical Center. They were pleased with the information and asked basic questions." Clio paused, knowing she was going to have to tell Baron Kanin the hospital wasn't the sole reason for her going to Oak Run. "They are ready to give Cascade their confidence."

"I gave them a week," a male voice rumbled. "We need manpower."

"Another meeting," Baron Kanin replied as his dark eyes lifted from her.

Clio twisted in her seat to see Director Kanin standing beside a bookcase, his hand resting on his gun, his darkened glare on her. With her nerves out of control, she hadn't seen him and didn't know he was there. Her incredible empath powers at work. And then his wall of tension leaked over her, its steel cables invading her senses, and puncturing through them she knew the meeting with Captain Wolt, minutes before hers, hadn't been good. In fact, it had been bad.

"You're sensing his tension?" Mistress asked.

"Yes. You had a meeting with Captain Wolt, and it didn't go well," she replied before she could stop herself.

"It went fine. Director Kanin is a stress monger." Mistress waited for Clio to look at her before continuing, "You're gathering information, Doctor, and your quick mind is organizing it, but you need to be careful. You don't want to overload. Strong emotions will bully their way in and cause chaos."

Mistress was an impressive actress. Her smile, glittering cocoa eyes, and relaxed disposition calmed and charmed, it was no wonder the Highguard made her one of their own. With a warning and a threat delivered as casually as if they were talking about the weather, she hadn't felt its sting. Clio was glad they were friends—there was no way she wanted the soothsayer as an enemy. While she let the quiet slip over her, smoothing the sharp edges of the director's tension, it cleared her mind enough she could think straight, and she explained, "The hospital wasn't the only reason for the meeting. They questioned me, and as Cascade expands, they fear they're too weak to fight against the pack if it tried to absorb them. They want to remain independent. The deception ... although it wasn't malicious, they did lie. It's the reason I didn't give him your invitation."

"Astute of you. And now Alpha Crevan wants to give his confidence?" Baron Kanin questioned.

"He called me this morning. They're prepared to do whatever they have to." His insistence struck her as odd but then there was the Emanation.

"He wants the protection of Cascade, our resources, and most likely open travel. Plus, any resources they might glean from Celestial."

"Yes." She watched the baron as his eyes saw past her and to his son standing at the back of the office. As silence settled, Clio felt there was more going on.

"He's moving fast considering they have never had any business with Cascade. It might be my lack of faith in them, but what if he wants his people to be part of the Collective?" Mistress asked. Giving Clio a sideways glance, the serene façade slipped from her face. At the same time there was a whip of fury slicing through the air. Mistress didn't like the idea of them being part of the Collective. Clio didn't fully understand the extent of the Collective besides it was the pack and its essence.

"He is moving fast. Like I said, I gave him a week. This could be an attempt to get close to us, and learn more," Director Kanin added. "Completely understandable."

"Since discussing the hospital was secondary, I asked why I was the one they wanted to meet with. They explained I would understand since I'm an empath and healer. I protect the weak. And I'm not part of the hierarchy of the pack nor am I part of its politics. I warned them about the deception," Clio replied. Suddenly, the folders and her recommendations seemed useless.

Baron Kanin sat back, his chair hissing with the movement. "You believe they were honest with you? They weren't deceiving you?"

"They left themselves open, leaving no question to their intensions and the honesty behind their words. As one, they apologized and offered their apologies to you." Clio took the folders and handed them to the baron, nothing to lose. "The first folder is my recommendation and endorsement for their confidence. The second, upon your acceptance, is the outline to help them with Promise Medical Center. Obviously, that's my priority."

"Obviously." The baron took the folders from her and opened the first one. "When they begin construction on the hospital, you'll need to create a team of doctors and nurses."

"Sir."

Baron Kanin looked up from the paper he held, then opened the second folder. His sharp, tawny gaze, much like Director Kanin's, scanned the report, the silence in the office spreading between them.

"Rutger, what are your feelings?" Baron Kanin asked.

"We accept his confidence. We can't reject him when the diversity in the sets will strengthen our statement. However, there will be strict regulations to his addition and those of the provosts. Travel will be limited and must be cleared through the Enforcer's office," Rutger replied.

"Jordyn, how do you feel about it?"

"I agree with Rutger. While I fear they want to be part of the Collective, it's clear they don't understand what's involved. To take that step, they would have to request inclusion, and Alpha Crevan would have to give up his authority to you. From what I know about him, there's no way he'll do that. Still, the truth of the Collective is dangerous," Jordyn answered. "I'm not prepared to explain to a stranger I'll know everything about him, his deepest, darkest secrets. Plus, my trait to read minds."

"I agree with you. Did he say anything to you about Jordyn and her traits?" Baron Kanin asked.

"No. He talked about the hospital, the pack, and the sets. You know everyone's secrets?" Clio asked, and again she didn't stop herself.

"Yes and no. If I wanted to, I could see you and I would know everything about you. Is it readily available? No. Do I have the information right now? No. You're safe, everyone is safe. While it's my word, and I can assure you and promise you I'm not going peek or I'm not going to invade your mind all day, for people it isn't always enough. No one wants their privacy threatened."

"No they don't." Clio watched her eyes glaze over to onyx and saw fathoms in them and it sent chills down her spine. Information was a weapon.

"It puts Jordyn's life at risk as well as anyone who could be used against her," Baron Kanin started. "I trust you to keep her traits a secret."

"Yes, sir." She was already keeping Mistress' traits a secret. From everyone, including the baron and the director.

"You did a good job, Doctor Hyde. Excellent work, you've completed your assignment. From here, Errando will be the coalition's contact. I'll inform Alpha Crevan of our decision. Like any appeal for confidence, there will be a background investigation, an interview, and if they pass, Alpha Crevan and the provosts will be brought before the Elders of the pack."

"Yes, sir."

"I understand congratulations are in order. You rescued Sheriff Samuels' daughter," Baron Kanin said with a smile, the mood changing from business to relaxed. "He called me to tell me how grateful he was for your help and to tell you his daughter is doing fine."

Clio felt heat scald her cheeks. "I was doing my job."

Chuckling, the baron shook his head. "Captain Barnes also called, thanked you for the assistance, and is looking forward to working with the enforcers. You and Captain Wolt make a good team."

Gods help her. "I guess we do." She wanted to die.

"All right, Doctor Hyde, I'll let you get back to work."

"Thank you, sir." Clio stood, thankful the meeting was over, and stepped around the chair.

"Doctor Hyde," Mistress said from behind her.

Turning around, she met cocoa eyes and a smile. The opposite of a second ago. "Mistress."

"Good luck with the house hunt."

"Thank you. I'm going to need it."

"A house. Are you moving closer to us?" the baron asked.

"Maybe. I'm just looking right now." The tension in her shoulders eased, and she realized she liked sharing her news.

"Where are you looking?" Director Kanin asked. He shut down his emotions and was actively blocking her, the sensation like white noise on her senses.

"Setzer Road." Clio waited for his reaction but saw none; not surprising when he trained his features like he had his emotions. He knew where it was, they all did, but maybe he didn't know about her crush on his captain.

"You know, Setzer Road," Mistress drew the words out as she raised her eyebrows. "Tall, dark, and handsome."

"I live on Mill Creek Road," Director Kanin replied with a growl running through his words and what might have been a rueful smile curving his lips.

"Yes, Wolf," Mistress replied an easy laugh rolling through her words. "The other tall, dark, and handsome, your BFF, twin, right-hand man, partner in crime. Isn't that right, Doctor Hyde?"

"He isn't tall, dark, and handsome. He is a pain in the ass and has terrible taste in furniture," Director Kanin replied.

He said it so serious Clio didn't know if he was joking or not. Instead of responding to him, she met eyes bright with humor and defended herself by saying, "Funny, ha, ha. It's the first on the list, I didn't pick it."

"Sure thing," Mistress teased and got a laugh out of the baron. "Go house hunt."

Clio shook her head and heard Mistress explaining what was funny to two men who had the weight of the world on their shoulders and rarely were allowed to relax. The door closed, cutting off the sound, and left Clio alone in the hall-way. She stood motionless for several seconds, trying to get her bearings, and to digest what had been said, revealed. Her association with the coalition was over as far as the baron was concerned. Until she was needed with the hospital. Her meeting hadn't created the same tension as Captain Wolt's, making her wonder what had been talked about. They were all good actors. No one giving away anything save for Director Kanin's stress, which could be anything. He did say they needed more manpower. Heading to the doors, Clio remembered the baroness never arrived with coffee; it sounded good, and she needed a pick me up. She would get a cup before her appointment with Mr. Starks and Setzer Road.

"Have a good afternoon, Doctor," Sadie said as she opened the door.

"Thank you. You too," Clio replied and walked into the afternoon's embrace.

Leaving the expanse of the covered porch, the sun blazed down to heat and exaggerate the scents of lawn, flowers, the pastures in the distance, and pack. It was comforting to smell them, something she hadn't been able to do in the past and was jealous of others for having it. She wondered what Pure-bloods like Mistress, Director Kanin smelled, and what information Baron Kanin learned from the air. Her thoughts held her attention as she made her way to her office where she retrieved her satchel, cell phone, and purse. She stalled, staring at the flannel hanging on the rack, and thought about leaving it; she wasn't going to hunt down Captain Good Mood. Or as Mistress called him, Tall, Dark, and Handsome. She groaned a curse and grabbed it; she would take it with her and worry about it later. Once in her crossover, the terminal dinging and beeping, she searched the parking lot, didn't see a silver 4x4, and left her parking spot. She drove the two-lane drive, intent on heading to a coffee shop when she really wanted a cool sip of tequila. Or a glass.

Setzer Road.

Then it hit her, and scarlet burned her cheeks. "Oh my gosh. I just confirmed to Baron Kanin, Director Kanin, and Mistress that I'm hopelessly infatuated with Ansel. Captain Wolt. Who doesn't know I exist. Great. Smooth move, Clio. Real smooth," she mumbled. "I'm an idiot."

How in the world did they trust her with their secrets?

Ansel feathered his fingers over the three delicate feathers in front of a sword, its tip pointed to the sky inked into his flesh. The Covey, Bronte, somehow it survived the fire. *"Brando, you love me."*

"I do not. Never have," he whispered as the blaze crawled up his legs, arms, chest, to lick his neck with its searing heat. The inferno burned through cotton and denim to melt skin, muscles, tendons, and he could hear the sizzle as it drank in the moisture of his body. The force crawled over him, and taking his face in its flames, he saw orange and red as it ate away at his eyebrows, eyelashes, and threatened to take his eyes.

"I should be dead," he sighed as he pulled the T-shirt over his head. The tattoo served as a reminder of his past as the medallion represented his future.

In the locker room, he checked to see if anyone noticed it, him, and told himself he didn't have to worry about that anymore. Cat was out of the bag, so to speak. Looking in the mirror, he saw his father's features and his mother's magic in his bronze eyes, and questioned if it was possible he was going to be free of Bronte, and then the Fellowship. His confidence had been secure, the baron was going to help him, Jordyn, Rutger, but after having time to think about it, he didn't know. He stopped himself from chasing the trail his mind wanted to go. He couldn't, wouldn't go back to keeping secrets from them, and if he changed strategies that's exactly what would happen. His wolf howled as it clawed his insides. It wanted its mate, and ignoring her, and feeling the blast of hurt as he left her standing in the parking lot pushed on his control.

After tossing and turning most of the night, the alpha's scent mocking him, his plan had been simple. He would spend an hour sparring and grappling with Luke and team Hades—he needed to burn energy, to take his mind off Clio and the jealously burning in him. He hated the other alpha. Then there was the call to Strong Lord, it was an ax over his head. All he saw was her in the other man's arms, her azure eyes with warm honey gleaming as she stared at the night. It made him want to punch something, so he hit the bags. However, that was two hours ago. He was late and the day was moving on without him. Adding to his already bad mood, an enforcer, Owen, told him he had a flat tire. At least a mechanic offered to fix it and it would be done by the time he was ready to leave.

Ansel picked up his cell, shoved it in a back pocket of his jeans, grabbed his gym bag, slung it over his shoulder, then took his tactical belt and holster from the locker. Off work, he wore civilian clothing. He headed out of the locker room and into the gym, which was empty, making his footsteps sound on the tile. In seconds, he was in the hall passing his office, communications, and through reception. When he left the meeting, the sun had shone bright in the cloudless sky, and was chasing the chill from the morning. He looked at the mountain ridges, the glittering snow on their peaks, and the thick, gray clouds as they slipped across the expanse of indigo. Pressure thickened the air with moisture, a stiff breeze moved the ends of his hair against his neck, and a chill skated down his spine. It felt like a thunderstorm. Another damn storm. Inhaling, he held the breath and tasted the sweetness of rain. Whether the sky would open today or the next he wasn't sure. However, he did know he was going to have to hurry if he wanted to get any work done. With a quick scan of the parking lot, he saw that the mechanic had done exactly what he said he would do. His truck was parked in its spot.

At the passenger side door, he opened it, put his things on the seat, and couldn't stop himself from noticing Clio was gone. Early in the day after a meeting with the baron. Did she have another meeting with the alpha? He didn't know. Didn't want to know.

"Gotta let her go," he reminded himself. Pushing his fingers through his hair, over his scalp, and to his neck he rubbed the knot in his tight muscles.

He wouldn't use the chainsaw on the fallen trees ... no, he was going to use an ax. A couple of hours of going head-to-head with trees, then stacking the wood, might exhaust him enough he would sleep. Though he doubted it. The diesel engine rumbled to life, and leaving the parking lot, headed down the drive. Out on the open road he drove through the industrial district, checking on Rutger's warehouse, the activity going on, then through Trinity's downtown, sensing its feel, the energy of humans and magic-born. With Cascade's crests on the sides of his truck, it made a statement, and created a presence. The force of the city always made his wolf howl while its claws threatened to score him if he stopped. Making his way out of the city limits, trees lined the two-lane road, creating a cover of shade, made darker by the cluster of gray clouds.

He lost himself to the scenery, his buzzing thoughts, and the familiar dings and beeps of the terminal. This was his territory, his land, and home. It gave him a foundation no one could take away from him, and an internal strength.

"I can't let her go. I'm going to fight for her," he promised himself and his wolf. They would find Bronte and end her. If he remained with the Fellowship as their dog on a leash, fine, that's what he would do. *And once she remembers what happened to her?*

"She's going to hate me," he told himself. Then what? He was going to grovel at her feet until she got sick of him, and giving up, forgave him. He wasn't going to live without his teacher, healer, the brightness to his dark, beauty to his beast. He needed her. Vow made, a weight lifted from his shoulders, a lightness shoved at the sadness saturating his middle and slipped over the tension knotting his muscles. Ansel relaxed, his elbow in the window frame, one hand on the steering wheel, and the wind cooling his heated skin. He felt good. If that was possible.

"What in the hell?" he growled and sat forward at the same time he let off the accelerator. His heart pounded in his chest then slammed against his sternum to fall to his feet. After checking for traffic behind him, the truck slowed, and easing on the brakes he pulled to the shoulder and stopped under the canopy of a cottonwood tree.

Clio stepped out of her crossover, and walking around to the passenger side, opened the door to retrieve two cups, then used her hip to close the door. Her hip. The sashay and motion making a growl rumble low in his chest. She was holding coffee; Ansel recognized the color and the logo from Triple Shot Coffee House, which was owned by a member of the Red River fold of foxes. She had to have driven across town, a special trip. For who?

Tony Reed had been a paramedic and med van driver of Med Two who worked with Clio and introduced her to the place. Bronte murdered and brutalized Tony, then left his remains at Ansel's house to further incriminate him. He didn't know she still went there. Jealousy burned in his veins while the green monster reared its ugly head. Clio started down the sidewalk toward the front door when a man met her, and laughing, she handed him a cup. She bought him coffee.

"Who the hell is he? And why is she there?" Between the man and the alpha, he was going to lose his fucking mind.

Ansel's senses targeted the man, a Wight, werewolf and human. His essence felt weak, and he wasn't in the higher echelon of the pack. Dressed business casual—slacks, polo shirt—his light red hair styled, Ansel didn't recognize him. A low growl sounded when he clinked his cup against hers, making her laugh again, then his hand was at the small of her back, and he led her through the open door and into the house. A second later the door closed. Inside. She was with a man inside of a house. Down his street. What was left of his sanity broke apart, the shards falling. If she wanted to go to Oak Run and be seduced by an alpha, fine. It wasn't in Cascade, he wouldn't have to see them, and it wasn't on his damn street, right under his nose.

With jerky movements, Ansel put the truck into gear, and gaining speed went by the house as fast as he could go. There were fallen trees waiting for him and he was going to take his fury out on them.

CHAPTER SEVEN

Clio sipped her coffee. The dark roasted notes added enough sweetness that she didn't use cream or sugar. Plain black coffee that healed the soul and reminded her of Tony. When she visited the coffee house, his cousin sat with her, and they talked about him—his rock climbing, effortless laugh, and his love for his family. It was the only way she knew how to say sorry and give back to them.

"Across the street is a ranch, and the house backs up to Forest Service land, so no one will ever build. You have five acres here, it's a comfortable amount of space," Mr. Starks explained as he gave her an easygoing smile.

"Comfortable?" Clio asked as she entered the house through mission-style double doors. The foyer opened to the living room and kitchen, and making a left she walked to a large picture window that looked out to the street and the plain of ranch land. She could get used to seeing it every day. "I'm leaving a townhouse, and an association. At this point the yard seems daunting." Sitting well off the road, the large front yard, mature trees shading the house, and the flowerbeds gave it a sense of privacy. She liked that. It was the exact opposite of the townhouse's view. Parking lot and cars. She wouldn't hear people at all times of the day and night coming or going or feel the energy of downtown. It would be quiet. Was she ready for it?

"Jess said you were taking the plunge," Mr. Starks replied.

Laughing, Clio said, "Yes, I am. Not sure this is the plunge I want."

She was staring out the window, semi lost with the amount of land, the clouds looking like granite as they moved in, blocking out the sunshine and covering the scenery in gray. Shards of sunlight cast spiderweb shadows through branches, the grass stretched out to the road and across to see more landscape and mountains. The vastness, its openness, eased the grip she had on her thoughts, and she let the meeting with the baron, Mistress' threat, and then Captain Wolt walking away from her drift. Like they weren't as dire right then. Still musing over everything, she blinked her eyes when she saw a silver 4x4 with Cascade's crest on its door fly by. *Speak of the devil.* Her heart stilled to cover her reaction to seeing him, and she casually sipped her coffee.

"That's Captain Wolt, he's an enforcer for Cascade. He's about a mile down the road. He just snatched up the last ten acres. His property borders the ranch, and Forest Service land. No one will be able build near him, making this lot equally safe from development. It's worth a fortune." Mr. Starks inhaled and exhaled, his respect for the enforcers evident, as was his respect for Captain Wolt. "You both work at Foxwood, do you know him?"

His shirt is in my car. He ignores me. *He didn't ignore you*, she told herself. "I've seen him," Clio replied, calmly.

"If anything happens, you'll have an enforcer close by. And the best besides Director Kanin."

Clio met pale green eyes and smiled. "Good to know."

"The downstairs has two spare rooms, the kitchen, one full bathroom and another one in the mudroom/laundry room, access to the garage, and formal dining room. There's room in the kitchen for a table, and there's French doors leading out to a deck," he explained as he walked to the kitchen.

Clio followed, her thoughts in a dozen different directions, and why Captain Good Mood was heading home early. Was it the meeting? Did something happen? Why was it bugging her? Captain Wolt and Director Kanin were like brothers, thick as thieves, and the tension rolling off Director Kanin had been palpable, telling her something wasn't right. It grated on her senses, and she felt the urge to fix it, but didn't know what it was to fix. Then the director turned it off as if he had a switch. It was a testament to his control.

"Custom concrete countertops, cabinets, stainless steel appliances," Mr. Stark explained as he made his way to a hall. "Mudroom/laundry room, door to the garage. Here are the stairs."

She trailed behind, looking at the craftsmanship, the wood flooring, the pale color of paint on the walls. She was going to have to change that. She needed bright, not boring.

"This is why you're going to buy the house," he began.

"Mmm." She wasn't so sure she wanted the responsibility. The house was four times the size of her townhouse. Maybe she could rearrange the spare room and make it work for her office. Did she really want to be near Captain Wolt? No. Especially after making a fool of herself in front of the director and the baron. Director Kanin had to know Captain Wolt ignored her, treated her like the plague, and treated her like she was a Cascade employee. "Less than an employee," she mumbled.

"What was that?" Mr. Stark asked.

"Nothing. What were you saying?" she asked. *Close one.*

"The master suite is on the right, you have a sitting area, and French doors to the deck. The left side is an open area. Jess said you needed a home office and we agreed this would be perfect. You have views of the front and back of the house."

She would see about that. Doubts and fear continued to creep over any excitement she felt. Clio took the last step and stopped when she found herself in a large room surrounded by windows and could see the mountains, the valley, could see everything from where she stood. "Oh my, this is incredible."

"Yes. Once it officially goes on the market, it'll be gone."

"It's not going on the market," she heard herself say. Clio walked to the front windows, her heels clicking on dark wood flooring—her vintage, red Aubusson rug would be perfect—then turning, walked to the back windows. The entire side opened to the deck and there was another set of French doors. A deck downstairs and upstairs. Oh hell yeah. Excitement raced through her like an electrical current. Walking toward a set of oak double doors, she opened the left side and walked into a bedroom fit for a king. Or queen. "So not going on the market."

"Told you," Mr. Starks teased as he leaned against the door jam, his eyes on her as she roamed the empty room.

"Yes, you did." Trying to keep her head and her thoughts from planning where she was going to put her furniture, the furniture she was going to buy, she checked out the bathroom. One problem and it was a deal breaker. A huge skylight over the walk-in shower with river rock bottom let natural light in, there were double sinks, a huge tub she could do laps in, with a window running its length. There was nothing wrong with the bathroom. She headed toward the French doors, and opening the right side, walked out to the railing of the deck. She could see the coming rain in the thick clouds as if they were carrying a raging river, could smell it in the air, and felt the pressure of the building storm. She let it work through her as she scanned the downstairs deck and found everything was new—the pressure treated wood, the forest green tin roof—then it ended, and the backyard was a tangled mess of brush and grasses that went on for miles. "Will the owner take less?"

"Why?" Mr. Starks asked from the doorway.

"I need money for landscaping," she replied. And a bull-dozer.

"Ten thousand?"

She was thinking five, but ten would cover all the expenses. Her dad loved working in the yard, and this would be a great way to get her parents over to her house. Barbeque, drinks. She was getting ahead of herself; she didn't own a grill, and hadn't been grocery shopping in weeks. Explained why she had a bottle of tequila, lunchmeat, and Crevan's to-go boxes at her townhouse. "Yes, that would be perfect."

"I'll add it to the offer. If they decline?"

"Then I'll pay full price," she answered. The house was hers.

"Anything else?"

She laughed as a thrill coursed through her. "Nope."

"Excellent. When I get to the office, I'll write up the offer."

"Sounds good." If they accept, she just bought a house. Okay. She wanted, needed to tell someone, the excitement of it buzzing through her, and it was going to be Mistress. She was safe. "Is there anything I have to do?"

"Wait for them to accept the offer, then pack your stuff," Mr. Starks replied.

With that, Clio told Mr. Starks good-bye, she would be waiting for his call, and sat in her crossover her cell to her ear.

"Doctor Hyde, how can I help you?" Mistress asked.

"Am I bothering you?"

"Not at all, driving to Butte Springs," she replied.

Butte Springs. Not only had the witches held Mistress prisoner there, but their leader also tried sacrificing her to their god, and Clio was sure she witnessed Mistress' death. The lack of heartbeat, the silence, it had nagged her for months. And Mistress was going there. "Are you going to be all right?"

"You know I hate that question, but yeah, I am. I'm meeting Rutger there. You didn't call me to talk about Butte Springs. What's up?"

"I put an offer in. If they accept, I just bought the house on Setzer," she gushed.

"I thought you were merely looking?" she asked, and Clio could hear her smile.

"It has space for a home office and views to die for," she said in defense. "You have to see it."

Struggling through a giggle, she replied, "Congratulations. You get the house, and we'll have a party. Maybe invite your neighbor over. Show some neighborly love."

Clio outright laughed. "Yeah, no. I didn't embarrass myself this morning, did I?" She was suddenly serious, the euphoria draining from her. First the meeting with Crevan, his ulterior motives, and then Captain Wolt.

"No you didn't. He's home right now, said something about cleaning up his pond because his geese weren't happy."

Clio heard Mistress' terminal as it beeped and dinged in the background; she had to be busy, was heading to Butte

Springs. She appreciated her time and the friendship they shared. Staring at the flannel, she thought about it. She needed to get rid of it. There was no way she was packing it up and moving it with her, and she wasn't going to hand it over to Tabby, the office receptionist. Then reality hit. "I have to organize my office, and Mr. Starks said he was going to call as soon as he heard anything, then there's paperwork."

"Sounds like excuses to me, Doc. Was just letting you know."

"Thanks." She couldn't take more rejection from Captain Good Mood. "Thanks for letting me share my news."

"I'm glad you told me. Congratulations again. If you need help moving let me know, I'll bring the drinks."

"I will, thanks." Clio heard the line go quiet and started the engine.

She wasn't going to go to his house. There was pain there and a level of fear she didn't feel like battling. Not when she was happy and had something to be excited about. Plus, she needed to tell her parents, and was sure her mom would ask her over for dinner. Pulling onto the road, she decided she was going to simply drive by his place to see how nearby the enforcer really was.

Sure. She couldn't lie to herself. Her heart thundered in her chest, her pulse sounded in her ears, forcing her to inhale and exhale to try and calm herself down. *Not going to stop.* She saw the entrance to his driveway. *Not going to do it.* Closer. She looked at his flannel. She was returning it. Plain and simple. She made a left, slowed the crossover to a crawl, crept up the drive lined with pine, oak, and fir trees, and to his house. He had to have heard her. She stopped beside his truck; he backed in, so the front faced the road, and she wondered why he didn't use his garage. Stupid thought. Why did she care?

The house she considered hers was a log home, the out-side tarnished by weather, with updated windows and doors, high ceiling with open beams and felt modern while fitting in with the mountains. Captain Wolt's house was a two-story farmhouse with raw cedar siding, red tin roof, covered front porch, and flowerbeds. She stared at it, her mind telling her she was asking for trouble and heartache, and she should turn around and go home. At the same time her heart fueled the courage needed to face him and hand over his property. She snagged the flannel from the passenger seat, and before she changed her mind, Clio got out of the car, and with weak legs walked to the stairs. The day Bronte found them came roaring back as she stepped up to the porch and she stopped.

"She isn't here." Scarlet eyes marred by white narrowed on her, then fear exploded and her instincts told her to get the hell out of there. "It isn't real. It isn't real," she repeated, and wasn't going to let fear rule her life. Mistress was driving toward her nightmare and facing a place of horror and pain, she could push her fear aside to return a shirt. And she was returning a shirt, not marrying the guy. The word marry and Captain Wolt didn't belong in the same sentence.

While she grappled for control, she knocked on the door and waited. One minute. Two. The clouds sat heavy with rain, the air thickening, bringing humidity with it, and she rubbed the back of her neck. Three minutes. He saw her and wasn't going to answer the door. Why would he? Clio was turning to leave when she heard noises and music from the back-yard. Mistress said he was going to be cleaning his pond for his unhappy geese. She expected a lot of things, but not that. She could put the flannel between the screen door and the oak door, and turning to leave, figured this way she wouldn't have to face him. "No way." He would think she was a coward. She would have to eventually see him at Foxwood, and she didn't want to explain why she left without talking to him. Like he would care. Shaking her head to clear them of her splintered thoughts, she grabbed the flannel and marched around the side of the house, the same way she had when they found Tony's body. "Stop."

With each step, she bullied her rabid thoughts back, and continuing around the house the music and hacking noises grew louder. When she reached the back, she walked the stone pathway lined with flowers to the deck where a stereo played a smokey blues rhythm from its place on a table. Beside it were two empty beer bottles, another one half full, and a half-eaten sandwich and chips. Why those simple details, and his choice of music, drew her in, she didn't know. Clio placed the flannel on the table beside a black T-shirt; didn't know why she picked up the beer and took a sip. After setting the bottle down, she went to the railing and watched him swing an ax, the hit splitting the fallen tree with a loud crack.

He wasn't wearing a shirt, leaving his bronze skin glittering under a sheen of sweat, the muscles in his back flexing with his movement, and his jeans, riding low on his hips, were dark around the waist. He lifted the ax, swinging it above his head—when his shoulders bunched, she saw the tattoo—and bringing it down, the tendons like cords in his arms, the head sliced through wood. The tattoo survived. It was the first thing she noticed when he was in the restoring chamber healing from burns covering ninety percent of his body. If the burns hadn't been bad enough, she thought she was going to lose him to organ failure and cardiac arrest.

She didn't think he was going to live. She would have lost him. And it would have destroyed her. She liked seeing him, knowing he was there. If he ignored her, did it matter? No.

He lifted the ax, it was over his head, then without striking he lowered it, resting the handle on one shoulder. Her heart went to her throat as he slowly turned around and nailed her with a bronze gaze.

With music playing in the background, Ansel had been mumbling to himself. Who the hell was the man, besides a Wight, and why was Clio seeing him? Not only seeing him but bought him coffee. An offering. And met him at his house. Where did the alpha fit in the picture? He didn't know. Didn't care. Didn't want to think about them. Her. He decided he was going to fight for her, a lot of good that did him; she shot him down before he had a chance to prove himself. With fury taking over, he brought the ax down, the steel slicing through wood like a knife through butter, the force making it sink into the ground beneath, the recoil vibrating the handle and going into his hands and arms. His muscles burned from exertion, he felt his back screaming as he lifted the ax, and swinging it down, hit the wood with a loud crack. Then a hum slithered over him, his senses cleared his mind, his wolf howled, and clawed at him with her presence. Lowering his head, her essence saturated the thickening air, making it hard to breathe and harder to think. He hadn't heard her, hadn't sensed someone was at his house.

It had been a fatal mistake to open himself to her when he searched for her. It created a breach in his defenses, allowing her to seep into him. Through him. He slowly lowered the ax, its handle on his shoulder, his muscles tense, and turned to face her. Her curls were loose over one shoulder, her black lashes framed her azure eyes, and she was staring at him. She wore a form-fitting blouse, slacks, heels.

Ever the professional. He had no idea why she was at his house. His wolf slammed into him, and bursting through his restraint sat under his skin, threatening to take over to have its mate. Ansel fought it as her scent of cinnamon, and spice like brown sugar and clove, and coffee drifted to him. His nose flared, and inhaling to catch it, hated himself for it—it pushed on his non-existent control—and at the same time he savored the combination. It was for him and him alone. Then he smelled the Wight, growled, and with his werewolf speed and strength twisted around to embed the head of the ax in the log. He needed to calm down, he couldn't talk to her with his wolf front and center. He didn't want to scare her. Taking measured steps, he left the log, his ax, and pond, and taking the stairs two at a time, stood on his deck with Clio four feet from him.

"Can I help you?" he asked, and was surprised his voice didn't hold a growl. Not being able to stand still, he went to the table, saw his flannel, took the T-shirt, wiped his face and neck, then grabbed his beer. He'd hoped she was going to keep his shirt. Taking swig, he tasted her. Spice and her wolf, like a honied elixir tinged with fear, and his mind went blank, save for the image of them kissing, his hand in her hair. "You didn't have to drink my beer. There's more in the fridge," he grated through clenched teeth.

"Are you offering me one?" Clio asked and told herself to shut up. This was not the time to play with an irritated wolf. And he was irritated.

He stomped his way from the rounds of wood to the deck, his fury out for her to feel, and she had to keep herself from taking a step backwards. Hell, to keep herself from tucking tail and running to her car and leaving. Part fear, part she didn't trust herself with him. His six-four height and build was sexy as hell when he was spitting wood, it became freaking irresistible when he stood in front of her, his bare chest, the line of auburn hair against bronze leading to denim and disappearing. She was having a hard time keeping herself from blatantly ogling him at the same time her irrational fear tried taking over. Pushing it back, she let her desire trump panic. She was an idiot.

"Why are you here?" Ansel faced her and saw the darkened honey eddying around her pupils and swirling in azure.

"I'm returning your shirt. You didn't stop this morning," she easily replied. God's honest truth.

"I had a meeting." Taking another swig, he finished the bottle, and with her taste on his tongue, he gently set it on the table, stopping himself from smashing it and sending glass everywhere. To keep himself from taking her in his arms, he put his hands on his hips, his fingers digging into his sides. "Thank you for returning the shirt. I'm sure you didn't want one of your male friends knowing you had it."

Clio stared at him with blatant confusion in her gaze, and anger replaced fear. What the hell was he talking about? She wasn't the one ignoring him. "I didn't think you wanted anyone knowing you could possibly be nice to me. That you acknowledged my presence. Might ruin your reputation for being an ass," she countered, her hands on her hips. Shaking her head, she didn't know where that came from. Talk about acting like a lunatic. She needed to straighten her thoughts, maybe shake some sense into herself. And no, she didn't know why she was there, but it wasn't going to stop her from continuing, "My apologies, I should have left it with Tabby. I shouldn't have bothered you."

"But you did." Ansel wasn't an ass, he passed that up some time ago. He was a sorry excuse for a person.

"My apologies." *Oh, great one.* Clio turned to leave, her heart dropping from her chest to crash and burn.

"You washed it? You didn't like my scent," he accused. He was making matters worse when he needed her gone.

Why was he doing this to her? Why was she letting him? "I wouldn't return a dirty shirt." She felt like a fool for having slept in it. "Excuse my manners."

"My scent," he demanded.

"What?" Clio tried to bury her emotions where his scent was concerned. What it did to her. How she felt wrapped in the smell of his skin and wolf. The feel of cotton on her bare body.

He was racing down a trail he shouldn't be on like a runaway train. "I want to know how it compared to Alpha Crevan's."

"What are you talking about?" she demanded. How dare he? He was the lunatic.

"You smelled like him." Ansel reined in his anger, quenched the growl, and couldn't believe what he was doing. "The alpha's scent was on you." He didn't have anything to offer her. Except his lies. Jealousy. The price on his head. He was a fucking prize.

Is he for real? "How would you know that? You don't pay attention to me."

He paid very close attention to her. The need to touch her was going to destroy him. "I was there when you got home. Needed to know you were safe. I saw you, eyes bright as you gazed at the night. Were you thinking about him?" His jealousy was in full control, he was losing all his self-respect, and his wolf was going to turn his human body to shreds.

At her townhouse. He was the headlights she saw. "Yes, I was thinking about him. I had a report to write and turn into Baron Kanin. I needed to think about what I was going to say." Clio didn't know where the interrogation was going or why she was being interrogated. And why did he care what she thought about his scent and Craven? Unless ...

"Right." Ansel shoved his fingers through his sweat-damp hair, rubbed his neck, and felt the humidity as it sat sticky on his skin. "Forget it."

"No. You started this, Captain Good Mood. You're going to tell me why," she demanded.

Captain Good Mood. Is that what she thought of him? She was mocking him. "Why what?" *Good, play dumb.* The energy to continue drained from him while the tension gripping his muscles tightened. He was going to seize.

"Why do you care if I was with Crevan? Like I said, you don't pay attention to me. You don't like me, can barely stand looking at me. You ignored me today," she nearly yelled.

Fury and rage erupted; they were on a first name basis. "I had a meeting," he lied for a second time.

"Fine, then tell me what your meeting was about?" Clio felt him shutdown and shut her out. Where Director Kanin's had been white noise on her senses, Captain Wolt felt like a blade scoring her to give her mental whiplash.

"Pack business. And it's none of yours," he replied. Strong Lord. Bronte. His lies. The spell holding her memories. Begging for help.

"If it's none of my business, then my life is none of yours."

"It doesn't work like that," Ansel growled. Her life was his business. Like her heartbeat and the breaths making her chest rise and fall were his.

"That's exactly how it works, Father Time. In this century we call it equal rights. You can't ignore me, then tell me what to do."

Father Time. This century. Did she just call him old? No one called him old. "I can, Clio. And I will." *Mine*. No, he wasn't going there.

Clio. Her heart melted and she was sure it seeped into the deck. She needed to stay focused and not let false hope sway her. "Why?" The word lacked the defiance she wanted it to hold. Instead, she sounded needy.

"You fucking know why." He saw her jerking on the chains fastened to her wrists as the flames swallowed him. "Because of me you almost died. I'm already broken. If anything happened to you, it would destroy what's left of me." *Tesoro, you're the only thing holding me together*. He felt blades slice through his flesh, turning him raw and exposing his ugly, scarred heart, the sins rotting his insides, their weight breaking him down.

"You're not broken," she whispered and met his gaze.

"Don't, Clio. You don't know." Closing his eyes, he raised his face to the cloud-darkened sky, felt the heaviness of the storm, the balmy air, and met her softened gaze. "You don't fucking know." The spell was keeping her memories from her, but it wasn't stopping her from facing her fears, and he wondered what her defiance was doing to the magic. Part of him wished she ended the spell, saw him as the fraud he was and walked away from him. Yet the thought hurt him. She was his precious, beautiful woman who stood up to him, never left him, and tamed his wolf as much as she possessed the skill to bring it to a frenzy.

"Is that it? I don't know. I could never know. I'm not good enough. Are you ashamed of me?" she asked, her voice sounding small. Clio sucked in a breath. She hadn't realized how much she hurt as every weakness became fissures in her confidence.

"Gods, Clio. No, you amaze me. Your strength, loyalty, accomplishments, the way you heal people, and your pure heart make me want to be a better man. My soul is stained with the blood of others, and my sins. My heart is black, yours is not. You're innocent, honest, and I can't destroy that. I won't allow anyone to destroy the purity in you. I can't give you what you deserve, nor can I protect you." From Bronte. *Myself.*

She hated Bronte with every fiber of her being and wished the bitch was dead. Then his words wove around her, his raw confession taking the air from her lungs while her heart, she thought had abandoned her, stopped, her blood turned cold, and the world paused. She wasn't infatuated with him. Wasn't pining over her phantom. She wore his flannel to keep his scent close to her, to have his wolf, the velvet caress of his magic, and his distinctive spice on her skin and in her head. Gods, she loved the silent strength with unhealed wounds standing in front of her. He was going to be her undoing.

I love him. Inside of her, something snapped, like a band pulled too tight, and released the tension holding ... what? Her fear? She searched herself for the truth and felt a piece of a barrier missing. Maybe facing him was giving her her strength back. "You don't have to protect me, Ansel. I didn't die. We didn't die. The pack found us and saved us." She turned in a circle as a toxic mix of frustration, determination, and desire forced her to move. "I refuse to live in fear. I. Re-fuse. It isn't you against the world. It isn't me against the world. We have a pack. Kith and kin. We protect one an-other."

He was a stupid, selfish bastard for even considering be-ing with her. He stared at her, the heated need in her gaze, the way she bit her bottom lip with her thoughts, all the while seconds ticked by with the beat of his heart. His skin warmed and a tingle cascaded over him when his wolf de-manded he take its mate. Ansel was being unfair when his lies were holding her memories captive, Bronte was out there somewhere, and the Fellowship was blackmailing him. Against his resolve, he believed every word she said and knew it couldn't continue. He couldn't risk her life.

"You need to leave," he grated through clenched teeth, and the shards of his heart turned to ash. As if sensing the twisted energy between them, sensual tension, and re-pressed need, the first drops of rain dotted the deck, their shoulders, and thunder roared across the sky. Adding to the volatile power was the slow rhythm playing.

He was right. She told herself she needed to leave. Get in the car and go home. Leave him to his demons. She needed to protect what was left of her heart. And pride. The morning came back. Everyone knew, and there was no more pretend-ing she hadn't given her heart to this dark mystery telling her to leave. *Damn you*, she longed to yell. *Damn you*. She wanted him like she never wanted anything in her life, and it made her stay where she was. "No. I can feel your desire, you want me," she accused, her voice throaty, giving away her passion and her fear. "Like I want you."

Want isn't a strong enough word. He felt his eyes reshape to his wolf's; he drew in her scent, felt her lust swirling around her, and the fight with his wolf intensified. "Negative. This can't be." His entire body vibrated with tension created from her stare at the same time cool rain drops landed on his heated skin, making him shudder.

"Why?" She took a step toward him, her breasts rising with her deep inhales, and she saw him trembling. "Tell me, Ansel, why?"

My lies. "You deserve better." Ansel didn't move, didn't take a step back, couldn't deny her. "The alpha." Saying it made his stomach turn and his wolf howl in sorrow.

"No. I decide what I want. I decided it was you."

Gods, woman.

Lightning shot across the sky, its electric spines slicing through clouds, turning the gray to white for a breath, and in seconds thunder answered the violence with its bellow. As if giving up the fight, the clouds opened themselves and rain fell as they stood staring at one another. Spurred on by the thunderstorm's energy, Ansel closed the distance between them, grasped her by her throat, his other hand on her back, and leaning down, held her azure gaze as he took her lips. When she gave into him, his kiss turned possessive, demanding, his tongue exploring her mouth, licking at her lips, her thin fingers wrapped around his wrist, tried to, and he smiled at her petite size.

"Why are you smiling?" Clio asked through a breath, her lips feathering his, while his heat seeped into her. The rainfall soaked her silk blouse, making it cling to her skin, sending chills over her.

"You," he whispered, his hand tightening around her throat. "You." His free hand drew her closer to him, her soaked shirt revealing the curve of her breasts. Against his chest the rain pelted his shoulders and back, the drops slipping over his skin, to his jeans, and thunder bombarded over them in wild chaos. He pulled back, caught his breath, and watched drops land on her cheeks, making her freckles glisten. Lowering his head, she gazed at him as he licked the tear-shaped water, his tongue grazing her skin to drink in her sugar and clove, and she closed her eyes and raised her face to the sky.

My tesoro. He wanted to say it to her, call her his treasure ... she was and much, much more. But wouldn't dare risk destroying the fragile filaments crisscrossing over her memories. Would he? Could he confess his lies? Affirmative. He didn't want anything between them. Even if it meant losing her. "Clio."

"Don't." Clio twined her fingers in his damp hair, her palm on the back of his neck, his muscles tensing, and held his bronze gaze. "Please."

Always. Her throaty voice, delicious mouth, lips a ruby red from their kiss, her hands on him, it was easy to obey her. He knew he would always obey her. The lies weren't going anywhere, they would keep. Touching her forehead with his, he whispered, "We should get out of the rain."

True. She lost herself in him, his hand on her throat taking possession of her, the other at her back, holding her tight against his strong body, and feral storm. Clio wasn't going to be the same. This was going ruin her. Sweet ruin it was going to be. Running her hands down his back slick from rain, like silk under her palms, she held his hips.

"Come with me," Ansel pleaded, the breathless sound quivering. His body vibrated with passion only Clio could sate, his muscles tensing to the point of pain, while he clung onto the shreds of his control. Their first time would be slow. He would treasure her, show her the man he wanted to be, the good she gave him.

"I will follow you anywhere," she replied, her words creating pressure against his palm.

He knew this and it scared the living hell out of him. Releasing his hold on her throat, he clasped her hand and took a step when she stopped. "What?"

"I'm going to melt before we get in the house. Your stuff. Do you want to take it inside?" she asked. The rain was getting stronger, the clouds darker, the thunder louder. She felt it in her chest, the echo drumming inside of her. Clio watched humor fill his eyes where raw desire had been, and he smiled. "I know. I know. Forever the responsible one. Don't make fun of me."

"Never. Do I make you melt?"

"You know you do. Every time I saw you. Just like you know I wore your shirt to have your scent on my skin. What did you think of my townhouse?" Pure arrogance veiled his face, his chiseled jaw clenched with satisfaction, and his wolf swirled in bronze.

"Neat, in order, but small. And, Doctor, tsk, tsk, your office is a mess. My shirt looked good on your bed." There was a question he couldn't stop himself from asking. "What were you doing at the house?" he demanded, his voice husky and laced with emotion.

"Jealous?" Clio challenged. He had searched her house, no doubt top to bottom and back again. She was sure he spent his time investigating her life.

"You know I am. Get used to it," he replied, his voice flat. "Why did you buy him coffee?"

It was Clio's turn to don arrogance and a smirk knowing he had been watching her. "He likes coffee. I got him his favorite."

A favorite from Triple Shot Coffee House. "I don't play well with others, beautiful. You're teasing a jealous wolf," he threatened, a low rumble in his words and holding a promise. His *tesoro* was his tempest. "Punishment will follow."

There was a subtle brogue to his words she hadn't heard before. The roughness told her she bet it would, and it would be divine. Her body trembled with the thought. Clio wanted to push him away, take out the months he spent ignoring her and the anguish she felt out on him, then tease him to watch his bronze gaze darken with his jealousy. But she wanted more of him. She needed him. Neither her heart nor her body could take waiting. "Darling, you can relax, he's a real estate agent. I put an offer on the house. I'm going to buy it," she answered coolly like she was stating the obvious.

Darling. He liked the way her lips curled around the word as it slowly left her, and it was directed at him. Ansel's sanity started coming back, the red haze clouding his vision from jealousy dissipated with her explanation. It was then he realized he wanted her in his bed, his house, and living with him. Insanity wasn't enough to let the thought take root. Eventually his lies were going to catch up to him, and when she found out what he had done to her, the betrayal, she might hate him and loathe their relationship. It was then he noticed she wasn't scared of him. Even when his six-four height loomed over her and his growling threat and promise of punishment, her desire flared, her heartbeat raced, and the sweetness of her arousal wrapped around her. The feel of fear and the sting of trepidation, he had known for months, since the spell, had disappeared. His tempest fought it and won. Ansel knew her strength, determination, and their intimacy was causing the spell to unravel, and having sex with her might destroy it completely. He would lose her just when he caught her.

"Did you hear me?" she asked as she pointed a finger and hit his chest.

Covering the spot where her finger left a bite from heat, he managed, "Yes. I'm stopping myself from picking you up, tossing you over my shoulder, and carrying you to my bedroom. Congratulations."

"Why stop?" His congratulations went right over head when her middle coiled into a tight ball of fire, and she saw him tossing her to his bed, and her body heated to the point she was really going to melt.

Ansel smiled, the devil in his grin, his plans for her in his eyes. "The stuff."

"Right," she mumbled. Forcing herself to walk, she grabbed the soaked T-shirt, flannel, and draping them over her forearm, picked up the plate with the soggy sandwich and chips. "Think you can handle the stereo?"

"Beautiful, you are going to pay," Ansel promised, the brogue back in his voice.

He was about to leave the apparatus in the rain—he could buy a new one, he wanted his hands on Clio, and her in his arms—then decided against it, he needed to take it slow. After unplugging it, he followed her inside, and carrying it across the living room, set it on a table and plugged it back in. A sultry melody began playing just as the sky opened its gates and a torrent of rain pelted the tin roof, the ground, and thunder and lightning danced together in a battle of wills. The fresh scent of earth, water on leaves and grass, drifted while the balmy heat amplified the smells of flowers. He went to the door, opened it, and locked the screen door. He wanted to hear the rain and smell the land, hoping it helped him to think. He couldn't help but fear the love he felt for Clio was going to swallow him whole, and when the spell finally released its hold, the woman he loved more than life itself was going to leave him. He would become a husk of a man. Maybe when the Fellowship decided it was time to see if they could tap into the monster that was his magic, it would kill him. Death would be a gift.

Clio watched him stand in front of the screen door and stare at the yard, the rain and mist gathering at the edges of the woodline for several seconds. His emotions were as dangerous as his damp hair on his neck, his board back, muscled shoulders, and narrow waist. The thunderstorm turned furious, wind blew through the treetops, and tossed the tumbling of water. It was wild outside as much as it was inside. The man she loved was a caged animal, his skin keeping the wolf from breaking through. She wanted to feel his raw passion her lips, his weight on her body.

"Made it just in time," she said as she closed the distance, and standing at his back, wrapped her arms around him.

As if they had stood like that for a hundred years, he covered her hands with his. Ansel closed his eyes, inhaled, and exhaled as the storm raged, its uncontrolled temper unleashing its wrath. "We did." He turned in her arms, her hands going to his hips, and he pulled her close. Nuzzling her neck, he licked up to her ear where he bit the edge, heard her whimper, then pushed his hand through her rain-wet curls, and clenching the thickness, pulled her head back and stared down on her with bronze eyes. "Time to pay, my tempest."

Clio's heart was going to jump out of her sternum, her breaths coming in heavy gasps, and she was sure she moaned when he clutched her hair, then his rough promise sent heat to flood her insides. No pride. She didn't have a response, couldn't think about anything besides her body, and the need overwhelming her senses. Her wolf rose from her depths, recognized the Domineer holding her, the threat he posed, and the ecstasy he promised.

Ansel's wolf responded to her, its fated mate, and without his consent, its essence reached out as if asking hers to accept him. To accept his heart, his spirit, and his love. To accept everything that made him a man and a wolf. Was it possible the instinct to recognize her fated mate hadn't been bound by the spell? "Do you know what's happening?" he asked, his words shaky with the truth and the commitment in front of them.

Yes, she knew. It had taken his wolf summoning hers with its primal need for its mate to free the instinct, the intuition she didn't know she had. "Yes." Her answer was ragged, her voice breathy. Clio had known it all along. Her wolf was no longer hers to control, it wanted, needed to love Ansel. Her fated mate.

"I'm a Pureblood without a crest. I'm Captain of Enforcers, that's all I have to offer you," he confessed.

His sincerity stopped her from laughing. She was a Wight. "I'll try not to hold it against you."

"If you don't want this you have to stop it now," Ansel demanded, the words leaving a chill in their wake. "If you stop this, you have to leave me, Clio. Cut me loose." His erratic heartbeat stuttered in his chest, and holding his breath he thought he was going to pass out. When her silence muted the gale outside and the music, and all he heard was her pulse in his ears, he prepared himself for rejection. Why would she want him? Why would she want to be tied to him? Forever? As if witnessing Rutger and Jordyn's pain wasn't warning enough. He had nothing to give her. The chill spread over him as the seconds struck his heart and with her rejection the wolf wasn't going to survive. The man wasn't going to survive. He would hand himself over to the Fellowship and hoped they killed him.

Cut him loose. Never. Clio freed her wolf, and opening herself to Ansel, their wolves' essences, as if they were ribbons made of smoke, entwined in the vapor. She let go of the breath she was holding as his feel filled her and a bond wove between them, rupturing her insides in a way she hadn't known was possible. She embraced Ansel's essence, his wolf, and with an inhale she felt his heartbeat and heard his wolf's howl.

Slowly releasing her hair, he cupped her face in his trembling hands, as a new heart formed inside of him to cradle Clio, and he saw his future and his end in her slate eyes warmed by whiskey. "My fated mate."

"My fated mate." It was real. There was no going back.

"Your eyes have changed. Where they were azure and honey, they burn slate and whiskey.

"For you. Kiss me."

"Your wish," he whispered. He would never deny her, and he took her lips.

CHAPTER EIGHT

Clio's heart raced with the admission, their forever commitment. She had never made a decision so quickly. She argued with herself, *This wasn't rash ... no, I've been waiting for him my entire life.* This she knew in her soul. Leaning into him, her hands moved to his back, then up tense muscles and over his shoulders. She held him like he might fade into the storm's mist. As their tongues explored one another, he lifted her, and she wrapped her legs around his waist, and kicked off her heels.

He heard two thuds and groaned, "Your shirt." She bit his bottom lip, and he felt dark hunger cloud rational thought. "Off."

Letting go of him, he whined at the chill left behind. She held his gaze as her fingers, nails painted a deep sangria, undid buttons, then shrugged the near translucent material off her shoulders, letting it fall the to the floor. Clio was his flower who wore soft fabrics like silk, chose pastel colors, then was his tempest with slate eyes, her lust eddying around whiskey. Ansel stilled, his gaze lowering to the swell of her breasts contained in the softest pink lace he had ever laid eyes on, their peaks a darker blush pressing against the thin threads. Tiny freckles dotted her creamy skin, that warmed and turned a rosy hue under his stare.

"You're going to kill me."

Clio laced her fingers behind his neck, licked his top lip until he parted them, then whispered, "You're going to be my ruin."

In his case it was true. He was going to be her ruin, and she was going to kill him when she left, and then loathed the unbreakable bond between them. He refused to let the fear ruin what they were doing when at that moment she was his tesoro, and he wasn't going to waste the time he had with her.

Holding her against him—one hand at her back, his palm on her skin, the other under her thigh and rear—he started for the stairs. As he stepped up to the first one another seductive pulse played while the rain pelted the tin roof, thunder rolled across the sky, and crashes of lightning created a crescendo to the carnal demands ruling his body.

She was counting down the seconds to when he would deliver them to his room when he paused and turning pressed her to the wall, causing a chill to seep into her heated skin. He kissed her, his tongue meeting hers to taste and savor, then he took her hand from his neck, gripped her wrist, and pinned it beside her head. Doing the same with her other hand, he restrained her with the weight of his body, his muscles flexing. Held against the cool wall, she felt completely under his control, while his kisses continued to conquer and enthrall her, taking her to a level of desire she hadn't allowed herself to feel. Hadn't wanted to know about because she didn't have the time, and they shut down Clio's thought process. As sensations bombarded her, she tightened her thighs around his middle. The warmth seeped from one to the other, the flames teasing combustion with their skin-to-skin contact as it ignited a hunger she didn't think she was going to survive long enough to quench. Ansel dipped his head, leaving her lips swollen, her breathing heavy, and kissed his way to her breast. Taking the peak in his mouth, he licked flesh through lace, stealing the air from her. Clio arched her back to him, his moan nothing more than a hot breath cascading over her nipple, making her stomach clench, and she rocked her hips.

With her hands pinned to the wall, her legs around his hips, her core pressing into his waist, and her arousal filling his senses, his head swam as he licked lace, the texture tantalizing on his tongue. He was drowning in her scent, her soft sighs, and having Clio to himself. Ansel growled, fearing going to his knees on the stairs. With regret, he enjoyed the feel of her, he released her wrists, pulled her to him and took the stairs, his footsteps heavy on the wood flooring as he walked the hall, then he was kicking his door open. She nibbled at the tender skin between his neck and shoulder, and teasing his ear, sent his control spiraling. Fearing doing something he was going to regret, or push her too far, Ansel paused.

Clio was taking nips of him, enjoying his taste, and having his skin under her tongue when he stopped and turned to stone. Stone. "What?" she asked as she met his hardened gaze.

"This," he growled as he closed his eyes and grappled for a shred of control.

"Why?" Panic raced through her. She knew it was too good to be true. This had been and would always be a fantasy. Her fantasy. Her phantom. Clio wanted to crawl into a hole and die, right after she gathered up her things and drove away. "Tell me."

"This will be our first time," Ansel confessed as he tightened his hold on her. "Our first time. I want it to be special."

Clio heard him and didn't hear him, her mind racing, her self-confidence sinking, and she giggled. "Special."

With his hunger in his eyes, he stared at her. "Yes, beautiful. Very special."

"I'm going to tell you this, and I don't expect you to say it me. I love you, Ansel Wolt." She knew she wore a grin and looked like a fool in love and didn't care. "I love you."

Ansel Wolt. He had never taken as much pride in his name as he did when she said it. "My tempest. Clio Hyde, I love you."

Those three words branded her heart in ways she couldn't explain.

"It's all right if you call me old fashioned. You already called me Father Time." He hadn't kept much from his past that he would bring to his present; nothing there except a century of pain and regret. So he assimilated to modern times—his kinship with Rutger helped—working with the enforcers helped him to fit in better, but this was different. His fated mate made him complete and changed everything. This was going to be unique to them. Clio Hyde was his, and his alone.

The inflection and brogue in his words was his age. The way he must have sounded. Gods how she wished she would have known him. "Father Time, I didn't know you were a hopeless romantic." It was breathy whisper as she kissed him, her lips soft on his.

He was hopeless. If he convinced himself he was in control he knew now for certain he was not. Ansel walked to the bed, and when his shins hit the edge, he lowered Clio to the dark indigo comforter, her cream skin a stark contrast, her blonde hair, its curls tight from drying behind her. *You're at my fingertips*, he wanted to yell to assure himself. "Unbutton your pants, tempest."

"Bossy," she teased. Obeying, she turned the button, the storm and the hiss of the zipper the only noises. "Unbuttoned and unzipped."

Ansel was going to explode. "Take them off," he ordered. His wolf was watching her, the way her hands slid down her sides to the waist of her slacks, then gliding them over her hips, and pulling them down her lean legs, she tossed them to the side with her foot.

"Off." She propped herself up on her elbows, the orders adding to the anticipation building between them. His eyes dropped to her breasts being held back by lace, and then her matching panties.

Ansel swallowed the lump in his throat and knew for sure it was his heart and growled, "Take your panties off."

"No," she countered and grinned. "Take your jeans off."

He was going to obey her, his muscles working to follow the order. "Beautiful, know that I'm a dominating wolf," he replied while he did as ordered.

She liked his subtle accent. It was hers. "I'll remember that, darling," she cooed as she laid back and slid her fingers to her waist.

After he'd unbuttoned every single one, he bent at the waist, tugged a boot off, then worked on the next, and when free, started pushing his jeans down his thighs.

Clio's heart stopped for a second and she blew out a breath as he straightened to his full height and in all his naked glory. "You have a thing against underwear?" She wasn't complaining, gods there was nothing to complain about. Muscled and cut, there wasn't an ounce of fat on him. Her eyes followed the plain of his stomach, the muscles contracting, and down to where the line of auburn hair ended, and she wanted to clench her thighs together as heat burned through her.

"Didn't want an extra layer if I had to wade into the pond. Your panties." Ansel remained where he stood, his eyes on her, absorbing her, the lace she was sliding down her thighs, and the scent coming from her. She wanted him, was drenched in desire, her ardor more intoxicating than any liquor. "Bra." Arrogance simmered in his order as she sat up, causing blonde curls to tumble over her shoulders, and she watched him with a hooded gaze.

"Off." Clio didn't know how much more she was going to be able to take. Her skin was hypersensitive, her body trembling from need, the hunger to have him, while his bronze gaze was drinking her in as it held his growing pleasure.

When she tossed her bra, and he saw the blush peak was a dark rose from his tongue and the lace, he thought he was going to lose his mind. She lowered to the comforter, her body on display for him, her vulnerability and lust burning in her eyes, which caused the threads of control he was desperately clinging to, to evaporate, leaving him his libido's victim. The drive to protect his mate and take her were like kisses from flames touching his skin. Ansel took a step, every muscle in his body contracting, and another, putting him at the end of his bed. His bed holding Clio. *Never thought I would see it.*

"Are you all right, Father Time?" Clio teased, her voice throaty from his stare, and the heat cascading through her. "Am I too much for you?"

When his eyes gleamed a dark bronze she had never seen before, and his muscles bunched, she knew toying with him was going to get her into trouble. Sweet trouble. Feeling empowered by his unwavering attention, and the confidence to be herself, she wanted to shove the knife of torment even deeper. With a wicked grin, she slid her hands over her breasts, her palms soft on the peaks of her nipples, the sensitive skin making her inhale, and arching her back, she glided them slowly down her stomach to her hips where she paused when she heard him snarl, a guttural rumble.

"Stop," Ansel growled.

Clio ignored his order, watched his eyes tracking her, and knew she should be afraid, very afraid. She didn't know anything about him. Was she pushing him too far? Did she care? Not right then. Still, she didn't know the simplest of things—his favorite color, his favorite food. What did he do on his days off? What were his fears? His strengths? His plans for the future? She didn't know. And suddenly their futures had become intertwined. Never changing. She was bound to Captain Ansel Wolt, who was a mystery to everyone. She did know she was sexually attracted to the man. Had been for ... entirely too damn long. Emotionally drawn to him as if there was a rope from his heart to hers pulling her toward him. She loved him. Her fated mate. Clio wondered if he was thinking the same thing as she feathered her hip with her nails. Did he understand the gap between them, the age difference? Then she stopped when his eyes went completely wolf.

"I said stop," he ordered.

Ansel wanted to roar like a beast celebrating a kill. He didn't. He possessed enough restraint to stop himself. Then he felt that slipping from him as she continued to ignore him and her hands skimmed her curves, her head pressed into the comforter, her back arching with her moan, as if his eyes were making love to her. Grabbing her ankles—her eyes widened, and she gave a soft whimper of surprise—he tugged her to him, her hair fanning out behind her.

"Mine," he grated through clenched teeth. He watched her eyes for fear, hesitation, a flicker to tell him he was giving too much of himself over to the wolf and was being too rough with her. He didn't see anything except raw need. Her lack of inhibitions stunned him and meant his wildest most sexual fantasies were going to come true. There would be no boundaries between them. At least not until she learned the truth. Another growl and he pushed the thought out of his mind, letting lust and his wolf's dominance rule him. Kneeling on the bed, he pulled her, and when her thighs were over his, he sat on his calves, and slid his hands up silken skin.

With a breathless moan, Clio rolled her hips and met him as he gently slid a finger into her core, and drawing it out, did it again while holding her left thigh in a calloused grip. His seductive strokes brought heated waves of pleasure roiling inside of her and had her fisting the comforter beneath her.

"You're hot, tempest, like white fire," Ansel whispered. He gazed down at her as she undulated her hips, matching his rhythm while clutching the comforter, and whimpers left her parted lips. Caught in the blaze, he watched his mate become a slave to the pleasure he was giving her, and her submission made his wolf howl. "Burn for me, my tempest."

Clio's body wasn't going to burn, it was going to combust, she knew it, could feel the pressure building with each of his caresses.

"Fondle your breasts, tempest," Ansel ordered as he teased glossy flesh reddened by his strokes.

Immediately obeying the command, giving his dominance a perverse thrill, Clio released her grip on the comforter, and cupping her right breast, her fingers circled the sensitive pink peak. "You're bossy," she accused as she licked her lips.

Enthralled by her body, her heightened response to him, and her dark sangria colored nails as they played with the peak, then pinched the rosy bud, he rasped, "Bossy turns you on."

Pure arrogance. The pleasure coiling inside of her was becoming an inferno, and giving into his touches, the pleasure and pain from the tight grip on her hip was bringing her ecstasy. But it wasn't enough ... she needed more, she wanted him. "Ansel," she sighed through a breath.

He closed his eyes with the sound of his name, the feel of her yielding to pleasure, and couldn't take it anymore. He needed to be inside of her, taking possession of her. Raising her hips, he held her, inhaled, and exhaled for a shred of control, then penetrated her sheath, her slick arousal drawing him deeper, and forced himself to slow down.

"Tempest," he whispered.

Clio met liquid bronze, and understanding what he wanted, held her hand out, and he pulled her to him. Straddling him, they were skin to skin, his heat inside of her, filling her, and she rolled her hips.

Ansel wrapped his arms around her to have her breasts against his chest, their heartbeats keeping time with one another, and kissed her. He knew sex with his mate was going to be different, had heard the rumors, but he didn't expect it to be powerful. And he didn't expect Clio to respond to every touch, caress, his demands, and then match him. Breaking the searing kiss, he confessed, "I could lose myself in you."

"Good." Grinning, she held his gaze and rolled her hips.

"Dangerous." Ansel nipped at her lower lip. "Wrap your legs around me." When she did, Ansel lowered them to the

bed, the comforter cradling Clio, and Clio cradling him between her thighs, and he gave her a hard thrust.

With his muscular arms beside her, his thick body on top
of her, she felt deliciously surrounded. Arching her back, she
rolled her hips, then breathed, "You feel too damn good."

Ansel sank into her tightness to feel her clamp around
him, her muscles milking him, and withdrawing, he thrust inside of her to hear her moan his name. Pleasure twisted
inside him, tighter and tighter, and unleashing his control he
plunged into her deeper each time and felt her shudder beneath him. "You're mine, tempest, mine. Surrender to me."

With his dizzying thrusts, Clio wrapped one leg over him,
her heel at his hip, her nails digging into his back, his hot
skin on hers, and his breaths at her ear. Ecstasy wove
through her while flames climbed higher and higher, sweeping her into their inferno. There was no stopping the storm.

"Surrender," he demanded. His wolf's essence threaded
in the bond, tying her to him, and he felt her. She was his.

"Yours. Always. Yours," she whispered. With his wolf
brushing against hers, the torrents battering her ecstasy into
a frenzy, she cried out with the force of the pleasure shoot-
ing through her.

His tempest's nails dug into his skin, inciting him on as
she kept pace with him, then the most sinful, carnal cry left
her parted lips, and Ansel couldn't hold on to reality. He
tumbled over the edge as her sensuality heightened his
pleasure and he rode the wave until he was staring at slate
eyes with swirls of whiskey. "Tempest."

"Darling," Clio returned, her voice husky, and she smiled,
knowing she was wearing her 'I'm a fool in love' expression.
Lifting her head, she kissed him. Gloriously sated, her body
relaxed. She didn't have a care in the world.

Ansel kissed her back, then leaving barely there kisses, worked his way down her throat to the soft curve of her neck and shoulder, and bit her. A nip. She yelped, and rising he looked at the impression, and his wolf howled with the possession of its mate.

"Really?" she asked as she touched the mark and felt a thread of heat with the dominate action.

"The wolf demanded it." Ansel rose to his elbows, then with regret left Clio to lay beside her.

"Of course you had nothing to do with it," she teased as she snuggled into him. His hand rubbed her back, his fingers going up and down her spine. They needed to talk about what they'd done, and what they were going to do. Like reporting themselves to Baron Kanin. They were a fated mate, and he would validate their union with the Highguard as well as the pack. They would be recognized as a couple. Good as married. It made her heart pound inside of her chest.

"You liked it. It made your heart speed up." Inhaling her scent, he caught another, and his heart swelled as his wolf's essence tangled within. It was him. She wore his scent, a sweet smoke. When he felt her stiffen beside him, her heart sounding like machine gunfire, he knew she was thinking about the same thing he was—their shared future.

"I'm not sure I'm going to survive you," Clio replied as she backed out of his arms and sat up. With her mind clear, or at least clearer than it had been, the consequences of their actions were like a weight on her shoulders. Pushing pillows against the headboard, she sat back, thought about getting a shirt to cover herself, then decided she was comfortable the way she was. There was nothing to hide from. With her change in position, Ansel stretched, like the wolf he was, his lean body all muscles and tendons, and then shifted so his head was at the end of the bed and his feet were beside her thigh.

"What are you thinking about, Doctor Hyde?" he asked as he propped his head on his hand to see her better. Clio wasn't accusing him of betraying her, calling him names, or running out of his house, which meant having sex hadn't changed the spell. He was grateful and disappointed. Now, as fated mates, the bond between them solidified, there was no more denying it. There was no going back.

"Us. You. I don't know anything about you," she replied as she drew circles on the top of his foot with her fingertip. He had over a hundred years of life she knew nothing of. "I want to know everything about you. I want to know what you were doing fifty years ago."

"Waiting for modern conveniences," Ansel replied through a laugh. "Ask away."

Clio giggled and couldn't stop herself from picturing him in clothing of the time and on a horse, maybe wearing a cowboy hat. Holding his dark cinnamon gaze, she decided there was no cowboy hat; no way would she want anything taking from his face and covering his hair. Where did she begin? Simple. "What's your favorite color?"

He raised his brows was sure it was going to be about his past. Bronte. She didn't know the Fellowship had him on a leash. "Silver, like my truck. What is your favorite color?"

"Pink. Having seen my townhouse, you could have guessed that," she replied as heat bloomed in her cheeks. She was such a girly girl.

Ansel slowly dropped his gaze to her breasts, and nodding his head, said, "I change mine to pink."

Clio laughed, heat spreading across her cheeks, and the empowerment from his attention swept through her. "Favorite food."

"You. Your lips, mouth, your—"

"Seriously," she demanded as she flicked his toes.

"All right. My mom used to make fresh mozzarella, it was divine. Days later, my dad would take deer fat, some meat, dandelion greens, and thick slices of cheese and warm it in a pan over a fire. It would just be the two of us. Such different times," he answered, half dazed, and didn't know why he told her that. He hadn't thought about the memory in years. Decades.

There were years of emotion in his confession that touched Clio's heart. She remained silent when Ansel's eyes darkened, drowning the laughter, and he went still as if drifting to the past. "Is that where your accent comes from? Your parents?"

"I don't have an accent," he countered. Did he? If he did, he hadn't noticed. No one told him.

"Yes, you do. It rolls through your words, gives them weight. It's only when you're threatening me or calling me your tempest. I like it."

"You are my tempest. If you like it," he replied absently, and holding her gaze, shook himself. "I like the change in your eyes. Do you think it's because of us?"

She held the memory, whether he meant to tell her or not, in her heart where it was going to stay. "It could be. My wolf was close to the surface, and I accepted you. And Mistress says I'm a Potent. My empath abilities are intensifying."

"An empath. Makes sense. You're a healer and a teacher with a beautiful heart. You're strong, always have been, always will be." Ansel's own heart was stained black with his sins, the blood he shed, and the monster that was his magic.

"It's there, Principe," Strong Lord mused. *"Know this, your legacy is blood, and your crest is stained scarlet."*

His sins were his offering to Clio. It was a mistake. They were a mistake. His selfishness put Clio's life at risk.

Clio watched him change, his demeanor becoming the untouchable man she'd known, while regret rolled from him. She didn't need her empath trait to know he regretted them and the bond tethering them together for eternity. She scooted to the edge of the bed as silence and tension thickened between them, while outside the storm seemed to have blown itself out.

"Where are you going?" Ansel asked, his voice strained, and rough from his thoughts. He sat up, swung his legs off the bed, and watched her look for her bra and panties. Panties, not underwear, the delicate pink lace fitting perfect over her rear and hips.

"I can feel you, Ansel. You regret this. I don't know what I was thinking," Clio replied. She heard the tremble in her words, the sadness that was threatening to break her heart, and felt stupid.

"It's true." Hanging his head, he stared at the area rug, the dark greens, blues, and reds not helping him. "I was selfish. This puts your life at risk."

He regretted them. She was going to explode with the ramped up emotions roiling inside of her. Heartbroken and pissed off. *Damn him.* Facing him, she put her hands on her hips. "You weren't the only one involved. I was here, and I made the decision to be with you. Don't be a martyr. So unbecoming," she seethed.

With her wild curls over her shoulders, she stood naked, her hands on the curves of her hips, and Ansel watched the smokey slate harden to stone and the whiskey hues fade. A martyr? "Bronte is still out there."

"You don't need to use her as an excuse to get rid of me," Clio countered. She was seconds away from having a melt-down.

"I don't want to get rid of you. I just had the best sex of my life with the woman I love." He inhaled and exhaled. "If I'm a martyr, you're a victim of *your* circumstances," Ansel accused as he stood.

"What the hell are you talking about?"

"You aren't good enough. The first thing you think is that I don't want you because you're a Wight. You think you're weaker than everyone. What excuse do you have, Doctor? What will you use to distance yourself from me?" Raising his hand, he stopped her from talking. "I want to protect you from a killer who has already tried killing us."

Stunned, she took a step backwards and stepped on her panties. Gods, they were having their first argument naked. Did sex constitute a relationship? The bond between them flared, reminding her their relationship was more than sex and dating. She wasn't going to walk away from him, and he was right. "Fine. I'll admit to resorting to my default setting if you do?"

Default setting. That's one way of putting it. Except his lies weren't going to go away, the Fellowship wasn't going anywhere, and neither was Bronte. He didn't want Strong Lord using Clio against him. "Done."

Clio opened her mouth to argue and stopped. He agreed with her, but she wasn't finished. She knew it was jealousy provoking her. "Stop using her." Clio hated the dhampir. "She's between us."

"Because she wants to kill us."

"What do we do?" Clio asked, the energy for the argument running on empty.

"You were right. We are pack. We protect one another. We'll tell Baron Kanin what we are and we're together. And you'll have the protection you need," Ansel explained.

"Sound plan, Captain. What do we do now?" It was a good plan, the baron needed to know, and they needed the pack. "Wait. Did you say you had the best sex of your life?"

"I did. It was magnificent, sensual, and who knew you were so pervy." Ansel took a step toward her. "We need to talk, Clio."

"I know." Picking up her panties and bra, she realized she needed a shirt. Hers was soaked and on the living room floor. With her shoes.

"Here," Ansel started as he handed her a T-shirt, his name and rank on the right side, and Cascade's crest on the back. When she took it, he grabbed a pair of shorts and pulled them on.

Clio watched him move around his room, then shove his fingers through his thick hair. After pulling the T-shirt over her head, she slipped on her panties, and headed for the door.

"Hey, wait. Where are you going?"

"To my car, I need my cell." Clio waited for him to say something, and when he didn't, she walked the hallway, noticed the photographs on the wall, and stopped. "Are these by the Mistress?"

"Affirmative. She gave them to me when I bought the house," Ansel answered. "She hung them there."

"Were you friends with her?" Clio asked, as jealousy burned through her, and continued to the stairs. Being Purebloods and the elite of the pack, the Kanins and Langstons were looked at like royalty. Clio had watched Mistress from a distance, her default setting making sure she knew her place.

"We were. When she left the friendship ended. I didn't take Rutger's side, not like the pack had, but the damage was done. Then when she came back, she stopped being Jordyn and became the soothsayer and Prime's scion. Not to mention Detective Langston, which I hope ends soon."

Clio stepped into the living room with Ansel behind her as a new song played. "I couldn't imagine giving up my passion ... being a doctor is who I am. She went from photographer to cop, mystical forces aside. What do you mean, you hope it ends?"

"Jordyn needs to quit the OPI and be part of the enforcers. She's a valuable asset, we need her. Plus, if she's with the enforcers, it'll keep Rutger sane."

"Are you friends with her now? You address her by her name."

"We are, but more, we're kith and kin. She thinks of me as her brother," Ansel replied with pride and remembered the expression on Strong Lord's face. Then he thought about their interaction, the comfortable feel of her company, and her insistence they hand over a list of her weaknesses to help him. "She's like a sister."

Clio listened to him talk about Mistress with respect and didn't know what went on behind closed doors to have their relationship change from a broken friendship to brother and sister. She was glad it changed, because it proved to Ansel the pack would protect them. At the screen door, she watched mist dust her crossover and Ansel's truck. "Looks like the storm is ending."

"It does." The balmy weight that had ushered in the gale was lifting, allowing clean, fresh air to take its place. Ansel saw her car as her escape and didn't want her to leave. Standing behind her, he wrapped his arms around her, and leaning down, whispered, "Stay the night."

Clio backed into him, his strength and his warmth. "Do you think we're moving too fast?" Was she giving him an out? Or trying to distance herself from him? He conceded when he suggested they talk to the baron, when he would have taken on the responsibility of protecting her and searching for Bronte by himself. He was being open with her, answering her questions, and sharing his life with her.

He ignored the blatant suggestion he wanted her to leave, or she needed to leave. "No. It'll give us time to talk," he replied, his lips moving against her hair. "Anyway, we passed going too fast when you screamed my name in ecstasy."

Clio giggled—she couldn't help herself—and her cheeks heated. She wanted to stay with him, but she still needed to check in with reality and that was her cell phone. "I need my cell. And if you want me to stay, I'll need clothes. We both have work tomorrow."

"Ever the responsible one. Let me grab a tee and shoes, and I'll take you to your townhouse in the city for clothing ... if you must have it. However, I prefer you naked." Ansel cupped her breast while his free hand went to her hip, and he waited to see if she remembered him talking about her townhouse. He was playing with fire, he knew, but didn't understand why. Was it to get his lies out in the open? Or hurt her to the point she didn't want him near her? He was his own worst enemy. There was no doubt he wanted her. Needed her. She had become part of him, and he couldn't deny her anymore. But he knew it was a matter of time before he faced the Fellowship, Bronte, and his betrayal.

Clio stayed at the door, Ansel's hands on her, the feel of his possession in their bond, then tore herself away. She flipped the latch, unlocked the door, and stepped into the full force of the storm's pressure. "Get your shirt and shoes," she said as she faced him.

"Ma'am." Ansel held her gaze for a moment, then headed to the stairs.

Clio watched him, felt the bond between them flare with life, and barefoot, picked her steps as she walked to her car. After opening the driver's door, she sat behind the wheel and saw herself in the rearview mirror. "Looking fly, girl." Her curly, blonde hair with strawberry highlights was a mess of tangles, her eyeshadow was smeared, and she wore remnants of mascara on her cheeks, not her eyelashes. She was going to have to wash her face before she went anywhere. Plus, she was wearing a T-shirt and panties. She took her cell from the center console, shoved it into her purse, then grabbed her satchel, got out of the car, and closed the door.

"Ready?" Ansel asked with a smile.

"Funny. I need to wash my face and get dressed. You could have told me I looked like a drowned poodle," Clio replied as she stepped into the house.

"You're beautiful, tempest."

Laughing, Clio set her purse on the coffee table beside a magazine about the outdoors while she shook her head and took her cell out. As she looked at her phone, she stilled, inhaling and exhaling several times. It was real, and getting really serious.

"What?" Ansel asked when she froze, and her feel in their bond turned cool and to caution. "Clio, answer me."

Turning slowly to face him, she gripped her cell. "I bought the house. It's mine. I have to sign the paperwork, and there are inspections. But it's mine."

"What about escrow?" he asked.

"Two weeks. The owners moved out of state and want it over and done with." Clio smiled and started laughing. "I get the house and the guy. Pretty damn good day."

"You scared the hell out of me. I felt your hesitation, then a quick bite of fear. Don't ever do that again," Ansel ordered. He was sure his heart stopped for entirely too long.

"Yes, sir. That is going to take some getting used to. Now we know why Mistress and the director block each other while they're at work."

"Yes, we do. Go get cleaned up and let's get your stuff." Watching her head to the stairs, her hips swaying under his T-shirt, he felt the bond and shielded her from him. Her empath trait combined with the bond was the reason she felt his regret, and he wouldn't have it happen again. Couldn't afford it to happen. When she was out of sight, Ansel went to the table and grabbed his cell. After he quickly checked his messages and emails, he typed out a message, asking if they prepared the list of Jordyn's weakness, then requested a meeting with the baron, no details given about why, and sent it to Rutger. He would explain everything in the morning when they met with the baron. The response of affirmative only took a second. Ansel's heart pounded, and when he heard water running, he dialed.

"Principe," Strong Lord greeted. "You better have what I want."

"I do," Ansel replied through clenched teeth. "You better have what I want."

"First, I'll see the list. How did you get it?"

"Nothing is free," Ansel replied, throwing his words back at him. "Where and when?"

"Remember who you are speaking to," Strong Lord threatened. "The ridge. Tonight."

"Negative." Wasn't going to happen, but he couldn't upset Strong Lord in case he backed out of the deal. He had too much riding on it. Ansel turned toward the stairs when running water was replaced with Clio's light steps, making his heart feel like it was going to seize. Rubbing his chest where the medallion usually sat, he was thankful he had taken it off. He didn't want Clio to see it. "I won't have it until tomorrow morning."

"Is it that or the doctor?"

Ansel didn't like being spied on, hated the superiority coming from him, being questioned, and the implied threat. He was going to kill Strong Lord right after he killed Bronte. "The doctor is helping me. The list is part of Mistress' medical records," Ansel explained, knowing he put Clio in the Fellowship's crosshairs.

Lies. Lies. Lies. One day he hoped he was free of them.

Strong Lord chuckled, his arrogance grating on Ansel's nerves. "Tomorrow night, young prince."

Ansel heard silence, closed the screen, and dropped the cell in his pocket just as Clio stepped down the last stair. Her slate gaze narrowed on him, and he couldn't stop from smiling when she tried to tame her curls, wore his T-shirt, tying the extra material at her side, slacks, and heels. Then he heard Strong Lord's voice, and it reminded him of his lies. He didn't deserve her.

"Ready?" he asked as if his leash hadn't been jerked.

CHAPTER NINE

They sat in silence during the drive to her townhouse, the terminal carrying on a conversation by itself; the light mist hadn't stopped, causing the rubber of the wipers against the glass of the windshield to add to the dings and beeps. Over them like shadows the thunderclouds remained thick enough to block the sun, leaving the early afternoon a deary pewter with dull white highlights. Clio knew Ansel had been talking to someone, the director most likely, and it could have had something to do with the meeting but didn't know what. His anxiety was like an impenetrable barrier around him, keeping her out. By the time they reached her townhouse, the silence had become riddled with tension, its weight tangible. Then he offered to help her, and she immediately declined and raced to her door to get out from under the weight of his disquiet.

As she packed an overnight bag, her emotions spun out of control, and she was torn between excitement and the feeling something had gone very wrong. When she felt him like a shadow in their bond, it confirmed her assumption, but rather than tell her, he retreated inside of himself, putting a wall ... more like a barricade between them. Did she expect him to open himself to her and explain? No. Their relationship, all of a couple of hours old, wasn't such they were going to start pouring their hearts out to one another. Then she thought about the bond they shared and knew it was a foundation for them, solid ground beneath their feet. It didn't mean they weren't moving too fast.

Clio walked through her house on autopilot, changed out of her slacks and heels and into loose lounge pants and flipflops, while keeping the T-shirt, and then checked to make sure she had everything for the next day. She stood in her living room, the one she was going to sell to someone else, and watching Ansel as he sat waiting for her, her gaze went to the parking lot, and she couldn't believe how her life had changed. In one day, she bought a house and was mated to Ansel. Her phantom. The man she didn't think would ever really see her. But he had. And had been watching her. Protecting her from the shadows.

"There's nothing safe about you, Ansel," she whispered to her empty house. She was going to lose herself in him.

The round trip took a little over an hour. The mist continued, the clouds remained, and by the time they returned to Ansel's house, her skin itched from the silence. She found herself standing in his living room, feeling like a stranger, her arms hanging at her sides, and her overnight bag by the stairs. Were they capable of changing? Was he capable of giving up his independence, his isolation? Was she ready to do the same? Clio didn't know, and with his silence didn't feel she had the right to ask him. She saw the marked tension tightening Ansel's shoulders through his soft gray T-shirt that had an off-road vehicle on the back. The fact he owned anything other than Cascade-issued clothing surprised her. Then again, everything she found out about him was going to surprise her to some degree. She didn't know him.

With his back to her, he stood at the table, his hands gripping the back of a chair, and she knew another minute and he was going to squeeze it into splinters. She didn't want to address the obvious, but it was clear he wasn't going to.

Inhaling, she began, "I understand if you're having second thoughts." *Can I sound any weaker?* she thought as she cringed from the sound of her voice. "I can go home."

"No, beautiful, no second thoughts. Not where you're concerned," Ansel answered, and turning, met a smokey slate gaze that usually challenged him but was riddled with doubt. It made his heart ache he made her feel that way. After talking to Strong Lord, and finding out they were watching him, he shouldn't have been surprised and shouldn't have cared. But it wasn't about him anymore, it was Clio, and he felt like an ass for retreating inside himself to sit in the cesspool of his thoughts. He had to think about her safety, and it tore his mind apart while he wanted to sound the damn alarm to have enforcers surround his house.

Rutger and Jordyn were the first fated mates in hundreds of years, and while it was a testament to their status and the strength of their magic, it appeared to be a weakness. When one of them was being threatened, the other was paralyzed with fear, their thoughts clouded by the feeling of loss, and they knew if one of them died the other was going to follow. Although, the last part was a blessed ending to a living nightmare. Rutger and Jordyn were a solid team, their actions and reactions synced to one another at the same time their love was a violent symphony of lust and possession.

Ansel's jealousy burned through him, then burned out, and he reminded himself being a fated mate was one of the most powerful strengths. There were things he thought he should say, needed to say, if he wanted to fix the situation. He loved her, wanted to properly court her, show her he respected her, and there was more to them than sex. There would be late nights on the deck, mornings together ... he was there for her no matter what she was dealing with, and he needed to give her the world before his lies tore them apart. Maybe if she loved him, depended on him, she would forgive him.

"Then what is it?" Clio asked. "I feel you blocking me."

"I have over a century of life, most of it not good, and I don't want to overwhelm you with my emotions," he replied and let her feel his truth in their bond. "I'm not used to being exposed. Damn, beautiful, I want to say so much. It's all fucking confusing me."

Relief like a cool breeze during summer swept over her. Beautiful. He was with her. If he stopped referring to her by a pet name, she would worry. "I feel the same way. Start at the beginning."

"I want to properly court you," he blurted out. "Take you out on a date, get to know you."

Her heart left her to go to him and she wasn't sure she was going to get it back. Clio felt herself getting caught in his web of attention and raw honesty. "Do you want to meet my parents?"

Ansel straightened, his shoulders going back, his eyes gleaming bronze, and cursed himself for having forgotten about her parents. Her family. He didn't have parents. He didn't have a real family. He needed to be a man worthy of their daughter, worthy of Doctor Clio Hyde.

How? He was lying to Clio, and was planning on trading intel for the location of a sociopath so he could murder her. The cherry on top, his mind was screaming at him, they hadn't dated ... in fact, he yelled at her right before he had sex with her. Damn good sex. Oh gods how he messed that up.

When he didn't respond, she asked, "It's all right if you're not ready."

"I am. It's just that ..."

"We did this backwards," she finished for him.

"Yeah. Ass backwards. What if they don't like me?"

A giggle started brewing in her middle. Maybe it was the stress, his silence, and/or the rollercoaster of emotions they were riding. Clio tried stopping herself and using every ounce of control, failed, crash and burned, and it burst from her. Then, staring at Captain Ansel Wolt, who wore a look of pure fear, fueled the force. Clio laughed, her hands covering her mouth, her eyes watering, and couldn't stop.

"I'm glad you think this is funny," Ansel grated. He wasn't good enough for her, and when he broke her heart, he would have wounded an entire family.

"They already like you," Clio assured through a breath. "You're Captain of Enforcers." Actually, they respected him because he was Captain of Enforcers. She hadn't discussed Ansel with them. Not since her recovery.

"I nearly got you killed," he stated. "I have a dark past."

"Stop blaming yourself. Bronte is the enemy, not you," Clio countered, making her voice carry her authority. "They don't blame you. Like I have never blamed you." She was sure they didn't blame him. If they wanted to see her happy, they would accept him ... right?

"I don't have a family," he admitted. "I'm a hundred and something years older than you and your parents."

"Sounds like you're scared, Father Time." Clio closed the distance between them, the tension easing from the air that had become suffocating and the comfortable feel from earlier returning.

"I don't want to mess this up." Any more than he had.

"Then don't, darling." Clio put her hands on his hips and

looked up at him.

What am I going to do with her? Love her. Ansel leaned down, kissed her soft lips, his hand going to her hair, the other to her hip. "All right, I'll stop worrying."

"Good. Now how about something to eat?" she asked.

Ansel smiled. "I can do that." Taking her hand in his, he walked around the bar height counter and into the kitchen where he grabbed her waist, and lifting her, set her on the counter. "Let's see what I have."

When he opened the fridge, she whistled. "You have a stocked refrigerator. All I have is the containers Crevan gave me and lunch meat."

"He gave you food?" Ansel asked, the question nothing more than a snarl.

"Your fangs are showing," Clio teased. The instant jealousy sent a burst of thrill through her, while fully understanding if a female went anywhere near Ansel, Clio would rip them to shreds. Clearly their relationship was too new and their emotions uncontrolled.

"Told you I'm dominate." Ansel winked at her with all the arrogance of knowing the alpha hadn't had a chance with her. "What did he fix you?"

"A luscious lobster ravioli, with mouthwatering stuffed tiger shrimp. Mmm ... yummy," Clio answered and fluttered her eyes, the grin curving her pink lips. "And for dessert he made tiramisu and chocolate-covered strawberries. Delectable."

Seeing the humor in her gaze, Ansel raised his lips to show her his canines and growled. "You were warned."

"Dangerous wolf." She couldn't stop herself. "Back to your stocked fridge."

"I don't shop," he started to explain as he picked through packages, then grabbed a beer, set it beside Clio's thigh, and looked back at the shelves. "I thought it was Baroness Kanin, then I overheard Jordyn talking to Toni. She was giving the young solider a shopping list."

"They take care of you. See, you have a family ... just saying," Clio pointed out. "Do you have something other than beer?"

Without taking anything else out of the fridge—he had no idea what Clio liked, this was not something he knew anything about, and trying to make a decision was giving him a headache—he closed it. Straightening, he walked over to a cupboard, and after opening it, took a bottle of tequila out and handed it to her. "Rutger. Although I'm prepared to blame Jordyn."

"They set you up. And I'm not complaining, it's my favorite." Clio pulled the cork and inhaled the smooth scent of citrus. "You have a glass?"

"Umm ... yeah." Ansel turned to another cabinet door.

"Going to take a guess and say you don't have a lot of guests?" Clio asked as she watched him wander around checking cabinets. Dark wood, stone, and industrial lighting made up his kitchen, with its many cabinets. She didn't have that many.

"I'm not a social butterfly that's for sure. Rutger comes over and we drink beer and order pizza. Unless Jordyn brings us food." So what if he didn't know where everything was? It changed without him being there. And with Clio watching him, it made him nervous as hell. "When I was released from Celestial, I came home and found my kitchen had been overhauled. Ah, glasses."

"Director Kanin said you had terrible taste in furniture," Clio teased as she accepted the glass.

With her nerves getting the best of her, she poured a

hefty amount, and couldn't stop thinking about Mistress taking care of Ansel. Over the last year Clio watched their interaction, when they were at Foxwood, and knew the director and Ansel were like brothers, she even teased they were thick as thieves, because they were never without the other. Mistress always kept people at a distance, treated everyone equal, no one more special than the other, and kept her emotions locked down to the point Clio feared she was bottling things up or was in denial. When she spoke to Dr. Carrion, he expressed the same worries. They had been wrong. Mistress didn't express emotion in public for fear of it being used against her and secured her relationships behind her wall of ice to protect them from her enemies. Ansel feared her parents wouldn't like him, when she feared if she did anything wrong, she would have to face Director Kanin and Mistress. Not a comforting thought knowing what they were capable of. Taking a sip, she couldn't believe Mistress made sure her tequila was at Ansel's.

"He always says that. You should have seen his house before Jordyn," Ansel countered. "He has no room to talk."

"You love them, and they love you. That must give you a kind of confidence."

Ansel grabbed his beer, twisted the top off, and took a drink. "I guess it does. I hadn't thought of it like that." He knew the family loved him and they welcomed him as one of their own. He never let himself believe it was real—Bronte was out there, a threat, and his lies were like a never-ending void between him and everyone he knew. Some of that changed and he was thankful for it. "Where Rutger is brute force, Jordyn is grace." Laughing, he could see the expression on Jordyn's face when he drew his gun on her, and her onyx eyes targeted him. "Like a viper. Don't tell her I said that."

"I'm thinking blackmail," Clio replied as she hopped off the counter. A viper who would protect them to the end. She headed to the refrigerator and opened it, unable to believe the amount of food. Good food. "How about a charcuterie board?"

Ansel did his best to hide his blank look, like he might know what she was talking about, and gave up. "No idea what that is."

"It's fancy talk for meat and cheese."

"Yes, sounds good and easy."

Clio started taking out the needed supplies—smoked meats, creamy cheeses, olives—and grabbed a bag of peppers that would go perfect with her tequila. "Cutting board?"

"I do know where that is," he mumbled, and after taking it from its place by the knife set, handed it to Clio. "I can make up for this. Would you have dinner with me tomorrow night? I'll grill."

"A date?" she asked as she began slicing cheese.

"Affirmative, a date." Ansel watched her grip the knife, her movements efficient, practiced, perfect, like a doctor. He wasn't going to make Clio angry if she was holding a sharp object. The thought made him smile at the same time it reminded him he needed to update Rutger about the meeting with Strong Lord. As if sensing him, his cell sounded from its place on the table, and they both looked in its direction. When he started over, Ansel realized she hadn't answered him. "Dinner?"

"Yes, I would love to have dinner with you," she answered over her shoulder and continued to add cheese to the board.

His heart swelled and pride filled him, making man and wolf happy. Taking the cell, he touched the green circle. "Captain Wolt."

She searched his cupboards, like he had, and finally found what she needed. While he answered the call, she began putting the cheese away, then started on the meat, and making a circle placed the small bowl she found in the middle and added olives to it. When it looked like a charcuterie board, she almost laughed ... Ansel hadn't even known what it was. Clio went to the pantry in search of crackers and found it was just as stocked as the fridge with everything a man needed. Only there was enough food for an army. As she went about her tasks, she noticed Ansel wasn't in the house, the screen door had opened and closed, and the stereo, which he had turned off before they left, was on and a bluesy rhythm floated.

It's business, she reminded herself. She wasn't going to shove her way into his life. At least not as much as she already had. After she set the cutting board and crackers on the table, she went back to the kitchen, then to give him space, she headed to the backyard. The mist had stopped, the thick, gray clouds had begun dissipating, and a chill hung in the evening air. Twilight was minutes away from taking the sky and she felt oddly satisfied and scared. What were they doing? Playing house. Is this what fated mates did? It was incredibly fast. Had it happened to Mistress and the director? At least she had someone she trusted to ask. And Clio was going to ask.

She took a sip, set her glass on the rail, and rubbed her bare arms. Gazing out at the valley and forest beyond, she thought about the morning. They were going to go to Foxwood to tell Baron Kanin about them. What were they going to say? Their courtship/argument had gone from cold to hot in seconds, then back to cold when Ansel shutdown, and back to hot. She loved he picked her up and set her on the counter. She had half a thought to tell him she didn't like to be handled, but then didn't—he would know it for the lie it was. The sex they had served as physical proof. She liked being handled by him. The memory of his body over hers created a ball of fire in her middle, and she switched it off as best she could. She needed to think without him near her, without him crowding her head. Was she giving up her independence? It felt like it was slipping from her, enough she paused to answer when he asked her to dinner. Then there was their bond. He wasn't used to being exposed. Neither was she. Clio was a private person, her thoughts her own, her emotions her own, not to be judged. She liked being alone. No she didn't. Was she resorting to her default setting? Probably. There were times being alone was necessary, and she enjoyed those times. Being *alone* was different.

Ansel saw the cutting board teeming with food on the table, made to look like it came from a high-end restaurant, and shook his head. Beside it was a tray of crackers. Then he saw the open doors. She was standing at the rail, her hands rubbing her arms, and he watched her. With the humidity in the air, her curls tightened and fought the hold of the band she imprisoned them with. He wanted to take the band off and let the mass of unruly tangles free, and then run the silk of them through his fingers. Before his imagination teased him and his wolf had him going to her, he needed to think. Rutger hadn't called to question him about the meeting with the baron. Instead, he explained the details in motion and the plan for the information transfer with Strong Lord. Besides feeling he was betraying Jordyn and the pack, he told Rutger his feelings and doubts he would have to leave in the middle of the night. If Clio was staying at his house—if it was up to him, she would be—he would have to tell her why. Would he tell her the truth? At least part. Clio kept Jordyn's secrets, so he knew she would keep the meeting a secret. No, he wasn't going to involved her. He would tell her he had enforcer work to do, which was true. Not an outright lie. Damn, it was too late to stop it from happening.

The importance of it made Ansel aware of what he was risking. His life. Clio's. Jordyn's. Strong Lord wasn't going to tolerate Ansel breaking his blood bond, or Cascade conspiring against him. It was bold to move against the Fellowship, but Baron Kanin possessed Jordyn, scion to Prime, and the territory knew Prime would protect what he considered his. It gave Cascade a level of arrogance and protection. Despite Strong Lord believing he was more powerful and with more influence. No matter what Jordyn said, Prime's protection didn't protect Ansel. And in the end, Clio could be mated to a bloody, broken mess when Strong Lord was finished with him.

I don't have to worry about the spell or her memories if Strong Lord kills me. He shuddered with the thought. For the first time since his parents passing, his death scared him. He had something to live for. Ansel's death meant Clio wouldn't be far behind. Their bound hearts and joined wolves would drag her to death's door, and he would have destroyed his mate and her family. He wasn't going to accept their mating had been a mistake. He loved her. However, he should have killed Bronte first, and confessed his lies to Clio, before trapping her.

Ansel held his bottle of beer by its neck, its sides slick with condensation, and stilled when Clio slowly turned around to face him, her smokey slate eyes with whiskey eddying around her black pupils narrowing. She had been thinking.

"Want to eat outside?" he asked.

"Yes." Clio trained her facial reaction, knew it didn't

matter when their bond flared with their feelings, and she smiled. "I don't have the option at the townhouse."

"You have it here."

As he cleaned and dried the table and chairs, she got the board, crackers, peppers, two plates, a couple of forks, and napkins. When he returned from putting the towels in the laundry, he discovered she had found several candles, their gold flames dancing in the light breeze, and was sitting, her legs crossed, her thin fingers around the glass, waiting for him. There were few things he needed or wanted to see, or places he wanted to go. He didn't live in that world and never had the opportunity. Had cut any fantasies out of his life, knowing Bronte might find him. But the sight of Clio waiting for him, at his table, wasn't something he expected or had anticipated. He wanted it. Needed it. Like he needed the blood in his veins to keep his heart beating.

"You found candles." Ansel sat down in the chair closest to her. Cinnamon and brown sugar mixed with the oak from her tequila drifted around him, pulling him into her web. How he lasted as long as he had was a question he didn't have an answer for. And when he crashed and burned it had been rapture. Rutger's warning reared its head, and he pushed it back. They had tonight. He would worry about tomorrow night tomorrow.

"I hope you don't mind. Knowing you're a hopeless romantic, I figured you would like it," Clio replied, wearing a smirk. When he saw her waiting for him, his pleasure smashed through the walls holding his emotions in check and found her. The intensity branded her like his kiss and body had. She made her mate very happy.

"I'm definitely hopeless."

Ansel woke up, and despite his heart racing, it was a quiet alert. He inhaled and exhaled, trying to calm his pulse while he pinpointed what caused him to wake up in a panic. Seconds ticked into minutes, and he couldn't find one reason, and his anxiety was doing nothing to help him. When Clio rolled to her back, a soft moan leaving her lips, the curves of her breasts barely covered by the blanket she insisted on sleeping with, he propped his head on his hand and looked at her. If it was possible for the heavens to open, he knew they gave him Clio. A benevolent spirit he was afraid he was going to stain with his sins, and then when she was corrupted, he would shatter her heart into so many pieces.

He was a bastard.

His musings went to Rutger and Jordyn. He hadn't thought twice when Rutger demanded Jordyn work with the slayers to become a trained assassin, Ansel was all for it. Why? Because Jordyn was going to see bloodshed, already had blood on her hands, and would become an instrument of death. Clio wasn't meant for that world. His world. She was an innocent, a healer with a pure heart. It stabbed his conscience while it hit him in the gut, and he knew that's what woke him up. His betrayal. It was taking on physical form and it was lying between him and his mate. Ansel brushed an unruly curl from her forehead, as a sliver of dove gray sliced across her face to capture her beauty.

"I'll always protect you, even if you hate me," he promised.

Clio expected to see her phantom in the shadows of her mind where he gave her his protection and eased the fears haunting her. He wasn't there. His protection was gone. And understanding he wasn't coming back, a part of her crumbled knowing he left her. She didn't wake from her dream.

Instead, she imagined bronze glowing in the dull light, and turning to her side, she felt him beside her. He held her hip and tugged her closer to him, her body against the length of his and his arm over her as if protecting her even in sleep. She didn't need the protector from her dream. The phantom who stilled her fears. She was with her mate.

I could get used to this, she thought as she drifted.

When she woke up and realized Ansel had been staring at her while she slept, his weighted gaze holding onto her as if she might be his phantom, she curled into him and slept like the dead. Which she didn't think was possible when she wasn't comfortable sleeping with anyone ... not that she had any lovers, and she absolutely didn't like anyone around her when she slept. She was at her weakest and most vulnerable. Dr. Carrion attributed it to Post Traumatic Stress Disorder, and Bronte. In Ansel's arms, Clio let her defenses fall to the wayside; she felt safe, secure, and at home. That scared her. More than she wanted to admit.

Now as Clio followed Ansel through the gates of Foxwood, she knew everyone in communications noticed they arrived together, and Mandy was going to have a field day. They all knew what happened. How could they not? What they did. What they were. There was no denying it, and she felt her heart lodge in her throat while her lungs stopped working. If she was in the right frame of mind, instead of drowning in future embarrassment, she would have identified the problem and diagnosed herself. Hell, she knew what the problem was, and it was Ansel and the meeting with the baron. And modern medicine couldn't cure her ailments. A fool in love. Cool, calm, collected Dr. Hyde was about to lose her mind, her dignity in front of Baron Kanin.

"Great. Just great," she mumbled with her future downfall.

She drove through the lot, parked in her spot, and sat back in her seat. She needed to take a breath, calm her nerves. Sure thing, wasn't going to happen. Not when she recalled watching Ansel pull jeans up his thighs, his abs constricting under his skin, then tugging a Cascade T-shirt over his head, causing a thick swath of auburn hair to fall over his forehead. Watching him get dressed for work was the most erotic thing she had ever seen. Save for when he undressed. Then he noticed she was watching, and after winking at her, said, "Get your fill, beautiful."

"That man," Clio mumbled as she shook her head. After grabbing her cell, she shoved it into her satchel, grasped the strap, then took the zip-up hoodie from the passenger seat and holding it, turned to get out of her car when Ansel opened her door. One day he ignores her and the next he was opening her door. The entire world was going to know.

And why is that bad? Oh hell, she had no idea. She did. She was scared to death.

"I can ignore you if this is too much," Ansel offered when he saw her face pale and then became stricken with panic. He thought their first morning went well. She showered, the scent of her body wash—vanilla and orchids—drifted to the bedroom where he stopped to inhale it. When he heard her humming as she went through her routine, he listened. He didn't leave the room, found himself straightening things, pretending to look at stuff in his closet to stay close to her. Then she sauntered into the bedroom, dropped her towel, dressed in a purple bra, matching panties, a black racerback tank top, and dark purple scrub bottoms with tiny flowers all over them. Matching underclothes and flowers were his Clio.

However, nothing beat waking up to her leg draped over his, and her hair on his shoulder.

"I'm having an 'I can't believe this is happening' moment," she replied as she glanced around. "They will all know."

"That's the point. You're mine," he said, his voice deeper than usual, the brogue tangling in it. Ansel took the satchel from her, and when Clio was clear of the door, he closed it. They started across the parking lot, him holding the back of her neck, possession blatant in his grasp.

"I can carry my bag." Clio shouldn't have liked ... loved his hand at her neck. She worked her ass off to earn the respect of the enforcers, soldiers, and pack, and being led to the baron's estate wasn't, shouldn't have been allowed. For all the world to see. It was going to take seconds for their relationship to spread like a damn wildfire. Her parents. She needed to tell them. She promised once she was in her office and safe from the outside world, she would call them. Or they would call her. Their daughter finds her mate and they find out through the Cascade rumor mill. Wonderful. Perfect.

"I can carry it, too. No one ever carry your books, Doctor Hyde?"

"No. I managed it all by myself, Captain Wolt," she grated.

That he didn't doubt. He often wondered why Rutger and Jordyn referred to one another by their titles, and now he knew. "Sadie," he greeted when the sentinel in a polo shirt, shoulder holster, tactical pants, and boots opened the right-side door.

Smiling, her eyes skated over Clio to Ansel. "Good morning, Captain Wolt, Doctor Hyde."

While she was sure she was going to die from awkwardness, the way Sadie eyed Ansel had Clio's claws itching. She shoved it down, hoping he hadn't sensed it. Stopping once they were in the entryway, Ansel hung her satchel on a hook, then replaced his hand at the back of her neck to guide her to the baron's office for all the world to see.

Leaning down until his lips were feathering her hair, he whispered, "Jealous. I like it, beautiful." Ansel's wolf growled a low rumble of appreciation, its arrogance flaring in the bond.

"Shut up," Clio warned. And smiled.

Ansel chuckled as he raised his hand to knock on the door when the baroness walked down the hall. "Baroness Kanin," he greeted.

"Ansel, good morning. Doctor Hyde," Baroness greeted. Her velvet caramel eyes rolled to a rich chocolate and her wolf sharpened her features. "Congratulations, Ansel Wolt, and Clio Hyde. May blessings be bestowed upon you and yours."

Clio stood motionless, stunned, proud, and wanted to cry. "Thank you." Was that good enough? She should have said something else.

"Baroness Kanin." Ansel stepped away from Clio and embraced his kin, to have her magic and wolf wrap around him. If anyone thought Laurel Kanin was as delicate as she appeared, they were wrong. Mate to the alpha, mother to Second, Third, and Fourth, and matriarch to the pack, she was strength, stability, and love. Her capacity to give unconditional love also meant she possessed the capacity to exact revenge with cold efficiency. And she wielded her blade with ease.

The embrace took Clio by surprise, and she couldn't help but think about Ansel saying he didn't have a family. He did, and they loved him. Baroness Kanin stepped back, her eyes gleaming from dark lashes, her soft, brown hair back in a loose braid, and she wore a casual white linen tank top, shorts, and was barefoot.

"I won't detain you. You need to see Healey." With her words she stepped around them and headed toward the formal greeting room.

"Now I'm scared."

"Don't be. Baroness gave us her blessing," Ansel assured.

"Not what I meant. While you're scared of my parents, I have to contend with the entire Kanin family," Clio explained. "And Mistress."

Ansel cupped Clio's cheek, grazed his thumb over her bottom lip, then lightly kissed her. "I guess you better behave." He feigned pain when Clio elbowed him, then knocked three times, and waited. And waited. They knew they were there, had known as soon as they drove through the gates. Why were they waiting?

When the door slowly opened, silence sat thick on the other side, and he knew it was about the upcoming meeting with Strong Lord, and the risks involved. He had pushed it aside, wanting to enjoy Clio for as long as possible before the real world invaded. Rutger stepped back, and with a wave of his hand, indicated the chairs, while Baron Kanin with his irrefutable authority sat behind his desk. When Clio didn't move, Ansel nudged her to get her into the office. Jordyn stood, like a sentinel, to Baron Kanin's right side, while Rutger stalked to the back of the office. Rutger hated the idea of giving Strong Lord Jordyn's weaknesses, knowing what he wanted them for, even if they were false, and Ansel couldn't blame him. He wasn't sure he would allow anyone to put Clio in danger.

"Doctor Hyde, Captain Wolt," Baron Kanin's low rumble greeted as they sat down.

Clio's heart was a rock in her throat, her pulse in her ears, and her nerve endings were raw with anxiety. She was going to make a fool of herself.

Ansel tried to gauge the mood in the room and couldn't get a lock on it, which meant Jordyn was involved, and didn't know why Rutger chose to stand behind them. The confidence they wouldn't discuss Strong Lord, the information, and his lies in front of Clio was the only reason he hadn't taken her in his arms and bolted.

Clio watched Mistress step up to the baron's desk, which was an odd place for her to be, and glare at her.

"Doctor Hyde."

"Mistress." Clio's voice held, but her hands, which she clenched and placed in her lap were shaking.

"I see you've taken love thy neighbor to a whole new level."

Clio was about to defend herself, from what she didn't know, then watched a suspicious smile curve Mistress' lips. She was being teased. "I was just doing what you advised, Mistress," she countered, and felt herself relax.

Chuckling, the baron sat back. "Fated mates. Jordyn, can you sense their bond?"

"Where their threads existed as single entities, they are intertwined," she replied, her eyes onyx, her cheeks sharpening.

Unable to feel her power, Clio gave her a questioning stare, and at the same time she couldn't fathom the immense magic contained in her petite frame. Dressed in a fitted, red T-shirt, jeans, her gun and badge at her slim waist—Clio wanted to tell her to eat more—and running shoes, she did not look like an all-powerful soothsayer. She looked like a normal person. As normal as Jordyn Langston could look.

"Doctor Hyde, I feel your doubt. Look at it this way ... your thread and Ansel's thread have created a double helix which carries the essence of your wolf spirits, much like DNA. Instead of carrying genetic instructions, it continuously revises your matter in the Collective. The pack knows you're fated mates and the bond between you is resolute. You have become One-Flesh."

Explained in terms she understood, it made her feel better. One-Flesh. "I don't know what to say," Clio mumbled. There was more information in the statement than she was prepared for.

"You don't have to say anything," Baron Kanin replied as he gave Mistress a sideways glance riddled with gold shards. "Congratulations. Are you going to celebrate with an announcement or wait?"

The room fell silent. Did she say wait and offend Ansel? Did she plow through and say celebrate and offend Ansel? With their eyes on her, she didn't know, and panic started to churn in her middle. As she was about to say something, only the gods knew what, a warmth filled her, and she felt Ansel in their bond and knew the answer. "We're going to wait."

"Good idea. Take it slow. There's no rush," the baron agreed. "When you're ready, let me know. We'll convene with the elders of the pack, and advise the Highguard."

"Sir," Ansel replied. He hoped he appeared calm and not the nervous mess he felt like.

Rutger stepped up to Ansel, placed his hands on his shoulders, squeezed, and said, "Congratulations. This is where the fun begins."

"You better mean that in a good way," Jordyn threatened as she rounded the desk.

"Always, Mea."

Ansel stood with a grin on his face and hugged the man he loved as his brother, then his sister who gave him a family. "Thank you." There was more emotion in the two words than he had expressed through the long years of his life. In response, he received a smile and copper eyes, their depth going to her soul.

"Come here, Doc." Mistress hugged Clio, her embrace confident and gentle, and magic hummed through her. Before releasing her, Mistress whispered at her ear, "It was the geese, wasn't it?"

Laughing, Clio let the stress flow through and out of her and took a step toward Ansel. At his side, he placed his hand at the back of her neck. "Yes."

"What's so funny?" Ansel asked.

"It's private," Jordyn answered and winked at Clio.

"And the plotting has begun," Rutger accused as he stood beside Jordyn.

There was more truth in the statement than Ansel wanted to admit to. At Foxwood they weren't fated mates, they were Captain of Enforcers and Doctor Hyde. Slipping into work mode, he was reminded Clio was responsible for securing Jordyn's medical records, making it impossible for even him to see them. She also left out vital information, and in doing so, the data wasn't added to the reports sent to team leaders. Her status within the pack gave her authority and she protected their secrets. He didn't know how they were going to talk about work when they both protected the Kanin family and the pack's soothsayer. Moreso, Clio had casually stated they suspected someone was spying on Jordyn. Ansel was surprised she knew, then commented it might be Tracy, Jordyn's disgruntled sentinel, and there were shadows working on the situation. His thoughts brought reality back. He wanted to bask in the happiness and comfortable feel holding the office, but knew it needed to end. He had a meeting with Strong Lord, false intel to hand over, and a dhampir to kill.

When Ansel's hand tightened on her for a mere breath, and his other hand rested on the butt of his gun, she understood the hint. *Work*. "Thank you for everything. I have appointments."

"Understood, Doctor Hyde." Baron Kanin stood, walked to the door, and opened it.

"I'll walk you out," Ansel started.

When Clio was at the door, the baron placed his hand on her shoulder, squeezed, and gave her a gold gaze in the shape of his wolf. She gave him a smile—her eyes didn't change, at least not like that—and with Ansel at her back, walked the hallway to the double doors. Picking up her pace, to stay ahead of Ansel, she grabbed her satchel from the hook, slung it over her shoulder before he commandeered it, and carried it to her office.

"I can carry that for you," he offered.

"You could. But you have a meeting, and I have work to do," she countered. Clio heard the door open and wanted them both to go back home. *Home*. Was that how she saw his house and not her own? Her earlier fears of losing herself tried infiltrating her and she shoved them down. She thought it, all by herself, no one forced her.

"All right." Ansel let it go and walked her out the door and stopped a couple of feet from the stairs. "Beautiful?"

"What, darling?" Clio replied as she met cinnamon eyes holding a flame of his passion and a glint she didn't trust.

"I'm going to kiss you, right now," he warned as he captured her in his arms.

She realized her retreat was too slow when he took her

mouth, the heat from his kiss searing through her as his tongue tasted her, and his hands clasped her to the hard line of his body. While fire from his branding and flames from embarrassment battled, she envisioned everyone staring at them. A spectacle. He made them a damn show. When Ansel released her, he bit her bottom lip, and Clio had a hard time breathing.

"That was a dominance show," she accused. Tried to. It was breathier than she wanted.

"Yes. You're mine and I'm a dominate wolf," Ansel growled. "You were warned."

My ass, she thought. Clio stepped closer to him, and in a low voice promised, "We'll see how dominate you are when we're home alone." Then she hit the stairs, scarlet staining her cheeks, and started across the lot, to the office where she was going to hide.

"Counting on it, beautiful," Ansel called after her. Damn, she was going to see him at home, not his house, her house, their home. It made his heart do flips in his chest. Turning back to the door, to stop himself from chasing her, he nodded to Sadie and Troy, and noticed the smirk Troy was displaying. "What?"

"Girl got you. Didn't think I was going to live to see the day, sir," he replied, his blue eyes sparkling with humor.

"Me either." Truth. He was his own worst enemy. Ansel walked back to the office to find the door open—it had to be giving Rutger a seizure, he hated open doors—and entered. His thoughts where they should be, on Strong Lord.

"I bet she loved your public display of affection. You know she's not like that," Jordyn pointed out.

"She liked it," Ansel replied with arrogance. Her rapid heartbeat was still in his head, her taste of cinnamon on his tongue.

"Now you know why I'm always in trouble," Rutger teased.

"Oh hardly, wolf." Jordyn sat down in the seat Clio had left and met the baron's gold gaze. "Rutger explained to him last night what the plan was."

"We're treating this as an active threat with hostiles and we're expecting a conflict," the baron responded. "This is the list of Jordyn's weaknesses." He stood and handed Ansel a piece of paper, Cascade's letterhead at the top to prove it came from the baron's office.

It felt like it weighed a ton and was soaked in his lies.

"I can stop this," Ansel began as he stared at the list. *Turn myself over to them.* Guilt simmered in his middle with his selfishness.

"No. If it's not now it'll be later. They've been waiting," the baron replied. "With the attention Prime and the Highguard have been giving us, I should have expected it. No one understands Jordyn's traits, the extent of her powers, or the extent of Prime's protection. While this is about you, and your connection to Bronte, they may be testing their limits."

"Testing the Highguard's limits. How far can they push before someone stops them," Jordyn added.

It did nothing to ease the guilt, like a cancer, eating his insides. But they were going to take every precaution and were on the offense, not taken by surprise and have to defend themselves. Or an innocent. Clio. "He didn't believe me when I told him Jordyn found Rutger through their bond. He knew the wards would have stopped her from sensing him."

"Does he believe in the bond?" Jordyn asked.

"He doubts its strength," Ansel replied. "He considers shifters weaker beings. He's egotistical, which is why he thinks you need to be *humbled*. But the wards scared him."

"Can I see the paper?"

Ansel handed it to Jordyn.

She stood, picked a space on the baron's desk free of books and folders, and taking a pen started writing. "Everyone knows I'm friends with Ava, and she serves Prime. They also know she was in town. I'm stating she broke the wards. They won't question her and risk Prime finding out they're breaking the covenant with Cascade, and the Highguard's canons. It would make them a direct threat to me." Jordyn straightened and handed the paper back to him.

"Excellent, Jordyn," Baron Kanin said, then looked to Rutger.

"Ares and Deimos teams have been briefed. Shadows are in place as we speak, and they'll remain in place until tomorrow. Hades and Charon are on standby, and extra soldiers and enforcers have been brought in. They're doing training and outdoor exercises to not attract attention. Patrols are making their presence known if there's fallout from the meeting, and to protect the Cloaked. That's priority. If anyone, like the OPI, have questions, we're training," he explained as he gave Jordyn a narrowed gaze.

"I'll be sure to tell Thomas," Jordyn countered with a smile. It was met with a growl from Rutger.

"Strong Lord knew Clio was at my house. He'll assume the spell failed to do its job and she is my mate. There's no other reason she would have stayed overnight. It puts her at risk," Ansel said with his wolf in his voice. The instinct to protect her drove through him, raw, primeval, and gripped him in its steel claws.

Jordyn turned in her chair to meet his gaze. "Shadows are at your place and will remain until the threat is eliminated. We'll watch her," she promised. "Does she work here all day?"

"No, she said something about the Hollow," Ansel replied. He was shaken by their sincerity and their willingness to extend their protectiveness to Clio. And then put their lives at risk for him.

"Here or there, she'll be protected. We can't let her go to Celestial, since we won't put innocent lives at risk or risk human inference. Maybe send her to the Hollow. The both of you are going to your place after work?" Rutger asked.

"Affirmative." *We're going home.* "We're supposed to have dinner. With everything going on, I'm going to tell her I have late training."

"Be careful with her," Baron Kanin warned. "She might have survived Bronte's attack and moved forward, but she hasn't released the shackles of fear it created. I can feel them."

Some of the fear was the remnants of the spell. Still, he believed she was strong enough. He wanted to argue but knew he would be defending his mate. And he needed to keep his thoughts straight and on the facts. "I promise."

"I'm going to check in with her," Jordyn started as she stood. "See if there's anything she needs to do at the Hollow."

"Keep me updated," the baron ordered.

"Sir."

"Try to get her schedule," Rutger ordered as he stepped toward her. "And let her know there will be night training."

"Copy, Director Kanin." With a quick kiss, Jordyn left the office, her power swirling in her wake.

He would have that with Clio. "Isn't she tired of the OPI yet?" Ansel asked, his stress level improving knowing Jordyn was going to be with Clio.

"Negative. I think she stays to irritate me. And one more story about Detective Watt, Thomas, or how he buys her coffee, and I'm going to have to talk to the man. A chit chat, if you get my meaning."

Coffee. Ansel did and would back him up.

"She's training at Butte Springs with the slayers, you two. Give her a break," the baron warned.

CHAPTER TEN

Clio raced through the halls of the enforcer's office, not wanting to stop and talk to anyone. It was bad enough they were staring at her. Yeah, yeah, she was Captain Wolt's mate. Yeah, yeah, Tall, Dark, and Handsome was unattainable. *Was.* Clio knew she wore the night of sex on her face, like a billboard. How else do you consummate a relationship? And they all knew. They. All. Knew. Her insides turned to jelly as embarrassment scalded her.

The dorm area was a blur as she headed straight to Nearctic where she pushed through the doors and into her world. "Doctor Clio Hyde, authority code One Heka." The med room came to life while LED lights came on, a computer hummed, and Cascade's crest filled the screen, then panels slid back to reveal touchpads. Clio looked at the instruments, the supplies, stainless steel counters, the computer, all state of the art, and a calm settled over her. This was her world.

Without thinking, she walked to the window with views of the parking lot, and the estate, her fingers playing on the strap of her satchel, and saw Ansel. He was standing with Director Kanin, his face devoid of the passion she had seen when he kissed her. She reached for him in the bond, felt the cold wall from him blocking her, and felt cut off. When he turned his back to the window, his head bowed, his shoulders slumped, and his hand on the butt of his gun, she didn't like it. She could almost see him begging for forgiveness.

That's my imagination, she told herself. Why would he beg Director Kanin for forgiveness? It didn't change the fact that there was something going on and she wasn't privy to the information. The pieces were in front of her, and she didn't know which one went where, and didn't know how to ask without thinking she was crossing a boundary. Like she was butting into his life.

The damn mate thing had her off kilter. A day ago, if she had a question, she asked. *That wasn't entirely true*, she admitted, as she walked to her office. She pressed her hand on the palm vein scanner, entered her code, opened the door, and went to her desk. After Bronte, there were memories she didn't understand or couldn't reach, and when she questioned Dr. Carrion, he explained the tragic events and Bronte's drugs triggered temporary amnesia. To protect herself from the horrors. It caused her to second guess herself, and she stopped asking questions. Stopped being herself.

Clio told herself she had moved on. The proof being Mistress telling her she was a Potent and the baron trusted her enough to send her to talk to Crevan. Her natural instincts came back, as if she was allowed to use them. Throughout her life, she was notorious for obsessing over small details, then picking them apart to find the root of the problem. It was her predisposition; she was a doctor, and it was her job to diagnose the cause of illnesses. The obsessive behavior fit her. Like being an empath, her intuitiveness came naturally. Was she going to question Ansel? She didn't know. While her thoughts chased one another, she typed commands, bringing up his medical records, the outline of the human body in the center of the screen, the left side column listing his injuries.

Organ failure.

Cardiac arrest.

Bacterial infections.

Hypovolemia.

Hypothermia.

Where there should have been a blue outline there was red—it was all over his body—indicating his injuries, and the column kept getting longer. She saw his bronze gaze, his clenched jaw as the flames crawled up his arms, and over his shoulders, the red and yellow tips racing over him to lick at his face. Then he closed his eyes, shutting her out. Where she would have stopped the memory from tormenting her, she let it play. Clio felt the pressure on her shoulders from the restraints, smelled the tang from kerosene, the sulfur from matches, and saw the crimson moon. Above it all was Bronte laughing at her.

"I hate her." Seconds felt like hours while she prayed he would open his eyes.

"Let me see you," she demanded.

"Tesoro," he replied as the blaze engulfed him.

"I almost lost him," she whispered. That fear coming from deep inside of her was the same she felt when she saw him with the director. He gave her his back because he knew she was watching him. Where did tesoro come from?

"Doctor Hyde."

Clio shook herself, closed the file, signed out, and left her office to find Mistress standing at the window. "Can I help you, Mistress?"

"Please, drop the mistress thing. My name is Jordyn and you're basically my sister-in-law. Kith and kin. I came here to get all the details."

Clio wanted to laugh, but the overwhelming feeling she was losing herself stopped her. Everyone knew ... well, everything, including the threat Bronte was to them, and with Ansel shutting her out, it was not helping her stress level.

"I can use voodoo, or you can tell me what's up," Jordyn warned her.

"You've warned me twice," Clio countered. Then she thought they had a weird relationship.

"Sassy. The first warning was real," Jordyn started as she went back to the window. Without looking at Clio, she continued, "As an empath with strong instincts you gather information about people's emotions. Sad. Happy. If they're lying. Like we wanted you to do with Alpha Crevan to know if their intentions were honest. Information is dangerous. Sharing it is more dangerous."

"I understand," Clio assured. She was staring at Jordyn's back, her raven hair, its ends near her waist. Quite a difference from when she had lost half of it, more on one side than the other when she fought a giant ant.

"Making assumptions about a detail can create a lie, and lies are destructive. You could be better." Jordyn faced her. "You need training, and we'll find someone. The second warning was a joke. I wouldn't use my voodoo on you."

"Really?" Clio raised her eyebrows in question.

"No, not really," Jordyn replied with a smile that didn't reach her eyes.

There was something going on, Clio felt it in her bones, and Jordyn was part of it. What the hell was she thinking? "Why are you here?"

"The details. You snagged Captain Wolt. I haven't seen him crack a smile in years. An actual smile, and he's brooding less than usual."

Clio reached out to sense the lie or the truth and didn't feel either. There was a wolf, power, then they were gone and replaced by a cold darkness. The kind of cold that burned like there were flames crawling over her. She needed to stop thinking about flames.

"I had to work on it, but it comes naturally now. You won't like what you see if you try to sense me. I manipulate your magic and give it back to you but with a little surprise. Something you fear."

The darkness from her nightmares. Fire. "How in the hell did you learn to do that?" Clio asked, her curiosity working overtime.

"My secret." Jordyn inhaled and exhaled. "Come on, Doc, spill the beans on Ansel. What did you do?"

"First, tell me what the hell is going on and why Ansel shut me out," she demanded. Smooth move, making demands to Mistress who could make her nightmares come to life. She needed to calm down and take a breather.

Jordyn smiled again, and this time not only did it reach her eyes, but they rolled copper. "One, he's at work, it shouldn't surprise you. Rutger and I do the same thing to save our sanity. Two, there's mass training going on. The soldiers, enforcers, and patrols are conducting exercises throughout the city, while reaction teams are practicing their urban maneuvers. It can be stressful to have so many people in motion, especially if humas get nosey. Don't be surprised if Ansel has to play enforcer tonight. Now spill it."

There you have it. That would explain why he was stressed. "We were supposed to have dinner."

"It'll be late, after midnight. He'll be checking for security breaches. Per Director Kanin."

Right. Now she felt stupid for not asking and jumping to conclusions. For making assumptions. She had to get a handle on her emotions. "I went over there to return his shirt.

Then he was in the backyard with an ax," Clio began. Sweat glistening on his sun-kissed skin, his muscles flexing.

"A man wielding an ax. Every woman's weakness," Jordyn teased.

"Apparently mine," Clio replied through a laugh. Sitting in a chair by the stainless-steel counter, she took a pen and started bouncing it on a pad of paper and spent the next fifteen minutes telling Jordyn their beautiful love story, including calling him Father Time and an ass. "I know it's a romantic tale. He's worried my parents won't like him."

"You're worried about something. Is it your parents?"

"Truthfully, I'm not sure what they'll say. They respect his position. But as my mate? My recovery was rough on them." Sitting back, Clio wondered how much she was willing to tell Jordyn. She wasn't one to spill her guts.

"Parents can be tough. Be honest with them. I'm getting the feeling you aren't telling me everything. What's going on?"

"I feel like I'm losing myself," she gushed. "They accepted my offer, and I bought the house. Jess, my real estate agent, is at my place taking pictures so she can list it. I'm going to sell my first home. That doesn't matter, just like the years of medical school are irrelevant because I'm Captain of Enforcer's girlfriend. I'm Doctor Clio Hyde. I worked for it and the respect of my peers."

"Don't ever doubt people's respect of you, Clio, and don't worry about what they think. You're not his girlfriend. And he isn't your BF. You're his mate as he is yours. Big difference. I understand you hate being the center of attention, but you work at Foxwood. It's like a small town ... everyone knows everything and what they don't they freaking make up. I know."

True. "I just feel I'm losing control." Clio met cocoa eyes and didn't know what Jordyn was thinking. "It happened so fast. Do you think I'm being hysterical?"

"No, it's an emotional time. It's like you're on a runaway train and the bridge ahead of you is out. I can tell you it's not. But it's an unnerving ride until you get your bearing." Jordyn stood and went back to the window. "What's your schedule like?"

"I'm working here most of the day. I have to check in with Danette, she usually has a to-do list for me," she replied. "Doctor Baines was supposed to do a routine check in with staff at the Hollow, to make sure they aren't going crazy and the soldiers aren't antagonizing anyone. The other day during training, they cleared a room and held the doctors and nurses hostage. I talked to Lieutenant Bouldin about it, and when he saw them, he gave them high fives."

Jordyn giggled; it sounded choked when she tried to stop. "That's the soldiers for you. Are you going to the Hollow? I might be able to join you."

That should have raised awareness and created questions, like the distant memory of hearing Ansel call her tesoro, a name she didn't know. Tempest. Beautiful. Not tesoro. She didn't know what it meant or why she was clinging to it like it might save her from drowning.

"Doctor, you in there?" Jordyn asked, getting her attention.

"Umm ... yeah. I was thinking of not going. Doctor Baines has been doing a good job, and he's been able to get the soldiers to talk to him," she replied.

"You're better off staying at Foxwood, closer to Ansel. And you're distracted. You know, you can lose yourself in your man and still kick ass."

"Did you lose yourself?" she asked, not sure why when it

was obvious. The director and Jordyn were in sync.

"I lost everything to that wolf, and he can bring me to my knees while reminding me I'm the most precious thing in the world. With him I'm Jordyn and not a title. The flipside, he lost everything to me. I battled with thinking my empathy, the need to protect, and my love was a weakness, something someone was going to exploit. Rutger did, too. You can't keep who you are buried." Nailing Clio with a hard copper gaze, she said, "My love is my strength and foundation. If I didn't love, I wouldn't make sacrifices for the pack. At least for the right reasons."

Clio didn't know what to think, her mind in the center of chaos. There was so much happening to her emotionally, physically, mentally—it threatened to destroy the order she coveted.

"You think about that, Doc. I have reports to complete, or Thomas will drive me crazy. When I'm done, how about cocktails while the guys finish working? Healey likes the company since Gavin is working out of town, and Laurel likes cooking for people. My waistline is proof."

"Yes, cocktails sound good," Clio replied absently as her mind drifted. She didn't hear Jordyn leave or the door's familiar swish, all she heard was Ansel's voice in her head, *"Tesoro."* And her heart started racing.

Ansel stood beside Rutger at the border of the lush, green lawn, marking the estate, and asphalt of the parking lot, watching team leaders give enforcers and soldiers orders. "I'm completely out of control. If I fail tonight ..." He trailed off, and as if Ansel could feel her watching him, he couldn't handle her eyes on him, he gave the med room his back. The instinct to protect her raged, and his wolf howled for its mate, clawing his insides. There were a million things he wanted to say, ask. His mind was a mess, his heart was beating too fast, and his body felt strange.

"Welcome to being mated. The edginess, the need to be with her, touch her, and protect her will eventually taper off enough you can control the urges and the frustration. As for tonight, you won't fail."

He didn't share Rutger's confidence. "What about her? What is this doing to her?" Ansel felt someone should have warned them, at least told them what to expect.

"The same. Doctor Hyde is two people. She's an empath, so she might be sensitive to every emotion and it's exaggerating the situation, but then she's a doctor who relies on order and facts. She's levelheaded, not prone to drama, so I'm sure while it isn't comfortable, she is making sense of what's going on. It's a highly emotional time for the both of you," Rutger explained, his hand on the butt of his gun, the sun highlighting his mahogany gaze. If he noticed Ansel giving the office his back, he didn't say anything.

That's exactly what they didn't need, not now. "Sounds like there was a psych workup done on her," he accused.

It meant shadows had tracked her day and night, watched her every move, recorded what they could, then handed their findings over to a team of psychologists, with several empaths involved, who analyzed the information, creating a preliminary profile. Following the initial outline, Clio would have been interviewed, the questioning witnessed by another psychologist, a profiler, and empaths to study her verbal answers, physical reactions, and behavior. Ansel felt anger blaze through him at the thought they invaded Clio's life, turned it inside out, examined her like she was bug, then made judgements.

"Affirmative. When she was being considered for Nearctic. Plus, you're Captain of Enforcers and she's your mate. There can't be a threat within our ranks," Rutger explained plainly, in a neutral tone.

Ansel listened to his explanation and worked to snuff his anger. "Sorry," he breathed the word.

"Now you know why Jo hates the freak file."

He did. And knew the freak file wasn't changing. "You think we're going to pull this off?" he asked, changing the subject.

As he cooled his anger and his thoughts cleared, his doubts multiplied by the second while the what ifs were spiraling out of his control. His mind fighting against him didn't focus on Clio, it targeted her, and he growled low in his chest as he fought to regain his mind and wolf. If he failed, Strong Lord wouldn't wait to stab a spike made of magic into him in hopes of taking what no one had been able to touch. His monster, his magic. There was a good chance Ansel was going to die, which would lead to Clio's death. He hated thinking about it, wanted to ignore the possibility they would use the bond—a beautiful creation between fated mates—to hurt her. A slow torture. Ansel handled pain, had been taught by Bronte how to survive and ignore the worst, but what he couldn't bear was them using him. The wall he built between them had come easy enough since he was used to shielding himself from others, but she wasn't. She was there, exposed, no way to protect herself from him.

"You aren't going to fail," Rutger assured.

"You have to do something for me," Ansel insisted.

"What?"

"If this goes to shit, and I'm captured, they'll use me, torture me, so she feels it. If my walls fail, Clio doesn't know how to block me. Someone has to protect her." Ansel knew he sounded desperate, and his eyes were bronze with his wolf, the primal need to protect darkening them.

"She'll be protected, I vow this, brother," Rutger promised with a growl in his voice.

"What do we do?" Ansel needed to be working, doing something, not standing around while every emotion bullied through to overwhelm him.

The question went unanswered, and they both went silent when Jordyn exited the office and made her way through the packed parking lot toward them. Her presence caused enforcers and soldiers to stop what they were doing to watch her, and after bowing their heads in greeting, outright stared at her. Responding to them with a smile, she held her shoulders back, and with her hand on the butt of her gun, acted like nothing was going on.

"Jo hates that," Rutger grumbled.

"It seems she understands it, like the freak file," Ansel replied. He didn't know how. He spent his life evading attention and couldn't imagine the stress from being exposed.

"She would be fighting an uphill battle if she didn't. Who is that?"

A woman dressed as a soldier—tan BDU pants, light beige T-shirt with the soldier's insignia, two wolves and a shield, on her back, Glock 21, .45 caliber pistol secured in a dropdown holster, and boots—stopped in front of Jordyn. Her jet-black hair with purple undertones was back in a tight braid, its end at her waist, while the sides of her head were shaved. Symbols were inked into her skull from her temples to the back of her head, then went down her neck. She faced Jordyn as if she had done so a hundred times, and the two began talking.

"I don't know," Ansel replied as he took his cell and dialed. "You wanted more manpower."

"Captain Wolt, how can I help you?" Mandy asked.

"Parking lot, row six, Mistress is talking to a female soldier. I need an ID."

"Standby."

"Since the baron created the Commission to oversee all petitions, I have no idea what's going on. However, if I complained, he would tell me the information is on my desk."

The Commission was a group of ten magic-born voted in by the pack, klatch, and the Cloaked. Their job was to receive then review all incoming petitions, what faction the aspirant requested inclusion into, and then conduct an inquest. If the aspirant passed the initial inquest, the requested faction leader was informed, and they proceeded with a thorough investigation and background check. The Commission also hired and placed men and women in the soldiers and patrol. They didn't have the authority to send anyone to the enforcers, slayers, and shadows. Baron Kanin was the sole person who could make those decisions. Since the female was at Foxwood, in uniform, and had been called to serve as protection with her team, it meant she passed training.

"Captain Wolt."

"Go ahead."

"Emory Bishop, Illuminate, werewolf and the Erinyes. She's been active for a week," Mandy reported.

"Copy." Ansel ended the call and didn't have to repeat the information since Rutger heard it. "She's Greek." The Erinyes, also known as Furies, were female gods of the earth, deities of vengeance, and capable of cursing those they felt violated their vows.

"Prime," Rutger growled.

"You said the edginess was going to taper off. You don't

give me much hope." Ansel felt the steel edge of Rutger's rage rolling off him.

"I'm not a good example of control where Prime is concerned," he grated, his gold gaze on Jordyn.

Giving him a sideways glance, Ansel grinned. He was half teasing, trying to ease the tension, and half serious. He understood what it felt like to feel helpless to protect one's mate. He spent over a year watching Clio, trying to be there if anything happened to her. With his weakness and need to have her, he put her in the Fellowship's crosshairs, and added Jordyn and Rutger who had their own threats, to the chaos. Would he change it? Negative. Did he regret it? Negative. She was his mate, fated to be his, and while his emotions, instincts, and his wolf were like a raging storm inside of him, he felt complete, as if his broken pieces had been bandaged. They might never be healed but they weren't bleeding lesions.

"Who is that?" Ansel asked. A male, his shoulders filling out a blue, V-neck T-shirt, and wearing jeans and boots approached Jordyn, his black hair cut close to his skull, military style, his crystal blue eyes bright as he smiled at her.

"Charles' younger brother, Kinsey. He finished his time with the Coast Guard," Rutger answered. "Jordyn mentioned it last night. I didn't know he was going to be here."

"After Justice Talbolt questioned her about her sentinels, she seems to have accepted them," Ansel remarked.

"Another uphill battle if she hadn't. And she won't have them punished because she doesn't want them around." Rutger's tone was flat, his gaze heated and shoulders tense under his black BDU top.

They both watched her talk to Emory and Kinsey, then she walked toward them, a smile on her face, her cocoa gaze on Rutger. Jordyn went to Rutger's side, put her arm around him, and met Ansel's stare.

"Doctor Hyde is staying here. Once I'm done with my reports, I'll come back and we're having cocktails with Healey and Laurel."

"Thank you," Ansel said and knew it wasn't enough.

"Who were you talking to?" Rutger asked.

"Do you expect me to believe you didn't check with Mandy? Yes, Emory knows Prime, it would be hard not to, but she is far removed from his circle," Jordyn explained. "Her father is a Pureblood and takes his status within his pack seriously."

"Why is she talking to you?" Rutger raised his hand, and placing it on her shoulder, drew her closer.

"A set of eyes and ears."

"And Kinsey?"

"Is here to talk to Healey. He has delusions of being a sentinel. I have the feeling Healey is going to grant his request and he'll take up residency at Charles' place. I'll have to deal with them both." Jordyn leaned into Rutger, and looking up, gave him a 'this conversation is over' look. When Rutger shrugged his shoulders in response, she turned her attention to Ansel. "If Doctor Hyde seems distant, don't worry, she's thinking about things."

"Like what?" Ansel hesitantly asked.

"Being a Wight and now your girlfriend," Jordyn replied.

"She isn't my girlfriend," Ansel argued. "And besides being an accomplished doctor, she's a strong empath."

"We all know this. I advise taking it slow," Jordyn started. "Let her get her bearings."

Ansel took a step back, and facing the parking lot, gazed at the soldiers and enforcers, his eyes skimming over the office and the med room's windows. He couldn't fail.

"Understood." Either way, failure or success, the chance of losing her was real.

Clio gazed down at the three of them, saw their close-ness, felt like she was on the outside, and wondered if she wanted to be a part of them. If she could be a part of them. They didn't have much in common. Then her conversation with Jordyn replayed. Practically a sister-in-law. Was she becoming part of them? Would she fit in? Jordyn owned her place. Director Kanin looked like he didn't have a weakness. Ansel's strength, love, and loyalty had pride welling inside of her, but at the same time her doubts wanted to force her to walk away from him. Was it possible? "No," Clio answered aloud. It wasn't. She was having a hard time being away from him.

Jordyn stood on tiptoe, placed a kiss on the director's neck, then facing Ansel, said something, and went to her truck. No doubt going to work and Detective Watt. The right side door opened, and Troy, a sentinel for the baron and baroness, stepped out, talked to the director, and went back inside. After a short conversation with Ansel, Rutger went inside. Standing alone, Ansel looked at the commotion, the two-lane road leading out of Foxwood, then started across the parking lot and she lost sight of him.

Clio remained where she was, her mind replaying every word Ansel, and then Jordyn, said, and finally her own scattered thoughts. She jumped when a shrill ringing broke the silence, its scream coming from her office. Giving the window her back, she went to her desk and grabbed her cell. "Like she has ESP." Clio inhaled and exhaled. "Mom."

"Blossom, how are you?" Evelyn asked.

"Doing well, I'm at work." Guilt simmered then boiled and her stomach turned. "I need to talk to you and Dad."

"All right," she replied with caution. "Is there something wrong? Did you lose the house?"

"Nothing like that, and I got the house. Be prepared for yard work, the backyard is a disaster." Clio sat down, the anxiety draining from her, her thoughts clearing. Maybe she needed to talk to her mom. "I have a couple of hours, was thinking about coming by."

"Then I'll make lunch."

"Thanks, Mom. See you in a little bit." When her mom ended the call, Clio set her cell down and looked at the computer screen. Names, listed alphabetically, and labeled by job title, stared at her. She needed to schedule a day to use the gym and have the soldiers recertify to keep their paramedic status. Taking her cell, she dialed and waited. "Danette, do I have anything today?"

"Standard tasks. There are no appointments, Doctor Hyde. The calendar is clear. Do I need to add something?"

"No. I was checking. Contact Mandy and schedule a recertification day for the soldiers, and I'll need the gym, then call Doctor Maki to assist."

"Yes, Doctor. Anything else?"

"No. If something comes up, I'll have my cell. I'm going to visit my parents," Clio replied.

"Noted."

"Thank you." Clio ended the call and set the cell down only to have it ring. "Doctor Hyde."

"I hope I'm not bothering you." As he spoke, his throaty voice sounded like his animal was in his words.

"Not at all, Crevan. How can I help you?" she asked. Picking a pen from the holder, she readied to take notes.

"Baron Kanin has given me the authorization to have one of our doctors shadow you. Is there an opportunity for him to do so?"

Clio wanted to say no, and explain she wasn't the right person, and then suggest someone from Celestial. But if Baron Kanin gave his authorization, she didn't have a choice. "I'm in charge of recertifying the soldiers in order for them to keep their paramedic status. It takes place at Foxwood, the Enforcer's office. He is more than welcome to attend," she explained, her tone professional. It would be taking care of three things at once; the doctor would witness the soldiers, he would see the office, Ansel, Director Kanin, and lastly the efficiency in which they work. The expanse of it would open his eyes, and he would tell Crevan.

"Do you have a date?"

"Not yet. When I have one, I'll let you know."

"Thank you. Looking forward to hearing from you, Doctor Hyde." With his last word, he hung up on her.

Clio looked at the screen, then clicking it closed, set her cell down. "Well damn." What the hell did she do? Replaying the call, she knew she was professional, she answered his questions, did her job, and hadn't said anything personal. Personal. She laughed a soft sound and couldn't believe what she'd done without even knowing it. The last time she talked to Crevan, she knew she flirted with him, and she complimented his cooking, and teased him about how good his shrimp and raviolis were. Clio had been stern, all business, a representative for the pack. She talked to the alpha as a woman who had a mate. No misunderstanding there. Her fears about being a girlfriend were unfounded when she recognized their bond. She was his mate. There was a difference.

With her thoughts focused on her mate, she stood, grabbed her purse from where it hung, shoved her cell into it, and walked out of her office. She wasn't going to bother

Ansel to tell him she was going to visit her parents, with the training and late night scheduled he wouldn't have time. And she wasn't going to risk him making time when she needed to do this by herself. Her dad would understand, he was a werewolf, but her mom, human, didn't always believe in the myths, as she called them, of the magic-born. And fated mates was about as myth as it got ... hell, she doubted it enough to research the subject. Plus, she didn't need a six-four Pureblood with copper eyes, a body of muscle and coiled power to hold her by the back of the neck with his absolute possession to intimidate her parents. She pictured the expression on her dad's face and smiled.

"Yeah, I'll save that for later," she said to the empty room. "One Heka, shutdown." Lights turned off, cabinets locked, and panels slid to cover touchpads. Out of the med room, she strolled through the dorm area, kitchen, and to the hallway, her earlier race to her office forgotten. In the hallway, she eyed Ansel's door, and passing it made her way out of the office and toward the reception area.

"Doc."

Almost made it, she thought as she turned around. Standing in the doorway, she met indigo eyes with slivers of violet. "What can I do for you, Mandy?"

"Don't play dumb with me, lady. You got the guy," she gushed as she smiled. "That kiss was something."

It was something all right ... had her heart racing for more than one reason. Clio loosened her hold on her worries, and smiling with pure arrogance, replied, "He's all mine."

"Congratulations, Doc. Where are you headed?"

"My parents before someone tells them. I don't need my mom going into cardiac arrest and then shock."

"Have fun explaining Captain Wolt will be their son-in-law," Mandy teased.

"Thanks. See you later."

Mandy waved, then began talking into the mic of her headset.

She wasn't going to have a hard time explaining Ansel—he held rank in the pack, the baron and baroness thought of him as their son, and it wasn't like there was something wrong with him. Besides Bronte. Clio nearly died. Tried quitting her job. There's that. Outside, Clio raised her face to the sky, soaked the up the warmth from the sun, and tried to put her thoughts in order. Her parents would expect her to explain to them, rationally, what happened. Did she know what happened? No. One minute she was returning his flannel, the next she was sharing his bed, and telling Baron Kanin they were fated mates. There was nothing rational about them. Not when Ansel promised her a lifetime of wicked nights and sinful mornings. Heat bloomed over her, and to stop from seeing him naked, she focused on the questions her parents were going to have. On her way to her crossover, she saw Ansel's truck, and heard orders, then enforcers and soldiers answering with hard responses.

In the driver's seat, she started the engine, and after maneuvering out of the crowded parking lot drove the two-lane road. Maybe she needed to get away from Foxwood, Ansel, and the commotion. It was high energy, hard edges, and held an urgency she didn't understand, and it added to her turbulent mood. She needed to be with her parents. She trusted them, and they were calm, confident, and at peace. There wasn't a war going on inside of them. Once through the gate, her anxiety eased, letting her think beyond the chaos tumbling through her head, and she thought about Ansel. He might be able to block her from sensing him through their bond and was good at building barriers to stop anyone from feeling his battle, but it was different for her when she felt the vibrations of his emotions. Was it because she was an empath? Maybe. There was another reason, one she didn't want to put into words let alone admit to. Ansel let her in. He opened himself to her and let her in his heart; she felt his raw self. He was hers as much as she was his. Jordyn said that, and until then, Clio didn't understand. She did now.

On impulse, she flicked the blinker, turned right, and chose the scenic route. She needed time to think before facing her parents and the drive would settle her nerves. She hadn't lied to him when she told Ansel they liked him—he would have sensed it—and they did like him as Captain of Enforcers Ansel Wolt, and from afar. Really far. Her near death, inept recovery, and the fact she had handed Baron Kanin her resignation, hadn't won him any fans. Then facing the Highguard's Prosecution Administration and having to have a psychological evaluation to return to work absolutely did not help him. Not where she was concerned. They almost lost their only child and daughter, then watched her nearly give up her passion and go through hell to recover.

"I can do this," she mumbled. *They'll understand.*

Forest bordered the two-lane road, while shrubs and wildflowers crowded the asphalt, and she rolled down the windows, put her hand out to play in the wind, and slowed down. As she turned up the radio, the breeze carried cedar, oak, pine, which reminded her of Ansel, his scent, his house, and the song a slow number with a hint of blues took her back to the day before and his passion. By herself and feeling a tranquility deep within her, Clio let herself get lost in the rhythm and the memory of Ansel's love and possession of her. Smiling with the thoughts she felt the fissures inside of her fill with purpose and Ansel's presence, and she didn't fear everyone knowing everything, or her parents' doubt. As shaken as she was with doubt weakening her resolve, Clio was doing this because it felt right, and she loved Ansel. Like a weight had been lifted from her shoulders she relaxed, the song ended, and a commercial with a female voice rattling on about vacation homes in the Sierra Nevada Mountains faded into the background.

Even with her newfound confidence where she and Ansel were concerned, she wasn't going to see her parents unprepared. That was a personality characteristic, always the responsible one, she couldn't and wouldn't change. She was a doctor and being prepared made her who she was. No different than being intuitive, an empath, and a healer. She heard Ansel's voice. *"You're innocent, honest, I can't destroy that. I won't allow anyone to destroy the purity in you."* While he protected her, she was going to be strong for the both of them, and the demons darkening his eyes would retract their claws. He would never doubt her love.

"Ansel Wolt is mine," she vowed.

Catching a shadowed shape racing from the woodline, Clio slammed on the brakes, attempting to miss it. A high-pitched squeal pierced her ears as the car skidded on asphalt, and seeing the person in the road, she jerked the wheel, causing the car to slide sideways. It hit the shoulder and the tires kicking up gravel. Greens, browns, and slivers of sunlight blurred as she struggled to gain control, prayed the person was safe, then the crossover crashed into a group of trees. Shattering glass and crunching metal blasted around her, and an instant later a violent spray hit her right side, and she came to a hard stop. The impact threw her into the driver's door as the seat belt tightened on her, holding her in place. Her head hit the steering wheel, then the seat.

Panic raced through her with her deep inhales and harsh exhales, and she quickly did a mental search of her body. Nothing was broken. She had that going for her.

Clio tried moving only to have her body scream in pain. Her right side was bleeding from the shards of glass, and she saw blood dripping to her shirt. It must have been when she hit the steering wheel. Turning her head, her neck felt like fire wrapped around it and was squeezing. She couldn't see anything through the fractured windshield; she didn't know where the person was or if she had hit them. To her right, the passenger side was crushed. The impact destroyed the seats so much so she could reach out and touch the trees. Fragments of glass peppered what was left, the sun glittering off them, while black and gray smoke floated from under the hood. Clio sat back, trying to get the world to stop spinning, and worked on controlling her breathing and letting her muscles relax enough the pain eased.

"Need to call for help," she mumbled and tasted blood. She raised her hand and touched her lips, and her fingertips came back scarlet. "Don't panic." First thing was first, she needed help. Without straining her neck, her head lolled to the right to see the terminal had been smashed into the dash, her cell phone crushed, and she had no way of getting help. "Taking the backroad wasn't a good idea." Without the terminal and her cell, she was going to have to get out of the car. Plus, she had to see what the hell ran across the damned road. And if she made it out of the car, she might be able to shift and heal the worst of her injuries.

Clio pulled the handle. Nothing. Tried it again, felt it budge, and pushed with her shoulder, causing fire to shoot into her chest. Using her wolf, she shoved all her strength into it, and opened the door. Metal groaned then grated against metal. If she had been human, she would have sustained life-threatening injuries or would have been dead.

"Half werewolf," she mumbled as her head spun and her eyesight blurred. Definitely a concussion, she decided. It took more strength than she anticipated, but she made it out of the car. Clio clung to the side and steadied herself when the smell of oil and car fluids met her nose, creating a wave of nausea that rolled over her.

"Quite a crash."

Clio knew the voice, its tone sending chills down her spine and turning her blood cold. Shifting until she was leaning on the bent fender, she met white eyes with scarlet staining them.

"I was going to drain whoever was in the car, but this, his innocent, is going to be delectable. Worth what I had to do to get here."

"Bronte. Nice sword. Did you escape the Middle Ages?"

"Wight. It's good to see you, too," she mused. Her dull, black hair was streaked with gray, her thin shoulders skeletal, her complexion ashen, her gait unbalanced. It should have told Clio something.

"There's a tracker. Emergency." Clio pushed through swollen lips, her throat feeling like it was closing, and her head spun. Calling her wolf, she tried to shift, to feel its magic, but failed. Her injuries were too extensive.

"I guess I better get to it then." Bronte casually closed the distance between them, and standing beside Clio, inhaled, then hissed, "Mated. His scent is all over you." Her eyes blazed scarlet for a second, then bled white. "I will make him hate you."

Clio laughed; it sounded insane. "You need a hobby." Gods, she was losing her mind. The quiet inched forward, its darkness creating the shadow at the edge of her mind, and it gave her a sense of strength. "Is this where you threaten to kill me?"

"No. And what fun would killing you be? Remember, I like the cloak and dagger of it all. Swords, sorcery, the drama and flair. Fire." Bronte patted the sword strapped to her hip, its hilt glittering in the spiderweb of sunlight, and Clio followed her broken nails covered in chipped red paint. She checked the road, tilted her head as if listening to something, her hair falling over her shoulder, then met Clio's gaze. "Come." Walking around the car, the heels of her scuffed boots dragging, she headed toward the woodline.

Clio wasn't going anywhere. If she wanted to kill her or not, she could do it right where Clio was standing.

"Wight, you're going to make me angry, and I don't have the energy for it."

"Wait while I try to care." Concussion. Head injury. The adrenaline dump wasn't helping her self-preservation and the quiet she depended on began to fade.

In a breath, Bronte was in front of her, fangs bared, her hair fanning out behind her, and her eyes a dark garnet. "I am not in the mood."

"I. Don't. Care." Clio smiled, knew there was blood all over her teeth; she felt it and drool sliding down her chin.

Closing her eyes, she inhaled. "Your blood. I'm starving," she whispered. "Control."

That got Clio's attention, and what was left of the quiet shattered and vanished. With it gone, Clio felt vulnerable. She couldn't let it weaken her, not when she could take threats, drugs, been there done that, and threats of death. Facing a starving dhampir was not what she wanted to do.

"Aw, yes, Wight, I'm going to feed." Bronte smiled, mocking Clio's. "I've fed on Brando and now I'll feed on his mate. It's a glorious thing. A complete circle if you will."

"No."

"Yes. Come." Bronte grabbed her by her hair and started pulling her away from the road, the car, and any chance someone would see her.

They would see the wreck, maybe search the immediate area, and then call law enforcement. She hoped what she said about the tracker was real, that it hadn't been destroyed in the crash, and communications was sending help. It would take time since she had taken a backroad. While that undermined her strength and confidence, she clung to the hope Ansel would find her. He would search for her.

Stumbling after Bronte, she struggled to keep from hitting the ground face first and tried to keep her feet under her—through brush, trees, shrubs, her running shoes dragging over pine needles and leaves, then down an embankment. Clio fell, her knees sinking in soft dirt.

"I don't know what he sees in you," Bronte seethed as she helped Clio up. "Weak."

"He doesn't see you," Clio spit back at her.

"He will." Bronte shoved her, and wrapping her thin fingers around Clio's upper arm, her nails dug into her skin like claws, and she took them deeper into the woods and farther from the road. "What do we have here? It's like this was fate. First you and now we'll have our own private cabin in the woods."

Her voice was edged with insanity, and Clio wanted to hold her hands over her ears to keep from hearing Bronte's manic laughter but didn't have the strength to fight the pain. She stopped, took her blurred gaze from the ground, and looking up saw a cabin. Instantly, the hope she might escape Bronte sank to the ground with her heart.

"I feel your melancholy. It makes me happy you're

hopeless. It's like dessert. I needed it." Bronte pulled her to the door hanging from a hinge and peered inside. "It's not a townhouse in the city, but it'll do."

Clio shuddered with her words. "They're going to find me."

"That's the plan, Wight. That's the plan." Bronte pushed the broken plank door out of the way, shoved Clio inside, and following behind her, closed it.

Splinters of sunlight reached inside, the dim slices doing nothing to take the dank feel from the air, while it smelled of animals, waste, and rot. Clio limped across the plank floor, still wet from the thunderstorm, and stood against the far wall while she watched Bronte check the one room cabin.

"Sit," she ordered as she faced Clio.

She was tired of standing—she wanted to ease the pain in her hips and legs—and with her side bleeding, Clio did as ordered. "Now what?"

"I'm going to tell you a story," she answered. Bronte kicked shingles and old cans out of the way, gazed at the flooring, as if trying to make a decision, then took her seat. Sitting cross-legged, her tattered jeans were loose on her thighs, her shirt hung off one shoulder, exposing pale skin over bones, and she stared at Clio.

"Not interested." There were signs Clio was missing, things she wasn't paying attention to. *Head injures did that,* she reminded herself. So did shock, and slamming into a cluster of trees going fifty miles an hour. Staring back at Bronte, she let her senses search her, and adding her trait, empathy, she laughed, and it sounded cold. "You're dying."

"I am, Wight." Bronte shrugged as if she didn't care.

Clio saw through it and felt her regret while her energy was draining her.

"Is this where the innocent doctor with a pure heart tells

me she can save me?"

"No. I want to see you dead," Clio replied, her voice stone cold.

"There's the person I wanted to see. Cold. Hate. Not his precious, little innocent. Brando is your demon, Wight. Your demon. He turned you into this."

"You did, the day you tried killing us." The day raced back—the smell of burning skin, the weight of the shackles, blood riding the air, his bronze eyes holding her. Had Bronte changed her? She was tougher. Stronger.

"I'm talking about the spell on your memories." Bronte waited for her reaction. "That's right, he did that to you, and it put him in debt. His life for your memories."

"I don't believe you." It sounded weak to her own ears. The missing pieces, scattered as if thrown into the air, and out of reach. Tesoro. No, she wouldn't believe that, not coming from Bronte. Ansel wouldn't do that to her.

"Shhh ... listen," she began. "I am the progeny of a powerful vampire lord and mage. They were not mates and they were not parents. They were chosen to breed for their physical superiorities, their magic traits, and the power of their houses. After my birth, when my physical appearance and traits resembled my sire's, he sent the mage back to her coven. I stayed to train with the vampires of my line."

Clio didn't want to listen, she didn't care, she wanted whatever was happening to end, but at the same time she felt herself being drawn in. As the story continued, Bronte's accent grew thick with an edge of cold determination like it was taking everything she had to continue.

"I failed the first mission. As punishment, I spent two weeks locked in a cell. Naked. Beaten. Starving. Isolated from the others and made an example out of."

"How old were you?" Clio found herself asking.

"Eight. I missed my target. The next mission was a success. As were the rest. I lived to kill. I was a finely honed instrument for them to use until I was no longer necessary, and I became a threat. No longer relevant. No longer validated. I had no reason for being. They tried assassinating me," she nearly screamed. When she calmed herself, she continued, "I returned to my sire, drained him, and those of his house, and when I found the mage, I drained her and her coven. I absorbed their traits, some knowledge, and their memories. Their voices are impossible to stop."

Clio watched her cradle her head in her hands and hoped they tore her mind apart. "When did you met Ansel?"

White and scarlet met Clio's gaze. "As a powerful Pureblood, his mother's traits were unmatched. She became a lord's wife, a priestess to his church, and with her by his side, their combined strength, Lord Alessandro conquered his enemies, became king of his territory, and she became the symbol of power to his kingdom. Their territory expanded, their powers increased, and the Highguard seeing their worth gave them status within the ranks of their elite echelon. Despite being warned, King Alessandro's greed ravaged the land, and those he didn't murder fled. When the stronghold was attacked, Gaia went missing. King Alessandro believed she died, and he mourned her and their unborn child."

Unborn child. Ansel. Clio's heart sank. Bronte breathed in and out, her lungs struggling, and Clio heard her heartbeat slowing. Conserving her energy and trying to buy time, Clio waited and listened while Bronte talked. Someone had to be on their way.

"She was forgotten until rumors of Gaia and her shaman husband started spreading. King Alessandro wanted revenge, and with the Highguard's help they found the family. As punishment, Gaia was divested of her magic and then effaced from the Highguard's chronicles. It had been a vampire with mage traits, the only being strong enough to contain her magic without going insane. I hunted this vampire and learned there had been no magic. However, there was a boy. I searched him out."

"You didn't want him. You wanted his magic?" Clio asked as shock and horror tumbled through her.

"Yes. As does the Fellowship. They told me he was here, and I was sent to retrieve him. They thought he would follow me. Then there was you." Bronte coughed, weakly covered her mouth, and lowering her hand, looked at the blood staining her palm and smiled at Clio. "When I found him, I thought I was going to have to fight them, kill them, had planned for it, but his father and mother were dead, and his family's farm was burning to the ground." Her gaze went through Clio as if she was reliving the day. "He was on his knees in the middle of the inferno, his skin melting from his skeleton, his thick hair gone, and the skin was curling over his skull. The flames had wrapped him in their deadly embrace. I saved his life and gave him a new one."

"You set him on fire," Clio whispered.

"I gave him back to the flames. Complete circle," Bronte corrected, half dazed. "In those days there was respect for a life and a death. Regrettably, his magic is beyond me. I couldn't access it, he couldn't access it, no matter what I did."

"What did you do to him?" Clio growled. Gods, what had the sociopath done to him?

"Time is slipping from me."

"What the fuck did you do to him?" Clio tried standing. Her head spun, nausea sloshed in her stomach, her legs gave out, and she slid down the rough wood wall. Splinters snagged her tank top, tearing holes in the cotton, and dug into her skin. She held back a whine, there was nothing she could do about it.

"What had been done to me. I trained him to be an assassin. To be one of mine." She eyed Clio, her lips drew back, and scarlet, like fresh blood, filled her eyes. "When I knew I had broken him, I pinned him down and took his throat. He was too weak, too scared, too dependent on me to defend himself. After I took his throat and his blood, I took his body. He was no longer Ansel Wolt, no longer his own person, but Brando and he was mine. I owned him. I own him."

Bile threatened her throat; she was going to be sick. Her body shook with fury. "You tortured him. You violated him!" Clio yelled, her chest seizing, as tears slipped down her heated cheeks and vehemence raged inside of her like a storm with the wrongness. With the evil that had taken advantage of him. She thought she knew anger. Thought she understood hate. She was wrong. So very wrong. She understood their definitions. What she felt and what was clouding her mind was pure loathing. Clio detested Bronte. Wanted to see her dead. Wanted to use her wolf's teeth to tear the dhampir apart and feel her heartbeat stop. Then Ansel would be free of her claws. And when Bronte was nothing more than a memory, Clio was going to hold Ansel and never let him go.

Ever.

Bronte stood on weak legs, her eyes gleaming scarlet, her cheekbones protruding from under pallid skin, the tissue tightening, and she crossed the cabin with a crocked gait. "When I'm done, when he looks at you, he'll see me."

"Leave me alone," Clio demanded. Panic tangled with fear to coil inside of her as she scooted backward to the wall, and there was nowhere she could go. No escape.

"The bond you share will cease to exist at the same time the spell will dissolve. You'll have your memories, but you won't have him. He's mine. Always was, always will be." Bronte knelt beside her, and reaching out, twined Clio's hair between her fingers. Holding a blonde curl, she declared, "Recognize me as Milanka Telep, dhampir, scion to Lord Dario Telep, and the last of his line."

"No." Clio slapped her hand from her hair. She didn't care about the spell, her memories, the reason he deceived her. Clio was going to lose the bond. Her mate. The feel of him. "I'm a werewolf."

"You're a Wight," Milanka whispered, her lips moving around the words.

Half human.

Clio gasped as Milanka shoved her back to the wall and straddled her, causing pain to sear through her. She tried fighting back, failed, her arms disobeying her demands, her body feeling weak and broken. Hissing, she gripped Clio's face, twisted her head to the side, and exposing her neck, drove her fangs into her skin, making Clio cry out.

"No," she whimpered.

Milanka moaned, her lips cold on Clio's hot skin. When her fangs pulled free, Milanka held her face in shaking hands and turned her, their gazes meeting—hers a deep garnet. Her lips were swollen, and scarlet slid from her mouth with her words. "Virgin blood. You taste innocent. Like Brando used to. His little pure of heart."

Milanka spent her life destroying Ansel and was spending her last minutes alive trying to destroy her. Clio weakly held the dhampir's shoulders and shuddered as she felt her blood, her life being taken from her, drained from her, but there was something else going on, more than Milanka taking her blood. The bite. Milanka was dying. Whatever made her sick was going into Clio's system and started to destroy her from the inside out. It was bad. Diagnosing herself ... she was hemorrhaging. She wasn't going to make it. Whispering with desperation in her breath, she begged, "Help me, Ansel."

His six-four height and broad shoulders stood in front of her as he stared down at her, his cinnamon eyes rolling bronze, his passion in their liquid depths, and his muscles flexing under sun-tanned skin. His strength enveloped her as his arms wrapped around her and cradled her in a protective embrace. Clio inhaled a ragged breath, her heart stuttered in her chest, then Milanka was twisting her, and fangs pierced the other side of her throat. She felt her pulse slow, and her body caved under Milanka's weight. Clio opened her eyes as much as she could to stare at the wall of the cabin as her hands dropped to her sides. She was losing. She was going to lose.

"You're dying. Bleeding internally," Milanka coughed the words, peppering crimson on lips resembling rotting strawberries. "He'll try to save you. He'll use my blood, our blood to save you only to poison you. Despite hating me, he'll seal your fate, and you'll become me. If you live."

From hooded eyes, wet with tears, Clio watched Milanka sit against the far wall, her legs out in front of her, her hair flat on her head, her ashen skin glistening as if a fine sheen of oil coated her, then she pulled the sword free. With clumsy movements she placed the fine blade across her thin thighs, then feathered the steel with her fingertips, her eyes glazing over as if remembering days gone by.

"It's his longsword. I've kept it all these years." Milanka met Clio's gaze. "A silent kill."

"He'll kill you." Forced to watch his mate die or do anything in his power to save her, Ansel would save her. There was no doubt.

"Yes. I failed my mission. The punishment is death." Milanka rested her head against the wall behind her and closed her eyes. "Complete circle."

Too weak to keep her eyes open, Clio closed them, blocking Milanka from her sight as a chill skated across her clammy skin. Shock. Blood loss. Whatever disease she had been infected with. Wanting to feel Ansel before she lost consciousness, Clio tried their bond. She was too injured, too sick to sense anything. Even her wolf felt as if it had abandoned her. Alone and dying, Clio tried wrapping her arms around herself, attempting to keep some body heat, and failed. She was too weak. She was cold and getting colder. Did she want him to find her? She didn't know. If she lost him, she was better off dead. Her jumbled thoughts became erratic, she couldn't think, and her wolf howled a sad cry as the darkness crawled toward her to take her.

She didn't know who she was going to be if she woke up.

CHAPTER ELEVEN

Ansel walked out of the office, Quinn, team leader of Deimos, right behind him as RV One, an armored response vehicle, left the parking lot and headed out of Foxwood. Why it was leaving had his imagination running wild and his heart thundering.

"Who requested a vehicle?" Ansel asked.

"Detective Langston. The report isn't complete, but her transmissions stated there was an elf from one of the courts harassing hikers near Mount Shasta. He threatened them, chased them, and yelled at them. Aggressively. Whatever the hell that means. The sheriff's department took the call, then handed it over to the OPI. After she took him into custody, it was determined he wasn't from either of the courts, and the OPI decided it didn't want responsibility of him, so she called an enforcer," Quinn explained. "The prisoner is Cascade's problem."

"She'll bring him here?" Ansel asked for confirmation.

"Affirmative."

It wasn't Bronte or the Fellowship. It made him feel better. But it meant Jordyn wasn't returning to Foxwood anytime soon, and he needed to keep Clio from leaving. When he turned in the direction of her parking space, he didn't see her crossover and his heart jumped to his throat.

"Where is Doctor Hyde?" he growled. Ansel didn't wait for an answer. He went back to the office, slid his card, and couldn't get through the security procedures fast enough. Once through the last door, he skidded to a stop when Mandy met him in the hall. "Where is she?"

"The emergency tracker alerted me fifteen seconds ago. I tracked her from the time she left Foxwood, and when she stopped. It's been thirty minutes," Mandy explained, her eyes bright violet and worry lining her face. "She said she was going to see her parents before someone told them about the two of you."

"You didn't stop her?" Ansel knew it wasn't Mandy's fault.

"I didn't know. Listen to me ... when she stopped, the system went black, there was a delay, and then the emergency tracker came on. It means—"

"I know what it fucking means," he growled. Opening himself to their bond, he felt her weakness, grief, and her essence slipping from him, the bond becoming a thin line, and the emptiness nearly caused him to go to his knees. "Get a med van to her location. Priority One. Code White. Ready the Purifiers. Have the Hollow's staff on standby, the med van will transport her." Priority One, full back up, with a response team. Code White, the situation would be concealed from the public, and it was the Purifiers job to eliminate the evidence.

"Affirmative." Mandy turned at the same time she started giving orders and received responses before she reached communications.

Ansel left the office, those inside watching as he headed straight to his truck, their murmurs going silent when the door closed behind him. Across the parking lot, he saw Rutger exiting the house and running in his direction.

"I have the details. I'll follow you. I'm calling Jo," Rutger said as he passed him.

"What about the OPI and her prisoner?"

"Fuck the OPI," Rutger growled. "Cassidy has the prisoner in custody and is awaiting transport. RV One's ETA is three minutes."

"Copy." Ansel got in his truck, started the engine, and headed out with Rutger and Aydian, team leader of Ares, following.

He couldn't help but feel indebted to the pack and was grateful for the support they were giving him. And Jordyn was going to be there. Through the gate, Ansel increased his speed, as the terminal dinged and beeped with updated information. Switching to navigation, a map came up to give him Clio's location, and it made his heart pound in his chest and a growl rumbled from him with his rage. She hadn't taken a direct route to her parents' house. What the hell had she been thinking? She was a free woman who had every right to see her parents, every right to drive wherever she wanted because she had no clue what was happening. He should have known she wanted to tell her parents about them. He was sure daughters did that. Sons, maybe. He was accustomed to not having anyone. Hell, he didn't have anything to tell anyone. Until now.

The farther he drove from Trinity, Ansel's fear raged out of control. He didn't know what he was going to find, what happened to her, and it scared him the living hell out of him. He desperately clung to their bond, as if he was physically holding onto her. Checking his rearview mirror, he saw Rutger and Aydian were with him. He didn't see Jordyn's red truck but knew it might take her a while to catch up to them. Their presence gave him the strength to keep from giving in and letting fear rule him. Mile after mile teased him, corner after corner threatened to destroy his control, then he rounded a curve, saw skid marks, her crossover, and his entire world dropped out from under him.

"Tesoro," he whispered, the air leaving his lungs. He pulled off the road, skidded to a stop behind what was left of her car, and after killing the engine, got out. Nearly stumbling to the shell, he saw the passenger side had been crushed into the interior, pools of fluids stained the ground, and shards of glass lay everywhere. The wreckage peppered the area but Clio was nowhere to be found. Ansel put his hands on his knees, bent at the waist, and stared at the gravel, dirt, skid marks and didn't know where to begin.

"Ansel," Rutger's stern voice sounded beside him. "She couldn't have gone far."

"I know. You're right," he replied as he straightened. Inhaling, he caught the sweet iron of Clio's blood—she had been hurt—there was her scent of sugar and spice, and riding low was another smell he immediately recognized. "She's here," he growled. He was going to kill her.

"I know she is," Rutger replied. "We need to look for her."

"No. I can feel Clio ... she's weak and getting weaker. The other is Bronte. She is here, I can smell her," Ansel corrected as he grabbed Rutger's arm. "Bronte did this. The Fellowship lied to me. Tonight could be a setup."

"Let me worry about that. Find your mate, and I'll direct the med van when it arrives." His gold glare met Ansel's bronze, and he nodded.

While Rutger grabbed the mic at his collar and started barking orders Ansel rounded the car, his senses picking up their scents, his instincts on high alert, his mind wanting to scream. Standing beside the wreckage, Rutger ordered a wrecker for her car, and confirmed the Purifiers were on their

257 CRIMSON STEEL   257

way to get rid of the debris. In a matter of minutes, it would look like nothing happened; there wouldn't be a sliver of glass, a dark spot in the dirt from oil, and they would botch the skid marks. The Purifiers would erase the accident. How that was going to help him with the Fellowship he didn't know. He kept his thoughts on Strong Lord, the possibility he had been set up, and how and why Bronte was where she was. It was better than imagining Clio hurt. Which was impossible when he was following the scent of her blood and the invisible thread between them, its weakness tugging on him, as it warned him he was too late.

He didn't have to track her. Didn't have to follow the trail of blood. Didn't want to see the crushed foliage. Someone had walked while the other had been dragged.

Clio. Through grasses and brush, his boots sinking in wet dirt, his patience was thinning and his fear escalating. When he saw an aged cabin, it sent every instinct blaring with a warning. Clio was there. Bronte was there. Both were weak, their heartbeats sporadic. Ansel unholstered his Glock 21, .45 caliber pistol, and with his free hand ripped the door from its rusted hinges. With his gun raised, he readied to fire on Bronte and made entrance. What he saw he didn't want to see. Clio was against the wall, her head on her shoulder, blood soaking her right side, her forehead split open, her lips swollen and bleeding, and bruises—deep purple and red— marred the skin around her eyes. The worst of it, the wound his eyes targeted, was the bite mark. Bronte fed from her. Almost killing her.

His chest caved with a piercing pain as if a blade entered him to puncture his heart. There was a chance what Bronte had done destroyed the spell holding Clio's memories. Was he scared? Negative. He didn't care, and if it had it would be a weight lifted from his shoulders. A lie put in its grave. As he glared at Bronte, Ansel understood exactly what she had done, knew how her mind worked. Like she counted on his reaction. After kneeling beside Clio, he straightened her so she was lying on the floor, her arms at her sides, and not slouched between the floor and wall, her neck at an odd angle. When she was breathing normally, he stood and walked over to Bronte. Her garnet eyes were sparkling white, then a pallid ivory as she watched him, and searching her he felt death taking her.

"What did they do to you?"

"Gave me to a SinEater. You can use your imagination," she replied flippantly, the shadows in her eyes telling a different story.

It was part truth, part lie, and he didn't care, not when she was dying. "Fed you your own sins. I think the sheer amount should have killed you outright."

Bronte smiled, her thin lips pulling into a grotesque curve, and she shrugged, as much as she could manage. "He's a bastard." She tapped the blade across her thighs with her fingertip, drawing his attention.

He eyed the hilt. The longsword was his. Silent death. It's image forever tattooed on his side. The one Bronte used to kill Dayton, her lover, and the shifter she used in order to trap Ansel.

"They want to use him to siphon your magic from you," she answered, her voice a rough whisper. "They call him El-chanan."

Ansel thought he recognized the name and stored the information for the future. "I made a deal with them, and they were going to hand you over to me," he said, ignoring the sword and hoping to bait her. He needed to know if the Fellowship set him up to take him to the SinEater—half angel, half human—who might be able to take what he wanted. "How did you escape them?"

Bronte coughed, blood peppering her lips, and shrugged again like she didn't care what they were going to do. "They betrayed me." She coughed again and cleared her throat. "I killed my guards. I am an assassin. You know that better than anyone, Brando."

The cold detachment holding her face was a lie; she cared, resented the people who betrayed her, and was struggling to accept her death. He didn't care, not with Clio behind him. But she told him what he needed to know. On his knee, he grabbed the sword by the hilt, and it fit his hand as it had ninety years before. He set it out of her reach—not that she was in any condition to take it—and grabbing her thin wrists he jerked her, and dragged her across the dirty plank floor. When they were beside Clio's unmoving form, he made her stand.

"You're going to save her." With her guttural snicker, he was tempted to take the sword and turn the steel crimson with her blood. He couldn't. Wouldn't. Ansel shoved Bronte, made sure she didn't move, then knelt next to Clio and held her face, her skin cold in his palms. "Tesoro, baby, wake up."

Voices drifted, and she swore she heard Ansel's through the freeze encasing her. She fought against believing it was real. Wouldn't allow herself to hope. Then contained fury laced every word, like he was trying to break through the ice spreading over her, creating layers upon layers, and she knew even if he was real, she wasn't going to escape her tomb. Clio tried diagnosing what was happening to her, it was the only thing she could do to keep her mind from freezing like her body had. She couldn't. Words were lost. Definitions cluttered in the mess of her head. It wasn't knowledge, it was instinct telling her was dying.

"Tesoro." Ansel pushed his wolf and strength into their bond, his need to strengthen her embedding itself deep within them both. "Open your eyes."

A small flame flickered, giving her hope, and soon warmth started to spread out from her middle, too weak to melt the layers of ice, but it was there, and she knew he was real. "Ansel," she whispered.

"I'm here. You need to help me," Ansel pleaded as he stared at her.

Without thinking, she nodded, or at least tried to. She mumbled, "Yes."

"That's my baby. I need you to drink something for me. Do you understand?" *Please understand.*

"Yes." Through swollen eyes she saw a blurry Ansel sitting beside her, Milanka across his lap, and raising her wrist, he took both hands and snapped bone, breaking it. Clio would have cringed if she could. Then he tore it open and crimson dripped from the break, white bone shone bright through the veil, and he held it over her. Poisoned. It was poisoned. He had no idea what he was doing.

"Drink, Tesoro," his deep voice ordered as his wolf's eyes begged her.

Tesoro. It struck something inside of her, unraveling a web, its ends fluttering then disintegrating as a wave of emotion and images saturated her broken mind. She battled to see them, remember them, and failed. All she saw were the crimson drops, like rain, falling toward her. She turned her head and felt them land on her cheek. No. No. If she didn't die, he was going to hate her. He was going to see Milanka and feel his pain every time he looked at her. She was going to lose him. "No," she whimpered.

Ansel wrapped his fingers around the leaking wrist, knew it wasn't going to be enough, but had to try. "Please, you have to. She's taken too much from you," he pleaded, his voice thick from fear. The pieces fell into place as Clio's heartbeat weakened. Stygian. The void between life and death where she was being held in stasis. Life. Death. Wight. Dhampir. Bronte sensed Clio was his mate and knew he would do anything to save her. Knew he wouldn't hesitate. He felt their bond weakening and her essence fading from him. "I can't lose you. I won't lose you, tesoro. Stay with me."

Tears welled and slid from the corners of her eyes as he repeated the words. She hated the desperation in his voice, the need, the loss, the pain. "No. Not like her," Clio cried.

Was he going to do this to her? Dhampir. To them? Was he going to make the decision for her the same way he did when he buried her memories? Was he going to take her life into his hands? Their bond gone. Never to feel her inside of him. She was going to hate him. Maybe it was for the best. Their bond would unravel, the threads fraying then decaying. She would be free of him, his lies, and his betrayal. Hanging his head in defeat and confusion, Bronte whispered something to him from her place across his lap, the frail words falling on deaf ears while a fight raged inside of his head. He didn't have a choice.

"I'm sorry," he growled. He couldn't wait any longer. With Bronte's wrist in his right hand, he turned Clio's face toward him with his left. "Forgive me."

Clio tried fighting his hold, and failed, and failed to stop him from holding her mouth open. The poisoned liquid poured into her, hitting her tongue and the back of her throat, its tang burning as she gulped it down for fear of choking. Fear, panic, and rage consumed every inch of her knowing she was going to be like Milanka. She would need blood to survive. She would feed. When Ansel looked at her, he would see the person who stole his innocence, turned his life into a nightmare, and tried owning him. He would see his enemy.

"Ansel, stop," Jordyn demanded from behind him.

"No. I'm losing her." Ansel squeezed Bronte's wrist, making bones shatter and crimson drip.

He felt a hand rest on his shoulder, her fiery power sinking into him, her force surrounding him with the comfort of the pack as if in an embrace. "It's enough. I can feel her leaving the Collective. If you continue, you will destroy the mate bond," Jordyn warned.

"Stygian." He wasn't going to watch his mate die. They weren't going to stop him when he was doing what he knew.

"I know. There's another way, and it might save her from crossing over."

Ansel risked looking away from Clio and met copper eyes with obsidian shards. He didn't know when they walked into the cabin, Rutger and Aydian, and hadn't heard the sirens that blared for a second then went silent. He had been focused on Clio and her heartbeat. "How?"

"Stop feeding her Bronte's blood," Jordyn replied. "Let Rutger have her."

"Negative. How?" Ansel demanded, his features shifting to his wolf's. He was going to guard Clio with his life. Without her he didn't have one.

"Clio needs your blood. You're pack and her mate. Your magic may save her."

"How do you know?" he questioned. Ansel didn't want to think about what Jordyn had done. "Our blood isn't the same. I'm not the same."

She didn't answer. Instead, Jordyn stared at him with liquid obsidian eyes, their depths roiling. "It's not going to matter."

Her voice echoed through him, around him, and shaking his head, he didn't know if giving his blood to Clio was going to work. They weren't the same and he feared the effect his magic would have on her. When Bronte consumed Clio's blood, she altered it, making it possible for Clio's body to accept it, absorb it, and then it would accept the vampire's sânge. Hunger for the element of magic that made a vampire, and when her body absorbed the blood, its magic would transform Clio's human DNA. Did it mean she was going to cross over? Was her werewolf half strong enough to fight the sânge? He felt their bond thinning, but it wasn't because the blood had taken her through stygian causing her to cross over. She was dying. Was it the SinEater? He didn't know. Damn, he didn't know enough to risk Clio's life and was too frantic to think straight. Feeling alone and helpless, he had nothing else.

"All right. All right." He let Bronte's wrist go as Rutger took her limp form from his lap. "What about her?"

"With the charges against her, by the authority of the Highguard, I, soothsayer for the Cascade pack, sanction the kill. Take her heart as proof. True death," Jordyn replied, her voice cold and sharp like a blade. "I know she's sick. Her body will be taken to the Hollow for testing, then held until the Highguard's regents retrieve it."

The Highguard. Jordyn made it a lawful execution. She protected him once again.

Bronte grunted. "You'll lose the Wight."

Jordyn grabbed her chin and squeezed, making Bronte cry, and growled, "You and those like you underestimate me, dhampir. I keep what is mine." Turning away from Rutger,

Jordyn crossed the room, picked up the sword, and handed it to Ansel as Rutger propped Bronte against the wall.

He met Jordyn's narrowed gaze for a brief second, understood the power she wielded, what she sacrificed, and there was only one way she would know anything about vampires. She would have asked Shadow Lord. He would find out the price the thousand-year-old vampire warlord demanded for the information and make it up to her. If it was possible. If he was alive. He nodded his head, made his vow, and turned his attention back to Bronte. She stood on weak legs, her hand hanging from taut tendons, her wrist seeping blood, her fingers turning black, and her eyes holding him as if she couldn't believe what was happening.

"Milanka Telep, it ends now. Complete circle."

"Brando, can you end me?" she whispered, stealing his name from him once more, while mocking his strength. "You cannot kill your master."

Master. He saw himself forcing the strength of his upper body, his arms, hands, and fingernails to dig and use as leverage as he crawled across the heated dirt and rocks as she walked backwards and away from him. The blistering sun beat down on him, his broken legs, shattered ankle, and bare skin. Around him the combined scent of his blood—she'd scored his thighs with a knife—and sweat saturated his nose, causing nausea to roll through him.

You're weak, Brando, undeserving of me.

Her laughter strangled him as he begged for her forgiveness from split lips covered in dust, his wounds secondary to pleasing her. He needed to be worthy of her. Nothing else mattered. Ansel gripped the hilt, his knuckles blazing white as he fought the feeling of helplessness, then battled his way back to the present. To stay in the here and now, he focused his attention on Paramedic Wyatt Gautier's presence, and Dr. Baines as he placed Clio on the gurney, her soft whimpers sounding loud in his head. With Milanka's pending death, Ansel slipped back to the past where he saw her raven hair curled in ringlets, her white eyes sparkling with scarlet jewels, her smile curving her rose lips, her whispers in his ear, and shook his head. He couldn't believe he allowed himself to be used, molded to be her slave, and felt her lips on his skin. He fought to see the sickened monster in front of him to break the hold she had on him. He didn't care about her circle, what she called him, what she thought was the truth. He knew the truth. He was Captain of Enforcers Ansel Wolt with the Cascade pack. Mate to Dr. Clio Hyde.

"I'm not Brando. I am Captain of Enforcers Ansel Wolt. I was never yours, Milanka." Driving the sword into her chest, he shoved, felt bone grate against the blade, and pushing harder, sent it through her heart and out her back, its tip sinking into the wood behind her. Her eyes widened with disbelief as her chest heaved and her body tensed. Fighting death, which Ansel knew was an eternity, she continued to stare at him. Then her knees gave out, and hanging on the blade, she tilted her head to look up at him.

"Peace," she breathed through crimson-stained lips.

"There's no peace in hell," Ansel promised with a growl. He held her gaze, her white eyes bled scarlet, life draining from their depths like a sieve, and with her final exhale she was gone. No cloak and dagger. No drama. Silence. Blood soaked her shirt, the crimson spreading, and he saw his past, their twisted past, and her torment play in front of him. The master of his fear and pain was no more. How did he feel? Disassociated. Scarred. Numb. Her death didn't take away the scars she etched onto his body and his mind. He would deal with the mess later. It wasn't yet finished … no, it had just begun. And it wouldn't be until he knew Clio was safe.

"Your reign of terror is over," he whispered as he pulled the blade free.

Milanka crumpled to floor like a broken doll, her pale face resembling porcelain, her perfect, ageless features frozen in time, and gazing down at her, he saw his freedom as he prepared to take her heart with crimson steel.

"Patient Doctor Clio Hyde, Wight, human/werewolf, injuries correspond with the confirmed car accident. Lacerations along the forehead and mouth. Bleeding has stopped. Contusions around the eyes, a subconjunctival hemorrhage in the conjunctiva of both eyes, pupils are unequal sizes, indicating a concussion. Multiple lacerations on the right side, there are shards of glass embedded. There are signs of abrasions from the seat belt," Dr. Baines began as they carried Clio out of the cabin. "Extreme blood loss, puncture marks on the left and right sides of the neck, both bleeding. High risk of infection. Aggressor, Milanka Telep, dhampir, vampire/mage, age unknown, illness unknown. Current state, deceased."

Clio sensed she was moving, being carted from the cabin on a gurney, and wanted to cry from relief. Then she recognized the familiar cadence of Dr. Baines' voice as he identified her injuries before he started giving orders. They found her and she was being rescued. Just as excitement and the feel of safety started to take root, dread poured through her, and tears burned her eyes once more. She heard Ansel's suffering, the bones of Milanka's wrist snapping like dry twigs, then tasted the venom from her veins as it landed on Clio's tongue. Fighting to stay conscious, she reached for the bond, needing to feel Ansel, needing to feel his strength, his support, and felt him drifting further from her. She was going to lose him. Milanka was going to take him from her.

"We're losing her," Dr. Baines stated.

No. I'm here, Clio wanted to assure them but couldn't find the strength. While Dr. Baines adjusted her and placed pads on her chest and arms, the quiet crawled closer, its comforting silence changing and twisting into a cold void of the monster she was becoming. Too weak to fight its force, she let it overtake her. The darkness wrapped her in its embrace, and she faded into the nothing.

"Sit there," Dr. Baines ordered when Ansel stepped into the med van.

Clio's face was swollen and stained with purple, red, and nearly black bruises, her split lips began bleeding, and she looked small, weak, and helpless. He failed to protect her for a second time. His heart raced when he saw she was hooked up to three monitors, each beeping and dinging. The cords stretching out from them looking like they were plugged into her did not help him. The sight unnerved him and began unraveling any control he might have had, and he started doubting whether he was going to be able to keep it together. Ansel couldn't fight for control over his worry and fight the need to touch Clio, so he gave in to the one less likely to cause her problems. Taking her small hand, stained in blood, in his shaking one, he held it and felt the chill of her skin, then raising it, kissed her fingers.

"Stay with me, tesoro." Bringing his wolf close to the surface, he once more shoved his strength into the frailness of their bond, hoping to feel her and it might strengthen her.

"What did you do?" Dr. Baines asked as he watched one of the monitors.

"We're fated mates. I'm giving her the strength of my wolf through our bond," Ansel answered. And prayed it kept her from crossing over.

"I didn't know, I'm sorry," he started as he eyed Clio, then Ansel. After clearing his throat, he continued, "It's not enough to stabilize her, however it is strengthening her. How long can you continue?"

He was a Pureblood werewolf, his magic growing in strength for over a hundred years, and would have replied for as long as he had to. However, what he felt made him pause, the unnatural strain as if he was pouring his power into a black hole and to secure its existence it needed to consume him. He feared it was the sânge—the word meaning blood, descent, birth—altering her DNA to ensure a cross over. "Unsure."

"We'll met you at the Hollow," Rutger said from the open door, getting Ansel's attention.

"I don't know what Jordyn did," he admitted, his voice weak. He was being pulled in a thousand different directions; Milanka was dead, and Clio was fighting for her life. But if Jordyn was indebted to Shadow Lord and the Highguard, because of him, he wouldn't be able to live with himself.

"What she had to. Kith and kin." Rutger didn't wait for a response. His eyes rolled gold as he slammed the doors closed, leaving Ansel with Dr. Baines, then he hit the side three times.

"When you're at your limit, stop. Now take off your BDU top, and I'll start the transfusion." Dr. Baines, working efficiently and with speed, began taking needles protected in plastic sleeves from a drawer, and setting them on the counter, took plastic line from another and unrolled it.

Despite the rushed orders, Ansel felt time slow down to an excruciating crawl—the transfusion was taking too long, the drive was taking too long, and he knew they wouldn't make it to the Hollow in time. Anxiety held him in its claws as he unbuckled his thigh holster, tactical belt, and placing them in a secured drawer, no one wanted an armed werewolf in the med van, started on his BDU top. He didn't notice the rough ride or the speed while he tried keeping his thoughts on the buttons and his fingers moving and not on why he was doing it. Clio. Cross over. Dhampir. Consoling himself with Milanka's death kept him from losing his mind.

She is gone, he told himself again, *I'm free.* He let the truth of it sink in while he draped the top across his lap and waited for Dr. Baines' order.

"Extend your arm."

On auto, Ansel did what he was told. Placing his arm underside up on the armrest, he watched Dr. Baines clean the area, then he inserted a needle with a catheter. After he attached the end to the tube, he prepped Clio's arm—she didn't react, didn't move—and repeating the process, attached the tube to her. To calm his worry and his wolf, Ansel kept her heartbeat and her soft breathing in his ears, and watched her chest rise and fall with her shallow breaths.

"Infusion is successful and functioning. Are you monitoring?" Dr. Baines asked no one in the med van.

"Affirmative. All readings are coming through. We're standing by," a male voice coming from a speaker replied.

"Inserting second IV."

"Why?" Ansel asked, his voice strained. Did it mean there was something else wrong? How many monitors and IVs did she need?

Meeting Ansel's gaze, he gave him a soft smile. "Painkillers and I'm sedating her. As soon as we arrive, they'll take her to OR, and start removing the glass from her side. Then they'll do a full body scan to make sure there aren't internal injuries."

Dr. Baines continued to explain while Ansel told himself he needed to calm down, the doctor was doing everything in his power to help Clio, and she was going to be all right. She was going to make it. When Dr. Baines noticed Ansel's attention hit its max, he went back to monitoring Clio and talking to someone at the Hollow. Ansel censored himself; it wouldn't do either of them any good if he exhausted himself and blacked out. Leaning back, his strength continuing to drain from him—as if she was drinking straight from his vein—he watched crimson flow from him to Clio. Every instinct rode him, telling him to take her in his arms, bring her somewhere no one would find them, and protect her.

"ETA fifteen minutes," Wyatt reported from the front.

"If I haven't stabilized her, you'll need to walk with us to the operating room," Dr. Baines stated.

"Understood." Anything for her. Ansel stared at Clio and didn't see the injuries from the crash; he saw her delicate features and the gentleness she embraced. He saw the woman he shared his night with and needed to share his life with. He wasn't willing to look away from her, fearing if he did he would lose her, as if she was a ghost sent to torment his heart. As time ticked down, he memorized every element of her, every freckle, the shape of her lips, the curls framing her face, the way she felt lying beside him. His wolf howled, his heart ached, as if everything they shared the night before, including their mating, was evanescent.

"She's a fighter, Captain Wolt," Dr. Baines started. "I've worked with her. And you can see here, she's already improving. Mistress was right when she insisted on the transfusion."

And it came with a price no one was talking about. Ansel pulled his gaze from Clio, met light green eyes stained with worry. The witch, Esme of the Lapis Lazuli coven's son, couldn't mask his feelings. Ansel looked at the monitor and nodded. He felt numb, powerless, empty, and didn't have anything to say in response. His blood would help her heal from the injuries she sustained from the crash, and replenish her blood supply, but would it be enough to stop her from crossing over? He didn't know. Didn't want to think about it.

To distract himself he checked his cell. By the time they reached the Hollow, the crew working the accident would have cleared it while the Purifiers sterilized the scene and the cabin, leaving zero evidence behind. To the outside world it never happened. He wished it was that easy. He wanted to go back and change the morning. While Dr. Baines worked in silence, the monitors beeping and dinging and recording information he didn't understand, Ansel grappled for control. He needed to be Captain of Enforcers—cold, determined, dominate. Fighting against the desire to fall into the pit of failure and grief, he reminded himself he had a meeting with Strong Lord. He was a dog on a chain desperate to capture Milanka, he wanted her dead, wanted to tear her apart for torturing him, and was going betray his pack by handing over Jordyn's weaknesses for the Fellowship to exploit. He straightened, pushed his shoulders back, and felt the weight of Clio's life settle on them. No, he wasn't going to buckle under the pressure, he had to ensure Strong Lord believed him, it meant he couldn't give away his fear for Clio and the growing satisfaction of knowing Milanka was dead.

"Entering the Hollow. Doctor Barsacq is waiting with his team," Wyatt reported as they entered the underground facility.

Ansel listened to the monitors, the terminal's notifications, the chime as security cleared them, and then the road swooped down, and darkness blanketed them. In an instant the med van's headlights came on at the same time lights along the wall lit the tunnel. After following the two-lane drive for another half mile, the med van slowed. Going to the left, they headed to the emergency entrance where Wyatt turned around and backed up to a set of double doors.

"Doctor Hyde is stabilized for the moment. I'm going to end the transfusion, but I need you to be there if she declines. Surgery might be hard on her system," Dr. Baines explained as he removed the catheter from Ansel's arm.

"I'll be here." He wasn't going to let Clio out of his sight until he had to leave for the meeting. Even then he was coming straight back.

Something inside of her stirred, a fire burning in her veins she didn't understand, not when she had been cold. Freezing. Buried in ice. She'd given into the frost as its chill coated her to entomb her and knew she wasn't going to live through it. Over the rushed voices sounding above her, around her, she knew if she could taste the heat, it would be Ansel, his wolf, his desire. She needed to see him. Forcing her eyes open, mere slits, she saw him. He looked worried, his hair shoved back, the demons darkening his eyes, and she was the reason. Would be the reason for eternity. "Ansel," she whispered through tears. She didn't want to lose him.

"Baby, I'm here." Ansel grabbed her hand, and holding it as tight as he risked, jogged beside her as the team of doctors and nurses rolled Clio down a hallway.

"Captain Wolt, you can't go any farther," Dr. Barsacq said, his dark eyes showing his empathy.

Ansel nodded his acknowledgement, then leaned closer to Clio. "I'll be right here, beautiful, waiting for you," he promised as he kissed her lips.

When he released her hand, he took her foundation from her, and Clio's mind raced with loss. She didn't want to be alone. She felt his fingertips on her palm and then he was gone, and she closed eyes. There was nothing else she wanted to look at. Keeping his image in her mind, because she feared it was going to be the last time she saw him, her heart ached and her wolf went silent. Without Ansel to hold onto, she couldn't ignore the orders and responses as they echoed. Someone demanded anesthesia, and she wanted to protest until they said the glass in her side was worse than they expected. Apparently, there was an infection. And the bite marks on both sides of her neck had started seeping liquid. Another infection. She wasn't healing, which gave her hope, as slim as the rational side of her warned, that whatever Milanka thought she accomplished hadn't been successful.

Maybe I'm going to make it out of this, she thought, prayed.

More orders were given, soft replies she didn't understand. It was getting jumbled in her head, and she was sure she couldn't feel her legs. She fought the cluttered mess of her thoughts and focused on key words—infection, Milanka, antibiotics. If that wasn't enough, she tried turning Clio into Ansel's worst nightmare. The bitch wasn't going to leave her alone even in death. Autopsy. Blood transfusion. Progress.

Clio would have laughed at the irritated demands if her mind wasn't failing her. She was sluggish, in pain, was struggling not to panic and her emotions were an out-of-control roller coaster while images teased her. Were they moving her? She didn't know, couldn't see clearly. The world was a blur as un-controlled tears slid from the corners of her eyes just as an oxygen mask was placed over her face. Above her, she recognized the nurse, Rena Foy, gazing down at her with soft brown eyes. Clio knew her well—Illuminate, wolf/elf, gentle, caring, baked cookies, she loved chocolate chip ...

CHAPTER TWELVE

Ansel paced the concrete hallway, windows and doors lining one side while the other was a solid wall, a gold glow from overhead lights softening the hard the surfaces. With each step, his boots were silent on the shiny flooring while his wolf prowled his insides and he waited for news. A nurse, Paul Collis, Wight, wolf/human, had taken two pints of blood from him, and he was prepared to give more, his very last drop if it saved Clio, but was denied. He pushed his body too far, and with the meeting with Strong Lord pending he couldn't risk being weak. The second time Paul met him, he gave Ansel a protein drink and several nutrient bars, then disappeared without telling him a damn thing about what was happening to Clio.

"How are you doing?" Rutger asked. His hand rested on the butt of his handgun, his board shoulders filled out his BDU top, and his confidence radiated from him, while his face held grim creases.

"I'm a fucking mess," Ansel answered honestly. "And I have no idea what's happening."

"The OR has been locked down and guards have been posted at the door. Once she is out of surgery, they'll transfer her to the intensive care unit."

"Locked down, guards?" Ansel asked as his heart sank.

"Affirmative." Rutger eyed him.

"She's going to cross over." It wasn't a question. It was an admission of his guilt. "I did this to her."

"Don't. If this hadn't happened the way it did, I wouldn't have believed it. It's the coincidence of all coincidences. Wrong place, wrong time."

It was. It made him question how Milanka had gotten there. They both stilled when Jordyn started toward them, her hand on her hip, her right hand on her gun.

"News?" he asked.

"They've done what they can. It's taking time for her to heal from the injuries sustained from the accident, then the infection and fever from the virus Milanka was carrying. It's aggressive, and destroying her immune system ... white blood cells and red blood cells. They fear it's suppressing her werewolf's abilities, while the fever could result in brain dam-age and febrile seizures. There are signs of a cross over, but it isn't progressing. Somehow, it's been neutralized, for the moment," she explained. "She remains with the Collective."

Ansel sensed Clio in their bond—weak, almost as if she was standing a distance from it. Feeling her, sensing her made part of him relax while it did nothing to the guilt filling his veins. She was going to cross over. "What's next? Can I see her?"

"Negative. They're putting her in a medically induced coma, then moving her to the intensive care unit while they try to combat the virus."

"Try to combat the virus." He didn't like the doubt in her voice.

"She is my mate. I have to see her," Ansel growled. He didn't want Clio fighting for her life alone, she needed to know he was there. His wolf howled for her, needing to protect her, to cradle her in his arms as if using his body to shield her from the world.

"She isn't completely under, and Doctor Barsacq believes your emotions in the bond will counter the drugs and she'll waken before her body is healed. No one knows how she's reacting to the virus and again no one knows why the cross over has stalled. They want to watch her." Jordyn's voice had taken on a cool tone, while holding her compassion, and her eyes gleamed onyx for a breath.

"I hate this," he mumbled. His rational mind understood, his wolf did not. Not. One. Fucking. Bit.

"We need to get ready for the meeting," Rutger advised as he went to Jordyn's side, and putting an arm around her, drew her to him.

If he hadn't been watching, he wouldn't have seen the look of pain scar Jordyn's face and her shoulders lower. He didn't know what was happening, not in its entirety. He knew what was in front of him. His mate was fighting for her life. If she died, he would follow. The mating bond had thrown him in waters way over his head. Clio opened his eyes and gave him a new world. Damn she was like a hurricane in his veins, and he couldn't get enough of her.

He didn't know what Jordyn was feeling, sensing, as a soothsayer, and he didn't know what Shadow Lord asked of her in exchange for information. He didn't know how she truly felt about him handing over a list of her weaknesses, fake as they were. It put her in danger and made her a target. He fucking didn't know a whole damn lot. But this wasn't the time or place to discuss it. He needed to find out if Strong Lord set him up, and if the leader of the Fellowship knew his prize possession had escaped him and was dead.

"Copy," he replied, his eyes rolling bronze. "Let's go."

An hour later, Ansel was driving up a single-lane logging road shrouded by trees, the truck bouncing over water breaks, making equipment rattle while the terminal, tracking his location, beeped and dinged. He was biting at the bit to tell Strong Lord Milanka was dead and buried, or dead and her remains would soon be in the hands of the Highguard's regents. It meant the Highguard was going to be in Cascade with Baron Kanin. Strong Lord's violations against the canons and covenant weren't Ansel's cross to bear any longer. It was a level of freedom and the weight decreased to be sure, but just as Strong Lord had broken the covenant with Cascade, Ansel had broken his with the Fellowship, and punishment in whatever form was sure to follow. Nothing they did could be worse than him waiting to hear if his fated mate was going to live and then live long enough to cross over. His mind chased the wrong memories, and he could smell cinnamon on her breath, feel her skin against his, her thin fingers wrapped around his throat, her guttural moans echoing in his ears as she fed.

Clio a dhampir.

His past crashed down on him, making his skin crawl like snakes slithered over him, the revulsion of it churning in his stomach before he caught himself and cursed. It wasn't the same. They weren't the same. Milanka had been bred to be a trained assassin, became a sociopath with bloodlust. Clio was a healer, pure of heart, a caregiver given the trait of empathy, meek and quiet.

Not the same, he told himself. Like night and day. And when she crossed over and they lost their bond, would she feel the same way about him? Would she change? Would she accept her fate and feed like a vampire? His skin chilled, his blood slowing in his veins, and he was sure his heart was going to stop. Gods, he didn't know, and doubt made his entire being ache with loss. Then the one thing he feared most and forgot about in the chaos of the wreck and Milanka's death was the spell on Clio's memories. Was it intact? Or had it lost its hold on her? He was going to have to wait until she healed and regained consciousness. And when she did, she might hate him.

"Keep it together," he growled. He couldn't show weakness, couldn't have the stink of it on him when Strong Lord would smell it, exploit it. He might be a dog on a leash, one Strong Lord thought he chained to a tree, but he wasn't scared. Checking his terminal, he saw Aydian and team Ares were in position and Rutger and Jordyn had taken their posts. The shadows had been at the meeting place for over a day, hidden, their cameras and listening equipment in place to record Strong Lord accepting the list and admitting he knew where Milanka was. Or had been. Everything caught on video to ensure Ansel's protection and the truth, he confessed his part in the deception to deceive Baron Kanin, the pack, and Jordyn. Since Clio opened his eyes to the truth of his relationship with the Kanins, Ansel wasn't going to risk losing his family, not now, not ever.

"The road ends. I have to walk the rest of the way," he reported to the terminal. After pulling over, he parked, the passenger side close to the mountain, and killed the engine.

"Copy. Stay alert," Rutger ordered.

"Be careful," Jordyn said.

"Copy." Ansel made sure the interior lights remained off, and getting out of the truck, shoved his cell into his back pocket and started up the red dirt incline.

With his instincts on alert for the slightest movement, his senses searching for magic-born, his wolf readied for a fight. His breaths came in even inhales and exhales, his heartbeat a steady rhythm, he carried himself with confidence. He wasn't going to let anything give away his fear, the arrogance knowing Milanka was dead and no longer a threat, and he was surrounded by his own. Kith and kin. It was almost over.

Ansel marched up the narrow path, which was lined by shrubs, and the red dirt looked ruby under the sliver of silver gleaming above him. A warm breeze glided over his bare arms and pushed against his black T-shirt, cooling him while bringing the wild scents of the forest to his nose. Being outside calmed him further, gave him a place to collect himself, and soothed the edginess of his wolf. It gave him a quiet in which to think clearly and to streamline the chaos of his thoughts and what was happening around him. That seemingly was raging out of control.

When it was over, he was going to devote all his time to Clio, to help her heal the way she had helped so many others. He would be by her side, nothing between them. With more confidence than he ever possessed in his life, he straightened his shoulders and embraced the authority bestowed on him by Baron Kanin. The next couple of steps took him to a rock outcropping overlooking the valley and the mountain ridges beyond bathed in sliver. This was his home. The place where he and his fated mate would become a family.

"Gods, Clio, you better heal. I love you, tesoro," he whisper-prayed into the night sky. Seeking her in their bond, Ansel inhaled a sharp breath when he thought it felt deeper, her presence stronger, and it added to his resolve.

He backed away from the ledge when a disturbance shifted the air, changed its purity, then added an electric hum. In a second a dragon swooped to his right, and eyeing him with emerald eyes, a woman slid off its back. It took off, flying higher and higher, its head searching left and right before it hovered, then landed farther from him as if taking its post. *Interesting.* Ansel kept the dragon, a Pukys, originally from the Baltic states, its other form a giant cat, in his line of sight. In front of him blue eyes glared at him from a perfectly sculpted face, her blonde hair hanging in ringlets down to her waist. They swayed side to side as she sashayed toward him. He didn't know why the Kaia—once a benevolent spirit now turned demon—was there.

"Crimson Prince," she greeted with an exaggerated bow that made her hair tumble over her shoulders.

When she straightened, she stood a few inches shorter than Ansel. Not unusual when he was six-four, but where Clio was five-four and fit his body perfectly, the Kaia was close to six feet tall. Wearing a tight, black top that hugged her curves, black leggings wrapped around her long legs, and flat boots, she dressed for the ride through the sky. Ansel noticed the boots, because he assumed they were easier to run in. As a female member of the Fellowship, and part of the Cloaked, her only companions were the creatures within the walls of their compound, prison. They didn't receive visitors, weren't allowed to circulate among the magic-born in the Cascade territory. It made Ansel a popular person when he attended the meetings, and the Kaia was always interested in news from the outside world, whether it be about the latest fashions, celebrities, or foods. He didn't consider her a friend, but he hadn't considered her an enemy.

"Fiala, where is Strong Lord?" Ansel asked, getting to the point, his instincts telling him he had been set up. When he scented another carrying the same smell—a severe sharpness like metal shavings, which all the Fellowship seemed to be drenched in—it solidified his suspicions.

"He wouldn't waste his time with such a trivial errand," she responded as she placed her hands on her hips and eyed him with a blue glare.

"If the list of Soothsayer's weaknesses is trivial then I guess you don't need it," Ansel challenged. She was mocking him, and he could feel her amusement on the air. "Tell Strong Lord this won't happen again."

"Little Prince, as if he needs the list. It was a test to see how badly you wanted the dhampir. Now he knows when he jerks your chain, you'll betray those who consider you their kith and kin. He owns you." She twirled two fingers in a blonde curl and smiled at him. "Being untrustworthy is an ugly character trait. You don't want it exposed, do you? Hand over the list and we'll hand over the dhampir."

You've jerked my chain for the last time, he wanted to roar. Keeping himself under control, he reminded himself they didn't know. "Negative," he growled. The accident, Milanka, the entire situation had been contained and erased as if it never happened. But it had, and Clio was paying the price for it, and he was wasting time.

"Don't disappoint him. You have no leverage here. Strong Lord granted your request, then you lied to Cascade, betrayed them and their soothsayer. You've betrayed your mate. What will your little Wight think when she finds out you're a traitor and stole her memories?" Fiala took a step toward him. "You owe your life to the Fellowship. Hand over the list."

"Negative. There is no list, like there's no dhampir," Ansel countered. "While I would have preferred to have Strong Lord, I'll take the three ... four of you." Prisoners were fine with him. The more the merrier.

Fiala laughed, a light resonance that drifted with her arrogance. "You're right about the dhampir, not that it won't be hard to get her back ... she is dying. Well used by the SinEater and Dallan, you know their appetites and fetishes. But there is a list, and I'll be taking it."

They hadn't protected her from him, the pack, the Highguard, and they weren't helping her. No, they imprisoned her, tortured her, and used her. Dallan, his full name Beast of Leetir Dallan, originated from Irish folklore, had a human head, but his lower body was that of a beast, and he carried a deadly virus. Ansel cringed with the thought and wasn't sure how he felt about it. His emotions were erratic, and he needed to get back to the Hollow. Thinking back to the conversation he had with Milanka, he realized she hadn't said anything about Dallan. Why? She was a liar and sociopath who knew it would take time for anyone to diagnose what she had passed onto Clio. Dammit, he needed to be by her side.

Focused on the task in front of him, he clicked the mic clipped to his collar. "Beast of Leetir Dallan infected Milanka." With the information, Dr. Baines would know how to help her.

"Copy. Relaying."

"Milanka. Are you trying to protect your lover?" Fiala stepped closer to him, and watching him with a humored gaze put her hands on his chest. Slowly moving them up his T-shirt, her pale skin a stark contrast to the black material, and over his muscles, she lifted the gold chain from around his neck and held the medallion in her hand. "Your lover?"

"Negative." The thought sickened him.

"You could have had me, Prince, but you chose another. Strong Lord has made you nothing but a dog on a very short leash and has given us the authority to jerk it whenever the whim moves one of us." Clenching the chain and tightening it around his neck, his skin pinching in the links, she held his gaze and laughed. "Give me the list."

"Negative." Ansel grabbed her wrists and squeezed, wanting to crush bones. Then she whined, and turning her around, her back against his chest, he held her. The sensation of her that close to him made nausea slosh in his stomach and set his skin on fire. It was the mating between him and Clio and how it remained active. She was his.

"You're making a mistake, Crimson Prince. Strong Lord will punish you," she threatened through clenched teeth.

"You're under arrest for harboring a fugitive from Cascade and the Highguard. You violated the covenant with Cascade, broke the Highguard's canons, attempted to extort information from a high-ranking officer within Cascade and an enforcer, and you conspired to use information to threaten the life of Soothsayer Jordyn Langston, scion of Prime. Charges of torture, rape, kidnapping, and imprisonment will be brought against the Fellowship of the Stone. Not to mention Dallan, who didn't alert Baron Kanin of his presence." Ansel knew he was going to face his own punishment, but he didn't care, because then he was going to cut his ties. Half of his nightmare was over.

The dragon unfurled its wings, flaring the eight-foot expanse as if it was going to fly when three wolves emerged, followed by Aydian, team leader of Ares, his steel blue eyes holding zero emotion. Aydian Collins had been medically discharged from the military after therian mountain lions turned savage and attacked him and his team. The attack left him unusable and unstable and with the military discharging him with the designation of *unsound mind*. It gave Patriot Angels, PA, the authority to take him into custody. Aydian spent three years being experimented on until the government disbanded the organization. His connection to PA hadn't ended with the disbandment. Aydian changed his last name to Riordan, taking his mother's maiden name, when he found out his father had been part of the organization.

"Stay where you are, dragon, and I won't shoot you out of the sky," he warned, his voice a low growl. He stood with a rifle tucked into his shoulder, and his demons in his gaze.

Seeing the situation was well under control, the wolves sank back into the night, taking their places among the shadows, their job of assisting them complete. They wouldn't shift into their human form, not around the Pukys, the Kaia, or the two others, to reveal their identities. No one knew the shadows' identities, their places among the enforcers, soldiers, slayers changing as needed.

"Enforcers. You've betrayed us," Fiala accused, the tremble in her voice giving away her shock.

"You can't be surprised," Ansel began, his lips by her ear. Letting a growl tangle in the discontent he felt holding her, he seethed, "This dog is no longer on a leash."

"Two have been taken into custody and are in RV One. The Kaia will be transported in RV Two," Aydian reported. "How the hell is the dragon supposed to be transported?"

"Eero is going to shapeshift," Ansel ordered. "Aren't you?"

"No he isn't," Fiala answered. "He is going back to the stronghold."

Like hell. Ansel tightened his hold on her, his werewolf strength easily overpowering her, and she dropped her head. "He's in Cascade custody, and if he doesn't shift, we'll tranq him," he threatened.

"You heard Captain Wolt." Aydian gave a sideways glance, his gaze turning cold.

Chenoa, her dark hair back in a braid that ended at her waist, her coffee eyes holding an edge of blackberry, stepped to his side, her tranq gun at the ready. If she noticed the disdain creasing her team leader's face or felt the reluctance radiating from him when he gave the order, she ignored it well.

Ansel focused his attention on Eero, and started, "Three seconds. Three. Two." He was about to say one when lights, like sun on glitter, sparkled, showering the dragon's form and lighting the immediate area. When it was over and the lights faded, a cat resembling a Eurasian Lynx—its amber eyes lined in black, with black fur-tipped ears—stood staring at them. "RV Two."

"Sir." Aydian clicked the mic clipped at his collar. "Rainey, escort the cat to RV Two."

With the order, Chenoa slung the tranq gun over her shoulder and waited for Ansel to release Fiala. The female enforcer then stepped up with a pair of handcuffs made from Cobalt 27, a synthetic metal capable of suppressing the magic-borns' power. Her gaze was pensive, the underlying dark purple of her wolf bleeding through as she placed the first cuff on Fiala.

"You're going to regret this," Fiala fumed. "You'll never get the dhampir."

"Milanka Telep died this afternoon. Cause of death, sword through the heart. True death," Ansel explained. His words were cold, flat, and carried the past that weighed him down for over a century.

With her hands handcuffed behind her, Fiala froze, stared at him with ice blue eyes, her face reflecting surprise then fear. "You're lying."

"I killed her." A twisted redemption. "You know I'm not. Since she was a fugitive, the Highguard sanctioned the kill, and is here to take possession of the body," Ansel explained. "One of our people found her. You don't take very good care of your prisoners." The accident would remain a secret. That was until Clio crossed over and they had to explain what happened to Cascade's premier doctor. And his mate. A dhampir. *Not the same*, he repeated.

"Who knew after what they did to her she possessed the strength?" Fiala said flippantly, her curls bouncing around her.

She could pretend to not care, her offhanded reply suggesting Milanka had been nothing but a toy to use then dispose of. But there was something in her eyes ... fear, lack of confidence, he wasn't sure and he sure as hell didn't like it. He would be able to find out more, with Jordyn's assistance, when they were at Foxwood and in the underground holding cells of the Enforcer's office.

"Walk," Ansel ordered, as he pushed her in the direction of RV Two and the waiting enforcers.

They walked in silence, Aydian with Chenoa at his side, and the five team members circling them. Ansel shook his head when Aydian tried putting distance between himself and the female enforcer. Chenoa Matten, Pureblood; her parents were elders in the pack. They didn't have the prestige of the Kanins, Langstons, or the Alexanders—another family with hundreds of years of history—however, they held status. Following the mandates of the pack, she served as a pack soldier, and after completing the required two years, she joined the military where she served for ten. When she returned to Cascade, everyone questioned why she didn't stay with the military, but she applied for the enforcers and took her place among them. Chenoa was damn good at her job; disciplined, strong, took orders, completed orders, and didn't challenge those around her to prove her strength or her status. Why Aydian was having a hard time with her was anyone's guess. It wasn't like he was interested in her outside of the job—he was seeing a mage, Ava, who was serving Prime. Plus, Chenoa displayed zero interest in him. If the distrust continued, he was going to have to tell Rutger about it and they were going to talk to Aydian. Or Chenoa was going to transfer to a new team. They couldn't have mistrust and doubt among them, it would weaken the unit.

"Your chariot awaits," Ansel mocked as he opened the back door to the vehicle.

"You won't win this game, Prince," Fiala threatened.

"It's not a game," he replied. "Get in."

When Fiala and Eero were in the vehicle, shackled to their seats, with guns pointed at them, and the doors locked, Ansel stepped back. He watched both vehicles, and then Ares team, leave. The dirt road stretched out in front of him, the lights and diesel engines fading as they took a corner and turned out of sight, heading down the mountain. Part of it was over. It was hard to believe he was almost a free man.

"Milanka is dead," he whispered into the early morning darkness as if he didn't believe it. He never thought he would live to see it. He never thought he would live to see freedom. His days of looking over his shoulder, hiding the relationships with his kith and kin, and not doing anything that would attract attention for fear Milanka would take her revenge out on whoever was close to him was over. He didn't know when he hungered for freedom, the freedom to live his life, and to shed the chains of his past. A dog on a leash. The entire Fellowship thought they could call him to heel. Not anymore. He would have what he wanted. If Clio didn't hate him when she found out what he had done, and Strong Lord's punishment didn't kill him. Ansel kicked the dirt with the toe of his boot. He was close to having his dreams come true. After making his way to his truck, he got in, started the engine, and when the terminal was active, made a call.

"Both vehicles are being monitored. I'm heading to Fox-wood, Jo is with me, and we'll question the prisoners," Rutger explained. "Tactical alert has been terminated. Teams, soldiers, and patrols are returning to normal duty. Shadows remain active and will continue to watch the Fellowship."

A wave of relief washed over him, taking some of his anxiety with it. Questioning? Ansel knew the truth. Someone would ask questions, seemingly a routine interrogation, maybe throw in a threat or two to make it believable while behind a two-way mirror Jordyn was using her trait to read their minds. She would get the answers they wanted, and the prisoners would never know. "Copy. Is this going to the Highguard?"

"We're keeping this, at least part of it. The elf Jo took into custody, after he tried inciting a donnybrook, which means a fight, turned out to be Dallan's handler. Neither of them are supposed to be here. With a report filed with human law enforcement, we can't hide it, we'll have to report it to the Highguard. Since we believe the Highguard knew Milanka was with the Fellowship the entire fucking time and didn't do a damn thing about it, we're not handing over the prisoners. Screw them. Keeping them will show Strong Lord we're not going to let him get away with threatening the pack, and they'll give us leverage."

Keeping secrets from the Highguard. Confronting and challenging Strong Lord. "Copy. I'm going to the Hollow." Ansel didn't know how to feel.

"Copy. If you need anything, let me know."

"Us know," Jordyn said right behind Rutger.

Ansel smiled. *My family.* Despite the night and the coming repercussions, he couldn't help but believe everything was going to be all right. "Will do. Have a goodnight," he replied. Ending the call, he headed down the mountain toward the Hollow and his mate.

With threads of consciousness teasing her, waves of nausea lapped at her head, stomach, and bile threatened her throat while a chill skated over her. She could taste the sour liquid at the back of her mouth, inching toward her tongue like acid boiling up to spill over. Was she crossing over? Was it the virus? Her injuries? How long had she been there? How were they treating her? She didn't know any of the answers, the unknown creating panic to race in her veins like her blood and couldn't discern what hurt and what didn't. Again, she didn't think she could feel her legs, the numbness reaching into her arms and torso, and she couldn't move. They sedated her. It had to be. Unless the virus paralyzed her.

A damn repeat of when Milanka drugged her the first time. She hated the thought and feared the nightmares.

As if in answer a warmth laced her arm and told her they were giving her a sedative. She had to assume they were going to keep her under sedation and it had her wondering how bad off she really was. Her injuries from the crash hadn't been life threatening, but then whatever Milanka carried in her in blood—the virus and a dhampir—had to have contaminated the injuries. Clio didn't know anything about vampires let alone whatever the hell Milanka was.

More warmth spread from her arm, and feeling its effect flooding her system, wanted to scream, "No, no!"

She struggled to listen as people spoke, their voices raised, giving away an urgency, causing her heart to race, and she tried opening her eyes to see what was happening to her. It was a jumbled mess. She was trapped inside of herself like her body was her prison. As the drugs pulled her further under, a fog crawled over her senses, numbing them, and it closed in on her. Clio sank into the bond with Ansel, needing to feel him and assure herself he was there. Time slipped from her as feathers of essence greeted her. Gods, she could feel him.

I love you. Don't leave me, she wanted to beg him. *Don't leave me in this darkness.* His strength and love surrounded her and held her for precious seconds, bringing images of them together, then she slipped into the deep where the nothing waited.

His palms flattened on the window, his forehead resting on the cool glass as Clio filled their bond with her presence, her need pulling on him, her love filling fissures between them. But then she faded away. As if she was a ghost. "Tesoro," he whispered, the breath rough with his fear. His strength drained from him, his knees threatened to give out, and he struggled to hold onto her while giving himself to her to help her heal. To live.

"You have to get some rest," Rutger said as he placed his hand on Ansel's shoulder.

"What happened to Fiala and Eero?" he asked instead of responding. He needed to talk, needed to take his mind off the void sitting in the bond.

Straightening, Rutger lowered his hand, and they faced one another. Director Kanin, his brother, wore his worry on his face, and he saw exhaustion sitting in the lines fanning out from his mahogany eyes. Ansel saw dark pain, a remembered emotion sitting close to his thoughts.

"They're in holding cells awaiting interrogation. Baron Kanin thought it would be better to let them think about their confessions. The two others, Gurvir and Petras, were low-class demons and they were sent as backup. Neither cleared their presence in Cascade. They're also in holding cells. Strong Lord talked to Baron Kanin and explained since the pack is increasing its hold on its territory and expanding, he was feeling pressure from the Fellowship to find a weakness they could exploit. He claims to not care about the list, he is more powerful, but was going to use it to pacify the group. Prove his power," Rutger explained.

"Right." Ansel didn't believe Strong Lord. "The Fellowship would have used the information, of that I'm sure."

"Agreed. With the recording of your meeting, his people detained, its chaos, then with the Highguard on its way, the Fellowship has gone into lockdown. Which is fine. They won't make a move, giving us time."

"Time." Time was something he didn't have. Turning back to the window, his shoulders sank with his mood, exhaustion, and from the multiple machines Clio was hooked up to. They were beeping and dinging, their displays bright with information. She looked small, weak, and alone. "What does all of that stuff mean?"

"The virus hasn't responded to the medicine and it's causing her injuries to worsen," Rutger replied.

"What about crossing over?" Ansel had to pull the words from himself like they came from his soul, and then fought to give them sound.

"There's no sign. Doctor Baines thinks it's your blood. With her injuries and the virus there's no guarantee," Rutger responded quietly, hesitantly. As if he didn't believe it.

He knew better than anyone there was never a guarantee, but it didn't stop him from hoping, then from knowing hope was a bitch. "Understood. I'm going to stay here just in case." Because he was not going home to smell her, their shared scent, see her things, and recall the memoires from the night before. It would kill him. "I should have told her, before I trapped her."

"We're all guilty of making decisions in the heat of the moment. You did what you thought was best, for her protection. If the spell has been destroyed, she'll confront you, you can count on that, it's who she is. Be honest with her," Rutger advised. "She covets respect, demands it. Be sure to give it to her."

"Yeah." Honesty. Respect. Easy.

Ansel watched Dr. Baines, Dr. Barsacq, and several nurses hover over Clio's motionless form, and it made his heart ache and his emotions rioted. When his parents died, and he faced his own death, there was no regret, no fear, only numbness from their loss, and peace knowing the end was nigh. Then Milanka saved him, and he wanted to laugh—she saved him from one death and handed him another. A life sentence his parents would have disapproved of, that was nothing more than a slow death while he damned himself with his sins and ruined the good left in his heart.

Hiding.

Denying.

He spent years praying she didn't find him while he lied to everyone who showed him kindness, honesty, love. Lying and protecting himself, not allowing himself to care, to need someone was what he knew. It was his life. Had been his life.

He hung his head, to semi block the action in the room, and knew what he had to do. He had to open himself to Clio, wholly show her he needed her. He was going to be honest, but he was going to show her without holding back.

Dhampir.

The word seized his thoughts, its meaning in his life sending a chill to slice down his spine and splinter out when it hit his hips.

Not the same, he reminded himself, quickly as if it would stop the onslaught of pain. Clio and her pure heart weren't capable of the horrors Milanka performed. Craved. *Not the same*. His heart understood, recognized the difference, believed what he was saying, while his wolf saw its mate, the warmth in Clio, had felt her silky skin, heard her voice rich with passion for him. But his mind latched onto the pain, the cold, embarrassment, belittling, the loneliness, his failure. He never stopped Milanka from taking him, from bleeding him … no, he was too weak to protect himself from her and obeyed like a trained dog. It made it impossible to put the nightmare where it belonged, in the past, to put the emotional scars in the grave with her body.

There was a chance the spell was broken, and Clio would possess her memories. If it happened, he wouldn't have to worry about what he was going do, how he was going to act. His feelings were a moot point. She would feel and see his lies and betrayal, feel the sting from the months he deceived her, and hate him for what he did, what he stole. Staring into the room, the stark walls, the bed, people, machines, screens, and wires all blurred. He imagined the sun rising, its warmth blanketing the land, and its rays taking the shadows as it traveled across the expanse of an azure sky. It moved on without him, without them. Time didn't care where he was, what was happening to Clio, or their lives. He focused on her, her blonde hair fanned out and streaked with crimson, the blood on her arms, the bruises staining her face, and whispered, "Fate damned us, tesoro."

CHAPTER THIRTEEN

Clio moaned as the dream held her in its trance, and she rolled to her side, her face cradled in the softness of a pillow, her hair covering the side of her face, blocking the dull light. She remained cuddled in a blanket, not wanting the delusion that she was at her townhouse, music playing, her glass of tequila sitting on the table while the setting sun cast rose and golds across the sky, to end. Then it did. She was at Ansel's, standing beside her car, his auburn hair hadn't grown out, his shoulders thinner than they had been, and he was leaning against a post, a ghost of the man she had seen on fire floating over him.

As if it opened the floodgates, images engulfed her. *"Tesoro,"* he called her as he held her to him, then she was straddling him on his couch. They were going to celebrate the Highguard's ruling, he was found innocent, and she was going back to work. Going to her back, she stared at the unfamiliar ceiling, the recessed lighting, while tears welled and slipped down her temples. Clio squeezed her eyes closed and saw a man delivering flowers push his way into her townhouse in the city.

"Let me see," he demanded. Fear drenched her, and then she was blind, and days of her life were missing.

"No. No. Not true," she whispered around her tears. Milanka had to be lying.

"That's right, he did that to you, and it put him in debt. His life for your memories."

"Why?" Clio wanted to scream from the hurt consuming her. Ansel took her memories, took a part of her, left her believing she was losing her mind, and treated her as if she was nothing. Nothing. Like he could get rid of her. Like her life had no value. Her love had no value. He didn't want her. Not a Wight. She clutched the blanket in both fists and fought the overwhelming pressure of tears, panic, and feeling exposed. Her heart was breaking, shattering with each second, and she struggled to control herself.

Inhale. Exhale. She wouldn't lose herself to chaos. She needed facts. Milanka was dead. Dead. Forever gone. And she was alive.

As what?

With desperate touches she checked her throat and felt smooth skin on the left and right sides, then kicking off the blankets, meaning to check her side, realized she was wearing a light blue cotton top, matching pants, and on the right side by the hip was Cascade's crest. She was at the Hollow. With shaking hands, she worked to untangle the white ties, then with jerky pulls at the waist she saw she was wearing a pair of white panties. Her eyes narrowed on her flawless skin; she didn't have a bruise, she was completely healed.

"Oh gods, how?" Clio knew there should have been bruises, discolored skin where the glass punctured her. She checked her chest for seat belt abrasions and saw nothing. It wasn't real. It was a nightmare.

"Think. Think." The crash. Milanka. Then Ansel. He was the first one there, he found her. "What happened?" Clio sat straight up and found herself in one of the observation rooms—the two windows, two-way mirrors—meaning someone was able to watch her. Might be watching her.

When a couple of minutes passed, and no one came in, she was confident she was alone. It made her question if it was night or day. And what day it was. How long had she been at the Hollow? Too damn long if her injuries were healed. Unless ...

She didn't want to think about it. Didn't want to contemplate the worst thing that could happen to her. When three soft knocks sounded, loud in the silence, her thoughts ceased, and she turned to watch the door open. Dr. Baines stepped into her room. They *had* been watching her.

"Good to see you're awake, Doctor Hyde," Dr. Baines greeted. "How do you feel?"

"Too perfect," Clio answered as she eyed him. She wasn't a good patient, hated being a patient, and wanted out of there.

After casually pulling a chair to the side of the bed, Dr. Baines sat down, crossed his legs, and holding a tablet, met her questioning gaze. She wasn't going anywhere anytime soon. "You can thank Captain Wolt and Mistress Langston for that."

Ansel. A combination of anger and regret worked through making her heart stutter as if it wanted to give up and die then came back. She didn't know if she wanted to hear anything about him. "Why?"

"His blood is the reason you've healed. Mistress advised us about the transfusion," he answered. "He is a powerful Pureblood."

"I don't remember that," she mumbled softly. "What about Milanka and the bites?"

"So far there's very little indication of change. Are you sure you feel all right?"

"Yes. No. I don't know. How long have I been here?" Clio rubbed her neck with her right hand, then drawing it through her hair, pulled on a ratted mess at the back of her head. She groaned, not knowing what she looked like.

"You have to understand what happened to you," he began as he took his gaze from her to look at the tablet.

"Cut the crap, and just tell me, Doctor Baines," Clio demanded. Cringing with the sharpness of her words, because she wasn't the person she sounded like, she shook her head and met his worried gaze.

With an exaggerated inhale and exhale, he explained, "Two weeks. Week one, you were sedated while we treated the virus Miss Telep gave you. Then there was blood loss, and you needed to heal. You were monitored, twenty-four hours a day, for any effects from the virus, transfusion, bites, and the minuscule amount of dhampir blood you ingested."

"It was more than minuscule." It poured from the wrist Ansel snapped in two. "Week two?" One week gone. Ingested dhampir blood. She stopped herself from shuddering.

"*I don't want to lose you, tesoro.*"

Breathe. Breathe. Clio fought for control as her emotions raged.

"Doctor Hyde?"

"I'm good. Continue."

"When your recovery was satisfactory, you were moved from isolation and intensive care to this room. You've been in an out of consciousness for six days. Today is day seven."

Fourteen days. "Have I been monitored here?"

"Of course. Once you were stabilized, the feeding tube and IVs were removed."

"What was I being fed?" she asked slowly, like the words didn't want to leave her mouth.

"Captain Wolt's blood." Her stomach turned and nausea flowed through her. She was going to be sick. "Nutritional fluids."

Here's some B12 to go with your type O Pureblood. Then she wondered if Ansel's blood was negative or positive. Feeling dizzy, she decided she was finished talking about it, she would figure out the details later. She would read her file, in private. "My parents?" They had to be going out of their minds with worry—the car crash, Ansel, if someone had told them they were fated mates, and Milanka.

"They were told you had been in a car accident, were attacked by Miss Telep, and you're currently being held in isolation. Because they don't have clearance to know about the Hollow, or are allowed on the premises, they believe you are at Foxwood. Baron and Baroness, Mistress, Director Kanin, and Captain Wolt have been here every day. Captain Wolt kept you alive by sharing his wolf's strength through your mated bond. I didn't know you were mated."

Trapped and bound to a liar for an eternity is more like it, she thought as the anger sparked.

"When can I talk to my parents?" she asked, ignoring him, her mind racing with what she was going to say. She stopped herself from thinking about him, discussing Ansel. She couldn't, not right then, not when she wasn't thinking straight. She needed time to get back to her life, needed her routine, needed to understand what happened to her, what it meant for her future. Then maybe she would think about what he did to her and how she felt.

"If you're feeling well enough, you may call them. Remember, you're at Foxwood, in isolation," he answered, his light green eyes narrowing on her.

She could see his mind scrutinizing every word coming out of her mouth and analyzing what she wasn't saying. "Do you know anything about my house?"

"Yes. However, Mistress is here and would like to talk to you. She is going to explain what has happened," he replied as he stood. "When she's finished there are tests that need to be ran."

She didn't want to see anyone, but she didn't think Jordyn was going to take no for an answer. Clio Hyde wasn't going to tell Cascade's soothsayer to leave her alone. "Understood. Thank you, Doctor Baines."

"It's good to have you back." With that, he left her alone.

Clio shoved the pillows against the headboard and scooted back. Might as well make herself comfortable, she was going to be there for the long haul. The door opened and a hand holding a cup appeared, and she smelled coffee. What a delicious smell. "If you're bribing me, it's working."

Jordyn stepped inside and smiled. "Good. Heard it was your favorite."

Of course she did. "So what news do you have for me?"

"Drink your coffee."

Jordyn handed her the mug, Cascade's crest on its side to remind her where she was, and she sat down. Clio watched her and saw nothing in her cocoa eyes.

Inhaling the roasted notes, the caramel and smoke, she couldn't help but allow her lips to lift in a slight smile. "Before I drink this, tell me it's not going to make me sick. It's been two weeks. And I've been fed ... well, anyway."

"It's fine. I made sure."

Clio sipped, the warm liquid feeling like silk as she swallowed, and wanted to purr with ecstasy. "Good. Very good. Now tell me what the hell has been going on."

"Do you know what happens when a vampire feeds on you?"

"No. Neither should you," Clio responded. And didn't want to know.

Jordyn smiled, and Clio didn't like it. "It's called sânge. It's Romanian, because all the really cool vampires hail from there, and means blood, birth, descent. To understand it better, you could call it a virus. It's in their saliva, DNA, skin, and it's what they transfer to their victim to prepare them to accept the altered blood. Milanka did this to you, and when she nearly drank you dry, she put you in stygian, it's a statis between life and death. At that point the vampire has a decision to make ... let the victim die or turn them. The victim must have the blood from the vampire in order to survive stygian. Ansel saved your life when he gave you Milanka's, now we believe his blood is fighting the cross over."

"How? Why?" She heard the tremble in her voice, hated it, and knew what was coming.

"He's a powerful Pureblood. Your mate. Your wolves are linked to one another. Magic. Really, Doc?"

Yes really, she wanted to reply. She needed facts, they made her feel safe. There was an absolute involved, not questions or something based on superstition. "Doctor Baines said there was very little indication. Am I going to cross over?" Clio asked. Her world stopped for a painful second while her future and the life she knew slipped further from her.

"Affirmative."

Clio closed her eyes against the truth, then opened them. "When?" In a heartbeat the life she knew had been placed in an hourglass and sand started falling. She was going to lose everything she worked for.

"I don't know. You should have by now. That's why we think it's Ansel's blood."

Clio laughed a sad sound, her throat feeling like it was closing on her, while her shoulders caved in defeat, and she felt exposed, vulnerable. She saw her seventeen-year-old self standing in front of a mirror, her blue eyes that would never change staring back as she questioned what she was. If she was ever going to shift. Would she remain human like her mom? Or shift into a werewolf like her dad?

With regret and fear in her voice she said, "I didn't shift into my wolf until my eighteenth birthday. It happened in the middle of the night. My wolf tore through my human body as it reshaped bones, muscles, tendons, and organs in agonizing pain." The first shift could be deadly, the human body fighting against the animal coming forward as it rejected its instincts. If she failed to fully shift, the primal instincts of the wolf would have taken over her mind and driven her to madness. Her parents would have had to make the decision to end her life. "My screams filled the house. That's when my mom called the baron, and with his help I shifted into my wolf form. I was a late bloomer. This doesn't surprise me." It reminded her she was inferior to Purebloods and Illuminates. More so now. "How old were you?"

"Minutes old. I shifted in my father's arms," Jordyn replied.

"You were powerful at birth. Somehow that doesn't surprise me either." Bowing her head, she fisted the blanket in her left hand and tried not spilling her coffee. The cream material with green vines and pink flowers covered the plain white sheets and she realized it was her blanket. "How did I get this?" As if it mattered.

"Ansel brought it for you. Said you insisted on sleeping with it," Jordyn answered. "He thought it would comfort you."

There was no comfort for her when she had a pending death sentence. She was going to lose her human half. "You know what he did to me." It wasn't a question. It was an accusation. Was she using her anger, the feeling she was getting fucked over, and her pending change to hate Ansel? Maybe. As if she needed to hate him more than she did.

"Affirmative."

Jordyn didn't make any excuses, she didn't try to lessen the blow, or defend Ansel, she stared straight at Clio, as if challenging her. Or being the soothsayer she was, didn't have to apologize to anyone. "Why didn't you tell me?"

"I didn't have to. Despite the spell's power you followed your wolf's instinct and your heart. You went to see Ansel because you couldn't stop yourself. Fated mates are primal, raw. The human element isn't part of the equation. We waited for you to break the hold it had on you."

"We?" She laughed a nervous sound, giving away her embarrassment. Everyone knew except her. She had been a fool led around by her naïve heart. "How many people knew?"

"Healey, Laurel, Rutger, myself. You have your memories, have they made a difference?" she asked. Was she was challenging her?

"I thought I was losing my mind. It made me feel ..."

"Like a Wight. Inferior." Jordyn held her gaze, the cocoa sharpening to a hard copper.

Clio knew she should keep her mouth shut she was falling, hell, racing back to her default setting. She wasn't going to yell at the pack's soothsayer, and what had Ansel called her? Prime's scion. She could be hung for looking at Jordyn wrong, and Jordyn knew it. She was wearing her arrogance like a second skin. But there was no way of stopping the fury sweeping through her, the fire wrapped in a fear so strong Clio thought it was going to cripple her and she was going to lose her mind.

"Yes, like a fucking Wight." Gods, she wanted to scream as rage started consuming her. "He. Us. We. All while fucking me, he knew. He lied to me. He took the decision from me. He sent someone to my house and had them invade my mind. He had no right. I handed him my heart and he broke it, shattered it. Ansel betrayed me."

Unruly blonde curls grazed her shoulders and cascaded down her back, while Clio yelled at Jordyn, his name on her tongue like a curse. Her flushed cheeks stood out from her pale face, scarlet streaked her smoky slate eyes that were wet from tears, and her entire body shook with her emotions. "She's right. I did this to her," Ansel growled as grief and guilt coiled inside of him with her words. "Like a damn coward." He should have told her. While the sky cried and its chilled tears pelted them, he should have told her the truth.

"You aren't the only problem here. While you betrayed her trust, she crafted her world and adhered to the rules she set for herself. It has been destroyed. This isn't going to be easy for her," Baron Kanin stated, his voice firm. "Clio found her footing before, she will again. It's going to take time."

"She's going to cross over," Ansel whispered. "She wasn't meant to be a dhampir. She's a healer, teacher, is kind and pure of heart." She was his girly girl who wore pink and slept with her favorite blanket. In Clio's eyes she was going to lose herself and it was his fault. He was to blame. How was he supposed to live with himself? How was he supposed to live without her?

"A werewolf or a dhampir, the designation changes, the person does not. When she crosses over, we'll be here for her. She isn't alone," the baron assured, his confidence in his voice, and he placed his hand on Ansel's shoulder.

With the baron's touch, emotions he denied his entire life, but was having hard time ignoring welled inside of him. "We'll lose our bond." Saying the words made his stomach roll and his wolf howl in agony. He felt the thread between them and could see it unraveling as the seconds ticked by.

"Ansel, son, look at me," Baron Kanin ordered as he dropped his hand.

He didn't want to, couldn't face the man who referred to him as son and let him see the weakness and the sins in his eyes. He didn't stop himself, the reflex to obey his alpha making his body move.

"You don't know what will happen. If and when something does, we have someone."

"Shadow Lord. It's not right," Ansel protested as he held dark eyes with flakes of gold. In them he saw the steadfastness that held the pack together and his power. There was a certainty Ansel was sure he would never feel, not when so many people, like Jordyn, were bearing his burden.

"She can handle herself."

By the tone of the baron's voice the conversation was over, and Ansel absently nodded as he turned back to Clio and watched the conversation on the other side of the mirrored glass. A rune protected the room, so no one would feel their magic, and it was soundproof ... unless someone turned the speakers on, like they had so they could listen.

Jordyn watched Clio, the intensity of her eyes drilling into her as she cried, then screamed about injustice, and it broke his heart into a million pieces. The jagged shards slicing him as they fell through him and out of his reach. She was going to lose her wolf and the bond between them would disappear like it had never been there. No matter what anyone said, he knew the truth. Only he would feel it and the void's absence, and would be forced to leave his mate behind as if she had died. It would be an open wound left to fester and never heal.

I'll add it to the others, he thought.

"Strong Lord has decided he doesn't want the Highguard to know he broke their canons, the covenant with the pack, and tried blackmailing you to get information about Jordyn. He conceded to the criminal charges, their treatment of Milanka, and having those we're holding, here illegally. He wants to negotiate for the release of his people," Baron Kanin began. "I'm going to keep his people, they will serve out a sentence, and force the others out of my territory."

Jerking himself out of his self-pity, he digested what the baron was telling him. The prisoners had been in the underground cells, out of the Highguard's sight, for two weeks while they investigated Clio's car accident, Milanka's death, and then their regents took her body. Milanka was dead and gone, he was free of one master. Ansel absently rubbed the medallion through his BDU top and T-shirt. He needed to deal with the one holding his leash.

"What do I have to do?" Ansel asked. He broke the covenant and there was going to be punishment. What it would be, he didn't care. He deserved it and more. Maybe it would stop him from feeling Clio.

"For breaking the covenant, you'll be punished. They cannot take your life. They cannot use magic of any kind to search you for your magic, and they cannot compel you to give them consent to search for it," Baron Kanin explained.

"When?" Ansel was overwhelmed and numb at the same time.

"When Clio is stable. I won't allow them to take you while your mate is healing," he replied. "Ansel, they're demanding two weeks. They cannot willfully take your life. However, the injuries sustained may."

Gods. Closing his eyes, he exhaled and lowered his head. He could imagine what they wanted to do to him for two weeks. The pain. Humiliation. Demeaning. He lived through worst.

"I understand." Ansel gathered what strength he could and watched Clio as she left the bed, and pacing like a caged animal, looked at the mirror. He felt her fury and pain when it flowed through their bond like lava, the cooling tips razor sharp.

Clio stared at the mirror, saw her reflection. Slate eyes with whiskey hues, her hair loose, the curls softening her appearance, the lack of makeup. She wasn't naked, wasn't covered in blood, and flinched. They bathed her. She knew the tub/shower stall, all stainless-steel, with a rack to hold the patient, and while grateful, added it to the 'never want to do that again' list. The thought enraged her. Then she sensed Ansel in their bond, knew he had to be close, but couldn't sense his presence as the room was guarded by a rune. Walking to her reflection, she stopped, put her hands on the glass, and through the bond she shared with him, shoved her rage, sorrow, and revulsion into it.

"I hate you," she whispered and felt her heart break. Had he been in the room he would have felt the lie for what it was. This was cowardly, she knew, but it was easier than him looking at her with disgust in his eyes when he looked at an enemy. Or pity at what he turned her into. Keeping her eyes straight forward and the tears from falling, she repeated, "I. Hate. You."

"I know," he whispered back. There was nothing he could do. Time was running out for the both of them.

"I understand you're emotional, you understand you're emotional, but don't say anything you'll regret. You may burn the very bridge you need," Jordyn warned from behind her. "The one person willing to sacrifice his life for yours."

Clio stared for a second, trying to hold onto her composure, took her glare from her reflection, and faced Jordyn, her stern gaze, the confidence she held, and her anger faded. She had a million excuses for acting the way she was—crossing over, becoming a monster, the past year had been a lie, she was going to lose everything including Ansel before she had a chance to have him. Damn him. Sucking in a breath, she held onto the flicker of anger and prayed she protected what was left of her heart.

"He took my memories to get rid of me. He didn't want me. And while I pined after him, he treated me like the plague, a child. He told me he loved me. Is that a lie, too?" she asked, the words tumbling from her as hurt wrapped its arms around her. "What will stop him from doing it again? How can I trust him?"

"I don't know because I'm not you, and I'm not him. I'm not going to defend him when it isn't my fight to defend. If you want his side of the story, and want answers to all of your whys, you have to ask him. Face him. Demand answers. Time isn't something either of you have at this point. Don't waste what you do have." Jordyn uncrossed her legs, stood with the elegance she possessed, and going to the door, her raven hair at her waist, turned her black-lined copper eyes on Clio. "Miss Malave from the pack's law office sold your townhouse, you got over asking price, and took care of the purchase of the house on Setzer. Your stuff is there. You're being released tomorrow, so they made sure the master bedroom was set up enough you can sleep in it. You can use the phone in the hallway to call your parents. Remember, you're at Foxwood. They don't know about you and your fated mate."

Fated mate. It was like a punch to the stomach. Without waiting for Clio to reply, the door opened and closed, and Jordyn, the one person she felt she could be honest with, left her. Townhouse sold, Setzer house bought, and her stuff moved. She spent a minute wondering about her car, but figured it didn't matter at this point. At this point. Her mind reeled.

"Time isn't something either of you have at this point."

What did she mean? Either of them. What was happening to Ansel? Clio knew Milanka's death made him a free man, she couldn't stalk him anymore. Did he know he was free? Turning in a circle, she saw the mirrors again and wanted to crawl under her blanket and hide. Gods only knew who was watching and witnessed her temper tantrum. Ansel. Baron Kanin. Director Kanin. Dr. Baines. Dr. Barsacq. The nurses ... no, they wouldn't be allowed to be there, thankfully. She might be able to keep a shred of dignity. She tested the bond, felt a chill where he had once been, and the nothing he left when he blocked her, and she felt his absence. He left. She hadn't felt him cut her off, he simply went silent, and disappeared like the phantom he was in her life.

"Dammit," she whispered as she paced the small room, her pants swishing as she walked, stomped, her bare feet on concrete. Regret rode her, and Clio didn't care who was watching, what they were thinking, not when her mind was in chaos. She knew Ansel would be her end, she didn't think it was going to end like this. Over the years he had been a constant in her life and she faced living the rest of her life without his feel. Damn him. He betrayed her. Stole from her. She hated him. The void was going to devour her. Torn to shreds by need and loss, Clio made another lap.

Ansel marched through the hallways, his boots heavy on the concrete flooring, his footfalls echoing off the walls, while his thoughts targeted Clio, her anger, and her hate. After passing through the automatic doors, he stepped out of the hospital, into the underground garage, and stared at the cars and trucks. He couldn't stop from shuddering and couldn't catch his breath. She hated him. Told him she hated him. He knew she would. He took and took from her and gave her nothing in return. Nothing but danger, fear, and now a cross over into a being he knew to be a monster.

He was taking a daughter from loving parents. A doctor from her hospital. When she said she hated him, he knew he ruined her pure heart. He was a cancer to her life. To the pack. He didn't know what he was thinking when he made love to her and bonded her to him when she deserved better. Like Alpha Crevan. Ansel inhaled as guilt continued to eat at his insides. He hadn't been thinking. He fought the need to have her, his wolf's demands for its mate, his building passion for her for a year, and couldn't do it any longer. Was powerless to stop himself when he was close to her. Damn the flannel shirt. And not when he saw every male as a threat. He had been blinded by his selfishness and jealousy.

"She didn't mean it."

Ansel froze, bowed his head, and placed his hands on his hips. "She did. You and I both know it," he replied as he met copper eyes glittering in the dim lighting. Jordyn spooked him for a minute with her stillness, weighted presence, and the seriousness in her gaze. He hadn't sensed her, hadn't known she was there. "I destroyed her."

"I felt her lie," Jordyn countered. "She's protecting herself the only way she knows how."

Was there hope? It didn't matter. Clio was going to cross over, extinguishing the bond between them, destroying them. She was going to resent him for what she was going to turn into. While she suffered, alone, he was going to be at Strong Lord's mercy. And he was sure Strong Lord wasn't going to let him live after Ansel broke the covenant and then turned him into Baron Kanin. "It doesn't matter. Not now."

"She's being released tomorrow," Jordyn started as she ignored him, her voice taking on a sternness. "There's a good chance she'll cross over within the week. You're going to stand guard over her, Captain Wolt. You're going to be there for her."

The implications made his stomach clench in defense and his skin crawl at the same time his wolf howled a song of grief at the loss. While his wolf understood his pain the nightmares Milanka gave him, it didn't understand losing its mate. Fated mate. The perfect half to make him whole.

Jordyn's eyes gleamed copper while onyx shards splintered the satin sheen, no doubt she sensed and smelled the revulsion he felt with the thought of Clio with fangs.

Not the same.

"Is that an order?" he challenged, his hand automatically going to the butt of his gun and his shoulders straightened.

"Affirmative." Jordyn smiled. It wasn't out of friendship or joy, it was menacing, dark, as if the part she kept hidden behind her barricade of calm façade was showing itself.

"Mistress." In the past, if anyone had given him an order, he would have confirmed it with Rutger or Baron Kanin. Not today. Jordyn had taken her place as soothsayer for the pack, and somehow became an extension of Baron Kanin.

Jordyn held his gaze for a breath, then nodding her response, raven hair falling over one slender shoulder, she met his eyes, turned on her heel, and walked to her truck. Ansel watched her drive away and had no idea what was going on but had a feeling she did.

CHAPTER FOURTEEN

Clio sat straight, and watched trees, mountains, and houses blur as the road stretched out in front of her. Its end would leave her on her own and in her new house, and she didn't know how to feel about it. She had been excited to leave the Hollow, get outside, to see the sun and back to her life. Then reality hit ... Ansel wasn't there, wouldn't be. She pleaded with Baron Kanin, promising she wouldn't resign and would continue to work if Ansel stayed away from her. She needed to settle into her new place and face whatever was going to happen to her.

"If you need anything, don't hesitate to call. Day or night."

Lazily turning her head, Clio stared at the side of Jordyn's face. "You didn't need to drive me home. My parents would have," she replied, halfheartedly. She was glad her parents hadn't; she wasn't prepared to explain Ansel, the crash, Milanka, the cross over.

"I know."

"Are you going to be my handler?"

Jordyn turned her head enough to meet Clio's gaze before looking back at the road. "Affirmative. Until you need an Eclipse and a Minor."

Her heart seized in her chest when she thought about feeding from someone, but it had stopped completely at the idea it was going to be a vampire. "Shadow Lord arranged it with the vampire council?" Clio asked. "La Morte." She didn't know the extent of the vampire lord's power but knew enough being indebted to him wasn't a good thing.

"Affirmative. Are you prepared?"

She wanted to say she was sorry. "As much as I can be, I guess."

Clio looked down at her hands, her cotton pants, the overnight bag at her feet and her running shoes. She had several sessions with Dr. Barsacq, a Pureblood elf and High Privilege empath with knowledge of all magic-born. They talked at length, and he explained what *might* happen, but no one knew for certain. It was the unknown she was scared of. Clio was a doctor, clinical, and liked knowing and having proof. No, she wasn't prepared at all. How does one prepare to cross over? And what was she going to be when it was over? Milanka? A monster. Gods no, it made her heart hurt. She wouldn't, couldn't lose who she was. The pain made her ache and tears well in her eyes.

"How am I going to explain the cross over?" Clio was sure the question was stuck in her throat. She needed to talk to her parents, who hadn't been thrilled after Milanka drugged her, then she would have to face the world as something else. Where did Ansel fit in? Did he fit in? She didn't know.

"You're going to tell them the truth. You were attacked my Milanka," Jordyn stated as she kept her eyes forward. "And assure them she was punished to the fullest extent of the law."

Clio closed her eyes and asked, "What happened to her?" Although she wasn't sure she wanted to know all the details.

"Ansel took her heart. True death."

"Gods," she groaned. *"My soul is stained with the blood of others, and my sins. My heart is black."* "He got his revenge." At what cost?

Jordyn didn't say anything as she slowed, then parked on the street and waited while a sporty, black truck backed out from the driveway, the woman waving as she drove by them.

"Who was that?" Clio didn't recognize the woman, which she should have. She was in charge of the physicals, and certification for all enforcer and soldiers.

"Emory Bishop, soldier. The house has been watched since Milanka's death," Jordyn answered. "You don't have a car. If you need to go somewhere, call me."

"Am I under house arrest?" Clio asked. She wouldn't be surprised since she was a threat, and no one knew how she was going to react when she crossed over. Plus, her house had been watched, meaning they thought she was in danger. Shutting down the worst of her thoughts, she considered her car. It had been insured, and she had money, it wouldn't be a problem to buy another one. Maybe after everything returned to normal, she would call her parents, have them over, and then she would get her dad to go with her to buy a car. Back to normal. Was that possible? She didn't know.

Jordyn tilted her head like she was sensing something. "Affirmative."

"Really?"

Nothing.

"Thanks for the ride," Clio mumbled.

"There are a couple of things you should know." Jordyn shifted in her seat, her arm on the steering wheel, and met her gaze. "I'm not defending Ansel, there's no reason for me to."

"Then don't. I don't want to hear it," Clio said as she started out of the truck.

"You'll hear this, Doctor Hyde."

Clio froze and lowered her head with the order. She didn't want to deal with whatever Jordyn, who wasn't talking to her as a friend any longer but as the pack's soothsayer, was going to tell her. "Mistress," she conceded as she sat back in the seat, her bag at her feet.

"I understand he lied to you, and I understand the hurt you feel." Her eyes darkened as if the confession was a knife in her heart. "You have a family, a career, friends, freedom. Ansel watched his family die, then when he thought he found one, she was a monster. For decades he's been hunted, stalked, and lived in fear if he got close to anyone, they would become Milanka's victim. And he was right. Your life was put in danger."

"He had someone put a spell on me. He took my choice from me," Clio protested, and it felt weak. "And when we were together, he didn't tell me." Her feelings for Ansel were weaving into her heart, her need, and her wolf wanted its mate. She didn't want to be alone. When she was with him, she felt safe, guarded. The night they shared descended on her, and she felt his body beside her.

No. She refused to give in, no matter how much it hurt, no matter how much the need burned through her, she couldn't, not yet. She needed to think. She needed time. Time she didn't have.

"What would you have done?"

Clio asked herself the same question and didn't have an answer. It infuriated her she would forgive him to have him. It enraged her she wanted to be escorted across Foxwood's parking lot with his hand at her neck knowing everyone was looking at them. It made her feel weak. "I don't know," she answered.

"Exactly, so don't hold that part against him. He made a covenant with the Fellowship to keep you safe. His life for yours, and he didn't hesitate," Jordyn countered. "He needed to know you were safe."

Milanka's words came back to her. *"Regrettably, his magic is beyond me. I couldn't access it, he couldn't access it, no matter what I did."*

"My safety for his magic. They want the magic he holds inside of him and used me to get to him."

Jordyn's onyx gaze narrowed on her. "Affirmative. He told you."

"No," she replied as she stared forward. "Milanka did. She said the Fellowship told her he was here and thought she could order him around the way she had when they were together. She bragged about owning him, being his master, like he was nothing more than an animal. They didn't consider his relationship with Director Kanin, the baron and baroness, and didn't know about me, and I got in her way," Clio replied. *Because he's my mate and he loves me.*

"They'll pay for that," Jordyn growled, her eyes gleaming onyx. "Ansel talked to us about the Fellowship, the covenant, and Milanka. Not only had they tethered him with a leash and collar, they were blackmailing him for information about me."

He was at their mercy. Then risked it all to protect her and the pack. Clio wanted them all dead. They were responsible for Milanka, Ansel being set on fire, and now her pending cross over. After opening the door, she got out, grabbed her bag, slung it over one shoulder, and met Jordyn's hardened gaze. Covenant. It was a binding contract, one that you didn't get out of without punishment. Ansel risked his life when he confessed what he'd done to Baron Kanin. It explained the meeting and why he blocked her from feeling him. If only she could take the day back. "What will they do to him?"

"For breaking the covenant, they have two weeks to do as they please."

Two weeks. Her insides fell apart, her heart hurt, and it was getting harder to breathe. "They'll kill him."

"Do you care?" she asked, her voice sharp, as if challenging her.

Clio stared at onyx eyes, saw possession and raw power in their depths. "What does it matter? I'll cross over and the bond will be gone. I won't be me." It was over before it began. She lost him. And she demanded he stay away from her. She told herself she needed time to think and get back to her life, whatever it was going to be. Clio was fooling herself.

"It matters. Fight for your wolf."

Jordyn put the truck in gear, Clio closed the door, and when she was backing out, walked to the front door and realized she didn't have keys. All her belongings had been taken from her and now she didn't have anything. ID, money, nothing. It was a painful reminder of her future. She held the handle, took a deep breath—this was her new home—and turning it, her house opened before her. Stepping inside, she saw her furniture. It wasn't haphazard, it hadn't been dumped in the first empty spot, someone had taken time to make it look like it belonged. They had stacked boxes along the right and left side walls, each labeled with its contents. Farther down the wall of boxes, she slowly moved through the room to the kitchen where more boxes were stacked, and her satchel, all the stuff from her car, and a bottle and glass, with a note on the clean counter. In a shaking hand, she opened it to read, Home Sweet Home, and no name. It was her favorite tequila, there was no doubt it was Jordyn. The note fell to the counter in silence as she turned from the kitchen and walked to the stairs. As if on auto she looked at the boxes, her office furniture, then went to the bedroom where the bed had been made.

Clio dropped the overnight bag on the floor, her arms hanging loose at her sides, and stared at the flannel shirt draped over a pillow. Her shoulders shuddered, tears built, and she fought back the raging emotions. He had been in her house. Most likely supervising whoever moved her stuff. She could see his bronze gaze tracking them. Her thoughts latched onto Ansel's pending punishment and her cross over, and she fought the pressure of building tears and panic. *Stop*, she ordered herself. Looking around her room at the boxes and furniture, what was she supposed to do? Pretend everything was all right? Pretend to care? Where was she supposed to start? She couldn't talk to Ansel, not yet. There was too much to think about. She needed to take a step, a baby step. Go to the kitchen and pour a glass?

Yes, she thought, *that sounds good. It sounds normal.* Clio waited a second and found she couldn't move as if her fear was holding her hostage. Inhaling and exhaling, she smelled him, then looked at the boxes and knew she needed to unpack and make her house a home. She had to start somewhere. Sure. In one day she lost herself, her wolf, and her mate.

"I never really had him," she told the empty room. He made sure of that when he took her memories. Clio wanted to harden her heart, to push him out until she was on solid ground. She told herself he didn't want her then, he ignored her. Even if she believed he loved her, he wouldn't want her once she became a reminder of his nightmares.

"When I knew I had broken him, I pinned him down and took his throat."

Milanka's voice played in her head. She broke him and took from him against his will, and he tried to keep those memories from her and then tried to keep that from happening to her. With her memories suppressed, she didn't consciously know she was his mate, but he knew. Every day he saw her he knew. What did it do to him? Part of her couldn't deny he loved her, and she understood why he did what he did, and there was another part, a desperate part, that reminded her of the hurt, betrayal, and the year she spent feeling lost. She needed to protect herself and concentrate on staying sane. Across the bedroom the skylights in the bathroom let sunlight brighten the spacious area and walk-in shower, while the window running the length of the huge tub looked out at the valley.

"I'll get a drink, have a bath, think about it later." Clio wanted to wash the stringent smell from the Hollow off her skin. As she went back to the kitchen, she tried to feel at home, tried to keep her thoughts focused on one thing, not the chaos waiting for her and the terror invading her. After pouring the silky liquor into the waiting glass, she stood at the French doors and gazed at the land that was hers, the setting sun, the gold and rose casting its veil over the valley and mountains. Night fall. What was going to happen? With the unanswered question, she turned and made her way back to the bathroom.

An hour later, the bath had gone cold, was drained, her tequila was gone, and she smelled like herself. Normal. Wearing a tank top and underwear, she couldn't bring herself to touch the flannel, she cuddled in her bed with her blanket. Relaxed and comfortable, it felt normal as if a piece of her old self was coming back. She grasped onto it as sleep drifted over her, and sinking into the bed, she decided she would live as normal as possible for as long as possible.

Would it be hours, days, weeks? She didn't know. While her tired mind trudged on, paths took off in every direction and she couldn't stop from seeing Ansel, his bronze eyes, and yawning she pulled the blanket closer to her, felt his hands on her, and let herself settle into sleep.

Ansel reread the date, the day they walked into Baron Kanin's office to tell him they were fated mates, then the report on Dr. Clio Hyde's accident, Milanka Telep's attack on her, and then Milanka's death. It covered the details of the cleanup afterward. "There's no peace in hell."

Next was Dr. Clio Hyde's treatment and release. The attached form stated Clio's pending cross over, the preparations being made, the names of the Eclipse and Minors from La Morte, the vampire council, their security clearance, and the signature of the person granting authorization. Jordyn Langston. He didn't want to think about that. As the doctor in charge of Nearctic, working in administration at Celestial, and in charge of personnel at the Hollow, eventually everyone in Cascade was going to know. Cascade, the Coulter Coalition, he wanted to growl as he thought about the alpha, the Highguard, the entire fucking state. She would have to face them all. Clio would be exposed. She hated being center of attention.

He pushed the thought down as his heart started beating a million miles an hour, his nerves unravelling as if he'd been struck by lightning and his breathing came in ragged inhales. His boot tapped the tile flooring while he played with a pen, bouncing it off the desktop. He wasn't looking at the paperwork in front of him, the reports about Fiala, Dallan, and his handler, Eero, and the demons they used as backup. Fiala and Eero would remain in custody, as would the demons. The others, according to the Highguard, were returned from where they came from and were being punished by their factions. His eyes lingered on Clio's report, his mind racing and keeping pace with his heart as he counted down the hours until he had to pull duty at her house. She ordered him to stay away from her, didn't want to have anything to do with him, had been granted time to be by herself, then he was ordered to stand guard. Made perfect sense to him.

He shook his head at Baron Kanin's order, and checking the time, noticed he had two hours to go. Ansel sat back in his chair, his hands in his lap, as if he was lost, his emotions tossed in a million different directions, and told himself it was regular guard duty. And if Clio needed time, then he would give it to her, he would wait for as long as he had to for his mate, the only woman he wanted, loved.

But she isn't going to stay the woman, werewolf, Wight, you know, she's going to cross over, his mind warned.

Not the same.

Clio wasn't Milanka.

Hell, he thought to himself, *she wasn't like anyone he knew.* She fit him. Where he was rough, she was soft. He was uncouth, set in his ways, she was sophisticated and refined. His life had been stained by the blood he spilled, hers was graced with the lives she saved. Then wearing his T-shirt, she made him a damn charcuterie board, and they sat outside surrounded by candles. He didn't deserve her, he didn't deserve that life, but he would be damned if he was going to give her up. The image of Clio's naked body in front of him as she feathered her hands down her stomach to her hips had his wolf howling for its mate, and his body demanding to touch her. He let himself have one thing—after moving her belongings, he made her bed and placed his flannel on her pillow. The side he knew she slept on.

Damn, he wanted to yell. He shoved at the demands, then shoved the concern and doubt down and focused on something that would send ice through his veins and over his body—his pending sentence with the Fellowship and Strong Lord. Two weeks was a long time. His saving grace, if he could call it that, was when Clio crossed over, their bond would no longer exist, freeing her from insanity and death when he met his end. It was a corrupted weight lifted from his shoulders. Looking at his cell, he saw the time and the minutes ticking down. He had five days until he turned himself over to Strong Lord and the Fellowship. Leashed and beat like an animal was his future. Maybe it was for the best. The alpha of the coalition was a better man. Just thinking it sent his mood deeper into the dark, if that was possible.

His head jerked up when there was a hard knock on his door. With chaos raging he hadn't sensed Rutger stopping. Ansel used the keypad to unlock the door, the mechanisms sliding, and Rutger opened it and walked in.

"When are you heading to Doctor Hyde's?"

"In an hour. She doesn't want me there," he stated, a growl in his voice.

"It's not up to her."

No it wasn't. An order had been given and the order would be obeyed. "Baron Kanin wants me there when she crosses over."

"Affirmative. In case something goes wrong, you have a connection to her," Rutger replied as he sat down, the butt of his gun clinking on the chair.

"Once she crosses, the bond will be gone. I won't have a connection," Ansel mumbled with regret.

"Don't be so sure. She survived and healed because of your blood. That has to count for something." Pushing his fingers through his thick hair, Rutger exhaled. "How are you going to deal with it?"

"What? Clio crossing over. She hates me. We'll lose our mate bond."

"Milanka was evil," Rutger said, his brows drawing in.

"Was. Clio isn't the same," he stated. Not the same.

"She isn't. But she'll need to feed to survive. Are you going to be there for her or make her choose someone else?"

His scars teased him as he met a gaze marked by gold and saw concern and doubt. "She is my mate," was all he could say because he didn't know. The thought Clio would touch someone else set his blood on fire and had his wolf howling in jealousy, making it an easy decision. It would be him.

But would it?

He could tell himself lies when he wasn't with her, she hadn't crossed over, and his life hadn't changed. He loved Clio, would give his life for her, but would he give her his throat? His blood? Milanka tortured him, took from him, made him her slave and a victim. He hadn't stopped her. Even as her fangs punctured his flesh, he wanted to be with her, needed her to see him, wanted the life of servitude where he wasn't responsible, wasn't a man, was a thing to be ruled and fed from. Shame oozed from him, turned to disgust, and then fury. Thinking about his weakness made his stomach turn and he stopped himself from shuddering. He fought against the onslaught of humiliation. He wasn't the boy who had been defenseless on his back as she dominated him to take his throat, and Clio wasn't Milanka. Would he let Clio take his throat?

"Remember that." Rutger stood, his right hand going to the butt of his gun. "You can leave now."

"Is that an order?" Ansel questioned, and wished he could take it back. Rutger and Jordyn were playing both sides of the field. Friend and authority.

"It's a suggestion from someone who nearly lost his mate," he replied, his voice tight, his eyes gleaming amber gold.

Ansel held his haunted gaze for a second when he turned and left. Yeah, he figured if anyone knew, it was Rutger. Hell had rained down on them more than once and they survived. After straightening the papers and folders on his desk, he stood. Yes, he was going to Clio's. To his mate.

Twilight frosted sunset's soft hues in colder blues and violets while the reflection of clouds decorated the upstairs' windows, turning them into nature's portraits. Ansel stayed to the left side as he drove into the driveway, then when in front of the garage, turned around so the truck faced the street. He had gotten into the habit when he had been called out in the middle of the night, in a snowstorm, and spent precious seconds trying to turn his truck around. Before killing the engine, he rolled down the windows, rested his elbow on the edge, and a gentle summer breeze brought the woods to him while the terminal beeped, dinged, and chimed. It was guard duty, nothing more. With the engine silent, the trees to his left standing as sentinels, the thick woods to his right, he sat staring at the street, the valley across, and the mountains as night slipped over the rolling contours, and wondered if she cared he was there or if she would forgive him.

Her forgiveness wouldn't matter if his past kept him from her. While he kept his wolf from the bond between them, and he kept his emotions locked down, Rutger's words sat in his head, playing over and over. Milanka was evil, and Clio would need to feed to survive. When he became part of Cascade, he worked to put the pain of his past behind him and told himself he had gotten over Milanka's abuse. It had been too many years and he wasn't going to let her hold him hostage. It was apparent he failed. He pushed it down where it festered and joined the lie he lived with every day. He had been hiding from her and denying himself a relationship with anyone.

It hadn't been a life.

There were two reasons he had a spell put on Clio, the first being he needed to know she was protected from himself and Milanka. They had been poison together and had become toxic separate. The second being he was scared of Clio, scared he wouldn't be able to give himself to her, and she would grow to hate him. Would resent his fear. He couldn't bear the thought. And yet she didn't hate him because he held himself back, she hated him for lying to her and taking a part of her.

Ansel gripped the steering wheel with his left hand, the skin of his knuckles gleaming white, and ordered himself to start the truck and drive away. To leave her surrounded by a family that loved her and those who wouldn't hurt her, wouldn't see her as the pain of his past riddling his present. That was the truth he couldn't admit to. Wight or dhampir didn't matter. He didn't think he had the strength to love her and give her what she needed. While the spell suppressed her memories, it allowed him to believe in a fantasy, and he did believe. Ansel opened the door, making it groan from the force, and using his senses checked the front of the house, the sides, and the yard. After all, it was guard duty. Everything was clear. Beside the truck, his hand on the butt of his gun, he stared up at the second story windows, the sky reflected, and felt helpless.

"I don't know how to ask for forgiveness. I don't know how to fix me," he whispered, his throat thick, his tears welling. "I love you."

When scenes of the crash jerked her awake, she felt different—her senses were heightened, her eyesight sharper, and her body felt foreign, as if her biology had begun transforming. Her insides felt heavy like her DNA was twisting and mutating to adapt to what she was becoming. That's when she couldn't fight herself any longer. She needed assurance, and with her wolf craving his presence, she tugged the flannel on and brought it tighter around her, drawing in his scent. Cuddled in the blanket and his shirt, she sat in the dimly lit room, and debated whether she was going to call Jordyn and alert her to the changes. No, she wouldn't. Not yet. They were changes. Not a cross over. Clio left her bedroom for space and took her post in front of the windows, needing to see the expanse of land, to sense its vastness, and her breath caught. She hadn't expected to see him.

Fear he was there to see her struck quick, fast, and sharp. Then his uniform told her he wasn't. The fear subsided and regret moved in. He was looking at her, his face stricken with worry and his eyes red and wet from unshed tears. His ruffled hair looked like he pushed his fingers through its thick, auburn mass in haste, the ends sitting at his collar. He wasn't happy. In fact, he looked conflicted, in pain, and it hurt her. Clio tested the bond, found he wasn't there—she couldn't feel him, or his wolf—and a part of her broke. She couldn't tell if he was blocking her, or if it was part of the change.

"What are you doing here?" Clio wanted to know when Baron Kanin had granted her request. While she could see him clearly, the lines fanning out from eyes holding bronze flakes in cinnamon, he couldn't see her since all the windows had a reflective tint on them. It gave her an advantage and allowed her to watch him for as long as she wanted.

Ansel rubbed his eyes, then taking the mic clipped to his collar began talking. When he gave her his back, he started walking and stopped by the front fender of his truck and looked toward the valley. She should have known the baron wouldn't let them have their space, they were fated mates.

Were. Once she stopped being a Wight and fully transitioned into a dhampir—she wanted to laugh at that—they wouldn't be anything besides the strangers they had been. Phantoms in each other's lives. The change would eliminate the bond between them. As a werewolf, would he feel her, feel the need to be with her, would his wolf demand its mate, while she would feel nothing? She was going to become a void. Watching him, she realized Ansel wasn't there as her mate ... no, he was there as her guard and there was nothing she could do about it. She grabbed her cell, dialed, and waited.

"Doctor Hyde," Jordyn answered on the first ring, her tone grave.

I'm not in the throes of the cross over, she wanted to say. "Why is he here?"

"He's an enforcer. He has guard duty, and you're on house arrest."

She was right. "How long is guard duty going to last?"

"As long as it takes. Have a good evening, Doctor."

Doctor. She didn't know if she could continue to work if her trait of empathy became another victim of the cross over.

"If your traits are centered around healing and empathy, I suspect your senses, instincts, and intuitiveness will

increase." Jordyn had told her. What else would the cross over take from her? What would it give her, she wondered as she walked between boxes to set the cell on a nearby table. She would face it when the time came. Worrying about it was going to drive her crazy, and she told herself she was going to live a normal life ... at least as normal as one could while on house arrest.

At the moment, she didn't know what Jordyn and the baron were doing as they manipulated people and moved them like they were chess pieces. Back at the window, she stared at the man who betrayed her, who would hate her with the same intensity he did the object of his torture, Milanka. And who she loved with every fiber of her being. Admitting that tore a hole in her heart and opened the floodgates to her tears, and they slipped down her cheeks to drop to the flannel shirt. With a fisted hand she pushed against her chest, her heart, felt its beats, and felt it break, the shards falling from her.

"I love you," Clio whispered as she placed her palms flat on the glass.

CHAPTER FIFTEEN

At sundown, Ansel parked his truck facing the street and took his post as he had for three nights in a row. And every night, he didn't see her, didn't want to open himself to her. He sensed her and heard her as she moved through the house while unpacking boxes or rearranging furniture. No one came to see her. However, Clio did make phone calls. To Jordyn. When he asked why her parents weren't allowed to visit, they explained it was part of her house arrest. They weren't taking chances of her being in an uncontrolled situation when she crossed over. Ansel absently touched the medallion, its weight a reminder his time was running out.

Two days.

There was nothing protecting him from serving his sentence with the Fellowship of the Stone. At least he would be free of them and the chain around his neck. If he survived. Which he was beginning to believe wouldn't happen. He felt empty, and in the hollow was cold pain. The overwhelming feeling he was alone dragged him under, and he knew surviving for himself wasn't enough. He hadn't slept, wasn't eating, was tired ... he ached and he needed more. He needed his mate.

If only it was that easy. He groaned with his weakness. Each night he told himself he was going to smooth out the scars Milanka cut into his psyche and purge her from his head. The minutes he did sleep, he dreamt of Clio, her laugh, her touch, then her scarlet gaze met his, his head turned, and her fangs penetrated his flesh. He woke up terrified, soaked with sweat, his heartbeat hammering in his chest, and fisting the sheets. Looking at the house from his rearview mirror, he realized Milanka's death hadn't set him free ... no, it damned him.

Groaning from the pit his thoughts plunged into, Ansel took his cell and hit the green circle.

"Captain Wolt."

"You could talk to her. Start with an apology."

If he was a man who rolled his eyes he would have, but he wasn't. He was, however, a pissed off, confused, Pure-blood werewolf who was going to lose his mate, so he growled. She didn't want to see him, and he wouldn't betray her trust again and wouldn't invade her privacy. "Negative."

"You have less than twenty-four hours."

As if he needed the reminder.

"And?" He waited for him to reply, argue, anything, and when he didn't, Ansel saw Rutger had hung up on him. That was fine. Just fucking fine. He didn't know how to overcome his past, his pain, his lies, and how the hell was he supposed to talk to Clio?

He silenced his thoughts and listened to the music that had been playing most of the evening, easily recognizing the tune. She was listening to the same music as he did, as they had the night they made love. Ansel got out of the truck, looked up at the house, at the open windows, and wanted to believe with all his soul it was because she missed him, wanted him, forgave him. Her presence was a light feathering along his instincts and softer brush against his wolf. His wolf clawed at him and fought to feel her, needing to have her essence and passion intertwined within him. It wasn't there. He felt hurt, loneliness, and her fear which made the man's heart ache. Fear. Ansel drew in a breath and caught her scent—spice, a honeyed sugar, woman—while trepidation laced the fusion. It had his wolf howling in his ears and his instincts blaring something was wrong.

"Talk to me, Clio," he whispered and took a step forward. "Please." Opening himself to their bond, he felt a thread of her, a weakened string fraying as if caught in the wind, and once the current took it, she would be gone. The cross over. He went to his truck, and after grabbing his cell, called Rutger. "She is crossing over. I'm losing her."

Ansel heard Rutger's deep voice as he relayed the information, then he replied, "We're on our way."

"Who?"

"Jordyn, Doctor Barsacq, an Eclipse from the vampire council, and two Minors," Rutger explained, his words rushed. "Code White."

Code White. Like the car accident, no one was going to know what happened. Then his mind targeted the Eclipse. From La Morte, the vampire council, he or she was an elder vampire, who would take Clio as their own as they guided her through the cross over. And the Minors were blood donors, trained to use their powers to calm the feeding or intensify it. Ansel knew sex was a part of feeding and didn't want any one of them near Clio. But that meant he would have to conquer his fear. He proved he was a coward, unable to overcome his past, was going to let Milanka win, and made everyone believe he couldn't help Clio. His mate.

"My mate," he said aloud, like it might strengthen him. The thought of a vampire feeding her made his wolf claw his insides. The thought of Clio feeding from him or her, another, made him sick inside, and his body shook. This night, whether he was ready or not, was going to force him to face his worst nightmare.

Twilight yielded to night, and she thought about turning on a light, then decided not to. Her vision wasn't impaired by the dark anymore. Over the days the panic and fear had subsided while the slight changes gradually coaxed her into accepting the transition.

I'm not going to completely change, she kept telling herself. She was a werewolf. She was going to lose her human half, and did that actually upset her? Yes and no. The part she regretted was losing the connection with her mom and it scared her. What were her parents going to think? She didn't know. Clio continued to sway to the music, the hem of her skirt brushing her thighs as she tried to keep her mind on the filing cabinet, the folders, and not on the smokey blues emanating from the speaker. The smooth descant wrapping her in its silky caress reminded her of Ansel. Like the flannel shirt, she fought against it, the need to be close to him, then she gave up. She wasn't one to hold a grudge, didn't have the hate in her heart to do so, or the energy. Instead of holding onto the pain she let herself indulge in her thoughts, the memory of his body ... even her dreams ceased to have Milanka in them and centered on him. And why not?

What could possibly happen?

For the three days Ansel stood *guard*, he didn't come near the house, kept a safe distance from her, was a cold shadow in their bond, and didn't do anything to invade her space. Her empty space. Part of her wished he stormed into her house and demanded they talk while part of her wasn't sure she wanted to see him and the disgust in his eyes knowing she wasn't going to be her for long. She would bet money Baron Kanin was using the house arrest to force Ansel to talk to her or her to him. And dang it worked to a point. She purposely left the windows open, the music on, louder than usual, had hummed or sang along knowing he would hear her, and used more body wash than normal knowing he would smell her. She did all of that as if challenging him to come to her. As if wanting him to see her before the cross over, because once she did, he would hate her. If she was going to admit to anything, she was over the spell he had placed on her, the year she spent thinking she lost her ever loving mind, and his distance. She understood the reasons. Plus, it was pointless to hold onto the anger. That was more dangerous than forgiving him.

What kept her from going to him or walking out of *her* house to *her* driveway and facing him and demanding answers was the cross over. She was going to be a dhampir. Caught by her thoughts, Clio's eyes burned with tears she swore she wasn't going to allow to fall, not for the mate she was going to lose and not for the life slipping through her fingers. She was going to come out on the other side. Alone. Maybe better.

"Dammit," she mumbled as she closed the drawer. Where did the endless optimism come from?

It's simple self-preservation, she told herself. She wasn't going to give up. If she did, she would go insane. And it wasn't totally about her, she needed to stay strong for her parents, her patients, and she was too damned stubborn to give up her responsibilities. Clio straightened, scanned the room, and was determined to finish the office. She wasn't going to dwell on Ansel or the cross over.

The damn cross over, she thought as nausea rolled through her with a vengeance. Holding her stomach, her eyes blurred, and her joints felt like they had turned to steel. She stumbled to the nearest chair, and falling into it, her skirt rode high on her thighs, her spaghetti strap tank top twisted around her, and inhaling and exhaling she worked to steady herself. It didn't work. Her skin flushed, her heartbeat was slowing, struggling to send blood through her heart and veins, and she felt life draining from her.

"No. No. No."

She knew it was going to happen, knew she was going to cross over, had accepted parts of it, but having it happening put her in fear and panic's claws. Blinking several times, she struggled to see the room, to stay focused, telling herself she needed to find her cell phone. She needed help. She feebly searched the office, the desktop, the top of the filing cabinet, and then a small table. Where the hell had she put it? Luckily, she found it. She needed to get to the table and call for help. Despite her efforts to fend off panic, it coiled inside of her, its sharp edges slicing through her resolve. She slid off the chair to the floor, got on her hands and knees, and with tears falling crawled inch by inch across the office. When she reached the table, she fumbled to get her cell, but it fell to the floor, skidded, forcing her to crawl farther, then reaching it, took it in a shaking hand and attempted to see the screen. Her vision was nearly gone, terror was pushing on her, and she was losing her strength. Her arms gave out, her knees were next, and collapsing, she forced herself to her back. Flat on her back, she tried pushing aside the pain and dread enough to remember the screen, and the numbers.

"Please. Please," she mumbled as she touched the screen.

"ETA one minute," Jordyn's stern voice reassured.

Relief washed over her at the same time there was an urgency to tell Jordyn she was upstairs, but she couldn't get words to form, couldn't get enough air. Her muscles began failing and her arm dropped to her side, the cell hit the floor, and without it she felt helpless. When a seizure gripped her, she rolled to her side, to have searing pain race from her head to her feet, its flames radiating from her middle, and drawing her knees to her chest her blood thundered in her veins. She wasn't going to make it, wasn't going to live through the fire consuming her, through the pain taking over every inch of her body. *Half. It could only take half.* To steady herself she reached inside of herself for her wolf, and feeling it weaken, feared she was going to lose her wolf too. Then the bond with Ansel lit up with his presence and strength, and the powerful combination began flowing to her. She recognized the feel, the safety it created, the need within them both, and grasped onto him. She didn't want to lose him, regretted not talking to him, and wanted him with her. She clung to the fact he sensed her, knew what was happening and called for help. When she heard rushed voices, she wanted to cry, then orders were being given, and she opened her eyes to see black. There was nothing.

"No. No," she begged. The pain engulfed her, leaving her writhing on the floor and waiting for them to find her.

Ansel watched as the Eclipse and the two Minors, dressed in black suits and wearing scarlet, the color of the vampire council, stepped out of a glossy, black, luxury sedan. Their eyes gleamed like obsidian as they nodded at him, then passing him followed Jordyn to the porch and the front door. Rutger remained behind, his eyes blazing gold with amber circling his pupils, and stopped when he was beside Ansel.

"Where's Doctor Barsacq?" Ansel asked as he turned to see the four of them disappear into the house. He should be there, at Clio's side, giving her his strength to go through the cross over, not just shoving as much energy as he could through the fading bond. And it was fading, weakening as he clawed at it to keep her near him.

Her last words rang in his head. *I hate you.* He didn't know how to change it. Didn't know how to overcome his scars, especially now when they felt as if they were amplifying. He wasn't going to be able to help her. She would never forgive him for allowing Milanka to control him and abandoning her.

"It was decided he wasn't necessary," Rutger answered.

"Who?" he demanded, his hand going to the butt of his gun, his words nothing more than growls. His control was slipping, and his patience were burning to ash. "La Morte? Shadow Lord? What the hell is happening?"

"Your mate is crossing over and you're not by her side," Rutger stated. "Are you going to have a stranger from the damn vampire council give her his blood?"

Ansel wanted to growl, then howl at the sky. No he didn't want another male touching his mate, nor did he want Clio's lips on that male. Nailing Rutger with a bronze glare, he inhaled and exhaled. "I can't."

"You can. Clio isn't Milanka, she is your mate."

"For how long? As soon as the cross over is complete, our bond will be gone. It's waning as we speak, I feel her slipping from me," he argued and knew it sounded like an excuse.

"The bond doesn't make you mates. She didn't know she was your mate and still she needed to be near you. Bond be damned. You make the choice. If you want her, fight for her. Do you love her?" Rutger demanded.

"Yes, dammit, she's my soul. If she wasn't I wouldn't be doing this ridiculous guard duty," Ansel yelled as he began marching back and forth. "Three days of listening to her singing, smelling her, sensing her, the need to touch her making it hard to be in my own damn skin." His wolf demanded he protect its mate, to be by her side, while his mind slashed open scars, releasing a flood of pain and fear that were too embedded inside of him to ignore.

Rutger laughed, but it didn't carry joy ... no, it sounded hard, raspy, irritated. "Then go to her."

"It's not that easy," he mumbled. "She hates me." It was another excuse, and he knew it.

Another rough laugh and he said, "She never called to have you removed. She likes having you here, to be able to see you. Said she couldn't face you knowing you were going to hate her the same way you hated Milanka, who you executed."

Ansel tore his gaze from the open second story windows, his imagination running wild with what the vampires were doing, what they were going to do, and looked at Rutger as if he had spoken a different language. "I could never hate her."

"She doesn't hate you."

Hope. It was there in all its cruel glory. He didn't want it. Didn't need it. Didn't want to hurt. Didn't want to remember. "Years. Fucking years and I didn't have the strength." Images flew through his head, her at his throat, his flayed skin lying on the ground, his blood surrounding him. No one needed to know, and he stopped his confession.

"You do now. Don't let her take your mate from you," Rutger replied softly.

Was it possible? Could he? With his gaze on the house, a scream tore through the night, making chills race down his spine and his wolf howled in his ears. Fear clawed at his heart, his throat, his lungs, and he didn't think, he reacted to the sound of his mate in pain and raced to the house.

At the end of every conversation with Dr. Barsacq and then over the days she convinced herself she was going to survive. With or without Ansel, and if it was without, she had to take from the vampires. It was part of what she was, no different than shapeshifting. Curling into a ball, blackness veiled her and she lost sense of where Jordyn and the vampires were. Then hands were on her burning skin, and fighting their hold, she tried to ride the pain as it cascaded though her. Clio's throat burned as she sucked in a breath and screamed at the same time her back arched off the bed. Agony lashed through her, its razor-sharp whips slicing across her skin while her insides felt like they were dissolving to become liquid, and a hunger struck her like a bolt of lightning.

I'm going to die.

"Clio, you have to drink," Jordyn demanded.

"No. I'm not this," she whispered as tears slid down her cheeks, and she held her stomach. "I told him not to save me."

"He saved his mate."

The wolf's primal need to protect, she told herself as her body seized with pain. He didn't want her, not now, not ever. She was the monster in his nightmares. Thrashing her head back and forth from the flames searing her, she decided she wasn't going to, wasn't going to touch the vampires. Not when it meant taking on a paramount. A sire from the vampire's council.

"End this," she begged.

Ansel stood at the bedroom door, his heart breaking with Clio's words. *"End this."* Fangs sank into his flesh. *No, tesoro.* Jordyn and the Minors were trying to hold her down while telling her she needed to drink. The Eclipse waited beside the bed, his sleeves rolled up to his elbows, and his collar open, revealing a tattoo inked in black. First she would drink from his wrist, less damage, and when the worst hunger pangs had been sated, he would feed her from his throat. Her head between his shoulder and jaw, he would hold her there. The sharing would create a bond between them, and he would become her sire and source of blood. As an emergent, she would be watched, then once she gained control over her hunger, she would become a blooded dhampir, cleared to feed from anyone she wanted. Desired. Is this what he wanted for her?

Humiliation rushed over him like frost on glass as her fingernails dug into his inner thigh, and piercing the skin, blood welled. Ansel saw her lowering, the ends of her thick, black hair feathering his hip, then her tongue flicked out to capture crimson. Gods, he was going to be sick.

"Ansel," Jordyn grated between clenched teeth.

His name jerked him out of the nightmare, and he saw Clio's strawberry blonde curls surrounding her pale face, her skin gleaming with sweat from shock as her organs mutated. Not into a full vampire, he reminded himself, she was half shapeshifter. There was the blood transfusion. The animal spirit and magic would protect her from a complete transformation.

She survived and healed because of your blood. It was a sobering thought, and one he should have been concentrating on. Maybe, and it was a big maybe, their bond, the bond between wolves would remain. The weakness he felt had been from the beginning stages of the cross over. Hope. It was there to tease him with his mate. Was he strong enough to help her, to keep her?

"If you don't do something, we'll hold her down and Christos will nourish her. He'll be her paramount," Jordyn yelled. Her onyx gaze held him, her anger rolling from her, and a swift wind had started circling her.

Her paramount. Her sire. Blood source. They would have an impenetrable connection. Nearly deeper than the bond between fated mates. She would be bound to someone else. Forever.

Clio groaned, her lips parted, and a feeble cry left her. He was vaguely aware of Rutger at his back, his power and magic as Second to the Alpha drifting around him, no doubt brought on by his mate's anger and worry. Ansel eyed the vampire, his obsidian eyes, and didn't like him, didn't want him—a male—near her. His wolf wanted to help its mate while his mind focused on the scars pulsing with his past that wanted him to fall into the pit they had created. Like a coward. He was being torn to pieces as his emotions tumbled into chaos. He didn't know what to do.

"Make a decision," Jordyn demanded.

"Soothsayer, time is wasting," Christos, the Eclipse, warned. "She can't continue like this. Werewolf and vampire, she'll go bestial. You'll lose her."

Jordyn hesitated for a mere breath, as if expecting him to take a stand, to rush to Clio's side. When he didn't, she replied, "Do what you have to."

As if in slow motion, Ansel watched Christos approach Clio, while her whimpers invaded his ears. He couldn't let it happen. He ordered his body to move—she wasn't the same, she wouldn't hurt him, demean him—and still he remained frozen. There was too much at stake, damned if you do and damned if you don't. Time was running out for them both. He reminded himself he wasn't alone, hadn't been for years. He had a family. Turning around, he met Rutger's gold gaze and began taking off his gear.

"The Fellowship knows we're bound, fated mates. If they learn she crossed over and I'm her paramount, they'll use it against me and her. They'll do their best to find a way around the parameters Baron Kanin has set. They want to see my blood spilled, meaning her life is at risk. Swear to me you'll protect her."

"Brother, she'll be protected, you have my word," Rutger swore, his voice thick with a growl, the hate he felt for the Fellowship evident in his gaze.

Ansel tossed his BDU top to a chair, along with his tactical belt, holster, and gun, and nodding faced Clio as the Eclipse took a step toward her. "Get away from her," he ordered.

No one was touching her. Swallowing hard, he was determined to not lose the woman he loved because a monster had her claws in him. He closed the distance between them. Jordyn lowered her head as she stepped out of the way, and when he glared at the vampires, they stepped back from the bed. Clio thrashed side to side, her hair over her face, arms flaying, her legs kicking, making the hem of her skirt sit at her waist, exposing her pink lace panties, toned legs, and creamy skin. He growled. No one was allowed to see what was his. And she was his.

Mine. Ansel opened himself to their bond, and bringing the wolf closer to the surface, its fur on his skin, let his power flow from him to Clio. One second. Two. Three. Four. And she stilled enough Ansel didn't fear hurting her if she struck out at him, then sat on the side of the bed, her body sinking into him with his weight.

"Tesoro, stay with me," he pleaded. Moving her hair back, he held her face in his hands to see slate eyes warmed by rich whiskey gazing at him.

Tesoro. The word thick with emotion and lit with his accent. The name had haunted her while possessing the power to calm her, but it didn't compare to having his hands on her, his heat sinking into her, and the comfort he gave her. A wave of hunger mixed with white pain rolled through her, making her teeth ache. Her skin tightened, and she knew it was going to tear to ribbons. To live. She was becoming his worst nightmare. To die. His pain would die with her.

"Not this. I can't be this," she whimpered.

"Yes, you can. You have to." Ansel moved over her, pinning her beneath him and between his thighs. He wasn't going to let her fight him.

"You'll hate me," she whispered through clenched teeth, her canines lengthening. With her words, tears slipped from the corners of her eyes and her body shuddered beneath him. "You'll hate what I am."

"No. I love you, beautiful. Always have, always will. Forgive me."

The brogue in his promise made Clio smile despite herself, and relief flooded her at the same time fire raced through her to consume her insides. Her teeth ached, and she was positive her veins were collapsing and her heart was going to stop if she didn't feed. The need disgusted her as the instinct pushed her, but it didn't matter, nothing mattered when she heard Ansel say he loved her.

"Find a reason to give me your heart, tesoro, please," Ansel pleaded, his eyes burning with unshed tears. If the bond between them vanished, then they would create their own.

He had given her his heart and his trust, and now he wanted hers. Needed to possess her.

"Yours," she promised. Clio handed him her heart and everything she was, including her future as his mate and a dhampir. Arching her back, as much as his weight allowed, with the next wave of pain, she knew it wasn't going to last much longer.

"Drink, my love," Ansel growled, the low rumble telling her he was as desperate for it as she was.

Clio watched, her heart fluttering in her chest, her breaths rough, labored, while one of the vampires drew his nail over Ansel's wrist. As if it was a scalpel, the sharp tip sliced through flesh, making crimson well then spill into her open mouth. Its heat and iron tangled with wolf while his unclaimed magic reached out to her. Dropping to her tongue, it burned like ice, then swallowing her body absorbed him. In an instant her mind filled with images, voices streaming through the bedlam in her head, while fire raged in her middle and every muscle cramped to the point of pain. Terror raced through, taking the air from her lungs when her joints seized, and her body became ramrod straight, then it was gone. She couldn't feel anything. As she eyed Ansel and held his bronze gaze, she couldn't feel him.

"I can't feel you," she grated, her throat burning. "I'm not going to make it."

"You are. I have you. I won't let go of you," Ansel promised. Holding onto the bond, he released his hold on the chains that had held him back.

On both sides of him the vampires were giving him orders while the female, her voice rising above the others, had begun chanting, the high-pitched lilt echoing in his ears. It was driving him crazy, they were getting into his head, messing with his thoughts, the increasing presto taking hold of his wolf's spirit to change it. Not understanding what it meant, he stopped himself from yelling at them. While he was distracted by the vampires' magic saturating the room, Clio pulled her arms free, and grabbing his wrist, tugged it down to her mouth and she latched onto him. Before he could stop himself, pangs of revulsion bowled through him, making his stomach twist in knots, his heartbeat pounded, and terror tore through his system. His mind flashed to Milanka, her scent surrounded him, and he needed to escape her clutches and the humiliation of being violated that always followed.

The scene played over and over again—she was going to hurt him, pain was coming. She was going to take his throat. Ansel battled back, trying to shove the worst memory from his mind, and felt himself failing as he always had. He was too weak to stop her. Sharp points impaled him, paralyzing him with fear as her fangs ripped through his flesh, the flash of pain overtaking him. Her laugh rough with her hunger, she licked the raw wound, his exposed muscles twitching under her touch and searing pain sending him into shock. His stomach rolled, his mind started to fracture, and he struggled to remember where he was.

Clio gripped Ansel's forearm, her lips moving against tight muscles, her tongue tasting the spice of his skin, his blood flowing into her and calming the hunger while bonding her to him. She understood she would always be his. Part of her railed against the possession ... paramount, sire, master, that's what he was becoming to her as she crossed over. The dhampir's instinct to accept him as her paramount overrode a lifetime of objections and her human half. The half she could feel dying as his blood filled her then seeped into her bloodstream to mutate her DNA, organs, her entire physiology. Heated tears slid from her eyes as she grieved her human half and the connection she had to the world.

In her mind she saw a scarlet gaze glittering from a pale face and Clio knew her. Would always know her. Milanka. She felt the weight of the other's presence and knew it wasn't coming from her. She wasn't creating the image. Ansel. His blood, his memories. The object of his terror. Wild fear blasted from him, his disgust saturating the link between them, while sad defeat drowned the feel of his wolf. It was the terror making her open her eyes to see his were closed, squeezed tight, his jaw clenched, the tendons in his neck straining, his shoulders bunched under the black tee. This was torturing him. She was doing this to him. It wasn't going to work. They weren't going to work. How was she supposed to fight a damn ghost that terrorized him?

Ansel felt Clio release him, her feel turning miserable, scared, as she looked up at him with slate eyes ringed in scarlet, her reddened lips swollen. "It's not you."

"I'm hurting you," Clio confessed as clarity teased her. The ends of his hair hung by his flushed cheeks, his hooded bronze gaze held her as if he wasn't going to let go, and his chest heaved with his breaths.

"Let me fight her," Ansel growled. He had to beat this. He wasn't going to let her win. She was dead. True death. "She's here." He made a fist and hit the center of chest. "Let me fight her."

"Not like this. I won't hurt you," she seethed through clenched teeth. Fighting against the numbness taking over her body, she struggled to push her hips up to squirm out from under him. In response, he lowered himself farther, pinning her to the bed with his weight. She couldn't fight her transforming body, him, his weight, and the surge of the hunger and need coursing through every inch of her. Unable to move, Clio's mind began spiraling out of control.

Gods, she was suffering and thought of him before herself. Ansel felt the raw tangle of need and hunger like a lightning bolt in their bond and wouldn't deny her. Ever. She was his. Pushing the pain and fear of his past to his dark depths, he leaned down, his lips feathering hers. "Kiss me, tesoro," Ansel begged. "We'll hold onto one another."

Clio inhaled his scent, heard his pulse, and while she fought to refuse him, to ignore his soft plea, her body betrayed her. Leaning closer to her, Ansel left a light kiss on her sensitive lips, causing heat to wash over her, and she couldn't stop a moan from escaping her. "Need you."

"Yes, tesoro, as I need you." Ansel took her mouth with a kiss to brand her while his tongue licked at hers and he tasted his blood. Spicy and tangy it covered his mouth, then it changed. She somehow made it sweet, like a nectar that made his desire burn through him.

She ran her fingers through his thick hair, indulging in the taste of him; his blood, his tongue, and his skin. Clio held him to her, needing to taste more of him, to feel his weight on her body, and his warmth on her skin. She kissed him back, praying they could be like this forever, when the hunger ripped through her, demanding blood. The cross over wasn't complete. He hadn't fully become her paramount. She was drifting between worlds and losing herself. Pulling back from him, she held his heated gaze and saw the wolf staring at her through the man's eyes.

Fight for your wolf.

Jordyn hadn't been talking about Clio's wolf, not exactly, she was talking about Ansel's wolf. The one he was losing to the ghost of his past. Her mind whirled around the blood transfusion. Ansel was a Pureblood werewolf, Eclipse, Minors, La Morte council, Shadow Lord, it had all been orchestrated by one person. Jordyn. She knew, had known. Clio fought the hunger, wanting to keep the clarity. There was more there, a sliver of information just out of her reach, but felt herself failing when the thirst continued to overtake her. The cross over was demanding her, the dhampir, needed to be fed.

Ansel lifted his weight from Clio, sat on his haunches, didn't allow himself to imagine what they looked like, and raised his forearm. Noticing the incision had partially healed, the Eclipse stepped forward, sang a string of words he didn't understand, then drew his nail along Ansel's wrist. Blood welled and dropped to Clio's mouth.

"Drink from me, tesoro. Drink from your mate," Ansel whispered, his voice a rough breath.

Clio wanted to cry from the raw truth she felt rolling from him at the same time she wanted to smile with joy from the emotions she was feeling. Taking his wrist with a shaking hand, she brought it to her lips, and holding his gaze, drank in his heated iron, its sweetness, and his wolf's essence. Stronger, as if he let his horrors go, it burned through her, setting her insides on fire and stealing her thoughts, her control, then it wrapped her in its magic, and black veiled her and took her over.

Her small hands with her pink-tipped nails gripped his forearm, her slate eyes lost their whiskey hues to scarlet, then slowly her grasp weakened, her hands releasing him and falling to the bed, her eyes closed. His senses zeroed in on her, her heartbeat slowed, her scent changed from sweet sugar and cinnamon to rust of a thunderstorm tangled in orchids, and her breathing became shallow.

"What's happening to her?" he demanded as he crawled from the bed, careful not to disturb her.

"You gave her your blood during stygian and she accepted your sânge. As her paramount, your blood has taken her under and she's crossing over," Eclipse answered, his accent curling around the words. "While it is not a true cross over because she is a werewolf, she has lost her human side. There will be changes, however slight."

"Changes," Ansel mumbled. His heart was beating a million miles an hour, his mind was reeling from what they were, what they had done. Reliving the moment where Milanka took his throat, nearly killing him, he wanted to believe he truly overcame her torture.

"You were mistreated by one of our own. Victimized. I apologize."

It is what it is, he wanted to say. "How long will she sleep?" He had twenty-four hours.

"Through until tomorrow night. When she rises, she'll need to feed. Captain Wolt, understand she is werewolf and vampire. She has become a hunter, she will be aggressive when she takes your throat. It will be your throat as you have become her paramount." Scarlet eyes held his. "The pain in your past cannot prevent her from feeding. As an emergent, this time is complex, and vital to her survival."

"I understand. I won't fail her," Ansel promised. He wouldn't fail his mate.

"The bond you have with your mate means she will need physical contact. Skin to skin."

"I understand."

Nodding his acknowledgement, he faced Jordyn. "Soothsayer, it is complete. Clio Hyde, dhampir, has been added to La Morte's chronicles."

"I am most grateful, Eclipse. Please give Marquis Ladolofo my venerations," she replied with a slight bow, her cultured tone giving respect.

"As wish you." He started for the bedroom door, the Minors automatically falling in behind him, then they stopped and the two parted to allow him to have a clear view of Jordyn. "How did you know?"

"She's one of mine," Jordyn answered. The lilt of her words was edged with her power and authority.

Ansel felt he missed part of the conversation, and he probably had; his mind had been elsewhere and not on Jordyn, Rutger, or Eclipse.

"Now she's ours. Shadow Lord sends his regards," Eclipse replied.

"In return, I respectfully send mine."

Ansel watched Jordyn's liquid copper eyes roll onyx as if she was sending a warning, one Eclipse didn't take offense to. There was a moment he felt death in the room while they continued their silent battle. He tried wrapping his mind around what was happening, and then fought to focus on the questions bombarding him. When he thought he was going to have to order them to leave, Eclipse and the Minors left the room, their footsteps on the stairs, then the front door opened and closed, and their presence ceased.

"What was that about?" he asked. "What did he mean by ours?"

"Your mate bond remains intact, and her wolf's spirit remains with the Collective. Her name has been added to their chronicles, meaning she belongs to the La Morte council, name only, and will serve under their council and obey their canons. However, you became her paramount, and as a Pureblood werewolf, they don't have possession of her.

Shadow Lord doubted me, hence Eclipse and his Minors," Jordyn answered.

"How did I become her paramount?" Ansel asked. It should have been impossible for a werewolf to become a vampire's paramount.

"She is a werewolf. You're a Pureblood, you're fated mates, and the blood transfusion," Jordyn replied.

"I don't understand," Ansel mumbled. He didn't think he ever would, and it didn't matter.

"Me either," Rutger mumbled, a growl lacing his words.

Ansel's mind raced in circles. He had to get a hold of himself, he was Captain of Enforcers. Meeting Jordyn's cocoa gaze, he saw a soothsayer. "You kept her in the Collective." It wasn't a question.

"Affirmative," she answered flatly, her eyes giving nothing away.

"How?"

Smiling, Jordyn replied, "That's my business."

Rutger gave her a sideways glance as a flash of pride streaked his face, then he sobered. No one was going to talk about it, and they didn't have to. Shadow Lord wanted Jordyn and would do what he had to, to have her. Eclipse had been there to watch her and would no doubt report everything from her heartbeat, the colors of her eyes, her magic, and her power to the vampire lord. Every time Jordyn acted reports were generated, added to the freak file, as she called it, and sent to every team leader. Baron Kanin, along with Jordyn, knew every faction had a file on her and was keeping track of her. She risked exposing herself and the extent of her magic when she protected Clio. He was indebted to the Kanin family, and Jordyn, and was grateful for their help.

"It's getting late. We'll leave you. If you need anything, call," Rutger offered.

"Thank you." Ansel put his emotions in his eyes, wanting them to see the rawness of his heart and the love he had for his family.

"Goodnight, brother," Rutger replied. With his hand at the small of Jordyn's back, he escorted her out of the room.

Ansel stood staring at the open door and listened as they left the house and then the driveway.

What the hell happened? he wanted to ask again and again. Slowly turning around, he looked at Clio, her still form, and watched the rise and fall of her chest and listened to her heartbeat. Its rhythm meant for him and him alone while it told him she was all right. As the confusion of the evening plagued him, he couldn't stop thinking about their bond. It remained. It was a blessing and a damn curse. Like being fated mates. With the clock ticking down he was going to have to strengthen his guards to block her while he was dealing with the Fellowship. No way did he want her knowing what they were doing to him. She saw too much of him, of Milanka and her torment, there was no reason to add more bloodshed.

CHAPTER SIXTEEN

Clio opened her eyes as if an alarm had gone off, sat straight up, her heart pounding in her chest, an ache spreading out from her middle, her chest heaving, and the feeling something was horribly wrong riding her instincts. Every werewolf and human instinct she possessed targeted the area, and searching she found there was no one there, no immediate threat. Then she searched the house, and felt Ansel and his wolf, his presence like a silent strength stalking the shadows.

It should have scared her, to feel him, her paramount, as completely as she did. Closing her eyes, she reminded herself her instincts weren't werewolf and human, they changed to werewolf and vampire. She blew out a slow breath and struggled to do something she never had to do before—rein in her chaotic emotions and rampant instincts while trying to bury her power. Her power. The vampire's essence wove through her, its filaments tangling with her wolf to strengthen her magic, and where she feared a divide that might tear her apart, there wasn't one. She felt complete.

Ansel was sure his heart was going to explode when Clio's feel erupted in their bonds, twofold, and her power saturated the house. The powerful blast gave him information he didn't have time to comprehend, save for she was scared, and panic was flowing through her. Racing from the kitchen, he took the stairs three at a time, ran through the loft/office area and into the master bedroom. He might have been gone for one minute, maybe less—he was going to grab a beer—and had no idea what could have happened.

When he entered the bedroom, scarlet eyes warmed by whiskey stared forward, her breathing was labored, heavy, and rough, but it was her eyes that drew him in. In fits of consciousness, he contemplated if he was going to be strong enough to give himself over to her, if he was going to be strong enough to endure having her head between his jaw and collarbone, and her fangs in his flesh. He obsessed over the decision, his nightmares, his coming punishment, and the future. Whatever it was going to be.

As if sensing him, Clio slowly turned her head, her creamy skin a contrast to her strawberry blonde curls tumbling over her shoulders, and her eyes narrowed on him. During the night he watched the change creep over her as the vampire's essence took the human pieces of her. Where her skin was satin and beautiful before, it glowed, her cheekbones looked carved, yet remained soft, her loose curls tightened nearly to ringlets, and a deep red threaded through. She wore a tank top from the night before, and he could see her body changed. Where she had been strong but soft, now her muscles looked toned, cut. No longer was she human.

When her crystal gaze met his, he knew he was lost in her. He would give himself to those scarlet jewels and never deny her anything she asked. Milanka was truly gone.

"Ansel," she whispered. Clio remained still, not sure what to do when she saw his bronze eyes marked with worry and tension gripping his bare shoulders. He wasn't wearing a shirt, was barefoot, his jeans slung low on his hips, and she believed with all her heart if she made a move he would sprint from the house. As is.

"Tesoro."

A silver of relief inched in. "I'm all right."

"I see that."

"My senses, instincts are different," she whispered, admitted. Clio was going to have to learn how to control them.

"Have you accepted the vampire?" he asked. As a Pureblood, he didn't resent being a werewolf, had never questioned why, had never wanted to be anything else. He knew humans who had been infected and hated what they had become, their self-loathing driving them to end their lives. Clio was a werewolf, had accepted that part of herself, as she accepted her human half. Even if it drove her to prove herself because she struggled with the designation of Wight. Would she hate being a dhampir? He prayed she didn't.

Did she have a choice? No. Did she accept it? Yes. She felt stronger. Complete. As the silence stretched out between them, awkward didn't describe the weird vibe. Then her memory threw what she had done in her face. She'd fallen asleep while sucking on his wrist. Damn how she wanted to crawl under the covers to hide and deny the heat flushing her face but couldn't. This was her new life. She was going to take it and live it.

"I accept what I am," she finally answered. "I'm not sure what do to."

Relief washed over him. Still, Ansel didn't know what to do. After the torture by Milanka's hand, he stayed the hell away from anything resembling a vampire, wanting to have zero to do with them, and not wanting to be their prey. "Eclipse stated you would need to feed when you woke up. Do you need to?" Had he kept the part about having to be close to her a secret? No. He wasn't going to lie to her. When she fed from him, she would be close to him. The Eclipse also warned she was a hunter and would be aggressive. There, he had been wrong. That wasn't who Clio was, and she wasn't displaying any aggression because she was a healer and em-path.

She listened to him, the matter of fact of the question, and the emotion it lacked. "Are you comfortable with this?" she asked instead of answering him. The night before was hazy at best, her memories jumbled. She thought she re-membered Jordyn challenging him, and he responded while under pressure. Would he accept her now, while they were alone? When there was no one there to make him feel guilty?

"I am. I will never deny you, tesoro. Not my blood or my throat. I am yours," he replied. He was sure his heart was in this throat and that's what made his words husky, rough. It couldn't be the desire coursing through him thinking about her taking him, because it wasn't possible. He may have cast Milanka out of his head, for good, but could Clio's need, his need overcome the scars left behind?

It wasn't their need, he corrected himself.

It was their love. Unconditional. He would sacrifice his life for hers.

Clio was too stunned to make a sound. How did this hap-pen? How did he accept her and not hate her? Hate her for what Milanka turned her into. The dhampir had been posi-tive Ansel would turn his back on her. Because she hadn't known him. She ignored the man he had become. She held his bronze gaze, letting silence surround them while her senses found his truth and the edge of his passion. He wanted her, and it called her thirst. The phone calls she had with Jordyn, the lack of hunger, the slow progression of the cross over. They thought it had been Ansel's blood, for a myriad of reasons. They explained the cross over wasn't going to be as violent or as extensive because she was a werewolf. They lied. Yes, it changed her human half, what there was of it. As her traits continued to mutate, she knew her human half was slowly fading. She always wanted to be something more. Who knew it would become real?

They kept saying the transfusion and bond was going to change her needs. They warned her. Oh, how they warned her. She prayed it wasn't true, prayed they were wrong, and then chose to ignore it. It wasn't possible. She wanted to believe someone, the gods, the vampires, the baron, they were all playing a cruel joke on Dr. Hyde, the perfectionist. Buttoned down and proper. The responsible one. Yet she displayed the predicted symptoms and acted on them. While trying to deny her feelings she had opened the windows, listened to the music he liked, and wore his flannel to have his scent on her. And she watched him. Her mate.

Gods, how did she tell him? "I need you."

It was a whisper as if she didn't want to ask. Because ... well, she didn't. That was his mate, stubborn and willful. The corner of his mouth kicked up in an arrogant male grin he couldn't hide.

"I need you." Watching her rection, Ansel approached the bed, and sitting down on the edge, reached out and held her cheek. "I love you, tesoro."

Clio's heart pounded with the three words she couldn't believe he said to her without hesitation. "I love you," she replied as she leaned into his hand. She told herself they were the same people, fated mates, and she had to believe that, had to believe she could be honest with him.

"What do you need?"

Maybe it was going to be harder than she thought. "I was counseled on what to expect. I don't feel like attacking you, there's no aggression and I don't feel starved," she stated, scooting back.

"You're a healer, an empath. Crossing over didn't change who you are at your core."

It was true, she felt her senses. "There's more to it than that." Clio met his gaze, hoping to see a reaction, an emotion to his thoughts, as if he wasn't comfortable or she touched on a sensitive subject. Milanka. She couldn't get the evil bitch out of her head. When she didn't see a negative response and he remained by her side, a solid strength, it gave her the courage to continue. "Your blood and our bond to one another altered my needs. My hunger may manifest itself another way."

Ansel couldn't imagine how. Again, after his experiences with Milanka, he didn't care to know anything about dhampirs, let alone what traits remained after someone crossed over and what it meant. He reminded himself he was starting over, no one was like Clio, and he wasn't going to compare her to anyone. "I'm not going anywhere, tesoro, I won't deny you. You can tell me."

Clio inhaled, sensed his truth, saw it in his bronze gaze, and exhaled in defeat. "Sex." Seconds ticked by, then a minute, neither of them moving, both barely breathing. And she wanted to hide. Ever the responsible one. Conversative Dr. Hyde. A hardass. No fun. Doesn't like to be center of attention. Was embarrassed when Ansel kissed her in front of the world. It was her luck she would feed off the physical act and his emotions.

"You mean to tell me your hunger is sex?" Ansel asked, trying his damned best to keep the smile off his face and his wolf from pouncing on her.

"That's what I said. And," she replied in her best doctor tone, forcing herself to push on, "I will feed, but mostly it's energy from emotions and physical contact."

Skin to skin. Ansel sat frozen with indecision, his brain splinting in half. Clio was like a succubus. He wanted to laugh until his sides hurt, then grab her and give her all the emotional and physical contact her heart desired.

With his silence she knew it had been a bad idea to tell him the truth about her *needs*. It made her look weak, desperate, non-professional. Despite how she felt about it, she refused to have lies between them, especially knowing the Fellowship expected to have him for two weeks. What she was going to do for two weeks she had no idea. It was another worry.

"I've hit the motherload," Ansel whispered as he looked at the comforter.

"What did you say?" Clio asked, her words clipped.

"Sex. It's every male's dream. Or maybe just mine. You're my mate and I am here for you. Always." The control over his facial expressions burned to ash, and the smile he wore, arrogant and self-satisfied, curved his lips. "I'm prepared to make the sacrifice."

"You think this is funny. Do you know who I am?" she countered. If she had been standing, she would have put her hands on her hips.

"Affirmative, Doctor Hyde ..."

"I'm respected. Respected by my peers. The baron and baroness. I've worked my ass off to get to where I am, and now, I'm ... I'm a dhampir who needs sex. What the actual fuck." Clio sat back against the pillows, her arms crossed over her chest, her heart racing, her heated blood coursing through her veins, and her desire for Ansel making her body rebel against her.

"Mate," Ansel said, raising his voice to get her to look at

him. When scarlet jewels with a whiskey hue held his, he continued, "Listen to me. This is between us, no one else. It's ours. Like our bond. And just like the magic buried inside of me is ours. We can't run from what we are."

She hated when he was the logical one. "It makes feel like a fool."

"Would you rather turn ferocious and have the need to attack and possibly cause harm to someone?" he asked.

"You know I wouldn't."

"Is sex with me so bad?" he asked with innocent worry, his eyes wide.

She looked at him, tried to see him through the eyes of the woman she had been a month before and failed. Did she want to be that person? Yes and no. She had wanted him then, but this was different. His skin begged for her touch, his parted lips wanted hers, and his eyes, liquid bronze, were drinking her in. And his wolf stared at her from inside of the man as if waiting to see what she was going to do. It was all too much, and Clio lost herself to the hunger and the need. Rising to her knees, she maneuvered herself over him to straddle him and clasped her hands behind his head, her breasts against his bare chest.

"I'm going to take that as a no," he said, his voice a low rumble, his accent thick.

"You're arrogant."

"And dominate. We discussed this." Grasping the hem of her tank top, he slowly lifted it. In response, she raised her arms. He pulled it free it, leaving her bare in front of him, save for her pink panties that matched her breasts. "Yes, pink is my favorite color."

"You're incorrigible," Clio breathed before his lips covered hers.

The slow sensuality of his kisses, the spice in his taste, his hips cradling her, and his hands at her back, opened her senses to release a part of her she didn't know she kept locked up. The subtle need and hunger from minutes before turned into an inferno that captured what remained of cool, calm, and collected, and torched it. She felt herself change as the vampire came forward, her eyes burned, and her teeth ached, but worse, her arousal seared through her entire body. While she thought she was going to burn alive, she needed to ease the concern threatening to douse the flames. She ran her fingers through Ansel's hair, her nails grazing his scalp, then gripped a handful and pulled it.

His head moved back, and she met his gaze. "If I do something you're not comfortable with, you have to tell me. I'm not going to hurt you, and I'm not going to take from you. I need your consent."

The dominate wolf in him growled when Clio fisted his hair then ease back when she stared at him with scarlet eyes ringed in white, the hues of whiskey drowning under her desire and hunger. When the tips of her canines touched her bottom lip, and the scent of her arousal flooded his nose, he thought he was going to lose his mind. He didn't understand how one woman could destroy and another could make him stronger than he was.

"You have my consent. Like you have my heart."

The purity of his truth and his consent, freely given, fueled the flames coiling inside of her. Clio was going to treasure his heart and pamper his body, and hopefully smooth the rough edges of the scars riddling him and darkening his eyes. She leaned into him, her breasts against his skin, her fingers tangled in his hair, and kissed him, slow, her tongue licking at him to taste him. His spice and wolf teased her senses, his heartbeat teased her thirst, while his flexing muscles teased her passion and turned the combination into pure bliss. Rocking her hips, his hands gripped her, and pressing her down on him, she heard a male moan escape him.

"Thought I was going to lose you, tesoro," he whispered against her throat.

Clio straightened to look him in the eyes and watched liquid bronze swirling around onyx. "Never," she promised softly. He wasn't going to get rid of her that easy. She would have demanded he promise to never betray her again, as if she needed the verbal confirmation, not just his presence, but Clio couldn't bring herself to say the words. Not when Ansel was going to sacrifice more than she could imagine.

"You're thinking."

"About you. This," she replied as she slid her hands over his shoulders. With her heightened senses she took in his muscles as they contracted under her palms, the way his breath hitched, and the curve of his lips. It made her grin. Then she thought about what she was going to do to him.

He knew what it was, his betrayal, his past, his pain, and as they tried to bully their way through to destroy him from the inside out, it was her presence stopping the assault. Not because she was straddling him wearing only a pair of pink lace panties, his favorites ... no, it was her softness, her awareness of him, the way she touched him, revered him, and the scent of her skin. She faced crossing over, survived the pain and physical changes, and was worrying about him. Her heart would always be true. Wrapping his arms around her, he drew her close, and buried his head in the curve of her neck and shoulder, and in the thickness of her wild curls. He could have stayed that way, her body clutched to his, her curves molded to him for an eternity, then he felt her hunger trickling into their bond. His dhampir needed to feed. The thought sent heat racing through him as images of their bodies intertwined filled his head. Ansel eased his hold on her, barely enough so he could stand, and turning them, gently placed her on the bed, and began unbuttoning his jeans.

Clio didn't say anything, didn't want anything to sway the mood. She watched in silence as his long fingers worked each button, then watched him shrug the worn denim down his sculpted thighs and saw he wasn't wearing underwear.

That will never get old, she thought. And he was all hers.

"Like what you see?" A low growl, giving away his desire, laced his words as he watched her eyes glide over him. Her shameless perusal of his body gave him a sense of pride, a kind of strength he ached to feel, and wanted to bathe in it. Ansel watched Rutger and Jordyn share their strength with one another, saw the esteem in their gazes, and always watched the baron and baroness. He longed to have some- one look at him as if he deserved the attention. Clio gave it to him.

"You know I do," she replied. "Come to me."

Clio hadn't finished the last word and he was on the bed, his weight on her lush body, her back arching to him to have her heat kiss his skin, and the lace of her panties an erratic tease to his sensitive flesh.

"Gods you feel good, tesoro." Going to his side, he held her gaze as his hand slid down to her hip, then to the waist of her panties, where he looped a finger and pulled the del- icate fabric down her legs. When she was free and bare, he stared at her curves, his dark skin a contrast to the cream of hers, like her innocence was to his sins, and couldn't believe she was his and there with him.

Heat emanated from him as his gaze roamed her body

and his hand, roughened by work, feathered up her hip, to her stomach, and then her breast. Cupping it, he gave the pink tip a slow lick, and arching her back to him, he took it in his mouth, his tongue circling, teasing, tasting her. Her fingers threaded through his thick, auburn hair, to his neck to touch his corded tendons, then back over his scalp, and she raised her hips. Clio was trying to enjoy his measured seduction, his devotion to her, and the luxuriousness of his mouth on her. But her hunger had been on edge when she woke and now it was riding her so hard, she forced the shakes back, and the shudder that wanted to shake her to her core. The once cool, calm, and controlled Clio Hyde was quickly losing control and drowning in need.

When Ansel's hand went to her hip, he gripped her, his fingers digging into her to send impulses of pleasure to her core, then it slipped to her inner thigh, and she rocked her hips. With the scent of his lust pouring from him, a moan, a rough sound saturated with sexual need and intensifying thirst, escaped her. Letting it roll over her lips she absently ran her tongue over her canines, no fangs, and moaned. The old Clio wanted to rebel, and she told herself if she had more time to understand the change and its effects she could control the thirst, the need to have him and to feed off him. She couldn't, wouldn't hurt him more than he had been. She wouldn't be the object of pain. With a sliver of control, she tried to fight him and the consuming need.

Ansel fought the marked fear, and taking her chin in his hand, he turned her face and their gazes met. "Do you need to be on top?"

"No. You need to be in control." Clio was aching, starving, the overwhelming need making her shake. Bronze challenged her as it swirled in his stare. "I don't want to lose control," she admitted. It was scary as hell, and she felt herself losing the battle.

"I don't fear you," Ansel whispered as he held Clio down. "Take me. Please."

"My dearest." The silent words curved her lips.

Ansel drew in the scent of her arousal, her heated skin, the iron of the thunderstorm and orchids she had become, and didn't have a reply. Couldn't form words with his heart in his throat and his own control burning to ash. Gods, his wolf wanted to take her, mark her, possess her thoroughly. Those thoughts had never occurred to him. Mark his mate. Where the hell did that come from? The wolf clawed him, howled as the essence of her being entered him through his pores to infuse him with her wolf and the vampire coursing through her veins. It was deeper than the bond between wolves, as if a primal part of the vampire wove its way into him. The intoxicating tangle seared his restraint, and releasing her, he cradled himself between her thighs and heard a whimper of pleasure as he lowered to her. There was nothing left in him except the need to have her, to satisfy wolf and man, a hunger eating its way through his flesh.

Clio gripped his shoulders, her nails sinking into skin as he entered her in one hard thrust, the sensation a slice of pain and fiery pleasure as he filled her completely. His heat spread out, igniting the shackles binding her to her fear and burning them. They fell away, letting lust and the voracious thirst take over. She couldn't stop herself if she tried.

Ansel drew back, his eyes on her, a sheen of sweat covering his forehead and cheeks, his muscles taut as he thrust into her. Hard. She was going to lose her mind. Wrapping her legs around his hips, she matched him, his thrusts harder, faster, and could swear she heard his blood pounding in his veins. As she arched her back, to have him deeper.

She couldn't wait any longer. Clio met his gaze for a breath, as if confirming he was all right, before nudging his head with her own to expose his throat and the sensitive skin protecting the throbbing vein beneath. When she licked the pulsing area, Ansel stilled, tension riddled his body, his muscles like rebar, and it made her pause, as her erratic heart threatened to burst. Worse, her body was in control, the need to have him driving her, the thirst desperate to be sated. They had gone too far for her to stop.

Ansel knew he screwed it up, just like he knew her senses were hypersensitive, and she was in the storm of hunger and sex, he felt her, and hated himself.

"It's the anticipation," he breathed through a growl.

Anticipate no more, she wanted to say. Warn. Clio was trying to grab at reality, to control herself, when he withdrew, making a chill caress her hot skin, and he thrust into her, bringing a cry to her lips. It pushed her over the edge. There was no reality. No thoughts save for the need to sink her fangs into him. And she did. Flesh gave under the points, her lips closed on his skin, and hot iron tinged with wolf, aged magic, and Ansel flooded her mouth, making white fire streak through her. Moaning from the intense pleasure, she drank him in, and clinging to him, Clio held him close to her.

Pleasure had taken him into its embrace, the shear madness of it threatening to carry him into rapture, then her fangs pierced his flesh and a flash of a nightmare blasted in his head. She held him in place, trapping him, and he fought the reaction, clenching his jaw. The pressure gave him an instant headache, was enough he knew he was going to crush his teeth, but he wouldn't stop her, didn't want her to release him, and he fought the rooted reaction.

As if sensing his uncertainty, Clio deliberately rolled her hips, taking him deeper while letting him go to slide her hands gently over his shoulders, down his back, and to his shoulders again in slow caresses. She might be drinking him in, however she released him. He was in control not being controlled. It loosened something inside of him, a link falling to the abyss, and gave him a shred of freedom. Without thinking, he turned his head for her, giving her better access, and in return she curled around him. Her body's curves fit into his, and a soft mewling sounded, and he felt her tongue flick and lick at his skin. He groaned as he let himself delve into the erotic sensation searing his body, and rolling his hips with her a bolt of pleasure ripped through him. Nothing compared to being inside of her, having her beneath him, and her at his throat.

Clio felt the edge of thirst fading then disappear altogether while the sexual hunger was blazing through her to tear her body apart. Releasing Ansel, she licked the two pin size punctures to close them and caught up with him as he rolled his hips, the friction creating sparks of delirium. When he rose above her to look at her, she saw raw arousal, the threshold he was balanced on, and his wolf. Their bond flared, their combined passion and desire like lightning bolts between them, and striking them, Clio understood on a primal level what Ansel needed.

Maneuvering to sit on his haunches, Ansel grabbed her hips and pulled her to him. With her wild curls fanned out behind her, her back slightly arched, her breasts with their pink tips moving, he thrust into her. When she fisted the sheet beneath her and brought her knee up the sight almost drove him mad. He wasn't going to be the same. He was holding his wolf back as much as he could. The animal stalked the surface, its instinct and urge to mark its mate pushing his control. Ansel needed to see Clio, her reddened lips, her hooded scarlet gaze, and the flush of arousal stain- ing her skin. He needed to see his fated mate. A gasp left Clio's parted lips, and the sultry sound burned through him to sear the wall his wolf raged behind. He wasn't going to stop, he couldn't, he could warn her.

"Mark. You," Ansel grated through clenched teeth, then felt his canines lengthen while the low growl muffled the words. He tightened his grip on her hips, the force leaving crimson prints on her silken skin. Gods, he needed to hold on. He couldn't do this. Something in his middle stirred to loosen another link and it fell to the abyss at the same time his wolf clawed at him. He had to do this to be free. Of what, he didn't know.

Clio felt Ansel's desperation in their bond, heard it in his voice, and sensed his wolf. It wanted her as much as she wanted him, needed him, while she fought for more. With her thirst sated, and her body drinking in the flames of his lust, she was so close to ecstasy.

"Tesoro," Ansel growled, his voice strained.

Clio met his bronze gaze, saw the animal staring at her, felt its pull, and understood they were connected by more than the bond between them, and he was more than her paramount. "I don't fear you."

She said his words back to him, the sultry fervor severing the last restraint, as if it had been cut by a blade and scored a piece of him. Ansel released her hips, grabbed her arms, and lifted her to him. Wrapping her arms around his neck, she kept the erotic rhythm, caressing him, stroking him as her breasts brushed his chest, sending shivers over his heated skin. He growled, the rumble vibrating between them as the final thread holding his wolf back frayed, letting the animal free. His features sharpened, his instincts refining, and he heard her breathing, her heartbeat, and her pulse in her veins. Rogue strands of her hair feathered his arms, and he heard the barely-there, throaty moans as the flames inside of her became red torches and burned wild. He was going to taste it, devour it, and it was going to incinerate him. Ansel grabbed her chin, held her as her glassy eyes met his, and turning her head he roared to feel his chest expand and his heart open to the woman in his arms. The world they knew ceased to exist as he bit into her soft flesh, his teeth sinking deeper and deeper while her cry, half surprised pain, half ladened with sexual heat flooded his ears. Her grip tightened on him, her pink-tipped nails clawing his skin, and swallowing, his throat convulsed as the rich elixir glided down, its iron carrying her storm. The wolf roared and raged as he possessed her, and his body absorbed her. When the spicy tonic hit his bloodstream, lightning blazed through him, forcing his head back. Bellowing, his mark crimson and glowing a velvety bronze, he rode the savage pleasure taking him over the edge.

He marked her as his. Clio clung to Ansel, the searing sting from his wicked bite sinking into her core to make her mindless as it burned a path through her while his heat pulsed inside of her. Her body absorbed him, the vampire's hunger devouring him while ecstasy swept her up in its beautiful chaos to carry her into bliss' sweet embrace. Inhaling and exhaling heavy breaths, Clio sagged against Ansel, her body's needs quenched, the bond between them blazing anew while the tie to her paramount wove into them. They were different. Would always be different.

"I've got you, tesoro," Ansel whispered. "I'll always hold you."

He held her as he scooted backwards, then resting against the headboard made sure Clio straddled him, her sheath around him, her head on his chest. As their passion began fading, their bodies slick with sweat, cooling, he marveled at what he had done. What she allowed him to do. And what it meant for them. He held her close to him, wasn't going to let her go, couldn't when there was something happening to him, something coming undone inside of him. He could feel the pressure increasing. He was having a hard time deciphering what it was, how his body was reacting, so he held onto her as if she was an anchor keeping him with her, keeping him from drifting away, or damn, falling apart.

"I could sleep right here," Clio mumbled lazily as she snuggled into Ansel, his strong arms around her. She thought she should say something about being marked—she felt pride—but didn't have the energy. The Eclipse warned her that after feeding for the first time she would experience fatigue, a weakness, and would need to sleep. She grinned, her lips curving against his skin, his spice in her head. She was tired and at the same time full of power and very much alive.

Ansel drew his hands up and down her back, her sides, then played with the ends of her silken hair. While she took comfort from his touches, he wasn't comforting her, he was fidgeting, the feeling of his being unraveling gripping him. "Sleep. I'll be right here."

"I love you."

"As I do you."

Clio leaned into him, her body becoming lax, her breathing coming in soft, even inhales with her sleep. He forced himself to stay where he was and fought the urge to get up to walk, maybe shift and run. Damn he wanted to claw at his skin. Not wanting to miss a second with Clio made him stay, made him quiet his mind the same way he had when Milanka punished him. Dread joined the unnerving descent into insanity knowing he would have to use the technique in the days to come. When he thought his insides had twisted into knots and his nerves were going to make him crazy, the prickling sensations started to ease, the panic and fear fading with it. His body was becoming his again, letting him relax, and hugging Clio to him, he moved her mass of curls to see his mark. He couldn't believe the impulse, his wolf's need making him mark her, and couldn't believe she received him. Accepted him and his bite. She was truly his. Now the four punctures would soon be healed and become invisible to human eyes, leaving magic-born the only witnesses to see the sheer pierces and the bronze glow marking her his.

He was a Pureblood with a powerful family but didn't think he was good enough to have a fated mate, let alone capable of marking her with the color of his wolf. He had to admit when Rutger marked Jordyn, and she wore his bite, the jagged edges, torn skin from his violence with pride, he had been jealous. Without his family, his past haunting him, and alone and isolated he wanted what they had. A true love. Something primal. Seductive. To belong to someone. And now he possessed it and a woman strong enough to endure him. If he survived. Ansel closed his eyes, rested his head on the headboard, heard the clock ticking down, and felt time passing him by. Through half closed eyes he took one last look at the veil of bronze over her slender shoulder, kissed his mate, inhaled her scent infused with his, closed his eyes, and prayed he lived to have her again. If Strong Lord succeeded in killing him, she was going to follow him, and he would be responsible for her death. The loss of an innocent soul taken to early. A beautiful, gifted doctor. Despite his best efforts, a tear slid down his cheek. Weakness wasn't an option.

Sighing, he realized he was the happiest man alive who was facing a death sentence.

CHAPTER SEVENTEEN

Clio moaned a sound of sheer pleasure, extended her arms above her head, twisted her body to have her muscles stretch, and rolled to her side to cuddle into the blankets. As wakefulness brought her out of deep sleep, she absently reached out at the same time the night played in front of her. The images drifted. They had fallen asleep, their naked bodies against one another, and sliding by in a slow procession she watched the display, then felt the impact of what they had done. She fed. He marked her. Without opening her eyes—she didn't want the slide show to end—she searched for Ansel.

The bed was empty. Cold. Clio forced her eyes open to see him, naked, sitting in a chair watching her, staring at her. His bronze stare held his torment, the shadows from his past, while worry creased his face, and his shoulders were tense. It cut through her like a scalpel, the incision allowing pain and fear to seep into the wound.

"Today?" she whispered, her voice shaking with emotion. Her heart was breaking, her soul crying out as he hesitantly nodded his reply, his eyes going from hard bronze to regretful cinnamon. "No." Clio sat up, the sheet falling to her waist to expose her own naked body. Neither one of them had dressed.

"It has to be," Ansel replied as he left the chair, and kneeling beside the bed, held her gaze. "Payment for my sins."

"No. No," Clio protested, shaking her head, making her hair hit her cheeks. "They'll kill you."

"They can't. Baron Kanin forbids it," he tried reassuring her. Red webbed her slate eyes warmed by whiskey, as her pink-tinged tears tore at his heart, making it seize in his chest. He said a quick prayer, and hoped the vampire half would save her from insanity and death.

She wanted to believe him, desperately wanted to believe the words, to believe Baron Kanin's order, but couldn't. It made her want to cry, burst into tears, and beg him to stay. That wasn't who she was, and she wouldn't fall apart now, not when she needed to be strong for him, to be there when he returned. "I hate this."

"I do too, tesoro. It can't be avoided." Ansel stood, Clio scooted backwards, and sitting on the bed, Clio crawled onto his lap and wrapped herself around him.

"I'll be here," she promised, her lips feathering his skin. His strong arms embraced her, drew her closer to him, then she sat up and met cinnamon with bronze flakes. "If they ... hurt you, I'll kill them."

"I know." Ansel held her scarlet gaze spiked with fury, and giving her a half smile knew his mate would do exactly what she promised.

Clio smiled back at him knowing if they killed him, she wouldn't live long enough to do anything. Her vow was an empty threat. Settling against him to absorb his heat, his scent, she needed to memorize everything about him.

"I marked you as mine. You wear bronze." Ansel slid his right hand up and down her spine, his fingers tangling in her curls, while holding her to his chest with his left.

"I wear it proudly." Reluctantly she sat up, her fingers at his neck, her right thumb caressing where she had bitten him. "I love you and I'm here for you. Always by your side."

"I don't deserve you," Ansel replied around the lump in his throat. The truth of her promise warmed their bond and he grasped onto it to savor it. "Do you need to feed?"

"No, I'm fine. But I promise to be starving when you get back."

He was actually sad she said no. He wanted her fangs in his flesh and her mark on him. He craved her ownership.

"It doesn't mean," Clio whispered as she kissed him, her lips lingering while her tongue lapped at his to have his taste, spice, magic, and wolf in her mouth and in her head, "I don't want you."

She didn't want to be without him. Didn't want to face the next two weeks alone, their bond a void, because she knew he was going to become a phantom. Her phantom. All the while her imagination gave her nightmares. For a painful second, she saw him staring at her as flames crawled over him, leaving a trail of burned flesh and singed hair, then she saw his strength, integrity, and loyalty. When Ansel's arms wrapped around her, and he tugged her closer to him and to the hard length of him, she gave in to him. Nothing separated their bodies, and rising, she slowly lowered herself down his length until flesh met flesh. It was going to be a sexual seduction, not a claiming like the night before. As she rolled her hips to feel him deep inside of her, she held his gaze and watched lust, passion, and dread swirl in the cinnamon darkened by bronze. There was power there, she recognized it, felt it in their bond, tasted it in his blood, and prayed it kept him alive. It kept them alive.

In silence, Ansel gripped her moving hips, his fingers digging into her silken skin, as she ground on him, giving him the sensual part of her, the vulnerable part of herself. Not the Dr. Clio Hyde everyone saw and assumed they knew. Opening himself to her, he knew it would be the last time for weeks desire, love, and flames flared in their bond. The inferno reaching out licked at their passion, kissed their desire, and embraced their love, the pure rawness of it overwhelming him. It didn't call his wolf, the animal that clawed his insides, roared with the need to mark its mate. It left the man alone to love. Sweat beaded on his forehead, making droplets slide down his temples to his cheeks as he fought to hold on to her, to see her cheeks flush, her lips swollen, and ecstasy sweeping her up and sending her flying. It filled him with satisfaction to give himself to her, to please her, to have her to himself.

As sensations cascaded through her, the pleasure and pain from his grip, the branding of his kiss, Clio twined her fingers in his thick, auburn hair and her body throbbed for more. Save for their heavy breathing, the sound of slick skin against skin, and their lust-ladened moans, silence held the room as if waiting to exhale. She broke the kiss, needing to see him, and from under her lashes she saw bronze blazing, his pleasure lashing at him, its whips leaving him breathless. She wanted to watch when he lost himself to pleasure.

Ansel held her breast to his mouth, his tongue teasing the peaked flesh. Their eyes locked on one another when her breath caught, and her head fell backwards. "Yes, tesoro."

White fire ripped through her, causing an eruption to spill within her. In the midst of the surge, Clio forced her eyes to Ansel and held onto him as if her life depended on it.

"Baby," Ansel grated through clenched teeth. Her breath caught as her eyes held him, and with her body clenched around him, he let go of his control and a wave of bliss rolled over him. They were still staring at each other, their breathing returning to normal, and as if sensing them the room exhaled through the silence letting the weight of the morning settle.

"I'm coming back," Ansel assured. He didn't know who he was trying to convince, her or himself.

"I know you are, or there will be hell to pay," Clio promised. If she wasn't capable, she knew Jordyn ... hell, the entire damn pack would make sure he, they, were avenged.

"My mate. Are you going to be all right?" He didn't need to explain he was worried about her feeding. Absently, his hands grazed her arms, her breasts, and then rested at her waist.

"Yes. It's been arranged," she answered, sitting straight.

"Who? Eclipse?" Ansel demanded, his frustration and failure in the words. A gift from Shadow Lord, he wanted to add. "If I was here—"

"No." Clio held his face and made him look at her. "You will be here. Listen to me, they have your blood stored at the Hollow, and between Baron Kanin and Jordyn, I will have enough energy," she explained, using her doctor's voice.

"This is my fault, I'm sorry." She released him, and he looked down, unable to meet her gaze. "If I hadn't done this—"

"Stop. Don't." She didn't want to have this conversation right before he left but there was no getting around it. After scooting away from him and off the bed, she grabbed a T-shirt he tossed over a chair, tugged it over her head, then met his gaze riddled with worry, fear, and the ever-present shadows. "Was I mad at you? Yes. You had no right to take my choice from me. It was wrong and it made me feel like I was losing my mind. I thought you didn't want me. I wasn't good enough. It was a way for you to get rid of me. I know that isn't true, and I understand. Milanka was a threat, a freaking demented sociopath who wanted to kill you. You felt there was nothing else you could do."

Slate and whiskey drowned under the scarlet coloring her eyes, turning them to sparkling jewels. Anyone else would have felt her anger and saw the change as a hint to back off, let it go, but all it did to him was make her irresistible. His tempest. His tesoro. His thunderstorm. He left the bed, and closing the distance between them, gripped her upper arms. "I'm sorry for deceiving you. The betrayal is inexcusable. I will live with knowing what I did. What I ordered someone to do. You said you hated me."

She wanted to roll her eyes. "You're forgiven. And it's obvious I don't hate you. Just so you know, Captain Wolt, martyr doesn't look good on you."

Ansel fought a grin and was going to give a retort when he was cut off by a cell phone, and since he recognized it, he knew who it was. He kissed Clio's forehead, lingered for a breath, saw the scarlet fade from her eyes, and leaving her searched through his stack of clothes to find it. "Captain Wolt."

Clio wrapped her arms around herself, turned away from him, and struggled to block out the conversation ... and failed. Her hearing, like the rest of her senses, had improved exponentially, and she was starting to hate it.

Yes, she was fine. No, there weren't any problems, side effects. Yes, they remained fated mates. With a surprise. She wore his mark.

When Rutger asked another question, Ansel touched Clio's shoulder—it had to do with her—and he saw her flinch. He hated himself for what he was going to put her through.

"No announcement. We'll wait until you return. It'll give me time to talk to my parents," she replied, and was happy her voice held. Her heart was aching, it was becoming real, and too soon he was going to leave her. In attempt to ignore the desperation taking over and the pain, she thought about the list of things she was going to have to explain to her parents. Fated mates. Dhampir. His mark. The Fellowship of the Stone. His punishment. What he stole from her.

"He said no one will discuss it until we're ready," Ansel assured her, then to Rutger said, "Affirmative, I'm ready." Ending the call, he gripped the phone, his knuckles whitening, and looked at her. "Rutger and Jordyn are on their way. If you want, Jordyn will stay for a while."

She needed to say yes, just to have someone there, so she wasn't dwelling on the next two weeks and what they were doing to him. "I'll think about it."

"Tesoro, I'm sorry," Ansel whispered, the rough sound grating from his throat. His chest caved with his guilt as his breath left his lungs and his heart sank.

"You have nothing to be sorry for." Clio hated seeing the strong, confident, silent force crumble in front of her. Flattening her palm on his chest, his muscles constricted, and his heat sank into her. She was going to miss him. "Let's get cleaned up."

Ansel held her wrist, lifted her hand from his chest, and placed it over his heart. "You're here. Always."

She wanted to cry and felt the tears trying to fall. "I love you, too."

After showering, dressing, and having something to eat, as if there was nothing going on, regular damn day, the mood changed from desperate to remain together, touching one another, to cold and distant, and he withdrew inside of himself. While she regretted it, she expected it. Clio sat on the top stair watching Ansel pace, the gold chain and medallion sitting against black, his long legs carrying him across the yard, his strides eating the distance, his jeans hugging his legs, his black T-shirt molded to his muscled torso. Every three steps he would look at her, his heavy bronze gaze targeting her, making her question what was on his mind, then he would continue marching, his boots kicking up dust. She sat silent, didn't know what to say, what to do, how to help him, and for the first time in a long time was unable to heal someone. Clio felt useless, helpless.

Ansel stopped and faced his mate. She wasn't wearing makeup, her mass of curls were up, while rogue strands sat long her neck. Her pink, sleeveless top covered his mark, and she wore a pair of gray, cotton shorts. With his hands on the waist of his jeans, his fingers making circles on the denim, he blurted out, "Marry me."

Caught by surprise, Clio giggled, knew it was wrong, and couldn't stop. Maybe it was the stress, the feeling of helplessness, or having to accept being a dhampir and facing the Fellowship ... she didn't know but she couldn't stop.

"Are you laughing at me?" he demanded, his eyes narrowing.

"No, I think I'm losing my mind," Clio replied through a breath. "Are you asking me to marry you?"

"Affirmative, Doctor Hyde."

"Well that makes it official." Standing, she placed her hands on her hips and glared at him.

"Will you, Clio Hyde, love of my life, please marry me?" He couldn't believe she was challenging him right then. Of all times. The fucking clock was ticking. And he needed something to think about, to latch onto through the pain and separation.

"This is impulsive. You're in a high stress situation and facing only the gods know what. Don't do this."

"What? We're already fated mates, I'm your paramount, what's a marriage?" he demanded. By the flash of scarlet she gave him, he knew he said the wrong thing.

"Let me explain. A marriage is a union between two people, a unity. There is a sanctity of which I take very seriously." Clio stood her ground despite wanting to yell yes and run to him. "The commitment isn't made in haste. It's definitely not made when you're facing an uncertain future."

"I didn't mean how it sounded." Ansel marched four feet, stopped, and faced her, his boots grating on the gravel. "I don't know what will happen to me. I need something to hold onto. Like a light at the end of a fucking tunnel," he confessed, and knew he sounded weak. He didn't want to be alone with his misery or his nightmares. Would Milanka come back and destroy everything he worked for? Would her terror rip his mind apart?

Clio descended the stairs, closed the distance, put her hands in his back pockets, and pulled him to her. "If you are all right, open the bond, I will be there. If you're not all right, open the bond, I will be there. I'm strong enough and I'm not going to break. You're not alone. You will never be alone."

Ansel's heart raced with her vow, her sacrifice, her love, and the strength she gave him unconditionally. He didn't deserve her.

Clio watched his emotions crease his face, darken his eyes, and wanted to help him. "I love you," was all she could say. Everything else seemed unconvincing, out of despair, and just words.

"I love you."

Clio closed her eyes and immersed herself in his scent and the feel of him when Ansel rested his forehead against hers. She hated the anticipation, the waiting, and the never-ending what-ifs. Hated them all. She felt Ansel's calm move over him, his feel in the bond weakening when they both looked up to see Rutger's black 4x4 truck rumble down the drive and park behind Ansel's. Clio blew out a slow breath, hoping it calmed her anxiety and eased the uncertainty fluttering in her middle.

"Ansel, Doctor Hyde," Rutger greeted, his mahogany gaze taking them in. Wearing a faded red T-shirt and equally faded jeans and boots, he wasn't the Director of Enforcers but Ansel's friend and brother.

"Director," Clio managed to say.

Jordyn took her place beside her mate, her clothing—fitted blouse, black slacks, heeled boots, and OPI badge—telling them she was expected to work. Detective Langston with the Organized Paranormal Investigations lived a multi-faceted life. Clio didn't know how she did it. Remaining silent, she gazed at them, her cocoa eyes listing between copper and onyx.

"I'm ready," Ansel said, breaking the silence, the roughness giving away the truth. He wasn't.

"We can leave. Time starts as soon as you're in the truck," Rutger stated.

Clio wanted to ask a dozen questions, the top three being why two weeks, had anyone confronted Strong Lord, had Baron Kanin used his authority to stop what was about to happen? And then the top question of all time, had Jordyn, soothsayer and all powerful tried to stop it? And had she tried talking to Prime, the leader of all magic-born? Surely if Jordyn asked, the powerful demon would have obliged. She couldn't make herself. It was unfair. She was shaking, and feared making Ansel, Captain of Enforcers, a Pureblood, a powerful werewolf strong enough to be an alpha, look weak, as if he would evade his responsibilities.

"He'll come home to you, Clio," Jordyn answered as if hearing her questions.

She probably did. "I know."

Ansel turned to Clio, took her in his arms, and kissed her. Not a searing kiss or a branding kiss, it was soft, a kiss of promise. "Two weeks. I'll be right here." He looked at his watch, then meeting her scarlet gaze with bronze said, "Nine."

"I don't feel like the cool, calm, and collected doctor I should be," Clio confessed.

"Your secret is safe with me, tesoro." He held her face for a breath, and hating it, Ansel let her go. Nodding to Rutger, he followed him to the truck where they got in. "Do you remember what I said?" he asked as he sat back and stared out the windshield at Clio.

"I swore to protect her, and I will. The pack will," Rutger replied.

Watching her as Rutger backed out of the drive, he kept his eyes on her until he could no longer see her. "Being without her is going to be worse than what Strong Lord has planned."

"It always is," Rutger answered softly.

"Tell me he is going to be all right," Clio demanded as she stared at the empty road, his silver 4x4, and felt the distance growing between them.

"He is going to be all right."

Meeting the copper gaze, the swirling fathoms it held, and the magic drifting from her, she doubted Jordyn was being serious. The flowing power prickled Clio's skin to send a shiver lacing down her spine. "You're extra creepy today."

Tilting her head to the left, Jordyn smiled. "So are you."

Clio gave a flat stare and shook her head. "Come inside, I have coffee." How did Jordyn appear normal one minute and supernatural the next?

"How is dhampir life?" Jordyn asked as they took the stairs.

"You mean as an emergent with enhanced senses and the need to feed?"

"Sex and blood. Kinda kinky, and not what I expected from you, Doctor. But you are an empath. Did you retain the trait?"

Clio stopped at her door and faced Jordyn. "How do you know?"

"I can smell it. Did you retain the trait?"

"Yes and its hypersensitive. Why don't I smell it?"

"You are the smell."

Maybe. Clio leaned close to Jordyn and inhaled. "I can't smell your wolf or magic. I can't sense you. Can scarcely hear your heartbeat. And the feel of magic from earlier is gone. It's like you're human."

Jordyn shrugged. "I don't know."

"You're lying," Clio grumbled as she opened the door and waited for Jordyn to pass. With her there the worry and fear for Ansel had been buried, not deep but enough her attention was on something else. As she walked into the house his scent of woods, man, and wolf met her, wrapped around her, then she heard his low whispers and his accent, and felt his breath on her skin. "I didn't think I could hurt this bad."

Jordyn faced her, her eyes going onyx. "Be strong, Doctor Hyde, it's day one."

"Day one," Clio repeated with a scarlet gaze.

CHAPTER EIGHTEEN

Oak, pine, cedar, and cottonwood trees lined the shoulders as if wanting to converge onto the asphalt as the two-lane road stretched out in front of them. The sun was rising higher and higher, pushing the day forward while it consumed the time he had left. Ansel felt the seconds as if the hands of the clock were slamming inside his skull.

Boom. Boom. Boom. He wanted to clasp his head in his hands to make it stop.

"You're going to be all right." Rutger's rough voice broke the silence and disoriented the dings and beeps from the terminal.

"Clio said if I died, she was going to kill them," Ansel said with a sliver of pride in his voice, then regret. She was his warrior. "It won't happen because she'll be dead or fucking insane. I did this to her. Just like I took her memories."

"She has her memories back, and from what I scented at her house she forgave you. It's time you let it go. You're not going to die." Rutger gave him a sideways glance, his gaze lingering. "I've never seen you scared."

Ansel knew his fear was saturating the cab, he felt it on his skin, and was inhaling it while Rutger's assurance that he was going to live battled back. He couldn't stop himself from clenching his teeth as his breath caught and his throat felt like it was closing on him, preventing him from defending himself or simply responding. Scared. He was scared. For the first time in his life, he was scared to death. *I'll lose Clio.*

Relaxing his jaw, he replied, "There's too much at risk."

"Having a mate and a family creates risk. At the same time, they're the ones who will protect you," Rutger stated. "Will walk through hell's fire because they love you."

True. "It's a foreign feeling."

"Get used to it."

Rutger made a left, the truck downshifting to climb the steep grade, the condition of the one-lane, dirt road looking abandoned and haunted and would make humans and magic-born alike reconsider going any farther. The thick trees, wild brambles, and boulders warned you if you stopped you didn't want to wander off, you didn't know what was lurking in the woods. As the truck continued a slithering feel of a presence—as if someone was watching them, following them—hovered in the air, making his senses go into overdrive. It was new. Every time he was forced to attend a meeting, this stretch of the road had been free of spells, magic. They either added something new or had activated a spell.

Behind them, clouds of red dirt sat heavy then drifted, the rocks the tires kicked up bounced off the road, while the sun breaking through the cluster of limbs cast spiderwebs on the black hood, their reflection on the windshield. His heart raced when he saw the two sentinels, one on the left, the other on the right. They weren't human or magic-born, rather they were two wooden poles with runes in multiple colors and figures in all shape and sizes carved into them. They stood as security, and when they drove between them, they entered a wall of magic and power. Strong Lord knew they were there. Pulling himself from his fear and the hell he was facing, his mind went to work.

"The poles," he mumbled.

"They're creepy, witchy shit," Rutger growled. "I've always hated them."

"Affirmative. Strong Lord demanded to know how Jordyn broke the wards shielding you. Because they have wards. They fear her breaking them. She would have known they held Milanka, and about the demons and the others. That's a lot of magic, power in one place."

"Affirmative. Could be they're trying to use their status and arrogance to get their bluff in. They're more powerful, forcing Cascade to back off. The baron wouldn't start a war with them when he would be putting innocent lives at risk. And he might lose his place as alpha."

Rutger's words were stern, sharp, controlled as if he had them restrained and was daring them to give away his emotions. Ansel knew the reaction well. The wards protected his location while they cut him off from the bond he shared with his mate. It had left him alone and given Kerrick time to brainwash him. Over the months Rutger had come back piece by piece, becoming himself with each new day. But sometimes, like right then, there was a sliver of the pain he dealt with. Ansel responded to the tension in the air by ignoring it and letting Rutger work through what he needed to.

"They were blatantly breaking the canons right under Baron Kanin's nose and Jordyn's. If they assumed she broke the wards, they might have been testing her abilities, strength. They want to know what she is capable of and what they can get away with. My confession and Milanka's escape fucked up their plans. Then the Highguard came to town."

"And backed the baron," Rutger added. "The Fellowship knows the Highguard will support Cascade and their sooth-sayer. I'll tell the baron our thoughts. When this is over and they have no claim on you they'll have to keep their distance or the baron will step in and things *will* get serious."

Ansel's reply went unsaid as the truck slowed and he watched the wrought iron gates slowly open. When they stopped, the Fellowship of the Stone's bunker, the strong-hold, and the mountain behind it came into view. The first story resembled a log home, money giving the impression there was nothing evil behind its walls. Not creatures from myth forced into hiding, creatures who had been mutated when magic left the world, creatures bent on revenge, or those who were serving a sentence for crimes against the Highguard. Which there were several. The asphalt beneath silenced the tires as Rutger drove up to the front where he stopped, put the truck in park, and sat back. Ansel's freedom had come to an end. Inhaling and exhaling, he buried his fear and panic. He would be damned if any one of them were going to sense him.

"I asked Clio to marry me," he blurted out.

Rutger laughed a humorless, low rumble. "She promptly said no."

"Affirmative. Then gave me a speech about the sanctity of marriage." The tension eased but the lighthearted feel wasn't real; it was a false veneer over the truth.

"Smart woman."

"She is," Ansel mused as he laughed at the reply. He wanted her to marry him, needed her, and felt, it sounded old fashioned to him, to bind her to him. She would carry his name.

"This is fucking stupid," Rutger's controlled roar declared as he hit the steering wheel.

"The consequences for my actions, brother. When it's over, I'm free. I have to remember that," Ansel replied, trying to reassure him. That was the light at the end of his tunnel. Clio. Freedom. Freedom to love her. Freedom to live.

"I'll be right here in two weeks," Rutger promised, his eyes rolling gold. "With a team if they fuck around."

"Two weeks." Ansel grabbed the door handle when Rutger gripped his upper arm. Facing him, he saw worry and fear in his mahogany gaze riddled with gold.

"I'll be here, brother."

"I know." After opening the door, Ansel got out, and standing beside the truck, held Rutger's gaze. "I know."

Before he did something out of desperation, that he would regret, Ansel closed the door, and started toward what would be his prison for the next two weeks. As the diesel engine and the crunching of tires over rocks faded, he found himself alone, and facing a set of double oak doors. They knew he was there. Knew the moment he crossed onto their territory. Why someone hadn't greeted him, and by that he meant put him in chains and escorted him to the dungeon, because there was one, he had no idea.

Ansel looked behind him to watch the gate close, as if sealing his fate, and when the locking mechanism latched the echo ended in a heavy silence that sank around him. His anxiety fed the tension rippling along his shoulders, up his neck, and into his head where it detonated with the building anticipation. They were screwing with him, watching him unravel, and he hadn't even gone into the house yet. Thinking about Clio wasn't helping him. He told the truth when he confessed to doing this to her. He wasn't there for her, and when he was, he took from her.

"Crimson Prince."

With images of Clio playing and guilt swirling in his veins, Ansel swung around, ready to face his capturers. "It's Captain Wolt, Shamyra."

Like Fiala, she was a Kaia, and where Fiala's skin was pale, was tall and blonde with blue eyes, Shamyra was petite with coffee skin, black lined her almond-shaped cocoa eyes, and her straight, raven hair ended at her pierced ears. She was exotic and moved as if she was part of the wind. He knew how dangerous the demoness was; she had been an assassin, and in no way did he believe she had ever been benevolent. Wearing a red tank top, dark jeans, and running shoes she looked almost human.

"Captain of Enforcers and traitor to the Fellowship," she mused. "Strong Lord is not pleased."

She didn't sound human. Her voice carried years of life, its timbre giving away her lineage while it held a warning. He instantly closed himself off from Clio, he had to, even knowing there were wards, and with his disconnect the fear, turmoil, and guilt from the morning cemented in determination. "I'm not concerned."

"You should be. We have plans for you, Captain," she promised, her eyes narrowing on him. "You have Fiala and Eero."

"They were arrested for crimes committed against Cascade, breaking the Highguard's canons, the atrocities committed against Milanka Telep, and protecting the magic-born who were here illegally."

Her laugh curled in the air. "You care about Milanka?"

He didn't. "Crimes were committed."

"How's your little Wight?" Shamyra questioned flippantly while ignoring his accusation of crimes committed. "Did she cry?"

"She is none of your concern." They didn't know and wouldn't know his little Wight was an Illuminate, a dhampir, and he was her paramount.

"You could have been part of us, Crimson Prince. Powerful creatures from myths. Purebloods. Illuminates. The victors." Closing the distance between them, she drew a perfectly manicured nail down the center of his chest. "You could have followed in your mother's footsteps."

The war Emanation, the rise in magic was going to cause. Only it wasn't going to be that easy, that clear cut, it wasn't going to be black and white ... no, it would start with small uprisings. Nothing to worry about. Life goes on. Eventually, it would become human against magic-born where sides would be taken, and lines drawn. The Fellowship believed they were superior, and so did others. After the scattered battles destroyed people on both sides, cities, and towns no longer existed, the true powers would be free to rage war. The earth would become a battle ground. A chill slid down his spine as he grabbed her wrist, held it, his fingers wrapping around her, and squeezed.

"Don't talk about my mother," he growled.

"Crimson Prince," Elchanan, SinEater, greeted. His flint eyes matched his gray button-up tucked into black slacks, which ended at his equally shiny black shoes.

"Tsk. Tsk. The prince prefers Captain Wolt," Shamyra advised through a mocking laugh.

Ansel squeezed her thin wrist, forcing her to meet his eyes, then let go of it as if it had burned him. "Elchanan."

"Captain Wolt, please come in. Strong Lord is waiting for you." Stepping back, he waved his arm and waited for Ansel and Shamyra to enter the massive foyer.

The bite from bitter smoke met his nose, and looking across the expanse a fire sparked and crackled from a stone enclave, its flames casting a glow over the leather couches. Above him, a chandelier with a wrought iron frame, crystals, and candle bulbs hung from the open beam ceiling, to add an elegance to the bare log walls, while expensive area rugs in rich colors covered the wood flooring. As part of the Cloaked, they lived in seclusion, but the Fellowship lived like prisoners. Some of them were, however they didn't suffer. Everything from the furniture, bathroom faucets, right down to the light switches proved the wealth of the group.

"Are you so cold, you need a fire?" Ansel asked. Temperatures had risen to the high eighties to low nineties and remained constant which was unusual for an area accustomed to the seventies. Ansel didn't think it was about the weather. No, he assumed it was for him, a not-so-subtle reminder of his beginning and his near death.

"Ambience. And I find fire cleanses the soul as much as it soothes it. Don't you agree?" Elchanan asked as he looked back at it, his silver and violet tinged hair grazing his collar.

"Negative." Ansel stood ramrod straight and searched the area, although the wards kept him from sensing anyone, where they were, what they were. He didn't have to guess where they were going to take him. He did expect to be treated like a prisoner ... they were like Milanka, drawn to drama.

"Shall we?" With an exaggerated bow, he waved his arm toward a hallway.

"Yes, Captain Wolt," Shamyra said as she took his elbow, "shall we?"

Ansel cringed with her touch and tried getting out of her hold to have her fight him. Resisting was useless when this was the game they were going to play. He reminded himself in two weeks it would be over, and when it was, his collar and leash would be handed back to his want to be masters. He was going to be free to have a life with Clio. As if responding to his thoughts, Shamyra tightened her hold, her petite frame concealing the strength she was capable of, as she followed Elchanan through the main living area to the hall. The house was empty, letting an eerie silence settle, and it made their muffled footsteps louder than they were. Leaving the façade of the house, they walked down a long hallway to a painting, he believed was from the 1600s, covering the wall from floor to ceiling and they stood in front of it. The stillness and quiet ate at the tension as Elchanan exposed a keypad and entered a code. Ansel had been given his own at the same time he was given his collar and leash. The light blinked green, the painting slid back into a pocket, and an open elevator sat waiting.

Stepping inside, the soft brown square large enough to accommodate the creatures and their forms, Elchanan held the door, while Shamyra guided Ansel inside, then nodded, and he chose the floor. The letter B lit up. Basement. It wasn't a basement, it was a throne room complete with dais, seating for an audience, and an array of torture equipment. A fancy dungeon.

Once we enter the bowels of the Fellowship it's over, his mind screamed at him. *I'll be at their mercy*. He wanted to laugh. A traitor deserved no mercy.

"That little burst in your heartbeat means you're scared," Shamyra teased as she leaned into him.

Nudging her away, he put as much distance as she allowed him to have between them. "Maybe I was thinking about my mate. Not this."

"Your little Wight." Shamyra's voice became brittle, the demoness letting her anger in her words.

"Mine," Ansel growled.

"Half human," she mumbled. "Weak."

"If what Milanka said was true about your training, Strong Lord will enjoy breaking you. *If* what she said was true. She was a bit preoccupied." Elchanan grinned, exposing a set of perfect, white teeth with sharp tips.

"What happened to you, Elchanan?" Ansel asked, his demeanor condescending. The once proud and respected SinEater had been a god to those who worshiped him and his abilities. People from around the world would give their last penny to save their deads' soul. He never expected to see him as a permanent resident of the stronghold. Before Elchanan could respond, Ansel accused, "I guess when you wallow with pigs you start to stink like them."

"Your association with Cascade has given you false confidence, Crimson Prince. Strong Lord and those of the Fellowship, pigs like me, own you," the SinEater countered, his flint eyes bleeding white.

"Gentlemen, we're here." When the doors opened with a whisper, Shamyra stepped ahead of Elchanan, letting her fingers trail down Ansel's forearm. The touch causing a chill to snake down his spine.

"Royalty first," Elchanan declared. Mocked.

Ansel buried his fear, wore his confidence like armor, and with his shoulders straight and his head held high, followed the demoness down the hallway. The walls were gray and blue stones, local to the area, specifically to the Fellowship's territory. Griffin had been Strong Lord of the Fellowship since its conception, feeding his magic into the land, to own it, manipulate it, sacrificing himself for its protection. What he failed to understand, and Ansel couldn't believe his thoughts were going there—maybe it comforted him—was Jordyn's blood flowed through Cascade's territory, making it hers and hers alone. Griffin's arrogance, like blatantly breaking the canons and then trying to blackmail Ansel, were going to be his downfall.

They walked in silence, the hall lit by candles, and he knew the warm glow was a lie. Beyond the stones was six feet of concrete protecting them, the elevator, several other floors, and the basement from the mountains. It also guaranteed several things; no one heard the screams, no one smelled the dead, and there were no interruptions. Plus, there were the wards they feared Jordyn could break, protecting them from magic-born. When they entered the throne room, heads turned to the muffled sounds of clothing, hushed murmurs broke the dead silence, and he refused to look.

He swallowed, stopped from shuddering when he realized they were going to make an example out of him. The weight of the truth landed on his shoulders, and almost sent him to the ground. After breaking the Highguard's canons and Cascade's, the Fellowship was allowed to punish Cascade's Captain of Enforcers. It proved they were superior, no one would dare go against Strong Lord or those aligned with him. Ansel had walked into it like a fucking lamb to slaughter. And there was nothing the baron, Rutger, or Jordyn could do about it. He singlehandedly fractured their authority in front of the territory and potential enemies. Anger, fear, and guilt twisted inside of him, roiling into an inferno he needed to control ... better yet, snuff completely or risk having it used against him. Like the need to protect Clio had been used against him.

With Elchanan leading, Ansel entered the sanctuary and the gold glow from wrought iron sconces, with a mix of candles. The plush, scarlet carpet cushioned his steps, and he felt the combined power flowing around him. He walked the aisle, passing pews, staring eyes, judging eyes, and thought the mock church was ridiculous. It always had been. The sconces, candles, black and red furnishings. Next he figured there were going to be men in black robes chanting. The absurdity of it all quenched the edge of the inferno. When Elchanan veered left to take his seat beside Shamyra, it left Ansel standing alone in front of the raised dais staring at the empty throne. Its size was indictive of Strong Lord's form, its feathers of gold, the eagle's head, and then rubies matched the rest of the décor, and the mural behind it.

At his back, Ansel heard their whispers, mumbles, accusations as their voices grew in strength, their trepidation fading. They weren't scared of him. He didn't have authority, status, rank, he was completely defenseless in the belly of the stronghold. A female was the first to sling an insult at him, her brittle voice calling him a liar, the next with more confidence came in form of traitor, the next coward. Cheat. A couple of others in a language he didn't understand and didn't care. Bastard. That one stung and he didn't know why. Foreign languages, the lit curling around whatever they were saying. Minutes turned into an hour as they continued to throw slurs at him, and he refused to move, to react to anything they were shouting. He wasn't controlling his anger ... no, there wasn't any, not when their opinion of him was irrelevant. Why would he care what they thought of him? Half of them were serving a prison sentence and the other half were content to simply exist. His concern targeted Strong Lord and the plans, future pain, he planned for him. If being verbally assaulted was supposed to unnerve him or hurt him, Strong Lord failed.

Their shouts, yells, threats, and insults cut off as if a switch had been hit, and an instant hush swept through the sanctuary telling Ansel Strong Lord was finally going to make his appearance. When the swollen river lined with cattails and tall grasses and the snowcapped mountains of the mural began sliding back, a hulk of a shadow emerged followed by heavy footsteps. Ansel forced himself to stand his ground. He wasn't going to give into the instinctual fear gripping him, especially in front of those who had spent over an hour calling him a coward.

At eight feet tall, his head a mane of white curls thick with feathers that cascaded down to end in the middle of his back, his yellow eyes gleaming, while feathers covered his broad chest that gave way to fur. His arms and hands were more lion than eagle, and brown fur lined his muscled legs down to the lion's nails. The only clothing, a kilt, hung low on his waist, emerald, green with scarlet, as he marched across the dais to his throne where he sat down. Ansel wore a mask of indifference as Strong Lord in his battle form narrowed his glare on him.

"Principe," Strong Lord greeted his voice crisp, clear for a being in his chosen form.

"Strong Lord." Ansel held his stare knowing his was bronze, his wolf close to the surface.

"I hope you're not offended by their vulgarity. They were expressing their discontent with your betrayal."

Ansel forced himself not to go into enforcer mode and point out they broke canons, tried to extort crucial information from him, and had betrayed Baron Kanin and the

Cascade pack. "Not at all. It was a pleasure to facilitate their contentment," he mocked.

"Their contentment hasn't yet started," Strong Lord mused, his nails clicking on the armrest of the throne.

"I'm sure I can handle more of their *vulgarity*," he taunted.

"Verbal? Physical?" Strong lord questioned. "You saw Milanka."

He allowed them to abuse her. Like he was going to allow them to abuse him. There was only one thing left to do. Ansel took the medallion, and unclasping it, held it in his hand, then let it drop to the rug. Gold on scarlet. "It's over."

Strong Lord tapped the dark wood of the armrest as he stared at him, his yellow gaze turning white with his anger. "No, Principe, it has just begun."

The entire sanctuary erupted in cheers and demands for his head. Ansel held Strong Lord's gaze, refusing to appear weak while his heart stopped in his chest.

CHAPTER NINETEEN

Day ten.

Clio shoved the shovel in the dirt, for what felt like the hundredth time, maybe thousandth, stopped when the reverberation sank into her arms from hitting a rock, and wiped sweat from her forehead with her forearm. She wasn't going to think about him or the empty feeling sitting in her middle.

No. Not going to happen. She was stronger than that. The image of him driving the ax's blade into the log, the muscles in his back rippling, his jeans tightening around his thighs, had her heart pounding. Then he was staring at her with a bronze gaze, the ax handle on his shoulder.

"Stop." She was going to die. Damn the dhampir thing.

"It's almost over, Doc" Jordyn said as she walked through the thick weeds, the thistles clinging to her jeans. Her hair was up in a messy ponytail, her T-shirt with *Go Hiking* across her chest fitted to her narrow waist. Even dressed down she looked like a powerful Pureblood.

"Did you come over to harass me?"

"Negative. Just making sure you're all right. What are you doing?" She looked at the ground Clio was currently digging up.

"Nothing." Her voice was sharper than it needed to be when she was talking to Jordyn. "Trying to burn energy.

Figured physical exercise would work." Sure she was. Being a dhampir with a need for her mate's touch and sexual energy was a damn place to be in and it was starting to piss her off.

"Is this like being hangry?" Jordyn asked with a smile. "Because it sounds like it. And you look like it."

"Funny, very funny." Clio took the shovel, and after placing it along the railing of the deck, sat on a stair, and wiped her hands on her denim shorts.

"Have you talked to Eclipse?"

"Yes. He states my control is commendable and he's endorsing the brand of blooded. I'm a real dhampir." It was good news. She proved she wouldn't lose control and threaten people's lives. And while she needed the endorsement to go back to work, it was overshadowed by Ansel's absence. "Any news?" she asked to change the subject.

"Negative. It's the same thing it's been for ten days. They don't have to tell Baron Kanin a damn thing." Jordyn remained standing, keeping five feet between them, her concern wafting from her like ribbons on the wind.

Clio's wolf picked it up, she was superior to Clio, but it was the vampire that understood it was more than simple worry over pack. "What's wrong?"

"Nothing. After speaking to you, Eclipse spoke to Baron Kanin. You've been given clearance to return to work. You'll start at Nearctic, and you'll serve a three month probation period. If successful, if you don't lose control and drain anyone, you'll gain full access. It means it's time to start telling people what happened."

"Damn," she mumbled. After every meeting with Dr. Barsacq, over a secured line, their faces on a screen, she waited to hear if she had been cleared, and nothing. Oh, he strung her along with doctor talk—keep up the good work, blah, blah, blah—but she got tired of hearing it. She exhaled a breath she didn't know she had been holding for a month and felt like the ax above her head had been retracted. They cleared her. She was back. And now she had to tell everyone Milanka attacked her, and she was a dhampir.

"My mom isn't going to be pleased." She didn't know why that was her first thought. Maybe it was the separation it would create. She had been a Wight, werewolf/human, two halves of her parents. Now she was something else and her mom wasn't part of it. Then there was Ansel. She couldn't explain being infected and crossing over without explaining him, their relationship, and where he was.

"Moms are like that. Mia thinks I'm evil, and Sloan called me an abomination."

"Harsh. How did it make you feel?" Clio knew she was going to face the same reaction … might not be as drastic, but it was going to be harsher than she wanted to deal with, especially having to deal with her *needs*. Seeing disappointment on her parents' faces wasn't something she was looking forward to. Though she couldn't blame them. She created the perfect person they saw—a perfectionist, intelligent, cool, calm, collected, never did anything rash, had a reasonable explanation for everything, every damn detail. From her townhouse to her luxury vehicle, she created an image and persona they depended on. Clio knew in her heart of hearts parts of that person had died the same time her human half slipped from her.

"Like an abomination. While Mia still thinks I'm evil, Sloan considers me all powerful but not an abomination. Hence the Lady in Waiting title," she replied, a grin curving her lips. "Have you felt him in your bond?"

It hit her senses like a blast, making her wolf howl and her fear snake through her. She should have known. "You're worried." And now she was worried. If she could worry more than she already was.

"They have wards, and I can't feel him. I can't fight the wards. You have no idea how angry that makes me," she growled through clenched teeth. "They're going to pay for messing with me."

Clio watched her eyes darken and believed every word she said.

"I haven't felt him. If the wards are blocking him from you, there's no way, even if he wanted me too, am I going to feel him." She promised him he would never be alone. That she would be there. And she failed. What if he had been trying to feel her, contact her the entire time she had been feeling sorry for herself and digging a freaking hole in her backyard? "I lied to him. I told him he would never be alone. I can't imagine being cut off from everyone."

"He isn't stupid, he understands. He is over hundred years old, has survived Milanka for decades, and is a trained enforcer," Jordyn reminded her.

"Yeah, doesn't make feel any better."

"Me neither." Jordyn took several steps, going farther into the yard before facing her. "What are you going to say to your parents?"

"Where do I start? You know I haven't lived my life in over a month. Maybe I'll just keep it that way."

"Sound plan. It matches the giant hole you've dug," Jordyn mocked.

Clio looked at the hole. It was getting pretty deep ... digging everyday did that. She knew she had to get back to life. Real life. Especially before Ansel came home. He didn't need to see the hot mess she had become. That while he was being held—she refused to think torture—she was doing nothing. "I'm going to tell them about Ansel and me first, then the rest. How will my situation be explained to the pack and Celestial?"

"There's already a rumor going around since you were attacked by Milanka you were infected and that's what delayed your recovery. Baron Kanin felt it was best to isolate you to make sure you were healthy and stable," Jordyn answered. "Once you tell your parents, he'll make an announcement."

She held her face in her hands, felt the dirt on her palms, and met Jordyn's questioning gaze. "Convenient. My parents have heard it?"

"They were given mere whispers, figured it would lessen the blow. Do you want me to go with you?"

"Heavens no. They see Cascade's soothsayer and they'll lose their minds and won't pay attention to what I'm saying. They don't know about us," Clio explained.

"About us. I feel used. Like a dirty secret."

Clio laughed, a real laugh, for the first time in weeks. "As your physician your safety is my priority, my soothsayer. Anyway, I can't get intel if people won't talk to me."

"Right you are. Then you'll have someone drive you."

"Not necessary," she protested as she stood.

"Yes, it is. You don't have a car, and as long as Ansel is with the Fellowship, probably giving them hell, you'll have an armed guard."

She forgot about not having a car. Clio had accepted her house arrest, Ansel's absence, and while her house was put together and immaculate, her front yard a thing of beauty, she hadn't bothered with anything else. Besides the hole in her backyard. The parallel of the waist-high weeds and unkept backyard and her life didn't go unnoticed. A pretty façade for people to look at and a total mess inside. *What an accomplishment.*

"And you'll want to fill in the hole."

"Why? Maybe I want a pond or something," she countered as she considered all her hard work, then eyed the other woman.

"Right next to your deck? I don't think that's in code."

"Maybe not. Know anyone with a bulldozer or something? The backyard is a mess."

"I'll check. Are you going to see them today?"

"Yes. I'll get cleaned up and go over there." Clio was going to call. They would ask her the first of a thousand questions, then offer dinner and cocktails. It would be normal for a second.

"I'll have Emory Bishop take you," Jordyn started as she held her cell. "She is one of mine and she's good. Plus, her rank among the soldiers will give you importance."

Clio thought she should have remembered the name, it sounded familiar, but she had been out of the loop for so long she was probably wrong. "You've covered almost everything," she replied.

"Almost?"

"You're forgetting about the seizure my mom is going to have."

"I can put Med Two on standby."

Two hours later, Clio was sitting in a truck, nothing like Jordyn or Rutger's full-size monsters with their diesel engines, grille guards, and equipment. This was a sporty vehicle, with black seats with red stitching, a stereo highlighted with more red, and its name made from chrome gleaming in front of her. She thought she recognized the name, Emory Bishop, then she saw the truck pull into her drive, music drifting before the volume had been lowered, and it came back. Emory had guarded Clio's house. The Illuminate with her black braid and the sides of her head shaved and inked with tattoos stared forward, only taking her eyes off the road to check her mirrors. Driving the speed limit, she took the corners slowly as if not wanting to scare Clio. She couldn't help but smile despite where they were headed.

"Nice truck." Clio wasn't the conversationalist type but needed to take her mind off her parents and Ansel.

"Thanks. I'm not much into cars and wanted something fast. It closes in on two hundred miles an hour and can take corners like they're embracing."

Clio looked at the side of her face when smokey wine eyes met hers for a breath, then went back to the road.

"Sorry, Doctor Hyde, you probably didn't want to know that."

"No worries. Kind of has me intrigued. I need a new a car," she replied. Clio tried to see herself driving the sporty truck to Celestial, the Hollow, then to Nearctic, and keeping it inside laughed at the image she came up with. She would look ridiculous. No, she was the luxury sedan type, because she liked it, and it didn't have red interior.

"Here we are, Doctor," Emory reported as she drove up the driveway. "I'll stay out here unless you need me."

"Okay. Good." Clio sat and stared at the house she had grown up in. "Good."

"Are you going to be all right? I can call Mistress."

"No." Clio turned enough to face her. "I'm a dhampir."

"Affirmative. Werewolf/vampire, Illuminate with empath traits, classified as a Potent. Your vampire traits will manifest over time. You have been blooded by the La Morte because of your exceptional restraint," she stated as if she had read it from a report. "Your paramount is Captain of Enforcers An-sel Wolt, Pureblood, your fated mate."

Definitely a report.

"I'm not allowed to disclose information, but I know, Doc-tor Hyde. I have never lived among humans, so their prejudice hasn't affected me. I can empathize with you and what you have to do."

Explains why she was one of Jordyn's. Sounded just like her. "Thanks." She had to get out of the truck before she de-cided to run for the hills. "They're my parents, how bad can it be?"

"I can't help you there, parents will be parents," Emory mumbled.

"I don't know how long this will take, are you sure you're all right with staying here? You don't need to go to work?" Clio asked. Actually, she wanted the soldier to leave because it would her give a little room. At least mentally.

"If I leave you here, Mistress will turn my brain to mush."

"She threatened you?" Clio asked, her voice rising with the question.

"Affirmative."

Of course she did. With that Clio got out of the truck—the gods forgive her if Jordyn turned their brains to mush—and headed to the house. The one-story ranch style home sat on an incline, and the large front yard, which sloped down, was covered in a sea of green grass, bordered by river rock and flowers, her mom's work. At the brick walkway she stared at the screen door, heard them inside, and paused to catch her breath. She didn't know how they were going to react.

With a touch of makeup on her eyes and cheeks, she wore a pale pink, sleeveless top, with a high collar to hide

Ansel's mark—no reason to scare her dad to death, while her mom would have no clue—a white cotton skirt, and sandals. She was attempting to look as normal as possible. They expected her to look a certain way and she would give them what they expected. To lessen the blow. However, she knew her slate eyes with whiskey hues would counter her attempts, and should they change to scarlet, it would be over before it started.

"You're a freaking doctor. And the personal physician to the Kanin family," she whispered. Giving up, she closed the distance, and when she was at the screen door, knocked lightly three times. She was shaking her head, she could have walked on in, when her mom stood on the other side and pulled it open.

"Blossom, you could have walked in," Evelyn stated. Her strawberry blonde with copper highlights was up, while stray strands feathered her cheeks.

Clio couldn't help but notice her crystal blue eyes narrowed on the deep red running through her curls and the way her body had changed.

"Habit," Clio responded with a weak smile and stepped inside. For the first time, the smells of the house met her to take her back to a different time and a different person. There was her dad, his aftershave, his wolf, the vanilla and peach air freshener her mom insisted on having, and her mom. Clio could smell the human, her blood, and the organic being her mother was. It was strange.

"Clio, poured your favorite." Smiling, Rhett handed her a glass.

When she took it from him, their fingers brushed one another's, and he stopped his smile and stared. His eyes narrowed, and she felt his werewolf senses. What they were telling him, considering he was a Wight, she didn't know.

When he trained his face, making it carefully neutral, his blue eyes darkened, she assumed the rumors had been confirmed. The visit wasn't going to be a good one.

"Dear, let her come in and sit down," Evelyn chided, oblivious to the tension building. "Come and sit, Blossom."

Taking several steps backwards he turned on the ball of his loafer, giving them his back, his neatly combed caramel hair not reaching the collar of his white button-up shirt. He must have just gotten home from work—he still wore his tie, it was loose, the knot lower on his chest, and his slacks wore wrinkles from sitting. Guilt slid through her, its dull edges catching on her with the fact she was going to pull their perfectly crafted world out from under them.

"Here, sit, and I'll get snacks."

Clio silently obeyed, and sitting across from her dad, watched him keep his gaze on her, his nose flaring as if he was trying to sort the scents surrounding her. She was mated, blooded, and an Illuminate. She knew his senses weren't strong, thankfully, and he wouldn't smell the blood she drank right before leaving her house. Explaining that would have added to her problems. When her mom returned with a platter of cheese, crackers, and assorted meats, she set it on the table, its clink the only noise. They were still staring at each other, alerting Evelyn to the unease. In response, she hesitatingly sat beside her husband, and together, holding hands and with twin looks of concern, stared at her.

"It's true then?" Evelyn asked, breaking the silence.

"Yes."

"Start at the beginning. It's the least you can do," Rhett stated, his voice deep. "For keeping this from us."

The tone took her back to her childhood where she begged for their forgiveness, then proved she was the perfect werewolf, controlled by cold logic, and the perfect human, humble and quiet, like they wanted to believe. But those days were long over. She was someone else entirely. Had been since Milanka tried killing her and she became Jordyn's doctor. Add in Ansel's acceptance of her and he loved her for who she was, she wasn't going back. She was respected and had been reinstated. She had a life and job to get back to.

"First of all, I didn't keep anything from you," she started, thankful her voice held, then raised her hand, quieting her dad. *Which I've never done*, she thought, *because there's never been a reason*. She met their gazes, the worry and betrayal sitting in them, and needed to calm down, straighten her thoughts, and proceed accordingly. Like Clio. She could give them that. "Last year after Captain Wolt had been cleared by the Highguard's Prosecution Administration, I went to his house. While I was there, we realized we were fated mates."

"Not possible," her mom began, shaking her head. "There's no such thing. It's a fairy tale Baron Kanin wants people to believe in. Like this Emanation."

Actually, it happened when Milanka was methodically setting him on fire, by then the drugs had started to wear off, and she knew then without a doubt he was hers. Again it was a detail she wasn't going to bring it up. "The Emanation is real, but you can believe whatever you like. I digress. While I was there, I received a call saying I needed to see Baron Kanin, so I left. At the meeting, the baron explained I had been reinstated. Excited about the news, I immediately called Captain Wolt and explained what had happened."

"Last year? If fated mates are indeed real, as you insist, why the year?" Rhett challenged.

She wanted to blurt out some stupid excuse, feeling the need to protect Ansel from looking bad, but knew neither of them would buy it, especially her dad. The apple didn't fall far from the tree. "He had a spell put on my memories."

"What?" Rhett shook his wife's hand loose, stood, and walked across the living room to the window looking out at the backyard. Facing her, he glared at her. "He took your choice away from you. He betrayed you."

Yes, he did. "He thought he was protecting me from Milanka," Clio explained. Defended. She was losing.

"Milanka. Bronte. His girlfriend," Rhett seethed. "The one who tried to kill you."

Clio wanted to roll her eyes, then felt his anger rolling from him at the same time she caught her mom watching them, her head going back and forth. "Yes."

"The spell wore off?" Evelyn asked, with caution.

"No, not really. I found the hiker." That's what started it, and she let her thoughts take her back to the side of road, then his backyard and the thunderstorm and his feel on her. Her dad was glaring at her when he grunted, and she knew the cue. Get on with it. "Besides cutting my legs on rocks and brush I tore my skirt, and my blouse was soaked with the girl's blood. She suffered an open fracture, her tibia, it was bleeding freely."

"Listen to yourself! You saved a life, and medicine is your passion. Are you going to give it up to be with him?" Rhett demanded.

How in the world? Clio stood, and facing her father wanted to explain in great detail, if she decided she was go-ing to do something else then she would. It was a free country. Of course it would make things worse. "No. I'm not. After successfully passing the Highguard's requirements, Baron Kanin reinstated me a couple of hours ago." La Morte's requirements. The vampire council tested her repeatedly. No reason to bring that up.

"There are rumors surrounding Director Kanin and his chosen, Clio. Captain Wolt takes lives. He is never held responsible. It makes him a murderer. You save people. You protect the weak. You're a healer." He wasn't trying to control his anger anymore or hide his dislike for Ansel.

"I've been reinstated." Another topic she wasn't going to talk about, Director Kanin's chosen. They did the dirty work no one else had the fortitude to complete or the stomach to handle.

"And it's good news. Rhett, let her continue," Evelyn insisted calmly.

She wasn't going to sit down, she couldn't. Her mom gave her soft blue eyes that had started to glisten with unshed tears, and for the first time in her life, she didn't know what they saw when they looked at her. "He gave me a shirt to wear home. After I washed it, I went to his place to give it back to him." Tesoro drifted through her and stopped her. She didn't know how to proceed.

"And?" Rhett demanded, his hands on his hips. "I know the pack, Clio, I know wolves. I know them well."

"So do I," she protested. He opened his mouth to say something and stopped. She got it like it hit her in the face. Her default setting. "Because I'm a Wight, I can't possibly know the pack as well as you. Is that it?"

"Not what I said."

It's what you meant.

"You don't know Captain Wolt and what he is capable of."

Clio shoved the urge to walk out down. Part of this was her fault. "The spell was supposed to make me fear him. To keep me from him. It didn't work. I went to his place, and we consummated our relationship," she pushed through thinned lips. Several times. She met pale faces and worried gazes, then her dad's hardened as his fury tried to escape. "The next day we went to Foxwood to tell Baron Kanin."

"Not your parents?" Evelyn whispered. "You went to the baron."

"I warned you, Clio. Warned you! Once Baron Kanin gets his teeth into you, you can't get away from him. He has you. The elite have you. The proof is in your lies," he accused. "Damn Captain Wolt."

Yes, she worked for the elite, the upper echelon, was treated as one, and because she was in the epicenter of the Cascade pack, she was aware of what was happening. Unlike her parents. "I never lied to you. I'm not going to listen to you criticize our alpha. And he is *our* alpha, which was why we weren't going to keep our status, fated mates, from him. We told him, and it was confirmed by Jordyn."

"The soothsayer? You know her?" Evelyn asked her eyes wide. "You're close to her. To call her by her name."

"I'm her physician." *And friend.* She hadn't realized her life had taken the turn it had and how much she kept from her parents. She didn't lie, she didn't say anything. When work was over it was time to enjoy her personal life. Simple as that. She didn't talk about Foxwood, Nearctic, the Hollow, none of the staff did, and she didn't talk about her relation-ship with Jordyn. It kept others from questioning her about Jordyn's medical records, her private life, and allowed Clio to learn intel. Clio held the secrets of Cascade and wouldn't be-tray the baron's trust. "After we told the baron, I called you and told you I was coming here. I was going to tell you. That's when the accident happened."

"God, Clio," Evelyn cried. "We didn't know. No one told us what happened. Said it was confidential. We're your parents."

"Baron Kanin doesn't care," Rhett growled. "So long as he gets what he wants."

Like protecting the pack from a virus Milanka had given her, and a possible blood-crazed dhampir. It took all her strength to keep fighting the urge to walk. They were upset, she got it, their emotions were rolling from them like giant waves, chaotic and frantic, and riddled with hurt. She wasn't going to stop, she needed to clear her conscience, and when she left it would be without emotional strings attached.

"Milanka was the reason for the crash. She infected me, and now I'm a dhampir. Werewolf/vampire. I have been added to La Morte's chronicles by an appointed Eclipse and Marquis Ladolofo," she explained, her anger simmering with her mom's tears and her dad's anger. She wasn't going to explain Ansel was her paramount, that would be a train wreck.

"Did Soothsayer have Shadow Lord help you?" Rhett asked. Accused. His eyes reflecting the accusation.

Clio didn't know he knew anything about Shadow Lord. *Interesting.*

"Poor, poor Clio," Evelyn whispered as she searched Clio's face. "My daughter is a dhampir."

"You've become part of the evil underbelly of the magic-born."

That was her. Before she had the chance to answer, with what, she wasn't sure, her dad kept going.

"Where is Captain Wolt now? Why isn't he here with you? Why isn't he by your side? Does he expect you to shoulder all the responsibility of your relationship? If you can call it that," he mumbled the last part.

"Do you love him?"

"Yes, I love him. Or I wouldn't be with him." She tried ignoring the disdain in her dad's voice, the disappointment, and the belittling he was throwing at her like daggers. She wasn't going to backdown. "He's serving a sentence with the Fellowship. He should be released in four days." It was like explaining he was doing time in county jail, and it had guilt spreading where anger had been.

"Serving a sentence. You can't trust him. He isn't a good man," Rhett protested. "He isn't a man. His girlfriend tried killing you. Do you remember the mess you were, Clio?"

"I remember, I was there. Nothing is going to change the fact Ansel is my mate. Absolutely nothing will change that. Nothing will change my love for him." She was half surprised they focused on her and Ansel and not her being a dhampir. Or Shadow Lord's help. She guessed it was because she was standing in front of them looking like her normal self. Human like. The thought struck her as funny. "Milanka is dead. She died shortly after she infected me." Sword through the chest and missing her heart. True death.

"Convenient. It took over a year to bring her to justice," her dad grumbled.

"Baron Kanin and … and the soothsayer, and that family has taken you from us," Evelyn continued crying, her face in her hands, the stay strands of hair feathering her pale fingers. "I knew it would happen when you went to work at Foxwood."

"Look what you've done to your mother. Is this what you wanted? Is this the outcome you wanted?" Rhett demanded as he placed his hands on his wife's shuddering shoulders.

"We've lived outside of the pack and have enjoyed freedom from their politics and drama."

They were going to be opposition, the side of her mind that collected intel warned. "You've lived in hiding. There's no escaping, we're pack. There's no escaping the future." How did this happen? When did the shit hit the fan? When did her parents change sides? There was a divide happening in the pack, no one could deny, and it was going to get worse before it got better. But her parents? Clio couldn't stop the fall of reasons from filling her head nor could she stop from piecing the puzzle together. "No one has taken me from you. I'm right here," she began and hoped her dad sensed her truth, and then convinced her mom. "You're upset because this is new and no doubt unnerving, but I'm not your perfect, little daughter. I'm not a Wight. I'm an Illuminate, a blooded dhampir, and mate to Captain of Enforcers Ansel Wolt." Part of her, the perfectionist part, thought she should explain she was Ansel's mate first, and that pissed her off even more. "If you can accept me for who I am, and my mate, then fine. If not, that's on you, not me. I won't be held accountable for your feelings."

Clio stared at them, her heart aching, her anger firing, her lungs threatening to collapse, and wanted Ansel with every fiber of her being. Damn she needed him. When they didn't say anything, seemingly standing their ground against her, she gave them her back, and walking, hoped they would stop her. *Don't let me leave*, she prayed. Clio pulled the door open, and letting it slowly close behind her, her heart sank as the afternoon's sun warmed her face while the scents from flowers and lawn drifted. Forcing herself not to mumble about injustices and her parents' reaction she stomped to the truck. As she approached, Emory quickly opened the passenger side door, and getting in, Clio's hope crashed and burned. Fine. That was fine. They all needed time to adjust.

Emory sat behind the steering wheel and started the truck, Clio noticed she replaced the tank top with a soldier's T-shirt, and wore a weapon tucked into a thigh holster. "Why are you armed?"

"People were staring at me like I was casing the house. I thought this looked more official," the soldier answered. "An armed escort."

"Great." That's what she needed. She bet money her parents' neighbors were calling and explaining there was an armed soldier in front of their house and *oh my what do you have going on*? Her parents would make the appropriate excuses, Clio was the Kanins' doctor, she had been in an accident, and wasn't driving. They wouldn't admit to Ansel and their relationship. Wouldn't tell anyone she was a blooded dhampir. It hurt and had her anger returning.

"Full disclosure, I heard every word. Just letting you know. My apologies, I should have said something."

Clio could only shake her head. "It's my fault. I did this and knew I was doing it. I adhered to the parameters given to me my entire life. Then Milanka tried killing me, and I struggled to accept my prefect world was no longer perfect. It became foreign, and I was a mess, and I cried on their shoulders. They saw their daughter hurting and felt helpless. Now they feel they have to save me from myself. Again. If I were them, I might feel the same way."

Emory remained silent, her concentration on the road, the rearview mirror, and traffic. Clio stopped herself from talking just to talk, letting the silence sit between them. "I need a drink."

Emory tapped her cell with a black-tipped nail, the screen lit up, and a second later she was talking. "Bishop reporting, Mistress. Meeting didn't go well, Doctor Hyde states she needs a drink. Affirmative." Emory touched her earpiece, ending the call, and made a right.

"Where are we going?" Clio asked. She wanted to go home, feel sorry for herself, psychoanalyze the conversation she had with her parents four or ten thousand times, and maybe burn energy by attacking the hole. Perhaps write a statement of apology.

"Mistress' house. She has your favorite."

Of course she does.

CHAPTER TWENTY

"Principe," Strong Lord whispered next to his ear, his hot breath making Ansel's stomach roll. "Do you know why we've kept you?"

Ansel didn't care. Maybe a day or two ago, he might have. Not that he knew what a day or two was, or how long he had been there. *Kept him*? It hadn't been two weeks. Baron Kanin wouldn't allow it. Would he?

"I've allowed the Fellowship, those who wanted to participate, to do as they pleased with you, while fully obeying the rules Baron Kanin put into place." He laughed, a quarter eagle's cry, a quarter lion's snarl, and the last half human.

It made his ears hurt.

"Now it's my turn, and there are things you should know," Strong Lord continued as his bulk stalked along the shadows of the cell, his voice echoing off its stone walls.

He didn't care. He wanted to say he didn't care. Ansel's chin rested on his chest, the blood and sweat's glaze smothering him like a second skin, while the chill from the cell tried eating into his bare flesh as it cooled blood welling up from new wounds. Opening his right eye—he lost the use of the left one, he couldn't remember when, his mind was behind—he tried to focus on Strong Lord and failed. A dark blur moved too fast to track, and he lost sight when he couldn't turn his head. Hell, he didn't have the strength to lift his chin off his chest.

The numbness did that, he reminded himself, and he sought refuge in its darkness.

Strong Lord clutched a fistful of hair, jerked Ansel's head back, and glared at his one good eye that was slowly swelling closed. "We interrogated Milanka. Do you know what she told us about you?"

With his head cocked back, it wrenched on his neck, constricting his throat, and he couldn't swallow, couldn't breathe. Panic lurched through him as black shadowed his vision and he felt his awareness slipping from him. His right eye closed, his body relaxed despite the manacles at his wrists, the chain dropping from the ceiling to hold his arms above his head and shoulder width apart. The restraints at his ankles were snug to the floor, eliminating any movement while they cut the circulation off to his bare feet. He'd spent countless days chained and beaten by *those who wanted to participate*, and when he lost his sight he memorized their scent, their voices, the way they inhaled before landing a blow, and was going to get his revenge. It stayed with him hour after hour.

Revenge.

"Come back, Principe," Strong Lord mused as he lowered Ansel's head. "There you are."

Consciousness flooded back. Ansel jerked, pain raced through his shoulders and into his neck to explode against his skull. The chains rattled around him, and swallowing hard, he inhaled and exhaled. In the position he preferred because it was less painful—his chin on his chest, hanging from his wrists, his legs limp—his mind screamed at him. Strong Lord wanted to tell him something. Did he care? Not a damn bit. He wanted to tell Strong Lord, promise the griffin, he was going to be the first to feel Ansel's hate. He was going to kill the creature, slowly, so very slow.

"Do know what she said about you?" Strong Lord questioned.

Drool slid freely from his between his split lips. What didn't cling to the torn skin slid down his chin and to his chest where it sank into several slices made by a knife. Fae. Male. Smelled of sage and lavender incense. The invasion into the lacerations would have stung if he could feel them. Shock had come and gone so many times he lost count, at the same time awareness had gripped him and waned in equal amounts. Then there was the numbness he invited to take him over, to drown him in its depths.

"Milanka said there were two sons, Principe. Gaia left her husband, King Alessandro, while carrying his unborn son and the babe died. Greif stricken and in vengeance the king petitioned the Highguard, and they found her guilty of deserting her husband and fleeing her church. They granted the request to punish Gaia by divesting her magic and then effacing both the shaman and Gaia from the Highguard's chronicles. Some high ranking official in the Highguard is in possession of her magic."

Gaia. His mom. King Alessandro. Sons. Ansel tried to shake his head to loosen the haze covering his thoughts and fought to connect himself to his body. It was going to be painful. Every open wound, bruise, and broken bone was going to become sensitive to flay him alive. As he pulled himself from the abyss he used to protect himself, his mind latched onto Milanka, his training, his weakness to stop her, and the numbness he embraced when she punished him. Sweet detachment from body and mind. He didn't have it, he was giving it up, ascending into a hell he didn't want to face.

"Did you hear me?" Strong Lord demanded as he slapped the back of Ansel's head.

When his swollen, dry lips refused to curve around his answer, he nodded his head. Almost there. His strained muscles warned him he didn't want to feel what hanging from chains was doing to him, or the lacerations riddling his torso, or his broken ribs. Drawing in a breath, his ribs shifted, he felt them grinding and moaned as the pain engulfed him and the sour smell of grime filled his nose.

"Coming out of it, are you? She warned us you were capable of putting yourself in a trance. It seemed to anger her." When Ansel didn't respond, Strong Lord ordered, "Look at me."

With pain like lava flooding his body, Ansel opened his right eye, felt pressure from his left, and saw a blur. A second later it focused enough he saw the griffin in his semi human form, his white hair pierced by feathers, and narrowed, yellow orbs.

"Usually, I would be inclined to believe her. While you were devoted to her, she tortured you for decades, and why would she lie to me? But I think the halfling was lying to protect you. Tell me, Principe, was she lying?"

Ansel was in no condition to answer a question he didn't understand. Halfling. Milanka. Torture. Yes, it was her. Protect? No. He grunted a response with what air he could manage to inhale.

"Watching you fight to breathe is tiresome."

Fuck you, his mind screamed.

"Get him down. He's useless to me like this." Strong Lord approached Ansel, and staying to his right, leaned down until a yellow eye was even with Ansel's. "Slip into the abyss, Principe. Enjoy your time there while you can."

Ansel growled a low sound of warning to have Strong Lord laugh, its echo fading then disappearing altogether as he left the cell. Ansel fought to keep his wall up so Clio didn't feel him, his weakness, and the white-hot pain saturating his body. He didn't need her worrying about him when she was dealing with being a dhampir. Suddenly, hands were on him, their grip tightening on his arms to increase the hurt while above him the chains rattled, orders sounded, and he dropped to the floor, landing on his left side while the side of his head smacked the cool stone. Blood spread out, soaking his hair, but it didn't hurt as bad as the blood rushing into his arms, hands, legs, and feet. In silence—he refused to give into his weakness, they wouldn't hear his cries—the sudden rush burned as it traveled, searing through his veins and into his muscles, causing him to roll side to side, attempting to alleviate the pulsing pressure. Overwhelmed by the lightning striking him, he rolled to his back, and he called the numbness to ease the storm raging inside of him. He would go to the abyss, he would see Clio there, and she would heal him. Slowly, as if was crawling from him, the world began to fade away.

"Wake up, Crimson Prince," a male mocked.

Not enough time. He needed more time. Ansel stirred, tentatively testing his limbs, when cold water sloshed over him, soaking his bare skin and jeans. The stark shock had him curling into a ball and wrapping his arms around himself, trying to conserve heat, as the chill drilled into his core.

"You stink of your own sewage, like the turncoat you are," he seethed.

Ansel registered the tone and slight accent and added him to the list of the soon to be dead. On his side, he turned to his stomach, and getting his hands and feet under him, got off the stone floor, sat on his ass, and met crystal blue eyes set in a pale face. His could see with both eyes. The superficial wounds had healed, while the deeper lacerations had scabbed over. Touching the side of his head, he discovered the cut there wasn't open. It told him he had been out for a while, how long he had no idea, like everything else since the beatings started.

"Three days," Strong Lord answered as if he had read Ansel's mind. In his semi human form, he walked around Ansel, his yellow eyes narrowing on him. "Get him a chair."

The man who threw water on him appeared with a chair and set it away from Ansel.

"I think he fears you, Principe," Strong Lord mocked through a laugh.

"He should. Death follows him." Ansel stood, scared his legs were going to give out, and when they didn't, he started toward the chair, his sideways gait hindering him. When he sat down, he exhaled, maneuvering to lessen the pressure on his right side, easing the weight from his ribs.

"Do you remember what I told you?"

He remembered. He dreamt about it and hoped like hell it had been a series of delusions brought on by starvation, dehydration, and shock. "You think Milanka was trying to protect me by telling you her version of my parents' lives. I don't believe it. I wouldn't believe anything she said," Ansel replied with defiance. "She opens her mouth and lies fly out."

"You doubt her version because if she was telling the truth your memory of your mother and father would be false? Or you believe she would never protect you?" Strong Lord asked.

He didn't need to say it, Ansel felt it in the weight of the question. Strong Lord knew exactly what had been done to him, and humiliation scalded him more than the beatings had hurt him. *"She warned us about you."* He bet she did. Milanka wouldn't risk herself for him. Throw him to the wolves, yes. Protect him, no.

"Protecting wasn't something she did."

A grunt came from the corner of the cell, where blue eyes stood his post. Ansel glared at him as he tried to place him and failed. It didn't matter, he knew the scent, the eyes, and his face. He was as good as dead.

"Ignore Liam. Her version means you had a stepbrother. That doesn't upset you?"

"You don't care if it upsets me. What do you want?" Ansel demanded. It sounded weak coming from dry lips and didn't carry the rage he was trying muster. Not when he needed to cover his reactions to the questions about his parents. Beaten down, starved of his mate, Strong Lord was trying to get him to confess to something. His magic. Ansel shook it loose and focused on the possibility he had a stepbrother. He didn't think it was true. It was Milanka lying to them. But why? What did she have to lose? She knew they were going to use her. Kill her.

"You," Strong Lord answered smoothly.

"You have me," Ansel countered. "For the moment." This was about his mom's magic. The demon living inside of him he had no way of using. He wasn't sure he believed it was there. He felt the void, the emptiness, the cold. As if she had carved his insides out. Was it magic? Was it a memory he clung to believing she was with him, so he wasn't alone? The grief and ache from their deaths roared to life and he saw flames swallow them.

"Don't drift away. Come back," Strong Lord urged.

Ansel ripped himself from his past and entered the present. If she gave him her magic, and she was as powerful as they thought, why was he half beaten and bleeding? Shouldn't he have healed? Shouldn't he possess powers beyond imagination? He laughed, a guttural sound that rode like knives up his throat, and knew he was losing his mind. There were only so many times you could get the shit kicked out of you before it fucked with you.

"What are you laughing at?"

"If I really possessed the magic you think I do, I should be more than this," he answered, his words slurred, his eyes grazing his body, the condition of it—dirty, stained with bruises, lanced with cuts, and marred by crusty scabs. Meeting his glare, Ansel hated what he was going to admit to, but he needed the bite from it to keep him sane. "Milanka took what she wanted from me. My blood. My throat. My body. Against my will. Where was the magic?"

"Her treatment of you means nothing. It has nothing to do with the magic of Queen Gaia," Strong Lord argued.

"She wasn't a queen." Ansel scoffed at the idea. "She was a priestess."

"That's where you're wrong, Principe. However, I'll admit there are as many tales about Queen Gaia and King Alessandro as there are grains of sand. They've become more myth than truth. I wanted to know what you had been told to compare it to what I have learned. I'm assuming whatever past you're clinging to isn't going to help me."

"I have the truth." *She told me.*

"I don't think so. I searched the Highguard's chronicles and found the Scared Writ belonging to King De Luca, Gaia's father. As a Pureblood werewolf with fae traits she was considered unique, and a bargaining tool for her father. The arranged marriage with King Alessandro would have united the two territories."

"I don't believe you." Ansel couldn't, wouldn't. He heard her talking to him, her accent curling around the words, as she told him of her escape.

"That's irrelevant. King Alessandro plundered his wealth and lost his throne during a battle he should have won. When the battle was over, it was believed the enemy had taken Queen Gaia. She had stood her post on the castle walls with the other fae, then they found evidence she had been killed. De Luca's Sacred Writ states he had cargo, family possessions shipped to the Americas on private ships. This was important because the possessions were leaving his home country. At the time, powerful magic-born were not allowed to travel, lest they take over another's territory. And certainly not a royal Pureblood with fae traits who was carrying a babe."

"And the men who ripped her magic from her, who were they? I saw them, I was there," Ansel argued as he struggled to sit up.

"It was a charade. Queen Gaia didn't possess her magic when they tested her. My question is, are you the child she was carrying? Or is there another who possesses her magic?" Strong Lord held his stare as if challenging him.

He had to have been the child. But that would make him older than his one hundred and forty-one years. He might be off by twenty, maybe thirty years ... hell, he didn't know. It might as well be a hundred years. He knew he shared his father's DNA. Native American. And he believed she gave him her magic. Was he sure? No. He wasn't sure of anything. His head was chaos around the nightmares that plagued him, the pain, and starvation. "I'm not. I can't be."

There was a painful truth to his words while the life he knew, the life he believed in turned to ash. His life. His past. His identity. Lies. He didn't have a crest and would never have one. The ache in his heart sank to his middle where it reached out like wires to tighten around his chest and slice through his strength. More threads grew from the hurt to whip through him, and unraveling his core it tore him apart from the inside out. It was the same sensation he felt after he made love to Clio. Maybe, it was her. He hadn't allowed himself to feel their bond and figured with the runes and spells surrounding the stronghold, the wards would prevent him from sensing her. But she was there, he had no doubt, and now he desperately clung to the feeling, letting it work through him to his wolf where it filled him with strength.

"That's what I thought. It means you are of no use to me," Strong Lord said with regret in his voice. "You are the son of an effaced Pureblood and a shaman, both deceased, nothing more. They might as well be ghosts. I have to believe the true son of King Alessandro is dead and with him Queen Gaia's magic."

"You have no use of me," Ansel laughed, his chest heaving, and turning it into a cough, he struggled to catch his breath. After everything, Strong Lord was going to throw him away like trash because he was nothing. "You've made my life a living hell."

"You've made your life a living hell. I just added excitement to it," Strong Lord boasted. "Our time has come to end anyway. Liam, I understand you've been patiently waiting for your chance with the fallen prince?"

"Yes, Strong Lord," Liam replied as he bowed his head.

Ansel met blue eyes gleaming from the shadows and saw the intent in them. He felt the threads continuing to weave and he could feel his skin heating, his wolf clawing at the invasion. He was going to lose his fucking mind.

Strong Lord gave a curt nod to Liam when the fae stepped forward. "You can't kill him." Turning, he met Ansel's gaze. "I understand your mate waits for you. It would be a pity if you succumbed to your injuries. As stated by the baron's rules."

Ansel wanted to put his strength in his glare and was denied.

"I guess the Cobalt is going to be overkill," Liam mused.

With his grip on reality slipping, Ansel made a mental note to kill Liam first. As the thought floated through his mind, reality vanished completely, and laughing, he heard it echoing off the stone walls at the same time the whistle of a weapon sliced through the air. Ansel caught the gray blur right before it connected with the side of his head, the crack echoing off his skull and ringing in his ears. He thought it was going to deafen him. Then, the lights shut off.

Warm air drifted over bare skin, drying sweat and blood, and inching into open cuts and scrapes, its bite jerked him awake. Opening his eyes, as best he could, Ansel saw a canvas of azure, disrupted by sleek white clouds, then sucking in a deep breath, he savored the clean air that took his stink from his nose. He laughed, his insanity sitting in the rough sound grating up his dry throat and it had him coughing up blood, the spray peppering his swollen lips. They dumped him outside.

Bastards. *They're going to die*, he promised himself. Turning his head, he saw the gate, the wrought iron with its curves intertwining to create an elaborate labyrinth within their confines and then emptiness on the other side. His eyes burned, his head throbbed, and his chest felt like stones had been placed inside. He didn't know what time it was, what day it was, but if he was outside, the two weeks had come to an end. Or Strong Lord accepted he wasn't the all-powerful son of Queen Gaia. The thought hurt him and brought back the lies he lived with his entire life. Why? He wanted to know why his mother and his father lied to him.

With heartache and rage fueling him, Ansel rolled to his side, rose on his hands and knees, and with his head hanging fought back the nausea rising from his stomach. His body demanded he lay down, the pain cascading through him making his limbs feel as if they weighed tons, but he wasn't, and pushed himself so he was sitting. Looking around he saw he was in the middle of the drive, and since he couldn't stay there, he scooted backward, sought the shade, and rested against a tree trunk. Despite his head feeling like a vise grip was trying to crush it, the conversation with Strong Lord played out. He didn't understand. Couldn't comprehend what had happened and why Strong Lord was obsessed with his mother's power. Another laugh worked its way to his throat. He was worried the horrors by Milanka's hand were going to destroy him when it had been the truth of his parents. Were the questions and their lies enough for him to doubt who he is?

Ansel paused when the crunching of rocks under tires and the rumble of a diesel engine, one he knew, the familiar sound making his heart pound inside of his chest, stopped at the gate. The wrought iron slid back, its mass concealed between trees, and he watched the black truck pull forward and stop when it was beside him. With the engine still running, the driver's side door opened, hard footsteps sounded, and Rutger rounded the front to approach him.

"You look like hell," he said as he knelt, his eyes blazing gold. "Doctor Hyde is going to be a very angry woman."

A wave of fury drifted from Rutger, and Ansel couldn't keep the cocked grin off his battered face. He could only imagine what he looked like. "She said she was going to kill them."

"She'll have help. Let's get you out of here." Rutger stood, made his way to the passenger side, and opened the door.

Using the tree to stand, Ansel realized he was barefoot, and the ground—covered in rocks, pine needles, and leaves—looked more like a battlefield than the woods. It forced him to wait for Rutger. Plus, he was starting to see double, and haze was crowding his peripheral vision. As he waited, his knees shook, and he knew his legs weren't strong enough to get him to the truck. He didn't need to make his injuries worse, and if he stepped on a rock his balance would fail him. If he had any balance. His head was spinning and was making the earth spin.

When Rutger returned, Ansel looped his arm over Rutger's shoulder and let him bear his weight as they made their way to the truck. At the door, Ansel stepped up, his muscles protesting, and nearly crawling inside, finally sat upright in the seat, and then he heard the dings and beeps of the terminal. They were glorious sounds. While Rutger rounded the front, Ansel relaxed his head against the seat and closed his eyes. It was over. He wasn't a dog on a leash. He didn't have what they wanted. He wouldn't have to obey their orders. He was free to live his life. Free.

Freedom.

"Doctor Hyde is waiting for you at your house. She thought you would be more comfortable there. Then said something about your geese returning," Rutger explained as he put the truck in reverse and began backing up.

Ansel rolled his head to the left to see two Rutgers fading in and out. "She would notice the geese."

"Affirmative." Rutger kept his eyes straight forward as he maneuvered the truck and headed out the Fellowship's territory. "It's good to have you back, brother."

With Rutger's use of brother emotions welled inside of him, the pressure seeking an outlet, then threatened to spill from his open wounds. Tears moistened his eyes, and for the first time in two weeks they rolled bronze, and he felt his wolf. The power of it coursed through him as it howled. In the chaos taking his body, the question repeated itself: were the questions and his parents' lies enough for him to doubt who he is? Negative. He had a family—the Kanins, Rutger, Jordyn—and a mate, his tesoro, Clio.

"Jo reported she couldn't feel you. She knew you weren't dead because your wolf's essence was with the Collective, but couldn't feel you. They have wards protecting the property, and by the rush of power coming from you, they must have had the cell reinforced."

If Jordyn wasn't capable of sensing him, it meant Clio wouldn't have been able to break through the wards. Which meant the threads burrowing inside of him, the alien moving in him wasn't Clio, never had been, it was something else. His mother's magic? His shoulders caved with the lie he was trying to cling to. Gods, why did they lie to him?

"The shackles were White 47, and their weapons of choice Cobalt 27. I was powerless." It took him back to Milanka. He had been powerless to stop the pain, torture, and powerless to defend himself. Without silver, wards, and their beatings he was gaining strength and was able to think clearly. They planned it. They knew what she had done to him and recreating the situation wanted to send him back to his nightmares, that no doubt would have broken him and his mind. It could have happened had it not been for Clio, and her strength. She was the light at the end of the tunnel.

"Why Cobalt? You aren't fae," Rutger questioned with a sideway glance.

"He assumed since my mother had fae in her ancestry, so would I," Ansel answered with hurt in his voice.

"Did he say anything about your mom?" Rutger gave him another sideways glance, the concern in his mahogany gaze sinking into him.

"It isn't important. Not anymore." Ansel closed his eyes and listened to the shift from dirt road to pavement, and the tires as Rutger increased the speed.

Day fourteen.

Clio paced Ansel's living room, her running shoes making whispers on the carpet as the weight from the last fourteen days was finally coming to an end. That was until she saw the condition he was in. Wringing her hands and talking to herself, she considered the med bag she brought with her. Inside sat a variety of bottles and vials of sedatives, painkillers, BioThropy to stop the progression of White 47, a synthetic silver, syn sanguine an artificial blood for shapeshifters, and every bandage she could shove into its pockets. She told herself, had Ansel's wounds been more than she could care for at his house, or he was mortally wounded, Rutger would have reported it and taken him to the Hollow. If he didn't report it, he would have told Jordyn. That hadn't happened. Unless he hadn't picked Ansel up. Or seen him. Or they haven't released him. Or ...

"ETA one minute," Jordyn reported as she shoved her cell in the back pocket of her jeans. "You can stop pacing, Doc."

"Right." Clio thought her heart was going to fall from her chest to sink to her feet while her lungs had stopped functioning, which she told herself was impossible.

Mentally starting a countdown, she forced a calm over her nerves, then she heard the rumble of Director Kanin's truck as it pulled up to the house. Clio lost all calm, and running from the living room raced outside, the screen door slamming closed behind her. She paused at the stairs when Ansel slid from the truck.

She was going to kill them. All of them. His hunched shoulders caved to his bare chest where lacerations sliced across flesh, ecchymosis discolored his sides, there was a protrusion on his right side, she was going to guess broken ribs, his jeans, filthy and torn, hung on the bones of his hips as if he hadn't eaten in two weeks, and his feet were covered in grime, his toe nails broken. Her eyes moved over the dried, cracking crimson veiling him and up to his face where more contusions stained his skin. His eyes were nearly swollen closed, his nose looked broken, and clumps and tangles twisted his shoulder-length, auburn hair. Then she met his gaze. She didn't see defeat. She saw his victory. They hadn't broken him.

Ansel stopped at the front fender, his feet in soft dirt, and stared at Clio, her scarlet eyes blazing with her emotions, her strawberry blonde hair loose, the curls with red running through them tempting him to twine them between his fingers. Lifting his hands, he looked at them to see the blood, dirt, and scrapes, then felt his legs shaking. Damn. He wasn't going to make it inside the house like he wanted.

"I'm a fucking mess, tesoro," he whispered as he went to his knees, the pain from hitting the ground sending lightning into his thighs.

Clio leapt from the porch, clearing the stairs and taking several steps. She knelt in front of Ansel, who was staring at her with eyes that rolled bronze. "I can fix that," she replied. Raising her hands, she tenderly cupped his face and kissed his forehead. "I've missed you."

He wanted to cry with the force of her love wrapping around him in a protective embrace as he inhaled her scent, and her heat sank into him. "I've missed you," he returned, his voice cracking, the words trembling.

"Come on, let's go in. You need a bandage or four, an IV for dehydration, BioThropy, and a bag or six of syn sanguine," Clio started as she stood and held her hand out.

Healer. He stared at her, reveled in her calm and felt the combination of wolf and vampire glide over him as he opened himself to the bond they shared. That he had blocked, and the Fellowship snuffed as if it was a flame. Clasping her hand in his, she gently helped him to stand, her strength surprising him. Once up, she went to his side. and looping his arm over her thin shoulders, let her help him to the house. He had questions about her transformation; she felt stronger.

Clio walked them up the stairs, through the screen door Jordyn held open, and to the couch where she waited as Ansel slowly lowered himself. "I'm going to start the IVs first, then I'll clean the lacerations. You know your ribs are broken."

"Affirmative, Doctor," Ansel replied as she turned from him to open the med bag.

Meeting his gaze, she smiled. "There aren't any internal injuries, despite what your torso looks likes."

"How can you be sure?" Rutger asked from behind her.

"I can smell it. If there was an injured organ or a rupture, there would be a scent."

"My dhampir," Ansel stated with more pride than he thought was possible.

"Turn your head." While she couldn't stop smiling, she remained in doctor mode. As Ansel turned his head, Clio saw the reason for the blood. The cut, from blunt force, was four inches in length. She was going to kill them for hurting her mate. "There's a gash. What the hell did they hit you with?"

"Not sure," he answered as he flinched. "It was Cobalt 27."

"Bastards. I'm going to seal it with a liquid bandage. You'll be able to heal."

It was the last thing either of them said as Clio worked on him for an hour. When she finished, there were six empty bags sitting on the coffee table—gauze, bandage wrappers, and cleansing wipes she used to clean him up, as much as possible. Before leaving him, Clio covered him with a blanket, and kissed his cheek. He desperately wanted to hold her, but couldn't keep his eyes open any longer, and couldn't remain sitting up. He leaned back and closed his eyes while his body absorbed the liquids and began healing from the inside out. Around him he heard Clio's voice, her silken lit, then Rutger's rough tone, and Jordyn's cultured timbre as they met in the kitchen, and after several seconds he could smell coffee brewing. He was going to have tell them what Strong Lord said; he wasn't what everyone thought he was. He was, however, a fallen prince. A nobody.

His parents had lied to him. Drifting into a light sleep, his mind went back to the day they died. The fire. The grief that gripped his heart. The need to follow them in death. Milanka's torture. He expected it to affect him the same way it had every time he fell into the nightmare's clutches. It didn't. Maybe it was Milanka's death, the end of his servitude to the Fellowship, the ease with which he accepted he was a nobody. But he doubted it. It was realizing he had a family. They were in his home, comfortable like they belonged there, and they did.

"Darling," Clio whispered, her breath warm next to his ear.

He rose from the sanctuary of his mind, but before opening his eyes, he let her say the endearment three more times. It was the way it sounded, like she was from the south, all drawn out and incredibly sensual. "Tesoro," he whispered back, and met her eyes with a hooded gaze framed by black lashes.

"Director Kanin would like to interrogate you." Clio wanted them to leave.

When Ansel found Rutger, he said, "It's a debriefing."

Ansel wanted to laugh, then met Clio's gaze rife with warning. "It's fine."

"Be nice, Director," Clio cautioned as she took her place beside him. "Doctor's orders."

"Affirmative, Doctor." With coffee cup in hand, Rutger sat down in the chair across from him. "What happened?"

Where did he begin? Ansel sat straighter, his body stronger, the weakness in his limbs abating, the pressure from his broken ribs nearly gone. The drumming in his head vanished, along with the irritating stinging from the cuts and scrapes. His mate was a miracle worker. He met Rutger's eyes and knew he wasn't being asked about the beatings, as the repercussions of those were his and his alone. "Strong Lord wanted to know about my parents. Milanka had told him her version and he wanted mine."

"He didn't believe you?"

"He didn't give me a chance to tell him," Ansel replied, then explained what Strong Lord said to him in painstaking detail. King Alessandro. The battle. An arranged marriage. "He believes Queen Gaia's son died and with him, her magic was lost."

"He is mistaken," Jordyn said.

CHAPTER TWENTY-ONE

Ansel stilled as everyone looked at her and she casually sipped her coffee. Sitting back in the chair, she acted as if she was talking about the weather and not his mother's secrets. Jordyn was turning into the calmest, coldest person Ansel had ever known.

"Why?" he asked to get her talking.

"There isn't another child."

The certainty in her voice had him believing her. But ...

"How do you know?" Strong Lord said he read the Highguard's chronicles.

"I'm part of the Highguard and have my connections," she answered.

Given her current statuses, it made it hard to doubt her. "King De Luca's Scared Writ."

Shrugging, Jordyn sipped her coffee.

Ansel didn't know what it meant and didn't want to. "If I have my mother's magic, why couldn't Strong Lord sense it, as he had before? And why can you?"

Smiling, her eyes rolled onyx, and she replied, "You're one of mine. Could be the wards, White 47, Cobalt 27, and the spell used to suppress your wolf. That combination would have equally suppressed your magic. To keep you from defending yourself, Strong Lord created a dead zone. And if he would have actively sought the magic, he would have violated the covenant, which he wouldn't risk when he wants his people back."

Could it be? "They didn't lie," he mumbled and was surprised he felt better, as if he had been given the foundation of his life back.

"Maybe they did. Parents lie. We lie. Maybe they didn't. If they did, could it have been to protect you? Strong Lord wouldn't have been the only person, friend or foe, vying for Queen Gaia's magic." Despite the calmness in her tone, he was aware she was challenging him.

There was a possibly it was the reason he accepted the tale Strong Lord weaved and believed. Parents would do anything to protect their children. He would do anything to protect his mate and his family.

"What is going to happen to me?" When she smiled, he frowned, and frustration from pain and emotional turmoil ripped through him. It's heat enough everyone in the room would have sensed it. "Do you think this is funny?"

"Affirmative." Taking another sip from her mug, she held his gaze.

"Explain it to him, Jo, and stop messing with him," Rutger ordered.

"Fine. When your mother passed her magic unto you, it would have merged with yours. It's not something that knows to stay separate. I don't think the wards and spells had anything to do with their inability to sense your magic. Additionally, you're a dominate Pureblood whose power has been increasing over the years. There's no doubt you have the capacity to shift into your Bestial form."

He heard Clio suck in a breath and thought he stopped breathing. The idea scared him and intrigued him. Rutger shifted into his Bestial form, lessening the fear of going bestial and turning primal. "And my mom's magic?"

"It's unclear what her traits were. Since her magic has always been part of you, you may have experienced an enhanced strength without knowing it."

Ansel's breath left his lungs as excitement coursed through his veins. Still there was the void, a coldness in his chest. Maybe it was his injuries. "When I was released from the chains it felt like threads reached out to my wolf, as if trying to strengthen it. Why now?" he demanded. Was he going to believe her?

"When was the first time you felt that way?" Jordyn asked, copper and onyx vying for their place in her gaze.

He didn't have to think about it. "I was with Clio. She had to feed." With his admission, Clio reached over, careful not to touch the tubes connected to the IVs, and placed her delicate hand in his. The contrast between his and hers wasn't lost on him. Leather and lace. Innocence and sin.

"You accepted her for who and what she is. Dhampir. Your mate. You don't fear her."

"Affirmative." Without question. Without her he wasn't sure he was a person.

"In the cell you accepted you."

"What in the hell are you talking about?" Jordyn wasn't sitting in front of him. The woman he knew sank back, letting whatever magic burned inside of her come forward.

"You. You've stopped holding yourself responsible for Milanka's treatment of you. You've cast off the guilt of your parents' deaths and for surviving the fire. You have accepted you," Jordyn replied as she stood like she needed to move. "You've accepted the pain of your past, your sins, and in doing so released the hold on the magic and your true strength. That's why they couldn't sense it. It's a natural part of you. Not a thing to be taken."

Silence filled the room as Rutger, Jordyn, and even Clio stared at him while he struggled to think of something to say. It was impossible when he was wrapping his mind around what Jordyn said. Acceptance. Forgiveness. Was he worthy of either? He didn't know.

Clio checked the last bag, and finding it empty, eased from her place by Ansel's side, then the couch, and began carefully removing the first catheter. While she worked, she kept an eye on him to watch his reaction as he digested what Jordyn told him. Which was astonishing. The truth of his mother. His true strength. Bestial form. There was a day he would have rejected the idea. It was dangerous, the chances of going bestial and losing yourself to the animal was too great. There were several centuries of written text to prove it.

After the meeting with her parents, and the days Ansel was gone, she used the time to reevaluate her belief system. Then when she went back to work at Nearctic, her senses were focused, her instincts heightened, and she accepted she was a dhampir and lived in a different world. Acceptance. The word carried the power to change people. She slid her gaze over to Ansel to see his thoughts cross his face, his eyes narrowing to have bronze shards float within cinnamon, and his wolf's strength gleamed behind the tangle of colors. After putting the used instruments in the biohazard bag, she cleaned up the rest of the equipment, and repacked the med bag. Silence sat heavy in the room, letting tension weave into it and add weight.

The silence and tension held the room prisoner for an hour its weight enough to make her skin itch.

Jordyn was standing at the French doors leading to the backyard, her raven hair at her back, the ends skirting her waist and seemed to be in her own world. Rutger was staring at Ansel with a gold gaze while Ansel stared back with bronze. What they were thinking, doing, seeing in one another, was anyone's guess. She left the living room for the kitchen, refilled her mug, then leaned against the counter and took a minute to sort through her thoughts. When she saw Ansel, her powerful mate, wounded and falling to his knees, she wanted to cry, and demand Strong Lord's head be served on a platter. She feared she would see shadows haunting his eyes, he would withdraw from her, and the traumas from his past would take their place in his present. Luckily, it didn't happen. He beat them. Sipping her coffee, she reveled in knowing they were stronger.

"Baron Kanin is giving you one week to recuperate and spend time with your mate," Rutger explained as he set the coffee mug on the table and stood. "I'm ordering you not to act. Do not make a decision until you return to work."

Ansel didn't want to acknowledge the order; it would make ignoring it harder. The decision he wasn't supposed to make had been made when Jordyn told him he was capable of shifting into his Bestial form. And having accepted his life and his mother's magic there was a chance he would be able to use the full scope of his power. He figured it was a slim chance, but a chance all the same. What it meant hurt him more than he thought possible.

"It's an order," Rutger warned.

Ansel felt the uncertainty coming from him and wanted to change it, assure him, but couldn't.

Clio watched them, their attention solely focused on the other, and the authority Director Kanin was trying not to use. When stillness glided through her, taking the heat and energy of Ansel, she knew he closed himself off from her. "What is this about?"

"You've been given a direct order, Captain Wolt," Jordyn enforced. "You'll be punished if you refuse to obey."

"I don't know what's going on." Clio found herself on the outside. Damn them, they were ignoring her, and she hated it. Hated wanting to be part of them. She also hated seeing Director Kanin and Jordyn gang up on Ansel, who had returned from being beaten and hadn't yet healed.

"One week." Rutger's gaze darkened to mahogany when he placed his hand at the small of Jordyn's back, the command in the air from his authority easing as he escorted her from the living room through the screen door and outside.

One week. A direct order. Ansel didn't move, his drive to stay awake dwindling. His muscles were weakening, making him more tired, and he wanted to go to bed. When he heard the truck start and the engine's rumble fade with the distance, he met Clio's scarlet glare. "One week."

"For what?" she demanded. "What the hell just happened?"

"Tomorrow. I'll tell you tomorrow. Give me tonight, tesoro, please." Ansel held his hand out to her, praying she took it and left the question alone.

She hated it. "Tomorrow." Clio closed the distance, and twining her fingers through Ansel's, she let him pull her to the couch and cuddled up beside him. His warmth seeped into her, easing the discomfort of the faceoff and tension it created, and snuggling closer, careful not to hurt him, she gazed up at him.

"What?" he asked, his voice rough, as a grin curved his cracked lips. From under lashes, he saw her staring up at him, her cheek against his arm, her curls feathering his skin.

"I'm glad you're safe. I'm glad you're home. I'm glad I can touch you." She didn't know touching him would make her feel safe, complete as if a part of her had been missing, and the energy coming from him settled within her. The pain, confusion, and guilt she lived with since seeing her parents felt less powerful, less controlling, and gave her clarity about what she was going to have to do.

"I love you." Ansel barely said the words before his eyes closed, his muscles went lax, and drifting into sleep, his last thought was he was home, with Clio.

Day three.

When she realized Ansel wasn't in bed with her, she crawled out from under soft sheets, not wasting time getting dressed—there was no one there, wouldn't be anyone there—and made her way downstairs. At the French doors leading to the backyard, she watched him go through several repetitions of exercises, each testing his balance, endurance, strength, and coordination. She told herself she was watching him in case he hurt himself, and that was almost funny considering he shapeshifted, healed his wounds, there wasn't a mark on him, and his strength had returned. He was good as new.

There were two things bugging her; one, he hadn't told her what the faceoff had been about and two, she wanted to shift and run with him and couldn't. It was the first time she tried and failed. She felt her wolf, knew it was there, and couldn't shift. After crossing over, her heightened senses strengthened her trait, and she was stronger than she had been. Most importantly, it made her a better doctor. But if she lost the ability to shift, she would be devastated, crushed. She would be missing a part of herself. She wouldn't be able to run with Ansel. Clio wasn't going to grieve yet, like she wasn't going to tell anyone, she would try again and then make a decision.

Then there was the last thing ... no, that wasn't true, she wished it was, could probably make herself believe it if the fantasy lasted. The third thing, while equally important, she was enjoying herself too much to bring the subject up. They were playing house, like a vacation in a fantasy. She liked it, but it wasn't going to last forever. Day seven served as the end of playtime, and day eight would see them going back to work. She would go to Nearctic, check in with the medical staff at the Hollow, and Ansel would meet with Baron Kanin. Damn, she wished she knew what it was about. Then there was the question where were they going to live? Which house? She had her office. He had his backyard that was a necessity if he worked out every morning.

The fourth thing. The last thing on her list. Her parents. She hadn't spoken to them, and they hadn't tried contacting her. Did she give them more time to accept her life? Did she let it go? Did she contact them? Did she wait until she could tell them where she was going to live? Or wait until after Ansel spoke with Baron Kanin?

That might be the best avenue, she thought as she sipped coffee. She wasn't going to face them with unanswered questions sitting between her and Ansel. When she faced them, she would have a solid plan, and Ansel would be with her, by her side. As backup.

Opening the door as silently as she could, Clio slipped through, and padding barefoot to the deck railing she set her coffee mug down. Under the sun its morning warmth on her shoulders and bare legs she watched him. She wasn't naked, although the thought was a tantalizing one. She wore a white camisole and turquoise silk panties, her hair—she had no idea what it looked like—was loose and down her back. After picking the mug up, she sipped as Ansel paused, shifted his position, and posed, his muscles contracting, straining, as beads of sweat rolled down his spine to his hips and the waist of his shorts. His short shorts that left his thighs bare and gave him freedom to kick, stretch, and shift easily between exercises and poses. She recognized the second set as marital arts. He went from one to the other with controlled skill, each movement making a different muscle group contract, tighten, to look sculpted.

As he spun on the ball of his foot he faced her, his chest gleaming, the line of auburn hair sinking below the black waistband. Her heart leapt from its place then beat wildly, at the same time her breath caught, and her body hummed at the sight of him. How many days had it been? Blood, five days. Energy, five maybe six. Too long. She had been side-tracked with Ansel coming home and making sure he healed. Clio stared at him, his cinnamon and bronze gaze seeming to see through her as his face remained neutral, calm, while chaos roiled in the depths of his gaze. Through bronze eyes his wolf was seeing the world, sensing it while Ansel was re-living something, feeling it, coming to terms with it. She felt the steel determination he was made from like an impene-trable wall. He was going to survive, and he was going to come to terms with their treatment of him. It didn't change her hate for Strong Lord and the Fellowship. Clio froze when his inhale expanded his chest, then his otherworldly stare turned molten, and focusing on her, her heart pounded in her chest. He knew she wanted him. Needed him. His wolf knew. The primal animal wanted its mate. Heat veiled her, coloring pale skin with a rosy hue, and making a sheen of sweat bead on her chest. Her camisole felt tight, while her body demanded she sate her hunger and thirst.

When the echoes of laughter and searing pain en-trenched his mind and body, Ansel woke and stared at the ceiling fan, its rotation cooling the early morning air and dry-ing the layer of sweat covering him. Despite wanting to stay where he was, beside Clio, her heartbeat in his head, the nightmare held him, and he couldn't shake the feel of hu-miliation or quell his raging emotions.

Forced to leave her sleeping soundly with her favorite blanket, he left the room and headed downstairs. He hoped walking helped him and the cooler air would erase the vivid images from his mind while it doused the tremors wanting to rack his body. It didn't work. Since he healed and his strength and energy had returned it became impossible to deny the two weeks he spent at the stronghold as their per-sonal whipping post. The smell of blood on stones drenched with others' deaths. The cuts. Broken bones. His own stink clinging to him while he hung from chains. He had to cut the nightmare loose, needed to get rid of it. He wouldn't saddle Clio with it, nor would he let it get between them. Not when he was considering changing their lives forever. That was a decision he couldn't make alone. He needed to talk to Clio, and while he wanted her to agree with him, to take the chance, he knew he couldn't keep the consequences from her. Cursing himself, his selfishness, and his weakness where the nightmare was concerned, he walked through his silent house, through the French doors, and outside. He thought his control should have been better ... after all, he was a one-hundred-and-forty-one-year-old werewolf, and it hadn't been the first time he'd been used for entertainment.

Ansel inhaled fresh air carrying pine, cedar, and water laced with cattails, water cress, and waterweeds, and taking it into himself let his territory, his land ease the tension grip-ping him. Then he thought of his family, his brother, Rutger, and Jordyn. Slowly, ever so slowly, the laugher faded, the echo of pain waned, and he relaxed his shoulders. But it wasn't enough. He needed to move. He had been deep inside of himself, his mind clear, his focus on his straining muscles as they burned with each drill, and his skin slick with sweat when the sun crested the mountain ridges its light chasing the shadows from his body. Its warmth wrapped around him, urging him to pull himself free, and when he opened his eyes, he saw her staring at him. She stood at the railing watching him, her scarlet gaze heated as it caressed his body and called his wolf, and his mark, a bronze veil over her slender shoulder proving she was his. He inhaled to capture her scent of thunderstorm and orchids laced with lust, the combination escorting his animal to the surface, its fur against the underside of his skin as he stalked to the stairs. Her breasts, covered in white, rose and fell with her breaths that had become deeper, and by the time he stalked to his mate, her eyes had bled crimson. His dhampir was hungry.

Clio watched, her insides shuddering with his slow approach, and struggling to remain still, she forced herself not to turn. Damn vampire side liked playing games. Why? She didn't know. Who did? The instinct to tease him rushed through with enough force, she shifted her feet. No, she was not going to run from her mate. Fated mate. A Pureblood werewolf. She wasn't a vampire. She was Dr. Clio Hyde. Cool. Calm. Collected. A perfectionist. Risking taking her eyes off Ansel as the primal animal beared down on her, she checked the distance to the deck railing.

"Tesoro," Ansel growled, his lips raising to expose lengthening canines. He tried warning her when he felt her need to run and the excitement coursing through her veins. Tried. He wanted her to run. He wanted to hunt his prey.

"Darling," Clio returned deliberately, as she tilted her head in denial. She wasn't going to do it. No, she wasn't. She could hear herself, *"Mom, Dad, the person who isn't a good man, Ansel, chases me around his yard."*

She laughed, and catching Ansel off guard, jumped to the rail. Facing him, she met the wolf in his eyes for a breath and it nearly had her heart exploding. Nothing was going to stop when her need to tempt him overwhelmed her, and jumping she landed softly on the grass and headed toward the wood-line. Behind her a deep howl, thick with man and wolf, thundered in the air, its force falling to touch her skin and burn her senses with his desire.

Ansel heaved in a breath as his temptress ran from him, like she was floating over the land, then he watched her disappear into the tree line, and the shadows wrapped around her to take her form. His dhampir. "Mine," he growled, the deep rumble vibrating his chest. He waited, drinking in the anticipation, and letting it tangle with his lust, while his wolf clawed him, its howl in his ears, his pulse quickening with the thrill of the hunt.

One second. Silence.

He couldn't hear her, meaning she stopped and was hiding. The brush was thick and healthy in that part of the property, the thunderstorms nourishing the trees and underbrush, giving life to several kinds of grasses. Forcing himself to wait, he heard birds singing, small wildlife scurrying over the forest floor, butterflies bouncing in the air, proving she hadn't disturbed them by her invasion. She might be an Illuminate, but she wasn't a predator, didn't seek meat or blood and wasn't hunting. Rather was being hunted. When he couldn't take waiting another second, he stalked after her, his bare feet sinking in grass, leaves, and stepping over fallen limbs he followed her scent of lust and iron, reflecting what she had become, werewolf and vampire. Pausing at the woodline, he drew air in to taste her on the breeze.

He took several cautious steps going deeper into the thicket while his senses were on alert and his thoughts circled the possibility of his Bestial form and its strength. It was another conversation they would have to have. The risk of going bestial and losing his mind was real. He wouldn't do anything to put Clio's life in danger or force her to make the decision to end his life, and potentially her own. Ansel followed Clio's scent, the barely marked ground, and brought his wolf forward. She had been trained as a soldier, was promoted to enforcer, and had worked for him for years. Then Baron Kanin removed her and gave her the position of doctor in charge of Nearctic. While he would always consider her an enforcer, she hadn't trained in over a year, her concentration focused on the hospitals and healing. Seeking shade in the crop of trees he saw her enter, he stilled to hear her. He sensed her, smelled her everywhere, knew she was there, but couldn't see her hiding in the brush. With his werewolf sight, stronger because he was a Pureblood, he should have been able to see her; she was wearing white, and her strawberry blonde hair with its wild curls and red streaks would have given her away.

The sunlight through limbs cast spiderweb shadows across the bushes, trees, and ground, making it impossible for her to remain wrapped in the shadows. So where was she?

Sneaky dhampir. Pride flourished, his chest expanded with primal male arrogance knowing she accepted her vampire half and embracing its traits, she grew in strength, and would continue to do so. It made his decision easier. He wouldn't have to worry about her when she would be strong enough to stand at his side, and the sharpest blade of guilt dulled. Slightly. He didn't know what she was going to say when he told her and what explanations he was going to give her when she questioned him. Because she would. His Dr. Hyde didn't do anything without knowing what was expected.

Clio sat on the limb above him, her right hand braced on the tree, her left on the limb beside her bare feet, and she watched his chest barely rise as he drew in air to scent her. And he would find her scent, she made sure of it. However, he wouldn't know where it was coming from. As a Wight, she had been an all right enforcer, working hard to keep up with the physical demands, and holding her own with the others. Being an Illuminate, dhampir, gave her agility, heightened senses, and sharpened her training. Her instincts sang with energy as she continued to spy on her wolf at the same time it ratcheted her thirst and hunger up more notches than she could count. A burn started in her stomach and reached out into her circulatory system where it set it on fire. This was fun ... hell, it was thrilling, but if she didn't take care of her needs, she was going to lose her mind. She had been warned about pushing herself to the edge of control, to the edge of starvation, and what the consequences would be. She couldn't hurt Ansel, to take him with violence and destroy the trust he had in her. She wouldn't become Milanka.

Ansel heard the barest scrape against bark; bare feet, she was above him. Without giving himself away, he found her position, and smiling with victory his canines lengthened. He thought about joining her on the limb when another muffled scrape sounded. Carefully listening, he sidestepped to the next crop of trees, giving her a clearing, when he heard the air change, as if someone was breaking through, and the breeze created brushed against his heated skin. In a heart-beat a shadow dropped from the sky, bringing iron, a storm, and the scent of his mate. She landed in front of him in a crouched position, her scarlet eyes gleaming with her lust and thirst. He liked the game, his wolf loved tracking her, but it was over. He wanted his mate. Refusing to let her evade him, he had her by the waist, and lifting her, she wrapped her legs around him.

"I knew you were there, tesoro," Ansel whispered as he licked the skin marked by his brand.

"I let you find me," Clio replied, a smile tugging at the corners of her mouth. Turning her head, she heard his low roll of laughter, and it trembled over her skin, sending chills down her spine, then his hand was in her hair and the other under her rear.

"I thought you liked me chasing you."

She did. It set her blood on fire. Clio nipped at his ear, bringing a growl to his lips, and countered, "It would have been fun to watch you wander around, but I have other things in mind."

"I'm all yours," Ansel mused. Carrying her from the open area and through a cluster of trees, he wasn't scared of any-one finding them, seeing them, no, he owned as far as the eye could see, and what he didn't, the Forest Service did. Deeper still, he didn't stop until they were protected by thick Manzanita, California sagebrush, Deergrass, Snowbrush, with dabs of color from Indian Paintbrush. Large oak trees added shade while California Oatgrass cushioned his steps. The ground cover starting then spreading after the thunder-storms moved through and rain saturated the area. Cocooned in greens and white blossoms he let Clio slide down the length of his body, the action causing her camisole to ride up her stomach, exposing toned muscles that flexed.

"It's nice here. Did you do this?" Clio asked as her toes reached the soft ground, the blades tickling her feet. She put distance between them, met a bronze gaze filled with questions from over her shoulder, then walked to the Snowbrush where she lightly touched white petals and emerald green leaves.

"Negative." He watched her stare at the flowers, pick at the leaves, and knew there was only one reason his doctor would be playing with petals. "You need to talk about something?"

"I didn't want it like this," she admitted as she faced him. She wanted him, skin on skin, the power of him flowing into her, and his blood in her veins. But she wasn't someone who could ignore a situation. Instead, it ate at her thoughts and invaded her mind like a virus. It also tested her patience. Like the burning in her veins was causing frustration.

"What?" he asked cautiously. There were a million things it could be. They had been dancing around reality as if ignoring it, it would go on its merry way, or play out and neither of them would be forced to make a decision. His mate might be standing in the forest wearing nothing except her top and panties, but his Dr. Hyde couldn't remain in fantasy land any longer. He hated it coming to an end at the same time it had to come to an end.

Clio's lips curved in a small smile when she saw the intent in Ansel's eyes and knew he had been thinking the same thing. It didn't ease the irritation like she thought it would have when she didn't have to explain herself or her concern. "This. We're playing house and there's a countdown to reality."

Using his left hand, he rubbed the back of his neck, then pushed his fingers through his thick hair. "Affirmative. The countdown." There was more than reality waiting at the end of their seven days. "What do you want to tackle first?"

Tackle, good word. "Housing." After watching him exercise in the early morning dawn, Clio had been thinking about where she wanted to live, how they would live, and had made a tentative decision.

"This is my territory. My land," he began, his voice low, assured, his eyes a dark cinnamon.

Was he serious? One of them would be giving something up and he expected it to be her. Of course he did. Captain of Enforces wasn't going to make a sacrifice. His domineering tone raked along her nerves, striking matches as it went and making her want to argue that she had her territory, her land. It also had her parents' accusations playing as if on a loop and ringing in her ears.

"But your office is at your house, and that's where you should be," Ansel finished. He stepped back and watched her reactions when he felt her anger lash out. Her gaze, slate and whiskey burned scarlet the bright red flooding her eyes.

Silence stretched out between them, him staring at her in confusion with a slice of wariness, and Clio giving him a death glare. There was no mistaking what he felt; Clio was on edge, and it wasn't so much death as it was hunger. When he returned from the Fellowship, he had been busy healing and trying to get his strength back, also he had been stuck in his head making plans, preparing the speech he was going to give Baron Kanin, and hadn't paid attention. Had she fed? That was a hard no. Her hunger was like a physical thing rolling out from her, its threads seeking his vein, the dhampir needing her paramount.

"What do you think?" he asked, making sure he didn't act dominate or the aggressor.

"What?" she demanded and cringed. Clio was losing her mind. Anger fired through her, heated her to the point of leaving a sheen of sweat on her skin, and her pulse was pounding against her skull. "What?"

"You're starving."

"I can take of myself. Just tell me what you said." She knew she sounded demanding and out of control, and reaching for her wolf, felt it slinking back as if knowing the vampire had taken over. *Is this what starvation feels like?*

"I'm going to tell you, then you're going to feed. I'm not going to argue with you about this. I won't watch you lose control of yourself," he warned. He would never, under any circumstance, use rank to force Clio to submit, but he didn't know any other way when the vampire was clearly gaining control. Ansel's eyes glowed bronze as he brought the wolf close to the surface, and exuding dominance became the Pureblood Dominate he was. But he wasn't only a Dominate and held a higher place in the hierarchy than Clio, he was also her paramount. He was her sire.

Clio felt his authority strike her—not hard, not gentle, with a warning and carrying a threat enough she pushed the vampire back and could think. Not clear enough. Lowering her eyes to his chest, she inhaled and exhaled, then replied, "Understood."

Ansel watched her fight. However, it wasn't the need for touch and energy, or sexual energy from him, she was fighting thirst and the vampire virus that had twisted her DNA. "Your office is at your house, that's where you need to be."

"Without you?" she accused. "You need to stay in your territory, your land." She was doing everything she could to block the thirst from taking over her mind and body and was failing by the second. This wasn't who she was. "Forget it. I can take care of myself."

"You can't. Not this. You need to feed."

"You're going to save me?" she demanded, her words shaky, her insides trembling. *I'm going to beat this*, she assured herself. The drive to be the best, that's who she was. She needed a minute.

"Listen to me. I'm here for you." Bronze eyes held hers. "I warned you." Ansel closed the distance between them, and slowly raising his hands, feathered her waist, then held Clio's upper arms. "You're not going to win, tesoro. It's stronger than you."

Unable to hold his gaze, she looked at her toes covered in lush grass, felt her body begin to tear apart from the inside out, the searing pain increasing with each passing second. She wasn't going to win. If she didn't feed, she was going to lose, and it was going to be painful, the logical side of her brain told her. But the fear she would hurt Ansel and add to the shadows in his eyes scared her worse. Meeting his gaze, she whispered, "I know." How did she apologize for failing? "I failed. I lost track."

"Shhh. How do you want me?" he asked with his wolf staring at her.

"You're trying to make light of this. What I've done. What I've said ..."

"You lost track. Now you know what it feels like, and you won't let it happen again. Will you, mate?"

An edge of dominance was back as he told her what to do. It grated on her frayed patience and pushed at her non-existent control. Swallowing the instinct to push back, to say something to cause a fight, she reached for her wolf, forcing the vampire to back off enough it wasn't in her words. "No, my dominate mate," she mocked with a bitterness to her tone.

Ansel smiled, his lips curving with her anger. Yes, she would stand at his side. The image of her fighting beside him had his blood racing through his veins, then the thought of her fangs in his flesh, her lithe body against his, had his wolf howling. "How do you want me?"

Clio slipped her fingers into the waist of his shorts, slid them down his thighs to the ground, and then slowly began lifting her camisole up her torso and over her head. She didn't move when Ansel held lace with his fingers and slipped her panties to the ground. When she stepped out, he picked her up, and she wrapped her legs around him. Clio nipped at his lips, her fangs holding the soft flesh for breath and leaving barely-there kisses on his jawline and lower to where his pulse beat against her lips.

The sensuality of Clio's kisses, the feather touch of the tips of her fangs, her possession of him, had Ansel's knees threatening to buckle and send them both crashing to the ground. Bending down, he held her against him, while he sat on the grass, and she was straddling him.

"How about this?" Clio made a mewling sound as she lifted then eased herself down his length and sinking to skin on skin.

"Tesoro," Ansel whispered.

"Shut up," she hissed against his throat. She received a growl in answer, and gripping her hips, he rocked her back and forth. Clio wanted to protest—he was pushing her control, she didn't want to rip his throat out—and failed when her thirst and desire seared her as if she been doused in fuel.

Ansel dug his fingers into her soft skin, felt her hips bones and muscles contracting as he rocked her and then sensed her unraveling. With her hands in his hair, he took her mouth, his tongue grazing the sharp point of a fang as he branded her, the primal part of his wolf taking possession of the vampire. The part of Clio weaving its way into her wolf, thoughts, decisions, and actions. Unrestrained. Unruly. As he licked and teased her lips and tongue, he created their pace, to have her curls feather his chest and arms.

She knew what he was doing. Sensed his wolf. He declared his authority not once, but twice, and was proving his dominance by controlling their rhythm. Clio was going to go mad, then his hand released her hip, blood flowing and bringing a sting, slid up her side to cover her breast. Unable to take anymore, she broke the kiss, met bronze eyes of his wolf, and with a fist full of hair, pulled his head to the left. She didn't hesitate ... she sank her fangs into his flesh, tasted the sweat on his skin as hot iron laced with wolf coated her tongue and the elixir slid down her throat. While her body absorbed his essence, it became another possession, a reminder he was her paramount, and a hit to her independence. Ansel's hands were at her hips, crushing her to him as she drank him in, taking him, marking him, possessing him. The sheer thought of it sent ecstasy rippling through her, and stealing one last sip to sate her thirst, her fangs retracted, releasing him from her hold.

Swollen red lips parted. Her cheeks were flushed, coloring her pale skin from his blood and the pleasure he could feel rising in her. As she sat back to fully ride him, he slowed their tempo, wrapped his arm around her, and getting to his knees, lowered until she was on her back, and he was cradled in the triangle of her thighs. He rested on his elbow, the length of him pinning her, while his other hand griped her hip, and holding her scarlet gaze, he thrust into her. Her left leg went over his hip, she closed her eyes, a moan leaving her parted lips, like music to his ears, and she arched into him. With her breasts against his chest their bodies met.

"Mine," he growled at her ear as he created a raw pace. "You're mine, tesoro."

Her entire body sang with ecstasy as he pushed her toward an inferno of bliss. "Yours," she readily agreed. Clarity cleared her frustration, and with her body nourished her back arched off the grass, the blades' tips prickling her heated skin to add to the sensations overwhelming her. Meeting each of his thrusts, it sent electric currents through her, and letting herself tumble over the edge rapture shattered her. A low growl tangled in a breathless moan left her.

The slices of sunlight breaking through the tree limbs warmed his back and made the sweat glisten on Clio's pink-hued skin. It also heated the scent of her, and mixed into hers was his. She wore his scent as if he had become part of her. It added fuel to his lust, and moving deep and hard, he felt her shudder, heard her husky moans, and following Clio into ecstasy, rapture detonated within him. With slow rolls of his hips, he slid in and out of her, pleasure cascading through him, and didn't stop until she lay limp beneath him. Removing his hand from her hip, he saw his print on her flesh. "Tesoro." He was going to apologize when it disappeared. She healed like an Illuminate. Pride filled him.

"Darling," she whispered lazily.

He didn't have a reply. Couldn't if he wanted to. In a breath his wolf brushed him, its force tangling with another, the magic overwhelming him and seizing him.

"Ansel." Clio rose to her elbows then scooted back from him when she felt the wash of power emanating from him, the constant flow like a river, and his eyes flashed bronze. "Ansel. What's happening?"

"I can't stop it," he growled. He needed to get away from her. Digging his fingers into grass and dirt, he tried to control the magic.

No. No. Bestial form. Why now? Clio wanted to ask. What happened? She wasn't going to get an answer until it was over. If Ansel survived. With blood and energy coursing through her, the vampire faced Ansel, his hardened bronze gaze, and his wolf's need to dominate. Staring up at him, she saw him struggling with the force of his magic and tried to call her wolf. Denied. Bad. It was bad.

"I. Can't. Stop." Bestial form. His wolf howled as he jerked back, and landing on his bare ass, he rocked forward, and went to his hands and knees. "I don't want to hurt to you."

The plea was pushed through clenched teeth, making Clio's instincts roar with a warning. "Don't fight it. Don't fight what you are."

He didn't want to hurt her. What if he wasn't strong enough and he turned bestial? What if he lost his mind and the primal animal went on a search and destroy mission?

"Go," he ordered. If he hurt Clio, his tesoro, he would truly lose his mind. His shift would push Baron Kanin to order Rutger to take him down, eliminate the problem, his brother would be forced to kill him. It was bad. And he didn't think it could get worse.

Clio met his gaze, his eyes sinking into their sockets as his flesh darkened and rippled over muscles and bones while his wolf fought to tear through the tissue of its human shell. Standing, she failed to shift, it meant she had to run. She grabbed her panties, pulled them up her thighs, then tugged the camisole over her head, and giving him a long look over her shoulder, his auburn hair hanging by his cheeks, the hurt creasing his face, and the fear rolling from him stabbing her heart, she raced away from him and toward the house. She didn't notice the branches and rocks, the edges digging into the bottom of her feet, or the sun as it crossed the sky. With her heart pounding inside of her chest, its beat keeping time with the passing seconds, she leapt the stairs, jerked open the right side of the door, and entered the empty house. Crossing the dining area and living room, she went to the stairs where her running shoes sat, and after pulling them on went to the closet beside the front door. His BDU top hung inside, and saying a quick prayer she pushed it aside to find his tactical belt. Clio pulled the Glock 21, .45 caliber pistol from its holster, removed the magazine, ejected the White 47 silver round, and made sure the chamber was clear. She felt time weighing her down as she searched for the non-lethal rounds, and when she found two magazines, she took one, loaded the gun, and grabbed the other.

When he lost sight of Clio, Ansel fell to the ground, and rolling to his side he curled into a ball. Pain seared him, his joints tightened to rebar, his tendons twisted, his lungs felt as if they were shrinking, while his mind erupted with information to overload his senses. He clamped the sides of his head with his hands, attempting to stop the deluge, and knew he was going to lose his mind. As the shift agonizingly progressed, he accepted he wasn't strong enough to complete the transition—to control the wolf's mind or the mind that would take over if he made it to the forbidden Bestial form. He heard Rutger's voice telling him he feared losing control. Ansel understood. With his back smashed to the grass, his body straightened, every muscle screaming as his legs elongated, his arms altering into their new shape, while a fine pelt of fur broke through sweat slick skin. He tried to moan, failed, he couldn't get enough air, then panic turned the blood in his veins to ice when he scented Clio. She returned.

No. No. He didn't want her there.

Clio entered the enclosure of brush to find Ansel half shifted, his arms and legs a mangle of human and wolf, while his chest expanded and reshaped, making his ribs stand out from his concave torso. Bestial form. She stood back from him, pistol in hand, inhaling and exhaling her fear, and felt helpless to help him.

"Run," Ansel breathed through tight lips, his eyes bleeding from hard bronze to liquid metal.

"I'm not abandoning you," she promised. Closing the distance between them, Clio opened the bond, felt his terror, and the doubt he wasn't strong enough. "You can do this." With the bond open, she shoved as much power and magic into it as she could, and adding her vampire side, drove defiance into him.

Ansel growled when he felt her vampire in their bond, cold, hard, mocking his weakness, its force shredding through him as if trying to help the shift tear him apart. With the last of his energy, he roared, shoved it back, its ice grating on him and leaving shards behind as he grasped onto his wolf. His claws dug into the animal, and diving deeper allowed himself to tap into the magic he believed was out of his reach, he believed he didn't deserve. Free from the restraints of his mental cage the magic exploded from within him, merging into his wolf. It wasn't his mom's magic, not her power, it was them. His father and his mother. Together. Inside of him. He felt their wolves as the shift flowed over him in a rush of sensory overload.

Clio didn't know what was happening when Ansel's magic swept over her, its feel like millions of pulses rode the air. When the initial volley faded and she caught her breath, Clio noted, felt the backlash of the intense aversion when the essence of her vampire entered their bond and challenged him. Now stumbling back, she tried to control the rejection of her vampire, and couldn't stop from smiling. Pureblood Dominate. He may have accepted her as a dhampir and let her feed from him because she was his fated mate and he trusted her not to hurt him. But he hated the vampire. Understandable when wolves lived, fought to live, and vampires took lives and embraced death, even their own. Ansel undulated from the ground, his grace and strength in every taut muscle, in the tendons straining under thick, dark auburn fur, every curve of his Bestial form—a seven-foot-tall combination of wolf and man. Clio took several steps backwards, confident she could outrun him, and meeting liquid bronze eyes, primal with their intent, raised the gun and trained it to the center of her mate's chest.

Ansel shook his head, making the fur ripple from his head and down his back as the air drifted over his ears. Several blades of grass fell from him as he stretched his arms, legs, and working to get his bearings, he settled into his new form. Information engulfed his senses, the overpowering sense of them had his instincts going crazy. He needed to control the intake and calm his wolf. He focused on Clio, her wolf, their bond, and the gun she had pointed at him. His gun. He could smell the non-lethal ammo she loaded in the weapon.

"I won't hurt you," he tried reassuring her, his jaw working awkwardly around the words.

"Are you, you?" Clio asked with caution. He hadn't gone insane. He stood before her, his massive chest rising and falling, his broad shoulders teaming with muscle, his torso narrowing at the waist to lead to lean legs built for agility. Maybe she wouldn't be able to outrun him.

Rather than try and talk—it sounded like there were rocks in his throat, and he didn't know how to say a word—he nodded his head.

Clio lowered the gun, letting it hang at her side. "How do you feel?"

"Good." Simple word.

"Anything hurt?"

He shook his head.

"You're in charge of your faculties?"

He nodded yes.

"Prove it," she challenged. Clio had no idea what he was going to do when he hadn't done anything indicating he'd gone bestial. If he did, would she know?

Ansel raised both hands, showing her he wasn't going to hurt her, and taking a step, watched her reaction. When she didn't flinch or back away, he closed the distance until there was a sliver between their bodies. Curling his clawed finger, he put it under her chin and met her scarlet gaze. "Love. You."

"You're a romantic even in your Bestial form," Clio whispered, as she let the repercussions of what he had done and what she witnessed filter through her.

Ansel nodded and backed away. Holding the form was draining him of energy and he knew he was going to collapse. "Can't. Maintain," he growled out as he swayed.

Clio moved to help him when he stumbled, and tripping, his massive body crashed to the ground, making an indentation. In the second it took her to reach him, his Bestial form melted to his human form, and he lay unconscious. She set the gun down beside her, to have both hands free, then gingerly working to make sure he hadn't injured himself, she saw there were no wounds. If she had any misgivings about being a dhampir, they were gone. Between the vampire and werewolf, she used her senses to check his vitals and confirm there was nothing wrong with him. Thankfully, he was all right. However, being physically sound didn't mean there wasn't something happening. While she examined him, he hadn't moved, didn't make a sound, and that worried her. She didn't know if it was simple exhaustion from shapeshifting into a different form or the magic that had pushed him to shapeshift. And she didn't know how long he was going to be out. It left her with no other choice but to leave him and go back to the house for supplies.

After returning his gun to its holster, she spied a backpack, and taking it raced upstairs, got dressed, then grabbed a T-shirt, sweatpants, running shoes, and a blanket. She shoved everything inside and headed to the kitchen in search of food. From the pantry she took energy bars, beef jerky, and bottled water containing electrolytes. Lastly, she grabbed her cell phone. If he didn't wake up, she was going to call Jordyn.

CHAPTER TWENTY-TWO

Day five.

Clio sat on the wood floor, her back against the wall, her knees drawn up to her chest. She fought sleep as she listened to Ansel's heartbeat while watching his chest rise and fall with easy breaths through slitted eyes. Having closed the blinds and covering those with thick blankets, she lost track of time and didn't know if it was day or night. She kept time by the levels of liquid in the IV bags hanging from stainless steel hooks. There were two; one for hydration and the other for nutrients. Keeping her focus on him, she sensed exhaustion, but hadn't sensed an illness or injuries.

When they were in the woods, she watched over him praying, hoping, demanding he would wake up and tell her everything was going to be okay, and when he didn't questions multiplied. Did she call for help? Did she wait? How long was she supposed to wait? He wasn't hurt, she kept reminding herself, and it stopped her panic from taking over and from calling anyone. And she didn't know what shifting into the Bestial form meant. Had he broken a canon? Would Bestial form eventually turn him bestial? Would he lose his humanity to the wolf? And the baron. What would he say? Because Ansel would have to tell him. Would he report Ansel to the Highguard? She didn't know. And it was the unknown that kept her mouth shut. There had been nothing else to do but wait. And she waited. Then he woke up, groggy, unsteady, and mumbling words she didn't understand, his accent thicker than it had ever been. While she tried to get him to talk to her, she helped him back to the house where he collapsed in bed, and he had been there ever since. A day and a half. A day and a fucking half. Clio fought herself every time her mind wanted to replay the day before, like it was a broken record player, and failing most of the time, she saw him fighting to shift. It was killing her. The silence was killing her. Not knowing what was happening was killing her.

"Tesoro," Ansel whispered, the breath grating his throat.

Clio's head lolled to the right as she drifted toward much needed sleep. *Just a minute*, she promised herself, then she would change out the bags.

"Tesoro."

The brittle whisper had her eyes snapping open, her body moving on auto, and she was at his side, staring at him. "Ansel." Clio sat on the side of the bed and paused when she saw his eyes were glowing. Glowing bronze. She really needed him to tell her he was all right.

He wasn't sure where he was, his vision was blurry, his senses erratic, his instincts trying to make sense of his surroundings. Was it night? The last thing he remembered was being in the woods. "Tesoro."

"I'm here," Clio assured. "I'm here."

Ansel felt her presence and it calmed the part of him wanting to panic. He tried talking to her, wanted to explain to her releasing his parents' magic had started a chain reaction that was changing him, altering his magic and his wolf, but he felt himself being dragged under. Darkness swamped him while in the distance he saw a sky stained with crimson and gold-tipped flames and knew what was next.

Day six.

With Clio's help, Ansel forced his tired body to a sitting position, and leaning against the headboard of his bed, asked, "How did I get here?"

"You walked," Clio replied, the words sharp, as she sat down in a chair she placed beside his bed. Where she spent the last couple of days watching and waiting. At least his eyes were their natural cinnamon, not the glowing bronze she met whenever he stirred.

Her anger drowned under the anxiety and fear drifting from her to him, and they surrounded him. He needed to fix it and reassure her everything was all right. "We need to talk."

"No. Shit." She crossed her arms over her chest.

"I don't know how long I'll be awake," he began. "I'm changing, Clio. My parents' magic is changing me."

She wanted to hold onto the anger, fear, and uncertainty, wanted to yell at him. Damn how she wanted to yell at him. She couldn't, not when she felt his truth. "How?"

"I don't understand how it's impacting my magic, my wolf, but it is. I feel complete. Stronger." It had been three days since his parents' magic pushed him to shift into his Bestial form. His parents' magic. He felt whole. The void that had sat thick inside of him was gone, as was the fear his life had been a lie. The truth was alive inside of him.

She didn't know what to say, ask. Instead, she sat there staring at him as his eyes closed, his black lashes resting on his cheeks for a heartbeat when he forced them open and met her gaze. "You need to rest. I'll remove the catheters and IVs. We'll talk tomorrow."

"Tomorrow," he mumbled as he sank lower. "Thank you for not abandoning me."

"I'll never abandon you," she promised. Clio watched for another minute, and when his breathing evened out, she adjusted the pillows, the blanket, and began removing the IVs.

Clio sat across the table glaring at Ansel as he drank his coffee as if nothing had happened. Like everything was peachy keen.

"Are we going to talk about it?" he asked as he set the mug down. When whatever had been happening to him ended, he woke up feeling like he slept for a week, which he almost had. While Clio slept soundly in the chair beside the bed, he used the time to take a shower. He wore loose shorts, no shirt, and he left his hair loose, its end at his shoulders. It was two inches longer than it had been.

"I don't know," Clio answered honestly as she sat back. "I think I need time. You just woke up." She crossed her bare legs, put her hands in her lap, and continued to stare. Glare.

Today is the last day, he thought. He needed to talk to her about his plan. But, if she was still upset by his Bestial form and what happened afterwards, she might not be ready. That was unacceptable. He needed her by his side. "We need to talk."

"Talk? This isn't talk material, it's a damned discussion." Clio stood, her nerves getting the better of her, and marched to the living room, then faced him and met his cinnamon gaze. "I watched you struggle to shift into your Bestial form only to see you collapse. You couldn't hold the shift. You were unconscious for hours." She refused to move him fearing she might hurt him. "You woke up, eyes blazing bronze, glowing. Ansel, they were glowing, and I helped you to the house where you collapsed again."

"Clio. I had just healed, and you fed. Shapeshifting took what energy I had left," he explained. "I shifted into my Bestial form for the first time."

"And I pointed your own damn gun at you."

"After loading it with non-lethal. You checked and saw I was all right."

"You scared me to death." Clio turned in a circle, then faced him. "You scared me to death. I thought I was going to lose you."

"I'm sorry. I truly am. I never intended to scare you like that. Clio, I need to talk to you about something." Ansel remained seated, not wanting to add to her anxiety.

"Besides your Bestial form and whatever your parents' magic has done to you?" she asked. Because it was going to be a no. Nada. Zilch. Dream on. She didn't want to know.

Ansel looked into his mug as if the coffee might tell him what to say, and when it didn't, all he saw was the reflection of his eyes set in a human face. He met Clio's glare. "I have to master it."

"No, you don't. Your eyes glowed for days. Is that natural?" she questioned.

"Unsure." He sat back trying to remain calm. "Yes, I do."

"Why?" After everything that had just happened, she wasn't going to listen to damn thing he had to say.

Then he started talking.

Clio listened to him, knew she was staring at him like he had two heads, while trying to hold back her fear, and reject the instinct to walk away from him. Leave him to his demise. She inhaled and exhaled. Inhaled and exhaled. She couldn't leave him, she was bound to him, loved him more than life itself, and if anything happened to him, she wouldn't forgive herself. If she lost him, the pain alone would kill her. Of course, if he died it would be a matter of time before she followed him. Outside of their relationship, a part of her comprehended what he needed to do was necessary, the right thing. The Emanation wasn't going to stop. If there was a chance to protect the pack, to secure the safety of the territory, no matter the cost, then that's what they needed to do.

"I have more strength, power, my magic is at its strongest. It's superior to my wolf form. No one knows, it gives me an advantage."

Her thoughts buzzed while he continued explaining what he needed to do, why he needed to do it, and the risk involved. But he was wrong. Director Kanin and Jordyn knew ... how, she had no idea, unless Jordyn read his thoughts, which she wouldn't do. How had she missed it? Easy. She was busy thinking about how she was going to deal with her parents and Ansel. She was thinking about how she was going to make her world perfect again. Because pleasing her parents had become priority. *This, though*, she thought as he continued, *never would have crossed my mind.*

"It's a risk to us both. If you're not in agreement, then I won't do it," Ansel finished as he stood.

"It scares me," Clio confessed.

"I know. It scares me, too." Ansel embraced her, held her to his chest, her cheek against his skin, and his face in the mess of curls. "This is about ending a power and its tyranny."

"I can't shift into my wolf form. I feel the animal, its claws, it wants out, but I can't shift," she confessed into his chest. "It could be a weakness."

Ansel listened to her, the words carried on her fear and worry floating to him. "We'll have time to understand what we are becoming. You don't know if it's permanent."

"I needed you to know." Leaning back to see his face, she saw raw determination, felt its force in their bond, and knew if she refused him, he would grow to resent her. Sadly, she would hate herself. Clio left the comfort of his arms and walked to the table where she took the mug, sipped her coffee, and contemplated her decision. Despite the possible results, death, and the possible end of their relationships with the pack and her parents, it was easy. Clio stalled for time, knew she was losing her mind to even contemplate it, and gently set her mug down. Meeting his heavy gaze, she replied, "I'm with you."

Ansel's heart stopped just as he released the breath he was holding. "Tesoro. You'll be beside me. I need you beside me."

When Ansel held her once more, Clio drew her fingers through his thick hair, relishing the softness, and the glow returning to his bronze gaze. "Yes, beside you."

"We'll tell the baron tomorrow."

"We still have unfinished business."

"What?"

"We haven't decided where we're going to live."

"If we don't die, we'll live in the stronghold," he answered. "Our territory."

CHAPTER TWENTY-THREE

Day eight.

The wrought iron gate rolled across the track, its length sliding into a thicket of trees where it stopped. Ansel checked his rearview mirror, saw Clio behind the wheel of her new silver, luxury SUV, her unruly curls restrained in a braid, and her sunglasses shielding her eyes. She wore a lavender, sleeveless cotton top, a pair of black scrub bottoms, running shoes, and he wanted her to turn around and go home. To *her* house. He couldn't believe he involved her the way he did. He was willingly putting her life at risk. As the selfish bastard he was, he couldn't do it without her. How did he know this? She was his mate. And it was instinct. For him to succeed, he needed her.

Letting off the brake, he entered Foxwood to the dings and beeps of the terminal, the screen refreshing with new information as he drove the two-lane road. Ansel couldn't help but relish the familiar sights, the treehouses, sniper points, and the feel of home and belonging. After nearly four weeks, he was finally back at work. He couldn't wait to be surrounded by enforcers, soldiers, their conversations, and their energy. There was always a buzz in the Enforcer's office that seeped into the body to change his mood from bad to good, even if he didn't want it to. It was the magic and power of the territory, and the loyalty of kith and kin. It made him inhale and exhale to control the tension and anxiety battling to take him over the edge where he turned around and drove home.

When his brake lights went off, she pressed the accelerator and followed him through the gate. She couldn't imagine what was going through his mind when hers was chaos, and having to face Baron Kanin made it all the worst. Their morning was as normal as it could have been, she guessed. Coffee. Breakfast. Showers. And they got ready for work, in silence. Each of them absorbed in their own thoughts. When they left, Ansel was back in his black BDU top with his name and Cascade's crest, jeans, boots, and thigh holster. His auburn hair was held back by a clasp in the shape of a crescent moon, with a gold star on the bottom point. The moon represented his father while the star represented his mother. Free of the Fellowship and Milanka's leash, he was able to embrace his past, his parents, and his freedom. Their essence embodied him, she felt his confidence and saw it in the way he carried himself. The chains that had once forced him to deny his true self were no more.

Clio was envious because she wasn't so lucky. She psychoanalyzed the conversation she had with her parents and decided a percentage of their hostility was caused by her actions, or lack thereof. She should have talked to them, told them about Ansel, and contacted them after the car accident. A small percentage of their opposition toward the baron was the direction he was taking the pack. Military strict. They weren't the only ones. And turning Foxwood into a compound. Another percentage, they honestly didn't believe the Emanation was real. And why would they? What proof was there to support it? Any indication it was real— giant ant, a group of magic-born determined to destroy

Jordyn and Director Kanin—was covered up. All they had was Baron Kanin's word. A display of their soothsayer's powers. The majority of the pack lived as humans, beside humans, enjoyed what they had and would, no doubt, fight to keep. If they embraced the Emanation, it would be like accepting the apocalypse and the end of the life they knew. It didn't make what they said to her, their dislike for Ansel, or their resistance to the Emanation and Baron Kanin right.

If she wanted her parents to believe her, to accept Ansel as her mate, and if she wanted to repair their relationship, it would be left up to her. Believing she chose the Kanins and the status Baron Kanin gave her over them, she would have to prove to them she didn't. She had chosen her career above all else, save for Ansel, and for him she was about to potentially give it up. But, her mind warned her, she couldn't face her parents and their judgement without a counter argument backed by the cold logic they expected and would believe.

"Wait until they hear about this," she mumbled to the inside of her car. There were no dings, beeps, or change in screens ... no, she had yet to have a terminal installed. It was freeing and disappointing at the same time. She wanted, craved her life the way it had been, just a piece of it. It wouldn't be the same, not ever, and not after today.

Ahead of her Ansel made a right, driving to his parking spot beside Director Kanin's black truck and Jordyn's red one. She continued straight toward the Enforcer's office, and after parking in front of the building beside Med Two, turned off the engine. Med Two sat silent, as did Wyatt's classic, dark brown truck. Sitting behind the wheel and staring at the office's rustic log exterior, she tried to put her thoughts where they should be—the meeting with the baron, and work. When she checked in with Danette, she relayed all updates, then downloaded her schedule to Clio's tablet. The download gave her a full day of paperwork, including signing off on several soldiers who had been injured in training. And there she sat, staring forward, her eyes blurring the longer she did.

Ansel stood at the driver's side door watching Clio stare into space. She was quiet most of the morning, which he appreciated as he also wasn't in the mood to talk. There seemed to be tension where there was too much to say, while at the same time there was nothing to say until they had their meeting with the baron. He waited another couple of seconds, watched the quick glances people were giving him ... they all knew where he had been, why he'd been there. He nodded his head when an enforcer waved, then knocked on the window. Clio's head jerked up, her eyes meeting his, and she lowered her head. Opening the door, he knelt down, put his hands on the edge of the chocolate leather seat, and waited.

"Just trying to organize my thoughts," she replied to his unasked question.

"I understand. We don't have to do this. We can meet with the baron, explain what happened, and go through our day. Normal. Nothing has to be said," he offered, his hand on her thigh.

Clio laughed as she turned in her seat to meet his cinnamon gaze spiked with a bronze glow. There was nothing normal about them. A blooded dhampir. Pureblood werewolf capable of shifting into his Bestial form. Normal had flown out the window. "I have to tell you something."

"What, Tesoro?"

"I love you." That was all she had, and she was going to cling to it.

"I love you. Let's get this over with," Ansel whispered, knowing he didn't deserve her love or her loyalty. Standing, he held his hand out and waited.

Clio stared at tan skin, long fingers, shook her head, and questioned, "What?"

"I carry your satchel or it's public affection, Doctor Hyde, your choice." Ansel wore raw arrogance, Pureblood Dominate, and the certainty he was going to get what he wanted. "Mate, what will it be?"

Clio smiled, a real smile, and it felt odd when their day was unfolding before them. Leaning over the seat, she grabbed her bag, then sat straight and handed it to Ansel. "The satchel, Captain Wolt."

"So be it, Doctor Hyde."

With Ansel carrying her bag, they walked across the parking lot, and received more than a couple of stares. They weren't malicious or judging—it was the first day Captain of Enforcer was back at work after serving a two-week sentence with the Fellowship and another to heal from the wounds inflicted. It was expected. Just like the stares she received on her first day back. With discipline being military strict, their eyes showed their concern and their thankfulness. The people working at Foxwood were loyal to the Kanins, and accepted things weren't always *normal*. It was a smaller family within a family, and they had their own ways. She wouldn't have it any other way.

"Captain Wolt, Doctor Hyde, good to see you," Maresa greeted, her brown eyes lighting up with the early morning sun. "Beautiful morning."

Ansel nodded at the young sentinel, a grin tugging at the corners of his mouth as he entered the foyer to the baron's mansion, his free hand at the small of Clio's back.

"What's so funny?" she asked as they walked the hallway.

"She gives Rutger the creeps. He says she is too happy. No one is really like that," he replied. "He thinks she is plotting against him. She might make him smile."

Why didn't that surprise her? Director Kanin was all business—serious, determined, focused—and not the beautiful morning type or the smiling type. She could only imagine the expression on his rugged face when he had to face the happy-go-lucky sentinel.

"Are you ready?" Ansel asked.

"Yes and no."

"Prefect. Me too." He raised his hand, cupping Clio's cheek, and leaning down, kissed her. Clio held the back of his neck as she deepened the kiss, wanting to have his taste on her tongue.

"Sorry for the interruption," Jordyn teased as she stood in the open door.

Ansel pressed his forehead to Clio's for a heartbeat, then straightened. "Jordyn."

"Ansel, Clio."

Sunlight poured in through the large window, its rays broken by Director Kanin as he stood looking out at Foxwood's grounds. His broad shoulders filled out his black BDU top, mahogany hair sitting at the collar, his black BDU pants ended in boots, and he wore his gear, tactical belt, gun, and holster. To his left was a bookcase filled with tomes, while to his right, beside the thick, chocolate-brown curtain, was an ornate walnut bar where a coffee cup and a carafe sat. The tension in the office was palpable, which told her they knew exactly why they were there, and no one, especially Director Kanin, liked it.

"Have a seat," Baron Kanin offered as he waved to the two chairs in front of his desk.

It looked as it always did when she was in his office, his desk—stacked with papers, folders, books, and a large monitor. It was a mess. How he found anything was beyond her.

"You know why we're here," Ansel started as he met mocha eyes with shards of gold. His heart leapt to his throat, his lungs collapsed when he tried to breathe, and his pulse rushed through his ears to deafen him. He needed to get himself under control.

"Yes, I know why you're here," Baron Kanin replied. "Why don't you explain it."

Explain it. He didn't want to say it out loud. It would make it real. It would change his life. Clio's life. Ansel met slate eyes with a whiskey hue and felt her love and assurance pulse in their bond. Facing Baron Kanin, he opened his mouth and was stopped.

"You have time. You don't need to do this," Rutger argued from behind him, his voice thick. "You're rushing into this."

Standing, Ansel faced the man he loved as a brother. He saw the emotion in his gold and amber glare, and the animal close to the surface. Ansel's eyes rolled bronze, the glow sparking in return. "You know I have to." Turning to Baron Kanin, he stated, "I shapeshifted into my Bestial form."

"Noted. Go on."

"Baron Kanin, Director Kanin, Soothsayer Jordyn Langston, under the canons of the Cascade pack, I, Captain of Enforcers Ansel Wolt, formally resign from my post."

A hush swept through the office as Clio's heart sank, then regret and fear slid in their bond. It hurt him. Ansel didn't want to leave his home. His family. Now there was no turning back. It was done. She watched him slowly take his seat with his shoulders slightly slumped.

"Once your resignation has been recorded, Ansel, you can't serve the pack in any capacity. You will lose your rank, authority, and security clearance," Baron Kanin warned.

Silence thickened the tension as he contemplated what he was doing. He would lose everything he worked for. The challenges he won to become Captain of Enforcers, the respect he earned. He wouldn't be fighting by Rutger's side. He would be barred from Foxwood, the Hollow, and the restricted areas of Cascade. He was a Pureblood Dominate without a crest, and now he wouldn't have status within the pack. Questioning himself, he wanted, needed someone to tell him he was doing the right thing. As if in answer, a warmth flowed to him in the bond, and it was all he needed. "I understand."

"Captain Wolt's resignation has been witnessed and recorded," Baron Kanin declared. "Jordyn."

"Witnessed and recorded," she replied, her voice thick, her eyes onyx.

"Witnessed and recorded," Rutger growled.

He forced himself to ignore Rutger. "I petition for the right to challenge Strong Lord of the Fellowship of the Stone," Ansel requested.

Baron Kanin closed his eyes, his emotions escaping his iron hold enough the room filled with his magic. Gold eyes met Ansel's when he began, "Doctor Clio Hyde, as his fated mate, if he fails, you will perish with him. Do you give your consent?"

With their gazes on her, she felt tears welling, the force burning her eyes, her heart fighting to push blood through its valves, and felt the strings of fear tightening on her. "Yes, sir."

"Ansel Wolt's verbal petition for a challenge has been recorded. As required by the Highguard the petition will be evaluated, decided upon, and a date and location will be determined. A covenant, explaining the rules of engagement, will be signed by both participants. The participant who defies the covenant will give up their right to the challenge, they will face defeat, and punishment and/or imprisonment. You've been counseled."

"Affirmative," Ansel replied. It was over. His nerves felt as if electric shocks were coursing through him while his entire world felt like it was drifting from him.

"If you fail, I'll lose a son," the baron said softly.

"I'll lose a brother, dammit," Rutger added.

"I'll lose Clio," Jordyn protested. "My doctor."

Clio met a copper gaze with onyx slicing through liquid metal and couldn't keep the stern expression from her face and the hurt from making her heart ache. She understood their concern for Ansel ... hell, their desperate need to make him change his mind—he was a son, a brother, a protector for the pack. Rutger's BFF and partner in crime, literally. Wasn't she more than Jordyn's doctor? Wasn't she? She heard her parents and her confidence dropped from her like a boulder. Maybe they welcomed her because she was Ansel's mate.

"Doc, don't be a fool. If I didn't adore you, I wouldn't treat you to cocktails. Or stick my nose in your business," Jordyn started, her hand on the butt of her gun that was holstered at her waist. Suddenly, the conversation narrowed down to the two of them. "I don't want to lose my friend."

"That's creepy," Clio mumbled and hated it when Jordyn knew exactly what she was thinking then called her out. "Thank you. It means a lot to me."

"You're welcome."

"I don't want to leave my position, not unless it's necessary."

"Doctor Hyde, you're welcome here, always," Baron Kanin assured. "Ansel, think about this."

"I have. If I succeed, I'll become Strong Lord, and you'll gain an ally and the Fellowship's loyalty," Ansel countered, his resolve returning with the baron's promise to Clio. If anything happened to him, they would protect her. She would always have a family. "Prince Hall, warlock, is a bishop with the House of Garnet, he has ties to the Fellowship. I could strengthen them and others. The Fellowship would be an extension of Cascade." He would put an end to the evil rooted within the group and no one would ever do what they did to Milanka. The thought surprised him.

"Why do I instantly think of mercenaries?" Baron Kanin mused.

Ansel shrugged. It was a good idea. They were creatures of myth. Bored creatures of myth. "That would be wrong, sir."

Baron Kanin laughed, his low rumble easing the tension. "Yes, it would. Remember that. Is there anything else?" the baron asked as he sat back, his arms crossed over his board chest. The gray button-up shirt was open at the collar, exposing the edges of the Kanin family crest, while the sleeves were rolled to his elbows.

"Affirmative. We do." Gods, were they going to do this? They had to. He wasn't going to lose Clio, even in death. She was his and she needed protection.

"Well?" Rutger demanded, his frustration leaking into his words. Leaving the window, he stomped to the desk where he faced Ansel. With dark eyes holding his emotion he glared at him. "What else could you possibly want?"

His heart pounded in his chest as his wolf howled for its mate. "A ceremony."

"Doctor Hyde," the baron started. "Do you agree?"

"Yes. Yes," she readily answered.

"That's something I can willingly agree to." Jordyn gave them a brilliant smile, her eyes gleaming copper as she stood beside Rutger.

"Agreed. Captain Ansel Wolt and Doctor Clio Hyde, you are granted a ceremony. The union between fated mates will be added to the Scared Writ of the Cascade pack. Afterwards, your resignation and petition will be recorded and added."

"What does that mean?" Clio asked.

"It means, there will be a territory wide announcement and then you'll set a date. Ansel, I'm giving you time. Have your ceremony and honeymoon, then plot against Strong Lord. During that time Cascade offers whatever resources you need to ensure your victory," Baron Kanin explained.

It was imperative she talk to her parents before the announcement went out. It would be a disaster if they found out from someone else. While she mentally made a plan to contact her parents, she knew there was something she had to fix, if she could. "I can't shift. I can feel my wolf, I can't bring it forward," Clio confessed, her words rushed.

"If we can't figure it out, we'll find someone who can," Jordyn promised. "And you'll start training with me."

"My parents' magic flows through me, but I don't know the extent of it. I also need to master my Bestial form," Ansel admitted.

"I can help you with that," Rutger assured, his gold eyes blazing. "I won't let you face Strong Lord until you're in control of your beast."

Ansel sat back, and looking at Rutger, Jordyn, and Baron Kanin saw his family. Soon the talk turned from training and planning to the ceremony, dresses, and tuxedos. It made his skin crawl; he hated the monkey suits. Eventually talk turned to work, and after dismissing herself, Clio left to go to her office.

CHAPTER TWENTY-FOUR

Clio set her cell on the railing, like a coward. She couldn't call them, not yet. She had to process everything that happened, and then when she was armed with a reasonable explanation for the ceremony, she would make the call. Rushing it would leave both sides upset and angry. As the sun began its decline behind the mountain ridges, gold and rose hues reflected on the pond's surface, the two geese squawked, and the breeze brought her the fresh scents of the woods. For the time being, they decided they would live at Ansel's; he had an alarm system connected to communications at Foxwood, and she liked the place. It gave her peace.

Ansel stopped at the open door to watch Clio and wondered how in the world he deserved her. Her strength, loyalty, and love amazed him. When she turned, her curls covering one shoulder, the red threading through matching her scarlet eyes, his wolf grasped onto his mate. "For you." He walked across the deck and handed her a glass of her favorite tequila.

"You kept your position. You can continue to work until the ceremony." Clio sipped, felt the heat, and tasted citrus and oak.

"It'll be nice. There are things I would like to finish. I want to spend more time there." Ansel raised the beer, drank, put the bottle on the railing, then after taking Clio's glass set it beside his. "Come here."

Clio was going to wrap her arms around him when he held her hips, and lifting her, stepped to the side and set her on the railing. "What are you up to?" she asked.

"I've never been free. I never felt like I had a family. Had a right to have one. And a place to belong. To have peace."

"You have it all," she whispered as she curled his hair in her fingers.

"Because of you." Drawing his finger along her jaw, he feathered her lips with his. "Tesoro, my treasure. I want this to be the first day of the rest of our lives," Ansel whispered, his words harsh with the depth of his emotion.

"Darling, this is the first day of the rest of our lives," Clio responded. She tugged him closer, wrapped her arms around him, and rested her face against his chest to have his heartbeat in her ear. No one was going take her wolf from her.

Ansel held his mate close to him, the woman fate gave to him, felt her heat, and looking out at his land, thought about the challenge. He was free of Milanka, and the Fellowship, and it should have been enough. He could resume his life as Captain of Enforcers with Clio by his side and not have to worry about a damn thing. Especially if he failed. His instincts told him he couldn't. This was his destiny, and like a fire it was consuming his insides. The Emanation. Those against Cascade. He had to help. When his body ached with the phantom injures from the beatings, and his nightmares woke him, he knew he had to stop the Fellowship. If he failed, Strong Lord would make an example of him, and using the bond between them, they were as good as dead. Both of them. If he succeeded, it was more than becoming Strong

Lord. It was becoming a power to protect his family and ensure Cascade's future.

THE END

M.A. Kastle is the author of Bone Chimes, Dark Awakening, and Warrior's Crown of the Cascade Saga, an urban fantasy that mixes paranormal, mystery, and romance. Bringing characters from the Cascade Saga to Crimson Moon, book one of the Cascade Wolves opens a new world of adventure. A dark urban fantasy, book one of the Moonlight Territory, Wolf Within, weaves intrigue, noir, and romance. Monica lives in Southern California with her notebooks, camera, her family, and two German Shepherds.

www.KASTLENOVELS.com
Facebook @Makastle
Instagram @Makastleauthor
Twitter @Makastle